# DEMONS OF GOOD AND EVIL

# BY KIM HARRISON

## BOOKS OF THE HOLLOWS

DEAD WITCH WALKING

THE GOOD, THE BAD, AND THE UNDEAD

EVERY WHICH WAY BUT DEAD

A FISTFUL OF CHARMS

FOR A FEW DEMONS MORE

THE OUTLAW DEMON WAILS

WHITE WITCH, BLACK CURSE

BLACK MAGIC SANCTION

PALE DEMON

A PERFECT BLOOD

EVER AFTER

THE UNDEAD POOL

THE WITCH WITH NO NAME

THE TURN

AMERICAN DEMON

MILLION DOLLAR DEMON

TROUBLE WITH THE CURSED

DEMONS OF GOOD AND EVIL

# DEMONS
## OF GOOD
## AND EVIL

## KIM HARRISON

ACE
NEW YORK

ACE
Published by Berkley
An imprint of Penguin Random House LLC
penguinrandomhouse.com

Library of Congress Cataloging-in-Publication Data

Names: Harrison, Kim, 1966– author.
Title: Demons of good and evil / Kim Harrison.
Description: New York : Ace, [2023] | Series: Hollows
Identifiers: LCCN 2022045761 (print) | LCCN 2022045762 (ebook) |
ISBN 9780593437544 (hardcover) | ISBN 9780593437568 (ebook)
Classification: LCC PS3608.A78355 D46 2023 (print) |
LCC PS3608.A78355 (ebook) | DDC 813/.6—dc23
LC record available at https://lccn.loc.gov/2022045761
LC ebook record available at https://lccn.loc.gov/2022045762

Printed in the United States of America
1st Printing

Book design by Kristin del Rosario

For Tim

# DEMONS OF GOOD AND EVIL

# CHAPTER

# 1

EDEN PARK'S OVERLOOK WAS ONE OF MY EARLIEST CHILDHOOD memories, not in its sun-drenched glory of a summer afternoon filled with dogs and kids cutting loose, but in the dark as it was now, the rumble of Cincinnati's lives muted under the moon's haze, the lights from the distant buildings an inviting glow. Far below and behind me, the Ohio River glinted as if a living thing, a welcome separation between the city and the more . . . unique citizens in the Hollows. Fixed between and overlooking both, Eden Park felt like the middle, which was where I had always been, surrounded by all, never quite fully belonging to either.

My dad had come up here when his choices lay heavy on him, invariably when my mother was at her distracted worst. I'd long been convinced that he had known who and what I was, and lately . . . the thought had occurred that perhaps he had brought me here to sit beside a ley line much as the woodsman had taken his children to the forest, not to leave them to starve, but to find someone who might be able to raise them to their full potential, because to stay ignorant of what I was might be more dangerous still.

Which might sound vain or presumptuous if I wasn't now sitting on that same park bench, staring at a ley line, a demon beside me instead of the man who had raised me as his own.

"My synapses are singed," I complained, and Al's expression became rife with annoyance.

"If you get caught in a circle by some wannabe magic user and can't jump out, it will be more than your head hurting," the demon said, hitting his affected, proper-British accent hard. "You're making us look bad. You are a demon. You should have at least one ley line memorized with which to jump to. That you have to stand within a line and translocate to get to the ever-after is embarrassing."

True, I was a demon, and as Al was fond of pointing out, it wasn't hard to make me vulnerable if you knew how. Just my luck that there was an entire university major devoted to it. "Yeah?" I said sourly. "Singeing my synapses to char isn't going to help."

Al's wide shoulders shifted in an unheard sigh. It was an unseasonably warm October night, and he had forgone his usual crushed green velvet frock coat for a lightweight and decidedly Victorian-feel vest. His high-top hat was gone as well, and the lace. But a new, silver-tipped walking cane rested against his knee—possibly holding a spell or two—and a pair of blue-tinted glasses he didn't need hung low on his nose. Seeing him eye my jeans and boots over them, I wondered if he felt he'd fallen to a new low despite his still-overdone appearance.

His mood, too, was off, being an uncomfortable mix of forced cheerfulness and dejection. I was fairly sure it wasn't my lack of progress. Honestly, the reason the demons had created gargoyles was that they couldn't master transposing, or jumping, the ley lines on their own. Gargoyles could "hear" the lines as easily as reading a book and, once bonded to a demon, could show them how to shift their aura to join with the ley line and pop out wherever they wanted, either here in reality or in the ever-after. But until I managed it, the only way I could get to the ever-after was by standing in a line and translocating myself there.

"The ley line is right there," Al grumped, looking at it on the other side of the small footbridge. "You can see it. You can hear it. Adjust your aura to match it—"

"And become a part of it, shifting my body to nothing but energy within its flow. Yeah, that's not the part I'm having trouble with," I smart-mouthed, and he mockingly gestured for me to get on with it. Losing myself in a ley line wasn't anything new, but trying to jump into it from halfway across a park was. I'd tried three times tonight already, failing miserably.

Frustrated, I sent my attention to Bis. The adolescent, cat-size gargoyle had perched himself in a nearby tree, on standby to snag me out of the line if I should somehow manage the jump and get myself stuck. Al's far older and larger gargoyle, Treble, had settled herself on a nearby streetlight as a secondary spotter. The craggy, hut-size beast appeared too large to be supported by the thin pole, but gargoyles, for all their stony looks, were relatively light.

Bis had bonded to me over a year ago, which basically meant he could teach me how to shift my aura to match any ley line on the planet. After a hundred years or so of gargoyle-aided practice, I'd be able to not only jump into a ley line from anywhere but jump out again at any location I wanted by using three or more ley lines to triangulate.

Unfortunately Bis and I had lost our instinctive connection when his soul had been stuck in a bottle. The first hints of our mental linkage were beginning to show, but until he could pass through my protection circle with impunity, the best I could do was learn the lines by rote. Trial and error. Which hurt and singed my synapses when I got it wrong.

Being fifty-plus years old, Bis was able to be on his own, and like most adolescents, he liked to sleep all day. His skin was dark and pebbly, though he could change its color at will to become almost invisible. All he had on against the night's damp was a red scarf, and he really didn't need that, either.

At Bis's encouraging nod, I resettled myself on the bench. Relaxing, I let my focus go slack as if I was using my second sight to see the ley line hovering like a red ribbon at chest height halfway across the park. But I wasn't. After an hour of this, I was tired and faking it. I was never going to translocate myself into that ley line, so I simply gazed at the moon peeking past the heavy clouds.

Between the ley lines and me were the two recirculating ponds and accompanying footbridge where I had spent my internship at the I.S. chasing out bridge trolls. The line itself ran over a small plot of concrete and a public Wiccan hearth, and beyond that was a wide space of open grass leading to Cincinnati.

The crescent moon did little to light the cloudy night. It would be a few days shy of full for Halloween, but that was more than a week away. I could hardly wait, and I'd already bought a basket of cherry tomatoes to give out to the kids along with their Snickers and Pixy Stix. The holiday spanned the entire week, culminating in a final, dusk-to-dawn candy hunt. Humans shut down before midnight, right when the party really started. It was for the best, really. They weren't made for the night.

The soft sound of approaching dress shoes drew my attention to the man walking his dog. "Go-o-ood evening," Al drawled, his threat obvious, and the man quickened his pace. "Focus," he growled at me, and I quit trying to coax the black Lab closer.

Bis dropped with a soft hush of sliding leather wings, pinpointing the back of the bench with an unerring accuracy despite the dark. "You're really close, Rachel," he encouraged, the white tufts of fur on his otherwise leathery-black ears standing out as he shifted them to listen to the people gathering in the field. "But you're too far into the, ah, lighter spectrum." Red eyes pinched, he looked up at Treble. "What's the right name for that sound?"

Treble's gnarled feet tightened on the light pole until the metal groaned. "It's not an auditory vibration. It's a visual one," she said, her deep voice rumbling like falling rocks and her lionlike tail switching. "And there isn't a name for it, which is why this study is useless until your aura again syncs with Rachel's. Gally . . ."

"Enough," Al muttered darkly, and I winced. I had a growing feeling that we weren't out here for me but for Al. I hadn't seen him jump the lines since he burned his synapses while trapping Hodin. Practicing along with me might be the only way for his pride to take it. "Your opinion on what is possible is not why you were asked to join us, Treble."

"Gally, if you would let me—" the old gargoyle said, her voice a pleading rasp.

"No." Al turned, one thick hand on the back of the bench as he glared up at her. "Take a break. Both of you. Go catch bats and do whatever you do when you aren't bothering us."

"Stupid hoary fart." With a downward thrust of her leathery wings, Treble launched herself into the air. The streetlight cracked and went out, and I flinched until I was sure nothing was coming down. When I next looked, she was high in the air, her huge, angled wings looking demonic against the city-lit clouds.

Shoulders shifting, Al put his elbows on his knees, his chin dropping into a cupped hand.

Bis sidestepped along the top of the bench to me, his craggy talons spaced so as not to leave a scratch. "Call me if you need me," he said, and I touched the foot he set on my shoulder.

I smiled, but inside, I was unsure. Our once indelible mental link was all but destroyed from Bis's prolonged connection to the baku. He would likely hear my mental call if he was listening, but if he was busy or asleep? It was chancy at best, and I was to blame.

"Rachel, you are alive," Bis said as he saw my heartache, and Al straightened, his own sour musings seeming to hesitate. "I'd make that same choice again. We will figure this out."

And then Bis was gone, his small shape vanishing over the yellow leaves still clinging to the trees. Embarrassed, I slumped on the bench, arms over my chest.

"I'd make that same choice again, too," Al said, a gleam in his goat-slitted, red eyes.

"Al."

"No," he said, a hand raising to stop my words. Behind us, a couple hurriedly coaxed their dog into their car and drove off amid a tense conversation. They hadn't been here for more than five minutes, and I wondered if we were being recognized.

"I'll get better at this," I said, instead of what I really wanted. *Talk to me. Are you afraid your skills won't return?* "I just need practice." Reaching a thought out, I tapped into the ley line, my jaw clenching at the mild discomfort. I'd been pushing too hard, and now I was singed.

"Practice, yes," he said, his thoughts clearly somewhere else as he fingered his cane.

The small group at the center of the grassy field was growing, and I frowned as an argument began to take shape, two sides clearly forming. *Weres?* I wondered, not sure how far I could push Al to get him to open up. If Treble was over four thousand years old, Al was far older. He'd lived countless lives: that of a wanderer, warlord, slave, magician, clever trickster, vengeful punisher, outcast, teacher. I wasn't sure what he was now. Perhaps Al didn't, either. Maybe that was the problem.

"The baku damage Bis suffered will mend," I said hesitantly. "Will you?"

Al stiffened. "Not your concern."

"Al." I shifted to face him square on. Two more cars had gone, leaving the park to us and the growing knot of people in the field. "I think it is. Why shouldn't I worry about you?" *I don't have anything else to do.* Other than keep the vampires in line, the witches off my case, and the demons from reverting to their old ways of dominating everything they coveted, which was a lot. The elves still wanted to take over the world despite being on the endangered species list, and the humans simply wanted to survive after the Turn had reduced their numbers to a thin fraction. Plague by way of tomato. Even forty years later, they grieved.

For the moment, everyone was behaving—hence me having the time for some practice. But Halloween was next week and the moon was waxing. . . .

Al's eye twitched as he scanned the milling, increasingly noisy mob at the center of the field. "I have been singed deeper than this before."

"When?" I countered, and his attention went to his hands, clasped and at rest.

"Not your concern," he said again.

"How long until you can tap a ley line?" I insisted.

"Not. Your. Concern," he practically growled.

"I think it is. If you aren't up to . . ." My voice trailed off as his eyes narrowed on me. I closed my mouth, turning to sit shoulder to shoulder instead of aggressively staring him down.

But the guilt remained, guilt that he had paid for my risky choice. He had protected me and suffered for it, burned his synapses as I captured his brother first in a ley line, then a mental construct that Hodin could never break even if magic should fail again. The smut we thought would protect Al hadn't been enough. He could still do earth magic, but demons were all about flash and bang—and though incredibly strong, earth magic wasn't it.

"It was my choice," Al said, softening as he recognized my mood. "And my task," he added. "I had much to atone for concerning Hodin. And you, perhaps."

My throat was tight, and I nodded, my attention flicking to the field when someone howled. It *was* a Were pack, and they were going to fur by the look of it. Weres could shift any day of the year, but they generally didn't do it in a city park two weeks from a full moon.

"Perhaps it is better this way," Al said lightly, but I could tell he was worried. "I'm not tempted to do anything demonic. Try to match your aura to my line again," he added, chin lifting. "I'm not helpless, but you are. You should be able to jump somewhere in case someone circles you."

"Sure," I said, voice a whisper.

But it was getting harder to focus as an aggressive howling became obvious. My nose wrinkled at the scent of wolfsbane, and I wondered if Bis and Treble were watching this. I doubted that the pack had gotten a permit to Were in public outside of the traditional three days around a full moon, and I was beginning to think that they, not Al and me, had emptied the park.

Al, too, squinted at them with an increased interest. "Your Were, David? Is he here?"

"I doubt it." I glanced at my shoulder bag and wondered if I should phone him. No one liked calling the I.S. on some loud weekday fun, but it was becoming obvious that this wasn't a companionable, laid-back get-together. There were three factions now, taunting one another as they slowly closed ranks while more shifted to fur. *A territorial spat?* I wondered. More than unusual.

Everyone in Cincy knew where they were in the grand scheme of things. Tattoos showed pack affiliation, and clothes and shades of tidiness did the rest. Graffiti marked territories, but everyone could freely go wherever they wanted. This show of aggression was downright odd, and my lips parted when, with a harsh bark and a yelp, two Weres rolled on the grass, snapping at ears and tails.

"I'm calling David." I reached for my phone. It could be an alpha challenge, but there were at least five packs out there now, and alpha challenges were generally handled in private.

"That's not a pack," Al said. "They are all alphas. Male and female."

"They can't be all alphas," I protested. Alphas *never* got together like this, and not without their packs behind them. Head down, I scrolled for David's number. "This is really weird. Why would Cincinnati's alphas cause trouble? Everyone is happy with where things sit." I hesitated, listening to my phone ring.

"You've reached Hue's phone," David's recorded voice said, and I grimaced. "If this is an emergency, please contact Were Insurance directly."

"Voice mail," I muttered. Ending the call, I hit the icon to connect again. "Maybe I should call Trent. He always knows what's going on."

Al's lip twitched, his stiff attitude a clear indication that he thought I could do better than an elf who had more money than God. "Everyone would be happier if you would stop punishing us by dating an elf," he said, and my brow furrowed.

*Everyone?* "If I wanted to punish you, I'd simply marry the man."

Al jerked his attention from the gathered Weres, horrified. "You wouldn't. . . ."

David's phone was still ringing, tied up with dealing with my previous call. "Seriously?" I scoffed, though a niggling desire remained. "I'm not about to live out in the middle of that planned forest of his. Now, once he gets into his downtown apartment?" I flashed Al a smile, enjoying seeing him sweat. But in all honesty, he had nothing to worry about. Oh, I loved Trent and would do ugly things if anyone hurt him, but I wasn't ready to be "mom" to two toddlers—as sweet, demanding, spoiled, and absolutely perfect as they were.

"Relax," I said as I gave up and closed my phone out. When David saw that I called twice, he'd get back to me. Contacting Were Insurance would only dump me into a phone maze of frustration. "Trent won't move until his apartment is finished. He's putting in a lot of safeguards, and he wants to spell them himself. The pool, too, is going to take time. The weight is an issue."

"Water abhors being forty-nine stories up." His gaze hard on the grassy field, Al snatched his cane in an elegant motion. "Oh, how grand," he drawled sarcastically. "The I.S."

I sat where I was, uneasy as the Weres, too, noticed the two Inderland Security cars now idling at the far end of the park. No one got out, and they didn't even turn on their blue and gold lights. The agents were wisely giving the Weres time to disperse. Gut tightening, I turned to the three black-and-whites pulling into the small lot behind us. Two-ways popped, and the tight, terse voice of dispatch made my pulse quicken.

But instead of scattering, the Weres dropped their squabble, banding together to taunt the agents: Weres in fur in the front, Weres in tees and jeans behind.

My thoughts went to Jenks, and a feeling of misgiving trickled through me for having told him to stay home. I could have used some skilled aerial recon. *Bis? Where the devil are you?*

"This is really odd," I whispered as the Weres became more confident, howling their defiance as the I.S. turned their lights on, and my lips parted as more stripped down in the come-and-go flashes and Wered. Fast. Too fast to be without a great deal of pain.

"Did you see that?" I said as I inched closer to Al, and the cruisers behind us emptied out. "That woman shifted in like fifteen seconds."

"Yes-s-s-s." Al's brow furrowed. "David must be down there. You cannot shift that fast without the aid of the focus."

"David wouldn't be involved in this," I said, glancing at my phone again.

"Time to go." Al stood, one hand on my shoulder, the other pointing his cane at the ley line between us and the growing pack. The ever-after would be a convenient escape. True, neither of us could jump to a line at the moment, but even a witch could stand in one and translocate realities. Once, the demon's practice of abducting witches for servants had stopped them. Now it was only a lingering fear that kept everyone out of the demons' realm.

"Unless Madam Subrosa wishes to help?" he added sardonically, and I stood as well. There were too few I.S. agents for what they were walking into.

*Help the I.S.?* It would go nowhere in improving my relationship with the vampire-controlled police force, but this was too weird. "And get hauled in for starting it?" I said as I sent a quick mental call to Bis.

As expected, there was no answer from the kid. It was as if I was shouting into a void, and I frowned, worried as five I.S. agents paced past us and over the footbridge to confront the growing pack. *Where the Turn is Bis?* I thought as Al and I followed them, heading for the ley line on the other side.

Weres were one of Inderland's most model citizens, even the alpha males and females law-abiding and easygoing. Oh, they tagged buildings to show territory and were not above mischief, but they always scattered when confronted, preferring to fight another day on territory of their own choosing. This outright aggression between multiple alphas was almost unheard-of. I'd only seen it once before, and a trickle of angst tightened my spine as I called David again.

"And now, the news," Al said dryly as an antenna-draped van parked sideways to take up three spots.

"The Turn take it, David, answer your phone," I said, eyes down as Al guided me to the footbridge. Even living vamps would think twice before confronting an entire pack of snarling wolves, and the five agents ahead of us slowed, waiting for reinforcements.

Finally David picked up, my first words catching as his low, pleasant voice filled my ear with his annoyance. "Rachel? If someone isn't on fire, I'm hanging up."

"Turn on your TV," I said, and the confident man sighed.

"Is it the vamps or demons?"

"It's the Weres," I said, both hoping and dreading that their aggression would keep the live camera feed off Al and me.

David's surprised grunt was joined by a higher voice, her words muffled. *Cassie?* I thought, recognizing her accent, not really surprised. David and the werefox had been dating since David had appraised her damaged casino boat.

"Try one forty," David said faintly, and then a louder "What the devil?"

"They are alphas, both the males and females," I said, sure he was seeing what I was seeing. "The I.S. is out here and no one is backing down," I added as Al drew me across the wide footbridge, my boots scuffing. "David, it's bizarre. I've never seen Weres do this before."

But I had, once on an island in the Straits of Mackinac—and my worry tightened.

"Where are my pants?" David said, but I was no longer listening. The I.S. had brought in a chopper, the wind and light only making the Weres that much more agitated. I stopped, pulling from Al's grip at the top of the footbridge when the chopper's moving light fixated on an angry older man surrounded by snarling Weres in fur. My pulse quickened, and a stab of fear shocked through me, funneled by memory.

White hair in a short military cut, camouflage pants and jacket, strong jaw, military bearing: it was Walter.

# CHAPTER

# 2

"DAVID? IT'S WALTER!" I SHOUTED INTO THE PHONE, JERKING WHEN the old Were shot a handgun at the chopper and it swung away. Son of a bastard, he shot at the I.S. They'd get mean now, and I looked behind me to see several more agents getting out of their cars.

"Walter?" David said tersely, and I heard a car door slam through the phone. "The guy you stole the focus from?"

"I did not steal it. Nick did," I said, but I was sure Walter didn't recognize the distinction, seeing as I hid it from him, knowing that in the wrong hands it would shift the balance of Were, elf, vampire, and witch too rapidly to prevent pushback. Weres were kept in check by their mild demeanor, their loyalty to their alphas, and their slow birth rate. The focus nullified all of that, making their alphas willing not only to look to one leader but to follow him or her into any number of aggressive acts. Even their population could skyrocket, as whoever held it could turn a human into a Were with a bite. I had given it to David. Walter probably wanted it back.

"This might be a problem," I whispered as Al dragged me across the bridge, and then Walter turned as if hearing me.

"Parker! She's here!" came his faint shout, the Were's eyes never leaving mine. His sharp whistle cut through the noise, and my worry grew as he began stripping in preparation to Were.

The chopper was long gone, but the I.S. didn't like being shot at, and the slick-looking vamp officers had moved to the outskirts to give their spell-toting peers room to work. Six witches in bulky anti-charm gear had gathered in a small knot at the statue of Romulus and Remus in front of us, probably prepping the spell to make a large, field-wide circle to contain the Weres in one go. At least, that's what I would have done.

"Rachel?" David sounded worried. "I'm on my way. Stay on the phone. Tell me what's happening. Are you close enough to see their pack tattoos?"

I heard a horn beep through the phone, but I think Cassie was driving, her unique, Australian-accented swearing faint in the background. "No, and most of them are in fur," I said, stumbling as Al led me off the bridge and to the ley line. "David, the I.S. is here, and no one is backing down. You need to hurry."

"Rachel?" Al drawled lightly. "You may want to put the phone down and engage."

"I am engaging," I snapped, freezing when I looked up to see a tall, blond figure standing amid the wolf pack like a shepherd minding his murderous flock. "Oh," I murmured as self-preservation tightened my gut. He was wearing an elaborate spelling robe, and a faint haze of gathered power wreathed him. He wasn't a Were.

*Walter has himself a magic user? Great. How, by the Turn, did he convince a magic user to help him get the focus?* Worried, I glanced at the witchy I.S. agents moving out—two to the right, two to the left, and one, the most powerful, standing where he was . . . staring at me as if this was my fault. "David, I have to go."

"You told me Morgan wouldn't be here," the robed figure was shouting, clearly ticked, and the woman beside Walter bristled, clearly not liking being yelled at. Her multiple tattoos put her as being a Were. Parker, maybe, seeing as Walter had called for her before he'd shifted. The age-silvered wolf lurching to his feet at her side was probably Walter himself.

"Rachel . . ." David said, and then I closed out my phone and tucked it in my back pocket. Not only was the guy in the overdone spelling robes clearly a magic user, but he knew who I was.

"I can't fight her and Hue's influence both," the magic user said as the Weres continued to taunt the I.S. agents, their teeth a clear warning. "Keep her busy."

*David,* I thought, my pulse quickening. Crap on toast, Walter *was* after the focus. I would have said even an independently united pack of alphas wouldn't be able to best the citywide obedience that David wielded with the focus, but with a magic user to help him, it might be possible. *And here I am, bringing David right into it,* I thought as I scanned the street running the length of the park, both dreading and wanting to see his little gray sports car. I had to warn him even if his presence might scatter the alphas and put an end to this.

"Interesting," Al murmured as he twirled his cane. "Whoever that is out there, he is trying very hard to look like an elf."

"He's disguised?" I blurted, squinting at the robed man arguing with the two Weres, one in fur, the other not. He was blond and trim, and now that Al had mentioned it, his voice, while having that musical cadence that most elves had, was also somewhat hollow—a sure giveaway for having been spelled. Even so, it was a very expensive disguise charm. Doppelganger spells were legal around the week before Halloween, and finding out who this was through store records wouldn't be easy.

Walter's lips pulled from his muzzle in an ugly snarl, the militant Were clearly not liking whatever the man was saying, his robe's sleeves furling dramatically as he talked. "Keep her busy, or you don't get Hue!" the man said as Parker began to strip. "I can't make it any simpler!"

Livid, the big gray wolf barked at him.

"You think I have a clue what you are saying?" the man said, his hands now dripping a purplish red magic. And then he turned to Al and me. "Fine. Ladies first."

"Look out!" I yelped as I shoved Al, knocking us both down as I invoked a protection circle. I hit the ground hard, the flats of my arms stinging as energy from the nearby ley line poured into me. The dizzying, roaring maelstrom bubbled and frothed over my singed synapses instead of the smooth rush it should have been, but my circle formed and held.

Al's annoyed grunt sounded loud beside me. "Mother pus bucket, Morgan," he said, his red, goat-slitted eyes inches from mine. "It is a wonder you have survived this long."

"Jenks keeps me alive," I said, jerking at a thunderous boom. *And Jenks isn't here.*

I spun where I lay, pushing my braid out of the way to see the parking lot. A car was on fire, struck by whatever spell Walter's magic user had thrown at us. Annoyed, clearly vampiric agents stood at a disgruntled distance while two of the magic-wielding witch agents jogged back to try to contain the fire with a spell.

*So much for a park-wide circle.* "Stay down," I said as I rose, breaking my bubble of protection as I pushed up through it. The energy from it poured in to fill my chi with a tingling confidence and send the stray strands of my hair frizzing. I looked over the chaos. Something had changed. Most of the Weres were fleeing, but I didn't think it was from that blast of magic.

"It's David," I whispered as I saw his little gray sports car at the park's far edge. Both car doors were open, and the flashing amber and blue lights played upon the good-size wolf in his prime standing on its roof. Walter had seen him as well, the militant Were barking for obedience as most of his alpha pack disintegrated.

They were fleeing the power of David's focus, and a shiver rolled down my spine when David lifted his muzzle, a confident howl rising high to silence the chaos as he called the packs of Cincinnati.

But it wasn't over, and my hands tingled with unspent power as the Weres who were left tightened into a defensive knot. That disguised magic user was in the center, arguing with Walter again, by the looks of it.

"Ahh." Al rested confidently against the foot of the bridge. "I do love a well-crafted curse. Thousands of years old, and the focus is as effective now as when Newt twisted it."

"Yeah, it's great," I said, my worry tightening even more as the I.S. began a slow, obvious retreat, content to let David settle this. The packs of Cincinnati were beginning to answer him. Cars had stopped in the middle of the street and people were jogging his way, stripping as they came. Tough and sinewy, most were rough around the edges with marvelously creative tattoos and scruffy faces, but they were crafty and intelligent, and instinctively knew how to work in a team. There were few I would trust more with my life or a task.

Walter, though, was clearly not backing down as he marshaled those left. A human couldn't best a one-hundred-and-eighty-pound wolf, but I wasn't a human. I was a witch-born demon, and I wasn't going to let David stand alone—magic user or not.

"You going to be okay here?" I said, and Al eyed me over his blue-tinted glasses. I felt my face flame. The ley line was within spitting distance. All he had to do was go stand in it.

"Right," I said, then broke into a run, the need to warn David rising high. "Where the devil is Bis?" I mused again as I nodded to the lead witch I.S. agent in passing and got a frown in return. "Bis!" I shouted, my pace slowing as two Weres in fur split from the main pack. They weren't fleeing. They were loping toward me. Unsure, I angled my path wider, annoyed when the Weres not only matched it but broke into a full-out run.

"Son of a pup," I muttered as memories of my last, disastrous alpha challenge swamped me. I skidded to a halt, slipping on the dew-wet grass as I pulled on the ley line. *Crap on toast, they're almost on me!* Power flowed, and I flung out a hand at the incoming Weres.

*"Rhombus!"* I shouted, my sharp word giving force to the molecule-thin barrier as it sprang into existence. As with all undrawn circles, I was at its center, and with a startled yip, both wolves ran into it, scrunching up comically as they came to a sudden and certain halt.

I dropped my circle, getting three steps closer to David before they regained their feet. *Parker?* I thought, remembering the woman stripping down. Behind her, the knot of angry Weres was growing. Lines had been drawn, and both sides were promising violence.

"Perhaps something more aggressive?" Al shouted from the bridge's footing.

I wasn't going to kid myself that Al was "allowing" me to handle this to show him my growing skills. He couldn't tap a ley line to do magic, and it was my fault.

"You are in my way," I muttered, my feet shifting to find my balance as the larger wolf with the tattered ear lifted her lip in a clear warning. *Parker.* Behind Parker, the second Were got to her feet, one paw held high as she limped forward. *More aggressive, eh?* Easy for Al to say. The I.S. wasn't looking for an excuse to bring him in, and self-defense didn't work when you were officially a demon. I had to be *gentle*, and Walter? Walter didn't.

"You aren't touching David!" I shouted. "You want him, you go through me."

But they were the ones standing between David and me, and my gut tightened in fear.

Parker growled, her lip lifting in a silent threat. Her haunches bunched, and I gathered a wad of raw energy in my hand. This was going to end now.

And then Parker jerked to a halt, her eyes going behind me.

*Al?* I wondered, then gasped as a red shadow streaked past me, headed right for them.

"Cassie!" I shouted, recognizing the tiny werefox. Legs stretched and her lips pulled from her muzzle in promised violence, she practically flew. *My God. She is beautiful,* I thought, and then her twenty pounds of courage collided with that enormous wolf, gold and gray mingling in an unreal motion and savagery.

"Cassie!" I lurched forward, unable to throw my magic lest I hit her, but the wily woman had dropped clear, and the pissed Were caught only air in her teeth.

High-pitched barks sounded as Cassie stood between Parker and me. Her foxy tail was fluffed and her back was hunched. Head low, she yapped at them, warning them off. She was tiny before the wolves, and I wondered why she'd left David.

That is, until a pop of magic flattened the grass and a yip of pain came clear over the sound of snarls and barks. David had sent her to find me. He needed my help. Alpha Were or not, he couldn't stand against someone capable of magic. Yeah, this was a problem.

"Rachel!" Bis shouted, and I looked up, relieved as his dark wings cut a sharp silhouette against the sky. "Some witch has David pinned down and is picking off pack members one by one. You have to get to him."

"You think?" I said, frustrated, and then I jumped when a rock thumped into the ground inches from the two wolves. Bis was lightweight but could carry a lot.

Startled, the smaller Were shied into Parker. The larger wolf turned, snapping. In half a second they were tussling in a fur-flying fight, but before I could think to move, the smaller Were screamed in pain and streaked away, dodging the distant I.S. agents to flee into the night.

Bis's laughter rumbled like rocks in a blender as he landed on my shoulder. What was left of my braid fell completely apart, and my hair flew wildly as he beat the air and wrapped his tail securely behind my back. "Leave," I said to Parker, but the huge wolf only shook herself, blood from an already tattered ear arching through the night like rubies.

Behind her, another wash of magic rose, and Cassie barked at me to hurry up.

Parker didn't move. She didn't have to engage, only prevent me from reaching David.

*More aggressive.* I reached again for a ley line. Power from the earth and sky roared into me, tingling to my extremities. From the field came a third thump of power. The echoing yelp of pain struck through me. I had to get to David. Now.

"Fire in the hole!" I shouted to warn Bis, and then, after giving Cassie a look to stay where she was, I swept my arm dramatically. *"Dilatare!"*

My breath caught, and for an instant, I gloried in the satisfying burst of force pushing out from me in all directions, flattening the grass in a sudden storm that carried a hint of my aura.

Yelping, Parker rolled, tumbling over the grass.

"Go!" I shouted, but Cassie was already gone, heading right for the worst of the noise.

I ran, dodging Parker as she found her feet. Bis took to the air, serving as an aerial guard. I followed Cassie's red blur, ducking when dark wings brushed my head. "You want me to drop a rock on that witch?" Bis asked as he made barrel rolls beside me, his eyes practically glowing in excitement.

"Stay clear," I said, slowing as I began to look for the swirl of charmed silk amid the fur. "Maybe check on Al," I added, and the kid winged up and away.

I slid to a bewildered halt. Like wild dogs, the Weres fought, engaging in brief spats only to spring back to bark obscenities. The park was gray and white under the ambient city glow, and Cincy's Weres were still coming in. I didn't see that magic user. Hell, I couldn't even tell friend from foe. *But Cassie can,* I decided as she landed right atop a Were and savaged an ear.

Yelping, the Were pawed Cassie off. Behind them, David and Walter fought. I was smaller than a Werewolf, but I had my magic. More importantly, I'd had enough.

Gathering myself, I pulled on the ley line. Tingling and warm, I faced the snarling pack. *"Lenio cinis!"* I exclaimed, and a bolt of line energy poured upward from me, hitting the low clouds and flattening out before bursting into a blazing light. A boom of sound followed, beating down on us in a physical wave. I.S. looked up from their phones, taking notice but not moving from where they were parked. Fine by me.

*That ought to push you out into the open,* I thought as yelps of surprise swamped the barks of anger. Car alarms began to warble, and I found my balance as David and the large gray alpha rolled apart, both panting.

Blood dripped from David's ear. Walter's one eye was swollen shut. Chunks of fur were missing from both of them, and I couldn't tell whose blood was whose. All too soon, the two lines began to re-form in a haze of dust—David, Cassie, and a growing handful of Cincinnati's Weres before a ragtag assembly of mistrustful, increasingly agitated alphas. Walter's alpha pack moved uneasily behind him, the moon and reflected ambient light making them swiftly pacing ghostly shadows. *Where are you, you little magical pissant?* I thought, jumping when Bis's light weight found my shoulder.

"Wow, Rachel. You lit the entire city!" the small gargoyle said, and I touched his feet clamped to me.

"Think I got their attention?" Satisfied, I tucked a strand of hair behind an ear and scuffed to a halt beside David. "Ah, you okay?" I asked, and he made a low, rumbling growl. It lifted from him with the sure savagery of the feral wolf, but it was tempered with intelligence, and I stifled a shudder, glad it wasn't aimed at me.

"Damn it, Vincent! I can't do this if Parker doesn't do her fucking job!" rang out, and my focus snapped up, searching until I found the disguised man, his spelled-blond head almost hidden behind the milling, snarling wolves. Now that I was closer, the odd, charmed timbre to his voice was obvious. *Yeah, I'd hide myself, too, if I was spelling for the city's subrosa.*

"Give it up!" Bis called out, and Cassie made an odd, yowling chortle of agreement.

"You aren't getting David while I breathe," I added, and the man in the spelling robes seemed to find that funny. Hands on his hips, he hardly acknowledged Walter and Parker as they padded close, both panting and ragged from the fight.

"Sometimes, even a fool gets the right answer," the magic user muttered.

And then he moved, arm swinging as he pulled on the line with enough force to make my knees wobble. My expression blanked as unfocused energy blossomed in his hand, purple and green and orange.

"Watch out, Bis!" I shouted, and he took off, wings beating for altitude as he sought shelter in the air. *"Dilatare!"* I exclaimed, almost joyous as a ball of force exploded from me in all directions, sending friend and foe alike tumbling in an innocuous but effective defense. I didn't have to hurt anyone to protect those who looked to me. I was better than that. *So far.*

The magic user, though, had felt it coming. He had stood firm behind a quickly raised protection circle as everyone hit the ground and rolled. I froze, horrified as I realized I had just knocked everyone free of David.

"Always thinking, huh?" the man said as the mass of energy in his grip flickered and grew. *"In articulo mortis!"* he shouted, aiming a fisted hand right at David.

Breath a quick intake, I lunged to knock David clear as a green bolt shot from a ring on the man's finger. It hit David square in the chest. "David!" I called as I slammed into him too late, my aura tingling as the curse flickered over me before sinking into the Were. "No!"

I pushed up, David beneath me as he made a choking gurgle. A whine slipped from him as he shook, and then he went still, his open eyes suddenly vacant.

Cassie slid to a terrified halt beside David. "He's alive," I said as she rounded on me, her lips pulled high in a snarl. "It's a curse!" I yelled as she barked at me, her back arched and tail switching. "He's alive. Cassie, he's alive! I can fix this."

"Get Hue in a car," the robed man said as he walked away. "We need to move."

"Ah, Rachel?" Bis said, his wings blowing my hair into my eyes. "Al left."

Surprised, I looked up. The footing of the bridge was indeed empty. And then I felt the blood drain from me. Walter's alpha pack was not running away. No, they were rallying. With David down, the focus was nullified, and with that gone, Walter's pack was gathering in behind the heavy gray wolf with a single, murderous aim: David.

Cassie yipped, and in a sudden rush, the Weres of Cincinnati closed in to make a protective circle about us. Cassie was at the front, her tiny form bristled with her ears pinned and black paws dancing. David slumped behind her. She was wolf chow. Because of me.

"Keep David safe," I said. "That witch is mine."

With a hard purpose, I wove past the assembled wolves to confront the magic user now calmly walking away. "Hey!" I shouted, my face warming when he didn't stop, didn't even slow down. "I said, hey!" I exclaimed again, each foot placed with care as I pulled on the ley line until my entire body tingled and my hair snarled in the magic static I was giving off.

That, he felt, and he turned as if surprised. "Really," he said as he saw me following, free of the pack. This was going to be between him and me. He had hurt David, and until that moment, I hadn't known the depth to which I considered him my family.

"You will not make it from here without leaving something behind," I intoned, my thoughts light in the demon collective as I picked my poison. This would be over fast. *So much for not hurting anyone.*

He halted, his heavily embordered robes furling as he yanked hard on the ley line. Energy coated him, hissing and bubbling as if in affront. "*Ta na shay, palurm!*" he shouted, his disguised voice hollow as he threw a glowing ball of purple and gold at me.

*He invoked the Goddess?* I thought as his curse crackled through the night air. I didn't move, my lips curling up in an ugly smile. "*Pacta sunt servanda!*" I said to bounce it back, and the man's curse jerked as if on a string, keening as it reversed and headed right for him.

He dove to the ground, spelling robes tangling as he rolled to evade it. Clearly alarmed, he staggered to a stand.

"*Implicare!*" I shouted to tangle his feet, and he lurched, going down again. "Uncurse David, you whining cur!" I exclaimed as I strode forward, eager to end this.

The man rolled, his robe hiding him. "Fuck this," he whispered, and the line twanged through me. "*Visio deli!*" he shouted.

I jerked to the side, but I was too close, and with a soundless flash of light, my vision went red.

Gasping, I flung myself back, arm over my face. I could not see. I could *not see!* "*Rhombus!*" I exclaimed, a breath of relief escaping me as my protection circle went up. I cringed, blind as I waited for the thump of a spell hitting my barrier, but there was nothing. My eyes teared and smarted, and my gut began to unclench as I realized the faint haze darting in and out of my vision was Cincy's lights. My vision was returning.

*Thank you, God.* Cowering under my circle, I blinked furiously, listening to the barks and snarls of the packs behind me turn into howls of success.

"Rachel, he's gone. Let me in!" Bis shouted, and I dropped my circle, sure he wouldn't ask if I was in danger. A twinge of heartache found me. Once, he could have passed right through. *And he will again,* I vowed.

"Where's David?" I asked when Bis's feet found my shoulder.

"Cassie has him," the little guy said, and I staggered upright. I couldn't see well, but Cassie's yip of anger kept me wobbling forward.

"Cassie?" I called when the scuffle of wolves and their panting breaths surrounded me. Slowly the night became clearer. Walter and his pack of alpha Weres were fleeing fast, and a ring of bloodied but triumphant wolves circled David and Cassie with more Weres arriving in twos and threes. Bis's tail tightened about me at the sudden roar of an engine, and I tensed.

"It's them," Bis said as a big-ass SUV bumped over the curb and rocked over the grass, its aim unclear but not headed our way. Weres dove in through the open windows when they could, leaving the rest to dodge the incoming I.S. agents and scatter into the night.

We had won?

I jumped when an eerie howl rose from a single throat. In twos and threes, the rest joined it, reasserting their right to live as they would, a warning as old as the moon that they claimed the ground they walked on. Wings shivering, Bis joined in, his low, rough howl bringing everyone to a momentary standstill that dissolved into a nervous dog chuckle. Walter might have nullified the focus by downing David in a curse, but clearly the city was still his.

But any thought of success vanished when I saw Cassie huddled over David. She had shifted. Not a stitch of clothing covered her, and her Black

Dandelion pack tattoo stood out on her shoulder, still red and peeling. Her brown skin was shiny with blood, and tears spilled from the small woman as she tugged David's head onto her lap, not a hint of embarrassment or self-consciousness showing. But it was her tattoos that drew my attention, and I stared at the body-encompassing peacock spreading its feathers across her back, the bright turquoise, green, and orangey red making a stunning show of art and detail.

"Is he okay?" Bis said, but I didn't know, and my gaze lifted over the park to where Al had been. *He left?*

I reached for my phone only to find an empty pocket. *Mother pus bucket*... "Bis, will you tell Jenks what happened? That I'm with David and will call when I can. I lost my phone."

"You got it," the kid said, and with a whoosh of wings and air, he was gone.

"David?" Cassie whispered, the pants of the pack an eerie backdrop as they began to shift painfully fast before the I.S. decided to do something more than keep people back.

"He's been cursed," I said, and Cassie's expression became stricken.

"He's breathin'," she said, her usually faint Australian accent hard in her worry. "Damn it, wake up, David!"

"Hey!" I exclaimed when she smacked his face. "Cassie, don't." I reached to stop her, halting when her gaze met mine. Fear was there, and anger—mostly at me. "I'm going to fix this," I added, and her expression blanked. But not until I saw her outright terror that I couldn't uncurse him this very second.

Someone handed her a pair of sweats, and she wiped her face as she tugged them on. Red, blue, and green stars decorated her thigh in a constellation-like pattern, the slow color gradations making me think it was where she had tested her tattoo colors. "Get him in the car," she said as she stood to put on the rest. "I'm takin' him to the hospital."

I backed up, awkward and feeling out of place as everyone else seemed to have something to do: getting dressed, handing out sticks of wolfsbane-spiked gum to alleviate the pain of shifting, hoisting David into an offered truck bed since lugging a wolf into the front seat of a sports car wasn't going to work.

*Hospital. Yes,* I thought as I hustled to catch up to Cassie. "I'm coming," I said as I closed the gap.

"They were all alphas," Cassie said as she scrambled up to sit beside David in the truck's bed, and I joined her. She was still angry, but I couldn't blame her. She wasn't the one who had slung a stupid spell and made him vulnerable, much less called him to come down here.

"I don't recognize this magic," I said as I put a hand to his shoulder. Senses searching, I sent a sliver of thought out to find his mind somnolent and still. The focus was still there, twined about his soul, but silent. Ring magic had downed him. He had invoked the Goddess. Bis had called him a witch, but he sounded like an elf to me. "Walter downed David to negate the focus," I whispered, but Cassie was too intent on David to listen.

The I.S. continued to stay out of the way as everything broke up, a single officer making the effort to get traffic flowing past the park again. Leaning over the side, I smacked the truck's door, pointing at the street to get us moving. I wasn't sure if I was more worried about the I.S. finding my phone, or not.

"Was it an alpha challenge?" Cassie sniffed back the tears as she wedged herself into the corner and dragged David's wolfy head onto her lap.

"No." I reached for a grip as the truck rocked over the curb and into traffic. Three cars fell in line before us, two behind, protecting us should Walter be waiting somewhere between here and the hospital. "It was Walter Vincent and some magic user I didn't recognize," I said. Walter didn't have much of a paper trail beyond the necessary entry in the Were database, but I had a feeling that Parker had been in the judicial system more than once. *I have a possible lead.*

"Walter Vincent." Cassie's fingers were lost in David's ruff. "The man you stole the focus from?"

"I didn't steal it," I said, still feeling the sting. "Nick, my dead boyfriend, did. I just didn't let Walter have it when it showed up on my doorstep."

Uncaring of the distinction, Cassie bowed her head. Hands never leaving

David, she whispered into his fuzzy ears, tears continuing to spot his fur. It took forever to get through the initial crush, and I felt relief as we turned into a brightly lit street and picked up speed.

But the closer we got to the hospital, the more pensive I became. Walter clearly wanted the focus, and this time, he had a magic user helping him. A powerful one.

# CHAPTER

# 3

I WASN'T KEEN ON HOSPITALS, BUT IF I HAD THE CHOICE BETWEEN A narrow bed with an oversize mug of water and rubbery Jell-O, or a chair in the hall waiting for news, I might take the rubbery Jell-O. Frustrated and anxious, I checked the hall clock again. David's room was across from the alcove of chairs I had settled in. The nurses' desk was between me and the elevators at the end of the hallway, and their whispery-soft voices and furtive looks in my direction were driving me crazy. I was sure they were talking about David.

*Though it could be me,* I mused, glancing at my low boots still sporting grass and dirt. Even better, my jeans were streaked from the truck bed. I didn't want to think about my hair, wild now that the charm to tame it had spent itself. The red curls were troublesome in the best of times, but in the dry air smelling of antiseptic and spells, my hair was almost a halo.

Sighing, I pushed myself deeper into the chair until the back of my head hit the wall. It was well after midnight, and I was getting antsy. I hadn't beaten Walter Vincent the last time we had met; I had survived him. Now he had someone spelling for him, probably an elf. That was why I had used the phone at the nurses' desk to call Trent. My worry that Walter's pack of alphas might continue to cause trouble on the street had been why I'd called Ivy and Pike. I'd called Jenks because Bis was fond of embellishing the truth and I hadn't wanted the pixy to worry. Jenks had been understandably ticked, swearing that I couldn't go out alone for a cup of sugar without coming back with a broken foot.

The elevator dinged and I glanced up, wondering who had made it here first. "Trent," I whispered in relief. I rose as he stepped out, looking more than good in his woolen, calf-length coat, a cashmere scarf about his neck and an unexpected drift of pixy dust on his shoulder. He had two cups of takeout coffee, and a pang of emotion struck through me as he raised them in greeting, his smile both loving and sympathetic. Jenks took to the air, the rasp of his dragonfly-like wings catching the attention of the nurses at their desk where the elevator hadn't.

Suddenly I was fighting unexpected tears, and I blinked fast, forcing myself to smile. It had been a very stressful evening, and Trent had somehow become my rock, the one person other than Jenks that I could be vulnerable around.

"Hi," he said as he set the coffee down and pulled me into a hug.

Exhaling, I sent my arms around his spare but strong form, the tingle of our internal energies balancing a sudden, not unwelcome spark. His birthday was tomorrow—or today, rather—and as we shared a quick kiss, I wondered why the universe saw fit to crowd the day with impossibilities.

"I'm glad you're here," I said as I breathed him in. I could smell coffee and the snap of invoked charms. A whiff of Cincinnati's river-scented air clung to him, a bare hint under his aftershave.

"Aw, you two make me want to puke sugar sprinkles," Jenks said, and I rocked away, smiling at the four-inch pixy hovering beside us. His wings made an unusually heavy thrum as he was working hard to stay in the air. Late October was often too cold for pixies, but Jenks had been shunning hibernation for five years now, wintering in the church and experimenting with pixy winter wear. Tonight he had wrapped himself in scarves and was head to toe in colorful bands of woven cloth. Come December, he and Getty might be the only pixies aboveground.

"Temps okay?" I said, and his sharply angular, tan face frowned.

"You sound like my mother, Rache," he muttered, but he was clearly uncomfortable as he landed on the rim of my cup and angled his wings to catch the rising steam.

Trent was still holding my hand as he sat, pulling me into to the chair beside him. "How is David?" he asked, but his gaze was on my wild hair.

I stared at the closed door, wishing I was brave enough to confront the two spellologists who had kicked me out. "Stable," I said. "Being examined," I added, reaching as I noticed Trent's ear. The sharply pointed arch was gone, and whereas he had spent most of his life with nicely rounded, pedestrian ear arches, he had regained his pointed elven ears after using a transformation curse. At least, he had until today. "What . . ." I started, and Trent's confused expression turned to understanding.

"Oh!" He patted his coat, then awkwardly ran a finger behind his collar to find a wooden charm. "I was at Other Earthlings," he said as he took it off. "Sylvia is fitting my Halloween costume." Smiling, he dropped the amulet into his pocket, and his ears became their pointed selves. "How is Cassie?" he asked as Jenks scraped a wad of caffeine-laced foam from my coffee with a pair of pixy-size chopsticks.

"Okay?" Again I looked at the door. "She's in with David. Thanks for picking up Jenks."

"Like I had a choice?" Trent's lips quirked as Jenks lifted into the air and went to sit on the wall sconce.

"You had a choice." Foam-laced chopsticks held clear, Jenks began to wiggle out of the body-length scarf. "Pick me up, or Jumoke shorts out your garden cameras." A length of fabric fluttered to the table, and Jenks shuddered, clearly glad to be free of it. "How come you're in the hall?" he asked as he one-handedly tugged his faded but elaborately embroidered sweater straight.

*Bluebells?* I wondered as I took up my coffee. "I asked too many questions," I muttered, then added, louder, "Family only at the moment." And whereas Cassie and David weren't married, they were the alphas of the Black Dandelion pack. It was almost closer than a spouse. "An auraologist is in there right now," I said, shoulders slumping as the coffee hit me and the nutty rich scent brought me awake. *Thank you, Trent. This is exactly what I need.*

"Auraologist?" Jenks asked. "What's wrong with his aura?"

"Don't know," I said, remembering the nightmarish ride through Cincy's midnight-busy streets to the hospital; Cassie's whispered, begging threats; the blast of horns as we ran red lights. "I never thought to check." My stomach began to knot. Auras sprang from the soul, and a soul curse was almost impossible to break.

Jenks's wings sounded better as he rose up, warm again. "I'll go take a look."

"Good idea." Pixies could see auras naturally. I'd have to use my second sight—something I wasn't eager to do in a hospital. No telling what, or whom, you might see.

"Back before you can say Tink's a Disney whore," Jenks said, then darted off, sparkles fading as he slipped under the door. He'd be okay. No one saw Jenks unless he wanted them to.

"Thanks for coming down," I said. "I know you're busy with party prep this week."

"It's David." Trent settled in, an ankle going up on a knee. "Besides, Quen is handling most of it. All he left me was to okay the caterers and find a costume."

That last held a hint of annoyance, and eyebrows high, I took in his shiny shoes, wool suit, silk tie, and perfectly styled fair, almost white hair. He was slowly regaining his status after having been accused of trafficking in illegal genetic medicines. Parties were a big part of that. Besides, it really wasn't a party so much as it was a twelve-hour charity event that brought in beaucoup bucks for Cincy's underprivileged.

"A thousand people?" I said, knowing he enjoyed putting it together more than he wanted to admit. "Three bands? How many caterers this year?"

"Six," he said with a sigh. "But it's going to be the last event at the old estate, and I want it to be memorable. I don't know how I'm going to pull this off at Carew Tower next year. Do you think the city might let me rent out Fountain Square?"

His brow was furrowed in real concern, and I found I could still smile. "Probably." I reached across the small space between us and touched his jawline. "But if you throw a party downtown, the entire city will crash it."

"Mmmm." Trent's vacant focus sharpened on me. "I talked to Takata this afternoon. Both he and your mother will be coming in for the week."

I stifled a wince. "She told me," I said, my feelings mixed. I loved my mother, but everything that came into her head came out of her mouth, and putting off her pointed questions as she camped out in my church for an entire week would be a nightmare. *How is your job going? When are you going to settle down and have me some grandkids? What's that burn circle in the floor from? Why is there a hole in your counter? Is there Brimstone in these cookies?*

Trent leaned to put his forehead against mine. "I offered them a suite. They said yes."

"Thank you," I said with a sigh, and he gave me a soft kiss, his gaze worried as he looked at David's door.

"I'd have been here sooner, but I had to put out a fire."

"I can see that," I said, touching his previously spelled ear. "You stand Sylvia up once, and you don't get an appointment ever again."

Trent's focus returned. "Sylvia I can schmooze. It's Lee. I send him an invitation every year, and every year he declines."

My eyebrows rose. "He's coming?"

Trent winced. "Yes, and I doubt it's to wish me a happy birthday."

I nodded. Lee ran the entire West Coast Brimstone trade, and though the two of them had known each other their entire lives—the arranged friendship intended to ease tensions between the two families as they vied for an ever-larger slice of Brimstone pie—I knew firsthand they seldom saw eye to eye. I'd say some of that was my fault, but their "friendship" had been combative and rather one-sided even before I had entered the picture. "I thought you had settled your distribution issues," I said.

Trent sighed, his attention on an orderly as she went into a nearby room. "He claims I've been dealing west of the Mississippi."

I took a slow breath. "Have you?"

Head down, Trent stared at his coffee cup. "His product isn't safe."

"Trent . . . you keep doing that, and he's going to try to take both sides of the river."

"It's not safe," he said again. "And until he ups his purity, I'm going to keep offering it."

I sipped my coffee, knowing better than to argue. Besides, I agreed with him. Unaltered, Brimstone was a dangerous mood booster and metabolism upper all in one. Making it work-safe reduced the mood enhancements to leave only a caffeine-like buzz without sacrificing the increased blood production. Living vampires used it to keep their blood capacity high enough such that their undead didn't have to go outside a small, known circle for their needs. I thought it stupid that humans had outlawed the very thing that kept them off the menu. But that was exactly why the I.S. and the human-run Federal Inderland Bureau, or FIB, looked the other way. It was an unenforced law that only came into play when you were wanted for something else they couldn't pin on you.

Trent's posture eased as he studied the depths of his cup. "Quen disagrees, but I plan on sharing my numbers with Lee. He needs to see the benefits of spending more up front to get a better number at the back. He'd up his sales by eight percent if he'd make his Brimstone work-safe. Do you have any idea how significant an increase of eight percent is?"

I smiled and took his hand in mine. "I doubt a week of partying is enough to soften him up enough to even listen. Lee is a stubborn ass."

Trent grinned, apparently enjoying the challenge. "True, but I've found him more pliable when money is involved." Slowly his smile faded, his eyes on our twined fingers. "This is important, Rachel."

"I know." A faint hum of magic cramped up my arm, and I gave his hand in mine a squeeze. The sensation was coming from the pearl pinky ring Trent had given me last year. It was sort of an "I'm dead and can't get up" spell. Trent had one, too, and they'd both turn black if one of us died or took ours off. Vivian contended mine was on the wrong finger, but I wasn't ready to move in with Trent, much less marry the man. Besides, if Trent had wanted it on my ring finger, he would have sized it for that. He'd made it clear he had no commitment issues, but he knew better than to push, having seen my pattern of self-sabotage when I felt emotionally scared.

"Hey, ah, mind if I ask Lee to help me put in a window ward on my porch while he's here?" I asked, sort of nervous. The ley line charm was complex, more art than anything else. Lee had installed the huge three-story window ward at Trent's estate when he'd been in his teens. My little eighteen by ten would be nothing for him.

Trent smirked, mischief glinting in his green eyes. "That's a great idea. Every time you ask him for help, he chalks it up as a win against me."

The elevator dinged, and Trent stiffened, his fingers slipping from mine as he sat back. *Ivy?* I mused, but my eyebrows rose when the doors opened to show Edden and Glenn, the older man in an ugly, rasping nylon coat, and his son in a flat black wool duster and trendy scarf. I hadn't called them, but Glenn had recently taken over his dad's FIB position of Inderland specialist and would have gotten more info than the news had.

Though markedly short beside his son, Edden carried his chair-weight well, his ex-military body moving with purpose and the expectation that things would go his way. His dark, fine hair had taken on a lot of gray in the five years I'd known him, and his neatly trimmed mustache was white. Though he was officially retired, I still had yet to see him in anything other than his usual creased kakis and button-down shirt.

Beside him, Glenn was positively polished, the Black man's step a little longer, his mien a tad closed, but I'd found his brooding presence hid an adventuresome spirit that kept him just this side of the law. Comfortably muscled, Glenn was tight where he should be. A glint of a stud earring gave him some bad boy bling. Edden had adopted him when he married Glenn's mother, but the two had been on their own for most of Glenn's life. And whereas they looked as different from each other as they possibly could, they were alike where it counted.

And I was really glad to see them.

"Edden. Glenn," I whispered as I stood, my worry for David returning as I pulled Edden into an earnest hug. "Thank you for coming." That was what you said, wasn't it? When someone you cared for was in the hospital and you were helpless to do anything?

My eyes warmed as the scent of Old Spice and coffee puffed up between us. Edden patted my shoulder as if he was my dad. Some days, I felt as if he thought he was. "How's David?" he said, and I let him go. His glasses had a new bifocal line, and a smile threatened.

"Stable." I waited for Trent to finish shaking Glenn's hand, and then I drew the taller man close, giving him a hug, too. After a four-year stint in the military, Glenn had landed at the FIB. Disillusioned, he left to work with a clandestine, humans-only government task force. Now he was back at the FIB, having been disappointed yet again but eager to take on his dad's old job and make the world the way he wanted to see it—one day, one case, at a time.

"Are . . . you here in official capacity?" I asked, seeing his FIB badge front and center.

"*I* am." Glenn glanced at his dad. "He's here for the ride."

Edden harrumphed and hoisted his belt. "I'm here because David is my friend."

"And that's why you're up at two a.m. using my laptop to print out a list of incoming alphas?" Glenn glanced over the seating area, then dragged a chair closer. The loud sound drew the attention of the nurses at the desk, but they didn't say a word, dazzled by Glenn's beguiling smile. "What happened?" he asked, his charm cutting off as he turned his back on them.

Head down, I took my seat, and the three men did the same. I sipped my coffee, stifling a shudder of the memory of Cassie's choked sobs. Trent had heard this when I'd called him, but it still made my gut tight. "Remember Walter Vincent? That militant Were from Mackinaw City?"

Glenn glanced at his dad. "The Were you stole the focus from?"

"I did not steal it," I said, ruffled. "Nick found it in Detroit."

Trent chuckled, eyes on his phone as he eased deeper into his chair. "A search funded by Vincent, whereupon Nick refused to give it to him," he said. "Leading to you pretending to destroy it and giving it to David."

My held breath slipped from me. His words hadn't been in recrimination. Trent knew how dangerous the focus would be in Walter's possession, and I shoved away the mental image of Nick tied to a sink, blood caked and bruised because he wouldn't tell Walter he'd sent the focus to me. The militant Were wouldn't stop with beatings and threats this time.

Edden ran a hand over his face in worry. "He's trying to gain the focus?" he said, and I nodded, understanding his confusion. Any alpha male could challenge David for leadership of the Black Dandelions, sure, but it wasn't as if they got the focus if they won. The sentient curse wasn't an amulet or charm. Not anymore. It was in David's very bones, where it would remain even after his death. At least now, melded to David's psyche instead of a hunk of bone, the curse had some say in how it was used. But perhaps killing David had been Walter's aim. Whoever possessed David's bones would possess the focus, able to wield and control it without opposition. *Shit . . .*

"That's my guess," I said. "His pack of alphas are predictably not very cohesive, but he's got a magic user this time to make up for it. A good one." *Smart.* "His second is Parker. It was a targeted action. If I hadn't been there . . ." But I had, and David had ended up cursed all the same.

I bit my lip, throat tight, and Edden touched my knee. "Take your time."

But I didn't have time, and I pushed the guilt down to deal with later. "I got a good look at him, but seeing as he was using a disguise charm right down to his voice, it won't do much good. He was trying to be an elf and one of his curses invoked the Goddess, but I don't know. His spelling robe was way over-the-top. Demonic, almost."

Trent's green eyes found mine from over his phone. True, the magic user had invoked the Goddess, but more telling was the curse that had downed David. *In articulo mortis.* At the point of death. That it was Latin meant the curse could be elven, demon, or witch in origin. I'd given it to the doctors at emergency, but they didn't know what it was. Al might. Maybe he'd left to go look it up.

"This was my fault," I said, guilt rising. "I accidentally knocked David free of everyone, and Walter's magic user downed him. It was Cassie who held everyone together and drove them off." Twenty pounds of will and snapping jaws—I'd never be that brave.

"Elven magic . . ." Trent's gaze became vacant as he mentally went through his Rolodex.

But it sharpened as David's door opened and the two doctors came out. Cassie was behind them, seeming tired and small, and I stood, my heart going out to her. She was still in her borrowed sweats, her short, kinky hair loose about her head to give her a little-girl-lost mien. A professional bandage was around her wrist, and she moved with a limp. One of her eyes was swollen, the skin around it beginning to purple. Even beat up, the slim, athletic woman was gorgeous. I just looked ugly after a beating.

Trent rose, moving fast to intercept the doctors. His pleasant confidence pulled them to a halt a mere three steps from the door, but I went for Cassie, giving her a quick hug before pushing back to search her face. "How is he?" I asked, and her breath caught.

"Um, about the same. They've tried a couple of things to uncurse him, but nothin' is workin'," she said, the way she pronounced her r's, lost her g's, and the slight rise in voice at her last word a clear indication of her fatigue. She worked hard to cover her accent. "That invocation phrase you gave them isn't known, meanin' it's probably demon."

"We will figure this out," I said as I gave her another hug and the scent of werefox pricked through me. "Are you doing okay?"

The frazzled woman looked over my shoulder to Edden and Glenn standing awkwardly nearby. "I don't know," she said, clearly suspicious of Glenn's badge. I could understand why. The FIB handled human issues. The I.S. handled everything else. "It's Kylie, Trank, Em, and Jedda all over again," she added, brow furrowed.

I felt my expression empty as my grip fell from her elbows. A ring amulet had been what cursed her employees, too, and the doctors still hadn't figured out how to untwist it. Me either, and I had better books. We might have caught a break if it was the same curse. The invocation phrase would be a big help in identifying it.

Cassie's silver-gray eyes flicked to the departing doctors, her jaw tightening when Glenn and Edden inched closer. "Why is the FIB here?" she whispered, and I turned to them.

"Cassie, this is Glenn and his dad, Edden. They're friends of David's. And mine."

"It's nice to meet you, ma'am," Glenn said as his dad leaned to shake Cassie's hand.

"She's a werefox," I said as the man tried not to stare. "From Australia."

"First-generation American," Cassie said, her accent gone. "My parents came over after the Turn."

"Um, nice to meet you," Glenn said again as he shook her hand.

"You said that." Cassie reclaimed her hand, still wearing that same smile I used when I was trying to disentangle myself from unwanted attention without being called a bitch. "I'd offer you some casino chips the next time you're down by the waterfront, but that might be inappropriate if you work for the FIB."

"I don't work twenty-four/seven," he said, but he was already backing down, shelving his obvious attraction to the dark-haired, brown-skinned woman with silver eyes. As did his father, Glenn saw a person, not their background, but unlike his dad, he also had no problem with getting to know them in the biblical sense, either. Cassie, though, was already involved in a relationship. Knowing David, it wouldn't be forever. The man was . . . well . . . yeah.

"Any friend of Rachel's," Cassie said, but I could sense her suspicion as she turned to David's door. I gave Glenn an encouraging smile as I followed her in, and he shrugged, used to being thought of as useless by most Inderlanders. Very few people knew it, but the FIB was hell on wheels when it came to research, investigation, and gathering information, especially on us paranormals. It was their special, paranoid-based gift.

But my faint smile vanished as I inched into the room. *David. I am so sorry,* I thought as Jenks rose from David's shoulder, where he'd been whispering into his bandaged ear.

I didn't see David much outside of his nine-to-five, which usually had him in a suit and tie while adjusting insurance claims. It might sound pedestrian, but his company insured witches, Weres, and vampires, and their claims often strayed from the norm. His job kept him fit, and his naturally feral grace was even more obvious when he was in fur and not his usual jeans and a crisp black shirt. Now, seeing him pale from a forced shift and Cassie arranging the white sheet about him, it was hard not to cry.

"You're going to be okay, David," I said as I angled past Trent to take David's hand. A faint tingling whispered into me. It was the focus, slumbering within David. His pack tattoo of a black dandelion gone to seed hit me like a cold smack, and I fought to keep my breath even.

"Is there anythin' you can do?" Cassie whispered from his other side, and guilt rose. There were too many people in here, but everyone wanted to help.

"I don't know what this is," I admitted as I gave David's hand a squeeze. "Walter's magic user isn't an elf simply because he invoked the Goddess. Demons can use elf magic." *Though only Hodin and I did.* "Witches, too, though they don't very often." *Which might be because every time they work with the elves, something really bad happens.* "The idea of asking a deity to intervene on their behalf doesn't sit well with them," I whispered. *A deadly, mischievous, capricious, unreliable deity. Crap on toast, we might be in trouble.*

Trent frowned. "I'm still going to look into it."

"Rache, take a squint at his aura," Jenks said. "It's the same as Cassie's people."

Cassie's breath caught, and I shifted nervously, nodding that I would.

*Ring magic,* I thought as I unfocused my attention to bring up my second sight. Hodin liked using elven magic. He liked storing magic in rings, too. But Hodin was safely ensconced in a tulpa, unable to escape what was basically solitary confinement. The mischievous demon had tried to get me to become his lackey before I'd gotten smart. That Hodin might have dangled the "student" card before someone else as well wasn't a big jump.

*Great,* I thought as reality went indistinct and the haze of the ever-after layered over it. It was dark in the ever-after—which made this easier—but I could still feel a hint of a breeze and smell the tall, wet grass. It had been raining there, too, and pushing the sensation of a chill, damp night away, I focused on the nebulous reality of everyone's aura.

Even using my second sight, I couldn't see my own aura, but Jenks's was a swirling, ever-changing rainbow. Cassie's was her expected green and blue, currently dull about her heart from her fear and worry. Trent's was a red-streaked gold, oddly similar to mine apart from the added sparkles. Glenn's was a greenish yellow, again holding slashes of red indicating a troubled childhood. His father's was a comforting blue, tending to yellow about his hands.

David's should have been a warm reddish brown with gold highlights, reminding me of a toad's eye. But today? Today it was an odd greenish yellow, nothing like Glenn's healthy tone. It was flatter, too, reminding me of the stolen aura of an undead vampire's. Not only that, but it wasn't covering all of him, thin at his extremities. It was exactly the same as Cassie's people.

"Jenks is right," I whispered, and Cassie sniffed back her tears.

"The auraologist thinks it's the same, too," she said, and I dropped my second sight.

"Hodin escaped?" Glenn guessed, having made the same connection as I had, and I shook my head, sure that if Hodin had, Dali would be screaming at me for breach of contract and demanding I put him back in his tulpa.

"Hodin could have been teaching someone," I said. "Someone stupid enough to think they can take his magic and run with it now that Hodin is gone. The good news is that Hodin wasn't that talented. He wrote everything down, which means if we can find the book the curse is in, it will probably have the countercurse as well."

But even as I said it, my shoulders slumped. The book might be in Hodin's old room, but I had yet to get past the door. *Maybe I should pick up a book on breaking magical locks.*

Jenks's wings hummed as he flew closer, and I swung my snarled hair clear. "You think Dali might let you talk to Hodin?" he said as he landed on my shoulder, and I shook my head again, feeling like a heel when Cassie's sudden, obvious hope crashed.

"Not a chance, and even if he did, he isn't Hodin anymore," I said. The demon was now hosting the baku, and both wanted me dead. I would learn nothing there. "We need to concentrate on finding the magic user. Glenn, I know it's a big ask, but can you get me access to the street cams? Maybe we can track where that truck went."

"You need somethin' to make a findin' charm?" Cassie blurted, cutting Glenn off.

"Why? What you got?" I said, pulse fast, and Cassie chuckled darkly.

"A wad of fur I ripped off the F-wit's face," she said, and Jenks smirked, hands on his hips as he landed on the bed rail. "It's Vincent's. I pulled it out from between my teeth when I shifted, so you might have to clean it. Find Vincent, you'll probably find that magic user."

"Perfect," I said as she reached into the pocket of her sweatpants, and I let go of David's hand to take the tuft of silver fur. "This is great," I said, the rough hair bumpy in my grip. "Find Walter, find his magic user, find the countercurse."

"Hot damn on a stick!" Jenks flew up and down, and then his expression hardened as his gaze went to the door. I turned, shocked to see Doyle standing in the doorway, his muscle-bound, thick-chested presence a threatening silhouette.

"Rachel Morgan," the I.S. detective said, his low voice seeming to drift in behind me as if to push me closer to him. "You aren't proposing to make an illegal finding charm, are you?"

"Hey, Doyle." My fist closed on the fur, hiding it. My voice was casual, but it was hard when his scrumptiously deep, sex-incarnate voice was swirling around in my brain. Doyle was a high-blood living vampire and looked it from his elegantly scarred skin to his perfect physique. It meant he had lots of potential, tons of drive, and a dangerous amount of sexual attraction. Unfortunately he was also a dime a dozen in Cincinnati, and without an undead sponsoring him, he was continually overlooked and passed over. And of course, he blamed me.

Trent cleared his throat as the I.S. detective pushed in, his dark eyes touching on everyone before settling on Glenn—with attitude. "Why is the FIB here?" Doyle said.

Jenks bristled. "Because unlike you, David has friends," he said, his wing pitch rising.

Doyle's insincere smile widened to show his short but very sharp canines. "I have friends," Doyle said, voice rumbling. "And you have no business here. This is an Inderland matter. No humans needed."

I took a breath, my words catching when Trent touched my elbow and nodded at Glenn. The FIB detective wasn't backing down. His time dating Ivy was standing him in good stead, and his relaxed tension screamed confidence.

"I'm the FIB's Inderland specialist," Glenn said. "All I need is someone to ask me."

"Ah, I ask," I said quickly. "I'm asking."

Doyle shrugged, his good-natured smile covering a hard anger. "Taking over for your daddy, mmmm? Up a little past your bedtime, aren't you?"

Glenn smiled to show his flat, even, human teeth. "I get more done after dark."

"Me too," Doyle said insincerely. "Morgan, I believe this is yours."

I fumbled to catch my phone as he tossed it at me, relief warring with suspicion. "Thanks," I said as I unlocked it to see that everything was as I'd left it.

"Ms. Castle?" Doyle gestured to the door. "You are the head alpha of the Black Dandelions at the moment, are you not? A word?"

Cassie touched David, bending to whisper something in his ear. It hit me hard, and my protective streak flared. "She's busy," I said. "Talk to me. I was there."

Doyle's smile widened. "If I want your deposition, I'll get a warrant and drag you in."

"It's okay, Rachel," Cassie said, and I exhaled, ticked. "I'll be right back," she added as she moved around the bed, touching the peak of David's feet in passing.

That last had been whispered to David, and I felt that Gordian knot about my chest tighten as her hand slipped away and she turned to Doyle, her expression a mix of hope and fear.

"Stay out of this, Morgan," Doyle warned me, his threatening bulk huge next to Cassie's diminutive height. "Those were not Cincy Weres. Which means they were probably new packs drawn in by the focus and were simply figuring out where they stood."

"You seriously think that was an alpha challenge?" I said. "That was an attempted abduction. If I hadn't been there to stop them, David might be dead right now."

"Rache . . ." Jenks muttered, and I flushed, following his gaze to Cassie. Her eyes were wide, and she was blinking fast, trying not to cry.

"Oh, God, Cassie, I'm so sorry," I said as I reached for her, but it was too late.

Doyle's hand was surprisingly gentle as it landed on Cassie's shoulder. "We know about Vincent," he said as he drew her off. "He's been in Cincy for a week."

Lips parted, I spun to Glenn, but he was as surprised as me. "And you didn't tell David?"

Cassie took a breath, held it as she looked over the room with damp eyes, then let it go. "I'm sorry," she whispered, then paced quickly from the room. Doyle strutted out after her.

Jenks's wings rasped as he hovered beside me. "If he makes her cry, I'm gonna pix him."

"Something is off," I added, not liking how fast Cassie had agreed to talk to him. Most Inderlanders didn't trust the FIB, but it felt like more than that. "Can you . . ." I twitched my finger in the "follow" gesture, and the pixy bobbed up and down.

"Easier than slipping on slug spit," Jenks said, his dust brilliant as he flew out after them.

Edden chuckled as he slapped his son on his shoulder. "Not too late to back out, Glenn."

"Not a chance." His dark eyes alight, Glenn rocked forward on his feet. "Parker," he said, focus distant. "Walter Vincent. Mackinaw. Could you excuse me? I'd like to talk to the nurses."

I nodded, but he was already striding out into the hallway, the door slowly shifting shut. I wasn't ready to leave, and I picked up David's patient tablet, relieved to see that he was scheduled for a daily chakra balance. Clearly the doctors had already made the connection between him and the four people downstairs. For what it was worth.

"I'll be back in the morning. Hang in there, David," I said as I gave his hand a quick squeeze. The four Weres in long-term care were not getting better. Actually, they were getting worse. Finding Walter's magic user might be their only chance. David's only chance.

I doubted that Cassie was going to leave, and as Trent said something encouraging to David, I rummaged in my shoulder bag for a phone charger. I left it on the table, hesitating to take in David's pale face before giving him a chaste kiss on his cheek.

"Bye, Cassie," I said as we hit the hall, and she gave me a preoccupied wave. I was eager to get home and search through my books to find something to bolster and balance chakras. Trent's head was down over his phone again, and I sighed, hoping he would put the thing away long enough to give me a ride home. Edden filed into place behind me, and the muted conversation of Cassie and Doyle was a soft murmur, indistinct and somehow comforting in its mix of high and low voices. *Like parents in the night,* I thought, feeling helpless.

"Doyle is a frog halfway down a duck's throat if he thinks I'm staying out of this," I said, frowning when I realized Trent had stopped just outside the door to finish his text.

Edden chuckled. "Glenn isn't going to let this go, either," he said as his arm went over my shoulder. "I'd appreciate it if you'd keep a watch on him until he finds his feet."

I glanced at Glenn leaning comfortably against the nurses' desk, Jenks on his shoulder as they chatted them up and possibly gained some information. "Absolutely."

But my mood soured when I saw Doyle and Cassie at the other end of the hall. The vampire had her practically pinned to the wall. She was holding her own, gesturing earnestly, but Doyle was clearly not happy, with his arms over his chest to make his biceps bulge.

"Glenn is so much better at this than me," Edden said, a wistful pride in him as he gazed at his son. "I'm honored that he wants to continue what I started, and I'm grateful that you will be here for him," Edden continued. "I'm not going to miss this—"

His voice broke, and I tugged him into a sideways hug. Retirement was going to be hard on him. "*I'm* going to miss this," I said softly. "I'm going to miss you."

His breath escaped him in a heavy sigh, and my throat tightened. "You were my first success," the older man said, and then he smiled as Trent joined us, his phone finally put away. "Almost nailed your ass to a judge's courtroom," Edden added.

The rims of Trent's pointy ears reddened. "I have no idea what you're talking about."

Edden grinned, but it faded fast. "I *am* going to miss this," he whispered, and then, after a nod, he squared his shoulders and walked to the elevators, touching his son's shoulder in passing.

"I'm never going to retire," I said as Jenks rejoined us.

"You ain't gonna live long enough to do no retiring," the pixy said.

"Can you stay the night?" I asked Trent, and he nodded, his arm going around my waist as we turned to Cassie talking with Doyle in the corner.

"Now that my calendar is clear." Trent touched his pocket where his phone lay. "I'm yours until morning."

"Thanks." I felt a frown take me. *Why the hell is Doyle arguing with*

*Cassie?* "Patricia's charm shop closes at two. Prepping the finding charm will have to wait."

Jenks's wings rasped as he landed on my neck, his winter wear spilling out over his arms. "And then we go kick some militant Were ass," he said as Trent found my hand and gave it a squeeze.

"Then we go. All of us."

# CHAPTER

# 4

EYES CLOSED, I STRETCHED, MY FOOT SLIDING AGAINST THE SHEETS as I searched for Trent. But all I found was a cooling warm spot where contentment once rested.

Breath slow and deep, I turned to the windows, squinting to see Trent dressed and sitting with his phone in the only sliver of light to make it past my closed blinds. He was texting someone, his fingers moving dexterously, head bowed and expression intent.

My words to tell him happy birthday caught. "Is it David?" I bolted upright.

Trent started, but his smile was reassuring. "Nothing, and no," he said as he tucked his phone away. "I haven't heard from Cassie, so everything is fine. Go back to sleep."

But the flash of adrenaline had quashed any chance of that, and I slumped into my pillow, fumbling for my phone and the time. "Ten?" I said, feeling the hit. "Good God."

Standing, Trent crossed the small belfry room, shuttered windows on all sides, oak floor beneath, and high rafters overhead complete with a bell. "Not everyone starts their day at noon," he said as he sat on the edge of the fainting couch. A bed wouldn't fit up the narrow stairs, and though it made for tight sleeping, we managed. My breath slipped easy from me as he brushed the hair from my face. "My God, you are beautiful in the morning," he whispered.

"With my hair in disarray," I started.

"And a hazy dream still in your eyes," he finished. Bending low, he kissed me, our lips meeting in a perfect sensation of belonging.

"Happy birthday," I whispered when he pulled back, and a faint smile found him. "You want your present?" It was a cookie cookbook, but seeing as it was demon in origin, each recipe held an earth-magic spell that did everything from cure pimples to put someone into an enchanted sleep. Even if he never made any, it was fascinating reading. I'd gotten it from Al, promising I'd help him make a tulpa in exchange for it.

"All I want is in this room," Trent said, his hand brushing the curls from my face. "Go back to sleep," he whispered, the dim light filtering past my blinds making him into a delicious temptation of magic and sex. "Lee has agreed to look at my profit and loss figures concerning a cleaner product, and I have to go."

My rising libido died, and I propped myself up on an elbow. "At ten in the morning?" I said in disbelief. "He's a witch. Well, he's a witch-born demon. I'm surprised he agreed to that."

Trent stood and tugged his sleeves straight. I could almost see him put on the convincing and utterly false mantle of upright businessman. "He didn't. I want to check my figures before we get together. I'm meeting him at one."

Which was not the best time for an elf, but Lee would know that. "The bastard," I whispered, and Trent chuckled.

"Yes, well, I convinced him to meet me at eight this Saturday at Cincinnati's coffee festival, so we're even." Mental ducks in a row, he bent to kiss me again. "I'll call you later," he said as he pulled the comforter to my chin. "I would just as soon ignore my birthday, but I think Quen is helping the girls make cards. Do you have time to get together today, or will you be camping out at the hospital?"

I thought of his present, then nodded, fully awake. "Not all day. I have to pick up some unprimed amulets at Patricia's. Make up a bunch. Glenn might be able to convince the FIB to drive them around." Getting together was starting to sound chancy, and I felt the need to get up, early hour or not. "If one pings, I'll be busy. Otherwise, I've got time."

"Sounds good. Keep me in the loop." Trent shifted to reach for his phone, frowning as he looked at the screen. The subtle tells that he was leaving vanished, and a stab of fear took me.

"Is it Cassie?"

"Ellasbeth." Trent settled his backside against the dresser as he studied the screen. "I should take this." And then louder, phone to his ear, "Good morning, Ellasbeth. Is the coffee shop going to work to drop off the girls tomorrow? It's on the way to my appointment."

I flung the covers off and put my feet on the floor as the worry line in Trent's forehead deepened. His appointment was actually a golfing date with Lee, and whereas I might have a problem with him playing golf when a militant Were was trying to abduct David, it was really two drug lords hashing out purity standards to everyone's benefit. Inviting Lee to the coffee festival, ungodly early or not, had the same kernel of need, and I wondered if Trent might appreciate some added security. I loved Cincinnati's annual coffee festival.

"You agreed to take them," he said, voice hard. "I made plans. Quen is engaged as well."

I tugged my robe on as I tried to listen in, but there was only a soft up and down of the prickly woman's voice. That, and Trent's pointy ears turning a rosy hue.

"You agreed," he said again, following it with "I'm not saying my work is more important than yours, I'm saying you made a commitment—" His words cut off as Ellasbeth interrupted, and he pinched the bridge of his nose. "I arranged something that requires Quen's presence under the assumption that you would be caring for them."

Trent was not a stranger to the word *no*, but Ellasbeth seemed to enjoy saying it, and I winced when Ellasbeth's voice became loud enough to hear.

"I'm not able to schedule my time as freely as you, Trenton," she said, hitting her faint Seattle accent hard as she was wont to do when feeling vulnerable. "I'm somewhat at the mercy of the university. I apologize, but I simply won't take them tomorrow. I can't walk into a meeting with two toddlers on my hips."

"But you think that I can?" Trent said, clearly angry, and my pulse quickened.

"You are golfing with a college friend," she said bitingly, and I winced.

"I'll watch them," I said as I found my slippers, and Trent's attention flicked up.

"I'm meeting Lee at nine thirty. You aren't even up then," he said.

*Nine thirty? Save me from crepuscular elves. . . .* "That's okay," I said, voice faint.

Trent hesitated for half a heartbeat. "Rachel has offered to step in for you."

I forced a smile, cringing inside. Nine freaking thirty? I'd have to get up with the sun.

"Rachel?" Ellasbeth's voice had gone high. "You said she was fending off a militant werewolf. You will not endanger—"

I lurched forward and grabbed Trent's hand to bring the phone between us. "You got that right, Ellasbeth," I said, my grip tightening when Trent tried to pull the phone away. "I can watch the girls for a few hours until Trent wraps up his purity standard meeting."

Trent yanked his phone back. "I'll see you Saturday a.m., then, as usual. At the estate."

"Saturday," Ellasbeth agreed, her voice tinny. "Please thank Rachel for me. I appreciate her being so accommodating."

*Good God, can she be any more passive-aggressive?* "I'll take them to the cider mill," I said, wondering if I could wrangle Jenks or Ivy into joining me for some added security. Ivy had a bittersweet relationship with kids, having the desire to have children but paralyzed with fear concerning their future. Being a vampire wasn't much fun when you parsed it all out.

Trent took a breath . . . only to let it out, his words unsaid. "She hung up," he muttered as he glanced at his phone and tucked it into a pocket. "Rachel, I can't thank you enough."

"It's going to be fun," I said, already dreading setting my alarm tonight. "We can pick out pumpkins and pet the rabbits." I tugged him into a last hug and kiss, but his thoughts were clearly already with Lee and his meeting. As my lips met his, his grip on me went from casual to posses-sive. That fast, he was entirely in the room, the scent of snickerdoodles and wine rising between us. A little shiver rippled through me, and his breath caught.

"I have to go," he said, but the heat in his eyes said he didn't want to.

His present could wait, and his hand slipped from mine with a reluc-tant slowness and tingle of line energy. "Don't forget to ask Lee about help-ing me with my porch window ward."

"I won't forget. Love you."

"I love you, too." *Desperately.*

Trent slipped out the narrow door. His steps were almost silent on the stair to the foyer, and I listened to him say something, probably to Jenks. A moment later, I felt the air shift as he went outside, and then heard the sound of his car rumbling to life and driving away.

I sighed, staring at my tiny, eight-cornered, peaked-ceiling room. "I really need to get a bed-in-a-box up here."

Slippers scuffing, I headed for the stairs as I mentally moved my scant furniture around to make room for a bed. Even with my spelling area now down in the kitchen where it belonged, there wasn't room for a double, much less the queen I wanted. Until I got past the ward on Hodin's room, I was stuck up here. I wasn't going to kick Stef out of my old one. Rude much?

It had been three months, and Hodin's door was still giving off a warn-ing tingle when I so much as went past it. The window had been even more strongly warded. It had been an annoyance before, but with the possibility that a cure for David and for Cassie's employees might be in there, getting past the ward had shifted from an annoying sliver to a driving need.

Thirty minutes and a shower later, I was on my back porch, my bare feet in a shaft of late-morning sun and a book on breaking magical locks at my elbow. I was still in my robe and pj's, but now I had coffee, and that made the early hour at least tolerable—especially when it was the good stuff Trent stocked my cupboard with.

It was one of those glorious late-October mornings when the air was still warm but you could smell the hint of bonfires in the yellowing leaves. The feeling of settling in, of slowing down, was heavy in the crisp air. It was a time when the sun's heat was sought-after, not avoided, and scrunching deeper into the three-seasons chair beside the unused fireplace, I sipped Trent's stupendously rich, nutty coffee and watched Jenks and Getty having a loud and dust-filled discussion deep in the graveyard. Come sundown, they'd be in the church avoiding the cold, but for now they could handle the temperatures and were likely bringing in the last of their stores.

With a sudden flash of dust, the two parted, their argument clearly not over. Theirs was a tumultuous relationship, what with Jenks used to planning a garden with outside opinions but being the deciding voice, and Getty not yet believing that she didn't have to fight to have her ideas heard and appreciated. Everything was a battle for her. But that the dark-haired pixy had even survived was a miracle.

Tucking my feet up under me, I settled deeper into the overindulgent cushions with my book and coffee. Jenks was headed for me, his shimmering dust a dismal blue and gold as he went from rock to tree, pretending to check on the state of the world as he inched closer.

"Good morning," I said, focused on my book when he finally lit on the chair beside mine.

Silent, Jenks gave me a sour flip of his hand, his wings dejectedly still as he eyed the sunlit garden. Clearly torn, he took a breath, then let it out as he fiddled with the embroidered hem of his jacket. It was worn, patched within an inch of its life. I figured it was one of the last that his wife had made for him, and I wondered if that might be where their argument started.

Though only twenty, Jenks had done more living and dying than many would ever do. His small size and large dreams had brought enough heartache and joy to have crushed a lesser soul. And still . . . he was only twenty, having worries and concerns that plague the young.

"Do you think the wind is too strong by the Davaros statue for holly-hocks?" he finally asked, and I looked up from my book, unsure how I should answer.

"Not if you plant something around them to serve as support," I said. "It might not be sunny enough, though. You may have to trim up that oak." Yeah. That was a good answer, vague and having enough conditions to leave my actual opinion open to debate.

Jenks's expression soured. "Yeah, that's what I thought." Wings blur-ring into invisibility, he rose up, his mood no better.

*Crap on toast, did I make things worse?* "Uh, before you go. If you are free tomorrow, I could use your help with the girls. I told Trent I'd babysit, and I'm taking them to the cider mill."

His dust brightened as I turned the conversation to something less . . . Getty. "Yeah, Trent told me," he said. "Sticky apple juice and wasps. I'm in. What time?"

"Early," I said with a sigh. "I'm picking them up at Junior's about eight thirty. It's supposed to be sunny, but I'll put a heat block in my purse. Any issues last night?"

"No," he said, touching the hilt of his garden sword, ever on his hip. "Not with the Were scouts that Cassie put at six points around the church."

"Excuse me?" I blurted, and the pixy's angular features eased into a laugh.

"Yeah, but they're like two blocks off because she knew you'd be ticked."

"Why? Walter is after David, not me." But as soon as I said it, I scrunched deeper into the cushions in a sudden doubt. *I can't fight her and Hue's influence both. . . .* The magic user's words resonated in my memory, and it was true. I protected David's position, and he protected mine. With one of us gone, the other was vulnerable. My subrosa position was a true balancing act, and I wasn't good at being political.

"Cassie knows you can take care of yourself," Jenks said. "But David counts you as one of his pack, the most vulnerable because you insist on being a loner."

"I'm a demon," I reminded him, eyebrows high.

"One who has to stand in a ley line to get to the ever-after," he practically snarked.

I set the open book down, my hand going to touch the back of my neck where my pack tattoo had once been. Grimacing, I curved my fingers into a fist. Last night hadn't done much for my confidence. "Are they still there?"

Jenks nodded. "Last I looked."

My feet hit the floor, and I stood as my free morning vanished. Cassie wasn't the only one who felt responsible for the pack. "Would you do me a favor and ask them to come in? I'm going to make them pancakes before I send them home." *Pancakes. Pick up some blank finding amulets. Visit Cassie and David at the hospital. Prime the amulets. Find Walter. Kick his ass. Sing happy birthday to Trent. Not all necessarily in that order.*

"Sure." Jenks rose up on a column of sparkles. "Save me some syrup. I'm going to need it to convince Getty we need to put the hollyhocks somewhere else. The woman has no idea how the sun changes from spring to summer to fall."

"She's never had a garden," I reminded him, and nodding, Jenks flew out and up.

"Weres," I mused fondly as I went into the kitchen, taking the time to open all the windows so the fresh, crisp air moved through the room as if I was cooking outside. Six Weres would eat about two full batches, and I went to get the flour out of the pantry. The stack of books that Trent and I had perused last night to find something to balance David's chakras had been shuffled about, and I wondered if it had been Stef. The smart woman was bored out of her mind as she hunted for work, filling her days by studying for her witch exam. For real this time.

"Salt, soda, buttermilk. Do I *have* buttermilk?" I wondered aloud as I moved competently about the kitchen. The contractor who had rebuilt the back had put in enough burners and ovens to feed a small army, the likes of which I wouldn't have normally sprung for except that we had been feeding a small army at the time. The church was a designated paranormal shelter, and I hadn't had a chance to use all the toys yet.

The griddle went down over the burners with a clang, and I turned at a scuff in the doorway. It was Stef, her cotton robe rumpled and her hazel eyes blinking sleep from her.

"Hi," she said as she shuffled to the coffee maker, her hands outstretched as if she was a zombie out for brains. "I thought I heard the shower. You're up early."

"Sorry. Didn't mean to wake you," I said as she poured herself a mug and leaned against the counter, deathly still until she downed her first gulp. "Ah, I've got a half dozen hungry Weres coming over for pancakes. You want some?"

The curvaceous woman glanced up over her mug, smiling. "Pancakes, no. Weres?" Her grin became randy. "Maybe. Can I help?"

"Nah, I got it."

The griddle was beginning to warm, and I set my biggest cooking bowl on the counter. But my lips parted in disgust as I looked inside it. Mouse droppings.

*Son of an everlasting troll baby* . . . "Damn it, Constance! Quit pooping in my stuff!" I shouted as I took the bowl to the trash and shook her little turds in.

Stef's eyes were wide as I stomped to the sink and washed the bowl. Twice. Three times. Still mad, I dunked it in the vat of salt water, and then washed it a fourth. "I swear, why hasn't she found some salt water and changed herself back," I groused. But in truth, putting up with viciously gnawed socks and finding mouse poop on my toothbrush was a hell of a lot easier than dealing with the transformed city master vampire in her true form. I thought it odd that Constance hadn't found a way to turn herself back, as careful as I was about keeping the lid on the dissolution vat when I wasn't spelling. Not that I was complaining. It had taken a lot of effort to curse the erratic, half-mad undead woman into a mouse in the first place. Why she hadn't fled when she escaped last July was a troublesome question.

It could be that Constance knew she'd lost her clout and had nothing with which to resume control over Cincinnati. Or perhaps she was still sulking that the DC vampires hadn't sent her here to rule but to die at my hand when her erratic "management style" caused chaos. It might even be that she was enjoying her downtime with no stress or responsibilities. Undead vampires liked to be the center of attention, but they were basically lazy.

But whether for her lack of clout, or sulking, or vacation, the vampiric mouse had clearly remained in the church after Doyle dropped her cage and she had escaped. I had no idea where she was spending her days. The crawl space was not lightproof.

"Constance again?" the dark-haired pixy asked as she flew in from the garden, and I nodded, flustered as I dried the bowl. Giggling, Getty pirouetted in the air, her exquisite skirt flaring to catch the light. She had spent much of her time the last three months spinning thread from spider silk and plant down, and the undyed fabric was a piece of the garden itself, all browns and golds. "Hang on a sec," she said as she darted to the pixy hole in the screen, jerking to a halt as she almost ran into Jenks.

"Excuse me," the small woman said, her dust shifting to a cold blue, and Jenks hovered before her, making an extravagant, sarcastic gesture. Skirts furling, Getty darted into the garden, her fading dust showing her path.

Jenks came forward with the scent of cold exhaust and dry leaves. "It's going to take them a few minutes to get here," he said, and I set the clean bowl on the counter. "If you ask me, I think Constance likes the church."

"Seriously?" I dumped the flour in, then the baking soda and salt. "I turned her into a mouse."

Stef chuckled, slurping her coffee as she hitched an ample hip up on the barstool chair before the books. "And kept her safe from the sun," she said as she drew one of the books closer. "Saw to her blood needs until she got loose. You bested her, then cared for her. That's what vampires respond to, according to my freshman class of Best Practices in Administering to Vampires. Even the undead ones."

"But she's an old undead. A master vampire," I said as I went to the fridge for the milk.

"Not a very good one." Jenks stood on the rim of the bowl, hands on his hips to look like Peter Pan. "I think she's afraid to return to DC. You were never cruel or manipulative even after you brought her down. Finnis was, and that's where she'll end up if she changes back."

"I suppose . . ."

Jenks's smile fell as Getty came in with a sparkly scarf. I recognized it as a test piece for her new loom, and it was stunning. Frowning, Jenks flew to the top of the fridge to sulk.

Getty spun to show off the scarf, somehow getting it around her neck without tangling it in her wings. "I'm going to give this to Constance," she said, her higher voice almost too fast to be heard. "But only if she promises to stop messing with you."

I hesitated, my batter-covered pinky halfway to my mouth. "You know where she is?"

Getty nodded, looking too pleased to live when Jenks frowned. "Since when?" he asked.

"Since I found her." Getty played with the fringe of the scarf to make it catch the light. "We had a discussion. Just the two of us."

I licked the batter from my pinky, deciding it was perfect. "Where is she?"

Getty smirked. "I can't tell you. That's part of what we discussed."

"She's in the garden. You knew it all the time?!" Jenks said, and Getty flew close, her wings somehow not tangling with his as she landed beside him. "Why didn't you tell me?"

Getty arranged his shirt, sighing at its worn state. "It was part of our deal. I don't tell you where she sleeps so you can't kill her, and she doesn't kill you where you sleep. I thought it was a good deal. If she broke it, I was going to stake her right through her shriveled heart."

Annoyed, Jenks backed up out of Getty's reach.

"It's okay," I said, willing to try anything to get Constance to stop. "I don't need to know where she is as long as I know she's alive—or undead, rather." I wondered, though, how she had gotten six feet down the night she'd bitten Doyle and he dropped her cage. Being a mouse did not negate her vampiric needs and drawbacks. Where she was getting her blood was a mystery I wasn't sure I wanted to solve. "Do you really think she'll quit messing with my stuff for a scarf?"

Getty beamed. "No, but it will open a dialogue." Her expression went severe. "Stay here," she said to Jenks. "I mean it. I don't want you following me. You do, and you will find worse than mouse tracks in your sock drawer."

Scowling, Jenks crossed his arms and slumped against the cookie jar. At least, until Getty leaned in and gave him a kiss on the cheek before zipping out the window again.

I stared, mouth dropping open. "She . . ."

"Yeah." Jenks's tan darkened in a flush as he wiped his cheek to look like a disgruntled sixth grader. "She's been doing that lately. It don't mean anything."

"It means she's happy," I said as I tested the griddle. "Something she probably has never been before. It's a good thing." I hesitated, thinking of his wife. "Isn't it?"

"I suppose." Glum, Jenks picked at the seam of his scabbard.

Silence took hold of the sunny kitchen. The soft hiss of the batter hitting the griddle was pleasant, and I breathed in the scent of cinnamon and nutmeg. He had been devastated when Matalina died defending the garden. I convinced him to keep living, just as Jenks had helped convince me when Kisten had died.

*Why is my life so full of change?* I wondered, melancholy as I sprinkled wolfsbane on the cooking batter. But life was change. Death was when change stopped.

"So . . ." Stef said as the silence began to get uncomfortable. "You're going through your books. Is this for David? You've got lots of sticky notes. That's good, right?"

Jenks slumped against the cookie jar, fingering the hem of his worn jacket. *It's going to be okay, Jenks. Give it some time.* "Yep. I'm pretty sure the curse that downed David is the same one that put Cassie's employees in a coma. I might be able to identify it from the invocation phrase."

"That's the good news," Jenks said from atop the fridge.

"Bad news is that it's not in any of my books," I said. "Al might know." It would explain why he ran off, maybe. Not knowing for sure, I wedged a spatula under the pancake, then let it fall. *Not done yet.* "Hodin is the linking factor between the two curses. You don't happen to know if he was working on anything in his room, do you?"

"He was, but I don't know what it is. Sorry." Stef winced. She'd narrowly escaped being the demon's involuntary familiar, and Hodin's "friendship" hadn't extended to giving her passage past the locked door. Even more frustrating was that she knew his room was as he had left it. The satchel she'd supposedly filled the night Hodin had fled had held nothing. She'd been too scared to put anything in it.

"And then there's what's behind door number three," I said. "Cassie gave me a tuft of Walter's fur. We find him, we probably find his magic user. Beat the countercurse out of him. Soon as Patricia's opens, I'm picking up a pack of blank finding amulets."

Stef took a sip of coffee. "Don't look at me to help you there. She won't sell to me, either. Patricia knows I'm your roommate."

"Which is why I only go in on Thursdays," I said, smiling. "Her day off."

Jenks's wings rasped as he went to sit on Stef's shoulder. It gave him a clear view of the garden, and I felt a stab of hope when Getty zipped in, awash in happy glitters. The scarf was gone.

"She will stop her inappropriate behavior if you give her a measured cup of diamonds. Real ones. Not fake," Getty said, beaming in satisfaction.

*Seriously?* "I don't have a cup of diamonds."

Getty shrugged. "Make her an offer."

"What does she want diamonds for?" Jenks's wings made a harsh clatter. "To sleep in?"

The petite pixy nodded merrily, but it was starting to make sense. No wonder the bling-loving vampire liked being a mouse. "I'm not asking Trent for a cup of diamonds," I grumped. "Will she settle for pearls?" I could give her the ones I'd taken from Nash. They were already unstrung, rolling around in the bottom of a drawer.

"I'll ask." Getty darted back into the garden. Jenks's eyes narrowed as he watched her dust slowly settle, and Stef smiled, hiding it behind a sip of coffee.

"Hey, ah, the hospital called me last night," she said, settling herself more firmly on the stool. "Wanted me to come in and fill in."

"That's positive," I said, and she smirked as if she had a secret. Stef had been looking for a job for over a month, but "filling in" didn't sound like her thing.

"Yep. The week before Halloween is always busy," she continued. "Costume malfunctions, decoration mishaps. That kind of thing. I told them no." Stef chuckled. "Actually, I told them to suck it. I'm not a temporary fill-in they can bring out when there's an emergency and stuff back in the closet when it's no longer convenient."

"Good for you," I said, even as I wondered if the intelligent woman would ever land a job with her aura coated in Hodin's smut and a two-slash demon mark on her wrist. *Not my fault, but still somehow my responsibility.*

"They offered me a full-time position instead," she added, and I snapped my head up in delight. "Fifteen percent raise and a parking spot. I'm in emergency starting tonight."

"Damn, girl! That's great!" I exclaimed.

"Apparently a hint of smut on one's aura calms the shit out of a vampire freaked out on a Brimstone overdose." Smiling, she looked at her hands as if she could see the dark tint covering her. "Never thought any good would come of it."

"Stef . . ." I started, and the woman took a steadying breath.

"If it works out, Boots and I are going to find a place of our own," she said firmly, and Jenks made a sharp nod of approval.

*He knew?* I thought as I struggled for something to say. I mean, I was happy for her, and it would be nice having a downstairs room again, but I would miss her. "You know you're welcome to stay . . ." I began.

Stef pushed her hair from her eyes, the strands still flat from her pillow. "It's time," she said, gaze dropping to her coffee. "I will never be able to thank you for taking me and my cat in when Constance kicked us out of our apartment, but your life—" She chuckled ruefully.

Jenks snorted. "Is going to get you killed," he finished for her, and I forced a smile.

"I was going to say 'makes it hard to keep a boyfriend,'" Stef said instead, and my smile turned real.

"You knew, didn't you," I said to Jenks, and he shrugged, his attention going to Getty as she came in, her dust a happy gold.

"She'll take the pearls," the four-inch woman said proudly, and I exhaled in relief.

"Thank God," I whispered, then flipped the pancakes. Yes, I was paying blackmail to a rodent, but I'd rather do that than continue to find her poop in my spelling bowls. *I really need to catch her.* "Deal," I added, still thinking about Stef finding a new place, and Getty darted out to tell her.

Jenks watched her go, frown deepening. "I thought Constance was in Hodin's old room. That's where she hid the night she escaped."

"If there was a light-tight chamber in Ivy's old room, we would have found it in the reno," I said as I went to warm up the syrup. "Constance probably expanded an old bolt-hole from the fairies. I'm still trying to figure out how she got under Hodin's locked door in the first place. You've tried, right?"

Jenks nodded, looking disgusted that he owned a room he couldn't get into.

*Maybe the repellent spell works via auras,* I mused as I stirred the remaining batter. The undead didn't have much of one, and the aura they did have wasn't even theirs. No soul, no aura.

"Rachel, you want me to keep those going while you get dressed?" Stef offered as she slid from the barstool, and I felt my expression brighten.

"Oh, man. Would you?" I tapped the microwave into motion and licked the stickiness from my fingers. "I'd really appreciate that. They shouldn't be here for . . ." I looked at Jenks.

"Five minutes?" he guessed, and I hustled to the hallway leading to the rest of the church.

Stef tightened the tie on her robe. "I'll make another pot of coffee. Put some wolfsbane in it."

I smiled, thinking Stef was more interested in the Weres than the coffee. "Thanks," I said. "I'm going to miss you when you move out. You know that, right?" I added.

"Me too. Weirdest seven months of my life," the woman said softly, almost to herself.

My thoughts were full of a light sadness as I started down the hallway, and I jumped when Jenks's wings sounded in the tight confines. "Hey, ah, Rache," the pixy said as he hovered backward before me, his dust an awkward blue and gold. "Could you, ah, pick me up something at Patricia's since you're going?"

I eyed Hodin's door as we passed it, the sudden cramping tingle in my gut warning me off. "Sure. What do you need?" The pixy-piss spell had slammed me into the wall the last time I'd tried the door, and I stifled a shudder as I continued into the sanctuary.

"Getty used up my stash of milkweed fiber weaving some stupid blanket," Jenks said. "Blew through it as if it was blueberry nectar. I should have stored more, but I haven't needed any since . . . for a while."

His words had faltered, and I felt a surge of sympathy. He hadn't needed any because it wasn't a buck's place to make clothes in the highly structured pixy society.

"I, ah, thought maybe if I got her some, she might focus on that and stop trying to help me plan next year's garden," Jenks finished, eyes downcast and fidgety.

"Sure," I said, my tone carefully neutral. "Why don't you come with me? Pick it out?"

"You think I should?" he said, and I nodded, a good feeling welling up through me. He didn't want the fiber to keep her out of the garden. He wanted it because she was a crackerjack ace at weaving and he thought it would make her feel productive and needed. And he was right.

"The weather will be nice this afternoon. I could use the company," I said, and his dust turned a contented gold.

"Okay." Jenks's gaze went to the front door to the church. "They're here," he added as the twin oak doors slammed open and six rough-hewn but good-natured Weres rolled in. "All right, all right, all right! Who's ready for some pancakes!"

# CHAPTER

# 5

"YOUR WINGS ARE COLD," I SAID AS JENKS PARKED HIMSELF ON MY shoulder and out of the wind. Patricia's was right in downtown Cincinnati, and the tall buildings had a tendency to funnel even the smallest breeze from the waterfront into an eye-squinting gale. Not a problem in the summer, but in late October it could be deadly to a heat-loving pixy, and I quickened my pace as I headed for Patricia's spell shop.

"Why do you think I'm on your shoulder, witch?" Jenks grumbled. "I thought you and Patricia were still on the outs."

I glanced up at the modest storefront sandwiched between a phone outlet and a comic book shop. "Patricia doesn't work on Thursday," I said, and Jenks snickered. Tomalin would be behind the counter, and Tomalin and I had an understanding—as long as I paid cash.

Smug, I opened the door and went inside. My slow, sedate breath pulled in the wonderful mix of redwood, musky herbs, and snap of ozone that all said magic. I'd always liked spell shops. They smelled so . . . delicious, a mix of power that went all the way to my bones. The chimes tinkled cheerfully, and the spell over the door flashed red from the lethal-magic detection amulet on my shoulder bag. Jenks's wings tickled my neck as he vibrated them to warm them up, and then he was airborne, darting off to do a quick recon. Pleased, I loosened my scarf, eager to wander the aisles and touch everything.

Patricia ran one of the best stores within fifty miles. Ley line equipment was upstairs, perishables and the pricier items down. In the rear by the register was a coffee nook holding a couch, two chairs, and a long table to give the home spell caster a place to spread out and plan a big project. But that was something I'd never been encouraged to do here, and my good mood took a hit. I fit in where I fit in, and where I didn't, it was obvious.

"Unprimed finding amulets," I said as two voices twined in a companionable conversation from the back. I was pretty sure I knew where the prepackaged amulets were. But I jerked to a halt when Jenks darted up, his dust an excited red and gold.

"You are never going to believe who's here."

"Be with you in a moment!" came loudly, and I froze. *Patricia?*

"Crap on toast," I whispered, heart sinking. "Tomalin was supposed to be working today."

"Yeah, but that's not the half of it," Jenks said as I paced to the end of the aisle and cautiously peeked around a stand of facial charms.

*It just keeps raining magic. . . .* I flushed as Patricia's expression shifted from welcome to animosity in half a second flat. Beside her at the couch going over an old spell book were two of the last people I'd expect to see.

"Vivian? Lee?" I stammered as I inched out of hiding. "My gosh, what are you two doing here?" *Together?*

"Rachel." Vivian flipped her short, straight hair out of her eyes and closed the book with a decidedly proprietary snap. "Wow. Small world."

Clearly surprised, Lee smiled, his oval face and straight black hair from his Japanese heritage looking more pronounced next to Vivian's blond and blue-eyed Midwestern vanilla. Trent's best childhood friend was of average build, average height, and had everyday brown eyes. That was where average left Stanley Saladan. The sharply dressed man gracefully rose to his feet from out of the deep couch. Dress shoes clicking, he came forward to give me an awkward, very fast hug. I could feel a hint of dark smut lingering in his aura, but it was less than I remembered. Clearly he had cleaned up his act. Marriage tends to do that to a person.

There was an uncomfortable tingle of ley line energy as our internal balances tried to equalize, and I flushed, embarrassed. "Wow, good to see you," I said as the scent of sand and redwood rose from his black button-down shirt and tie. He had an enviable deep tan, and my gaze went to the tiny scar on his eyelid as his thin lips held his initial smile. Like me, he was sensitive to sulfur, making me wonder if it was an artifact of Trent's dad's tinkering. We had both survived the Rosewood syndrome, but unlike me, Lee couldn't pass the cure on.

"Hi, Rachel," Lee said as Patricia gaped, clearly shocked I knew him. "Is, ah, Trent here?"

I grinned at his slight unease. "No. He's getting ready for his meeting with you, actually." I nodded at Vivian, now sitting with her small hands clasped in her lap. Waiting. "Wow. It's great to see you. How have you been? Family okay?"

Jenks's wings hummed as a flash of pain crossed Lee, quickly hidden.

"Out. Now." Patricia stood, her jeans and sweater rather pedestrian next to Vivian's exquisite outfit and Lee's loosened tie. "I can refuse service to anyone."

"Patricia," Vivian coaxed. "Rachel doesn't have to leave. I'd like to talk to her, actually."

I stifled a wince. Vivian had left a polite but stern request on my voice mail last week, wanting to see that curse I'd spelled Pike's brother with.

"That . . . *person* trashed my store!" Patricia exclaimed, arm shaking as she pointed at me, and Lee's eyes widened, amusement easing his expression. "Get out!"

"Rachel trashed your store?" Lee goaded, and Jenks snickered.

"Technically, it wasn't her," the pixy said. "It was Minias and Al."

Embarrassed, I tugged my bag higher up my shoulder. "What is your problem, Patricia? I know for a fact that your insurance covered it despite the demon clause."

Patricia's jaw tightened, her face becoming even more red. "My shop smelled like burnt amber for three weeks! I lost good customers because of you."

Jenks was on Vivian's shoulder, his whispers making the small woman smirk. "I am so sorry about that," I said, not liking her stifled laugh. "The free publicity from the news didn't hurt, though, did it."

Vivian cleared her throat to hide a chuckle, her evaluating calm as steady as always. Her fall dress suit was a crisp gold and brown, and her fingernails were polished to match. A diamond-encrusted Möbius strip pin glinted in the shop's lighting, and her heels didn't have one scuff on them. It had to be a spell, even though the head of the coven of moral and ethical standards probably didn't have much to do with running the bad guys down. She was an administrative figure now, and I wasn't sure she was happy about it, having once been the coven's go-to for solving complex problems quickly, quietly, and with lots of magic. I know I'd miss it.

"She doesn't seem to be trailing any demons now," Vivian said, and Patricia's attention flicked uneasily between us.

"I just need a set of unprimed finding amulets and a package of milk-weed fiber," I said, not willing to give up. Not when Vivian was sitting there, calm and composed, clearly seeking Lee's advice. I wasn't sure what to think. Why was Vivian asking Lee for help? *Maybe I should have answered her texts.* "And maybe a book on auratic locks," I added sourly.

"What are you stirring?" Vivian asked, her childlike voice high in question, and Patricia fidgeted, stymied. Kicking me out was harder after a coven leader asked me something, and as the older woman clenched her hands into fists, I eased forward so I wasn't hiding behind the amulet rack.

"Finding charms for the FIB," I said, not wanting to elaborate. The charms weren't legal without a judge's order, and everyone in Cincy knew about David's mishap by now.

"And Getty used all my milkweed fiber," Jenks added, still sitting on her shoulder.

Vivian glanced at Lee, something unsaid passing between them. "Oh," she said, voice calculating. "I was hoping you might be working on that countercurse for Brad Welroe."

Worry pinched my brow. "I ran into a snag," I said, then stiffened when Patricia took a large breath.

"Patricia?" Vivian said, and the woman jerked to a halt, hearing the warning as clearly as I did. "How long has it been since your stock was inventoried?"

"Um, last April," she said, eyes wide in question.

"Can I see the paperwork?"

Jenks snickered as the woman went red. "You want it now?" Patricia said, and Lee hid a smirk behind a quickly raised hand and a cough.

Vivian never lost her smile. "Or, you could get Rachel's order," she suggested.

Lee flashed an uncomfortable red as Patricia stared at me. And where I usually might have done something to irritate her, like give her a vampiric kiss-kiss, this time, I only felt a growing dread. There were far too many high-end magic users in this tiny shop.

"Excuse me." Patricia turned on a heel and walked to the back room.

I exhaled. "Thanks, Vi," I whispered as Jenks followed her to make sure she didn't spit in anything. "But I'm not sure I can trust anything that crosses her counter anymore."

"It will be fine. Sit." The coven leader patted the couch. "I insist."

I smiled weakly, wincing at the sound of a muffled tantrum. "Sure."

Lee, though, sort of bounced on his toes, clearly eager to leave. "Vivian, can we finish this later?" Vivian nodded, and the elegant man swooped forward to drag his coat from a nearby chair. "I'll see you later, Rachel," he said as stuffed his arms in the sleeves. "I, ah, am sorry about your pack leader. I hope he's okay. Is there anything I can do?"

"No, but thanks." I inched deeper into the tiny alcove full of books. "Ah, hey, if you have time before the party, my new porch—"

"Trent told me," Lee interrupted, grinning to flash his very white teeth. "I'd love to help. Tomorrow night okay?"

"That would be great." I sat down beside Vivian, a little nervous. She was one of the premiere spell slingers in North America, but it was the law behind her that made me uncomfortable. "Should I pick up anything?"

Eyebrows high, he smirked at the noise coming from the back room. "No. I got it. It's mostly ley line manipulations and some chalk. See you later," he said as he adjusted his scarf around his neck. "Madam Coven Leader," he added formally to Vivian. Scarf furling, he headed through the stacks to the door. "Thanks, Patricia!" he shouted, and then he was gone, the door chimes clinking merrily.

"I should probably go, too," I said, glancing at the thick book Vivian had on the table. I wasn't sure I liked that Lee and Patricia were on a first-name basis.

"I'm glad I ran into you," Vivian said, and I slumped. "I'm beginning to think you're avoiding me," she added, her voice a mix of mocking accusation.

I had been, but I wasn't about to admit it, and I reached for her book. "What are you working on?" I asked. I'd found that the coven of moral and ethical standards had no qualms about using white spells in ways that would land anyone else in Alcatraz. So unfair, but I was curious.

"Ah." Her voice shifted, and she seemed almost embarrassed as she moved the book out of my reach. Not before I caught the title, though. *Ley Line Regression Studies. Wow.* "The I.S. gave me the invocation phrase for the curse that brought down David, and Cassie's employees," she said. "Asked me to find the countercurse."

"That's what I'm doing," I said, feeling the hit. "And you thought Patricia might know? Why didn't you come to me?"

Again she hesitated, the confident woman actually wincing. "I was talking to Lee, actually. This was merely a convenient place to meet."

Not to mention Patricia's was the one place I wasn't likely to be. Upset, I scooted farther down the couch—away from her. "Which still begs the question of why you didn't come to me. I'm the one with the demon books, and it is a curse."

Her gaze darted to mine, a pinch of apology in it.

"You think I did it?" I said, aghast, and she reached out, touching my hand for a second.

"No, of course not," she said. "But I'm not the only voice in the coven."

My mouth was open, but I was too stunned to say anything. "David is my friend," I finally got out, and the polished woman had the decency to look embarrassed.

"Yes, but David is not the first person to be hit by this," she said. "Cassie's employees were holding Pike hostage when they were struck down. As you say, it's a curse. If you can untwist it, there's a chance that you were the one who cursed them."

The I.S. thought I had cursed David?

"It is in your best interest if I don't involve you. Rachel, please," she begged, brow furrowed. "Don't take this personally. I've been working with Lee since Cassie's employees were brought in. He came in early for Trent's party so we could move faster on it."

*She can work with Lee, but not me?* The reason was obvious. He was a witch-born demon, too. If he could do the curse, I could, as well.

I sat stiffly at the far end of the couch. It had gotten quiet in the back room. "Am I a person of interest?"

Vivian slumped. "I would appreciate it if you would stay out of this and let me handle it."

My chest hurt. "That's not going to happen. David is my friend. If it takes a curse to fix them, look the other way and I'll do it. I don't want any credit for it, and your aura stays nice and white." Okay. Maybe that last had been a little bitter, but I was tired of the coven doing things that I couldn't get away with.

"Don't get pissy with me," Vivian said, her own anger beginning to show. "This is your fault. If you were transparent about what you cursed Brad with, I could foster a feeling of trust with the rest of the coven. You're asking me to convince them with no proof that you cursed Brad by accident. That you trusted the wrong person. How can I do that when you won't share what you did?"

I suddenly realized where her suspicion was coming from, and I felt my face go cold. *Brad?* This wasn't about the chakra curse that had downed David. It was about Brad? I couldn't show Vivian the curse that I'd used on him. At least, not until I found the cure. It was a memory curse, one of

Newt's old ones, and it was bad. Even Newt hadn't used it. The monstrosity was progressively eating away at Brad's memory like a disease, and it would land me in Alcaraz.

"Vivian," I started, but my tone said it all. "I showed you Brad's curse before I even twisted it. You said its legality hinged on how it was used."

"I saw an adjusted version. I want to see the original," Vivian said stiffly as the tingle of line magic began to become obvious in the tense air.

Patricia was watching us from the register, a package of wooden amulets in her hand, and I warmed. "For God's sake, Vivian. I'm working on getting Brad uncursed. One of the ingredients is a little difficult to find."

"Is it illegal?"

"No. It's three thousand years old!"

"Really?" she said primly, her hands on her book white-knuckled. "I think you won't show me the curse you used on Pike's brother because you think it might get you in trouble."

Trouble? She said that as if I was going to be sent to the principal's office or kicked out of college, and I pushed deeper into the couch, frustrated.

"You will let him become a vegetable because you are afraid to pay for your magic? Maybe I can help."

"I'm not afraid to pay for my magic," I said bitterly. "I'm afraid of Alcatraz. Have you seen what they do to their inmates? You really want to get into this?"

"Don't change the subject," she said, and I grimaced.

For a moment, neither of us said anything, the snap of ozone sharp in the air. Vivian hadn't tapped a line, and I sure as hell is hot hadn't. We both knew better than to bring magic into this—but my hair had gotten staticky and little coils of freed energy played about Vivian's fingertips until she noticed and shook the tension from her hands.

"I need to see that curse, Rachel. All of it. I'm running out of excuses for you. The only reason shunning papers haven't been filed is because I'm here watching you."

A little rill of panic dropped through me. If they were going to shun me for accidentally using a dark curse, I wasn't about to give them the proof.

"If you show me the curse and evidence of attempted resolution, I can stall them until the first of the year," she said, sounding apologetic.

But if I showed them the curse, they might file the papers this afternoon.

"We all make mistakes," Vivian said as I drew my shoulder bag onto my lap.

It sounded insulting the way she said it, and I stood, tugging my coat closer. "I have to go. I'm watching David this afternoon so Cassie can get some sleep."

Patricia was smirking as she came forward, a plastic bag from the local grocery store in her hand. She didn't want anyone to know I had purchased from her. "Here are your amulets and milkweed fiber. That will be twenty-four fifteen. Cash."

Jenks hovered behind her, shaking his head, and Vivian delicately cleared her throat.

"Patricia, if those amulets have been tampered with, I am going to shut you down. You will be selling braided luck charms from the back of your SUV at Findlay Market."

Face white, Patricia pulled the bag close. "Let me check the expiration date," she said, retreating to the storeroom again. Jenks was a soft hum behind her, and I blinked fast, my emotions swinging wildly. He would keep me safe.

I stood awkwardly before Vivian, appreciating what she was doing, but knowing it wasn't ultimately for my benefit. "You saw what went into Brad's curse apart from a broken bone and some dust. Hodin slipped them in when I wasn't looking."

Vivian's lips pressed. "It makes a wand, if I remember correctly. If you surrender—"

"I'm not giving that to anyone," I said, flustered. "It's buried in my backyard."

Vivian stood, her slight form stiff with conviction. "Then I can't help you," she said, clearly frustrated. Energy snapped between us, but neither would tap a line. We knew better. "Get Brad uncursed, or you will be in Alcatraz by the first of the year."

"Alcatraz!" Jenks echoed, clearly upset, and I felt my jaw clench.

"I'm not going to Alcatraz," I said, more for Jenks than Vivian, but we both jumped when Vivian pushed herself into motion, clearly headed for the door. "Vivian," I called, but the proud woman didn't even slow. "You're right," I added as I followed her, Jenks a tight hum at my ear. "I'm afraid to show you the curse. I'm hurting Brad because I'm afraid of what you will say and how you will look at me. Can you promise you won't think of me any differently? Will you remember what I've done and not punish me for what I'm capable of doing?"

But Vivian kept walking, the chimes a wild tinkle as she went out and slammed the door hard enough to make the glass rattle.

I halted between the aisles, my anger no less potent, but knowing better than to follow her. Patricia was waiting when I turned, her smile ugly. "Not enough money in the world," she said, the bag of unprimed amulets and Jenks's milkweed fiber held behind her back.

My lip twitched, and I tried not to give in to my baser instincts. "You are inconveniencing me," I said, remembering what my dad used to say. "But you are hurting yourself. And I feel sorry for you. Jenks? Let's go."

Silent, Jenks took refuge between my scarf and my neck. My legs felt like water as I walked out, stiff-arming the door and letting it close naturally behind me. It would take about an hour out of my day that I didn't have, but I could get what I needed at the university's bookstore.

But my pace slowed when I saw Vivian sitting on the bench where I had once talked to Hodin, the small woman uncharacteristically hunched over her knees, her brow furrowed in thought. She looked up as I scuffed to a halt, her blue eyes holding regret—and perhaps fear.

Slowly, Vivian pushed from her knees to find her usual elegant posture. "I heard you went wolf yesterday. Lee says the curse to turn into a wolf requires human ash."

My lips parted in understanding. *She thought I twisted a dark curse to Were?* Perhaps this was the root of her mistrust, not my reluctance to show her Brad's curse. "I didn't shift into a wolf last night," I said, feeling cold. "But if I had, it wouldn't have taken human ash. I use salt as a substrate to get the same result. The original curse that the demons used to start the Were race used human ash to give a second DNA pattern in order to rub out any errors so they could breed true." The origin of the curse was ugly, but David and the other Weres were not.

"I didn't realize that," Vivian said. "How is the smut payment? Ah, when you go wolf."

"Marginal," I said, beginning to relax. "No more than a standard earth-magic transformation potion. Where do you think the witches got the recipe?"

A smile flitted and was gone. "There is a lot I don't know, and I'm supposed to know everything." She tilted her head, squinting at me through the sun. "You could fix that. If you weren't so secretive about demon magic."

I thought of Newt's books in my belfry, feeling as if they were lost, tortured children now in my loving care. "I can fix that," I agreed, stifling a shudder when Jenks's wings tickled my neck. "If the coven wasn't so hell-bent on limiting what the demons are legally allowed to do. I could lift you. You could lift me. I just need you to trust me for a little longer."

Vivian's shoulders shifted in a heavy sigh and her focus went distant, seeing through the passing traffic. What I was asking would require her to stand up to the rest of the coven. It might get her removed from office. It might get her shunned.

"Wait here." Vivian stood, purse in hand.

Jenks tugged my scarf as he peered over it, and we both watched her go into Patricia's store, door chime jingling merrily. "You think she's getting our stuff?" he said, and I shrugged.

It wasn't even thirty seconds before she came out with that bag. Breathless, she halted before me, her blue eyes wide. "If she tampered with anything, you let me know," she said, extending it.

She was giving me more than what Jenks and I needed. She was giving me her trust, and emotion welled up through me, heady. I wondered if this was how Al had felt when I first trusted him. Perhaps we were even more alike than I had ever thought. "Why?" I asked as I took it.

"Because you're right," she said, her expression fixed. "We aren't the baddest practitioners this side of the ley lines anymore, and trying to bring you down to our level is stupid when you can lift us higher. Please, Rachel. I need to see what you did to Brad. It is imperative. I won't let you land in Alcatraz. I promise."

It wasn't her asking, but the coven. Even so, I was scared. So was Vivian. We were both on dangerous ground, her trying to sell my innocence to the rest of the coven, and me basically letting a coven member in on demon magic. Giving the coven a deeper understanding of demon magic might be a Pandora's box. Or it might be the way for demons to integrate once again. That's all witches were, really—demons whose blood lacked the complex enzymes needed to kindle the higher magics.

"How do your next few days look?" Vivian asked, but the fear and anger were gone, replaced by a worried resolve. "I need to see that book."

*It never rains, but it pours,* I thought. "Busy, but I can make time."

Vivian exhaled, her posture returning to her usual upright stance. "Okay. Saturday, then. After two? Your place." Her gaze went to the bag in my hand. "You owe me twenty-four bucks."

Lips quirked, I nodded, and after giving me a smile, she turned and walked off.

"Huh. That went well," Jenks said, and I exhaled as I ran a hand over my energy-crackling hair. "Your phone is going to ring."

"Is it?" I said, familiar with his almost psychic ability to hear the electronics switch over. "It's Cassie," I said when I took my phone from my back pocket and hit the accept icon.

"Hi, Cassie." Pace fast, I went the opposite direction as Vivian, heading for my car. "I'm on my way. I've got the blank finding amulets and am ready to go."

"Good, because you were right," Cassie said, her accent making everything into a question.

My smile faltered as my pace slowed. *What kind of life do I have when being right means I'm up shit creek?*

"Ow!" she shouted, clearly not talking to me. "That is still attached, you bloody butcher!"

Jenks inched farther out of my scarf, his dust making my neck tingle. "I'm hearing a lot of commotion in the background," he said.

"Cassie? What happened?" I asked as I held the phone high and dug for my car keys.

"Walter Vincent happened," Cassie said, and a cold drop of reality skated down my spine. "He's got wolf balls. I'll give him that. I left David for ten minutes. Ten cur-blasted minutes to grab a shower in David's bathroom. I didn't even close the door. He and that alpha bitch Parker waltzed in and walked out with David. Pretended they were takin' him down for some tests."

"He's gone?" I exclaimed, stopping dead still on the cold sidewalk. "When?"

"Ten minutes. I would have called you sooner, but I was *tryin'* to catch 'em."

And got herself hurt, from the sound of it. *Walter has David.* The thought sent a ribbon of panic through me, and I quashed it. My gaze went to Jenks as the pixy darted from my scarf, a chill red and gray dust spilling from him. "What is the I.S. doing?" I said, thinking of my blank amulets.

"I don't know."

"Glenn," Jenks said, and I nodded. We had to find David. Now. If we got caught using an illegal finding amulet, Glenn could play the plausible deniability card.

"Ah, I'll be right there," I said, spinning to look at the skyline and place the FIB building. "Scratch that. Meet me at the FIB."

"The FIB?" she blurted, and I broke into a jog as I headed for my car. "What does the FIB care?"

"The FIB," I said again as I hung up to call Glenn. He might be working nights, but he'd come in for this.

Cassie was right. I had to find David before Walter or his magic user killed him. The I.S. was too slow. I needed a human. I needed the FIB.

# CHAPTER

# 6

UNLIKE THE I.S., WHO SEEMED TO DERIVE A PERVERSE JOY FROM making it difficult to get in to see them, the FIB maintained an adequate amount of parking, and I easily snagged a spot in the visitor lot after talking to the guy in the attendant hut. Apparently Glenn had dropped us on his electronic calendar after my call, which was then fed out to the entire building. I wasn't sure if I was impressed by the efficiency or appalled at the lack of privacy, but being told to "find a spot, ma'am" definitely put a spring in my step as I went in the main entrance, Jenks on my shoulder.

"That's not a spell detector," the pixy said as I scanned the open-floor area with its plastic orange chairs left over from the Turn and the long front counter. There was no line at the metal detector, and I headed that way. "Gotta love their innocence."

"They don't need one," I said as I put my bag on the conveyer belt, keys and phone on top. I gave the attendant a smile, knowing the efficiency, dedication, and pure guts the humans had who went toe-to-toe with their Inderlander counterparts. They couldn't compete with the natural skills and heightened abilities that witches, vampires, and Weres took for granted, but humans made up for it in other ways, ways that weren't apparent to most Inderlanders even when they were brought down by them. And they were brought down. Occasionally.

I was still wearing my admittedly smirky smile as my wandering gaze landed on the orange chairs and the guy sitting there. Er, cuffed there.

Thinking I was interested, he leered, going ashen when he saw Jenks and he realized I was an Inderlander. No one else would be coming in with a pixy.

Somehow, that made my day better. Hips swaying, I halted before the woman behind the VISITOR placard. Behind me, people were coming and going, everyone intent on the task of putting foot-into-gut of the bad guy. It was comforting.

Finally the woman looked up, her almost-there smile freezing when she saw Jenks. *That's right, sunshine. I'm not human.* "Hi," I said brightly, and Jenks mockingly saluted her. "We're here to see Detective Glenn. He's expecting us. Rachel Morgan, Jenks, and Cassie Castle. She's going to meet us here."

"Mmmm, Detective Glenn works nights," she said, her smile a little too wide. "Would you like me to make an appointment for you?"

"I already have one," I said, smile just as stilted. "I called him ten minutes ago. He said he was here." He'd never gone home, apparently. "Can you check again?" I mean, really. The guy at the car lot got the message.

"He won't be in until tonight," she said instead of taking thirty seconds to glance at her computer. "If you want to wait, you can sit over there."

My breath came in and out, and still, she stared at me, unmoving. Jenks sniggered, knowing what was going to happen next. There was no way I was going to sit in the orange chairs. Once you sit down, they forget about you as if there was a time-distortion field on them.

"Nah," I said, smiling to show my teeth, and Jenks spilled a bright dust, scaring her. "I'll wait right here." Elbows on the counter, I leaned forward, staring.

"Rachel?" came a high-pitched voice, and both Jenks and I turned to see Cassie struggling to get through the metal detector. "It's licensed," she said to the attendant. "Of course I have a permit. Like hell I'm leavin' it here. Fine. Fine! Keep it. I have an appointment."

Jenks's lips quirked into a smile. "I didn't know she was packing mundane steel."

"Good to know," I said, shifting to make room for her at the counter as she paced forward, scowling as she shoved a tiny piece of paper into her purse where her pistol belonged. Her curly hair was shiny and wet, and she seemed deathly tired.

"I don't know why I'm here," Cassie said as she joined us. "This is a waste of time."

I smiled, draping my arm over her shoulder and turning to the woman behind the counter. "Detective Glenn?" I said pleasantly. "We have an appointment."

The woman's gaze lingered on Cassie's bandages and swollen eye. "Just a moment," she said flatly as she engaged her headset. Suddenly her lips parted and her attention shot back to us. "Sir. Yes. I didn't know you were in this morning. Are you expecting—"

"Rachel Morgan and Cassie Castle," Glenn interrupted, his low voice barely audible. "Send them up. It should be in my appointments."

I beamed as the woman flushed. "Sir, they have a pixy—"

"I would hope so," Glenn barked. "Get them their IDs and send them up. If you are going to make me use this ridiculous app, you'd better darn well look at it."

Cassie cleared her throat, and the woman stiffened. "Yes, sir," she said as she clicked him off. "IDs, please?"

I dropped my bag on her counter and began pawing through it, careful to not show off my cherry-red, high-density-plastic spell pistol—which had *not* set off the metal detector. "Hang on. I know it's here."

Jenks had taken to the air, hovering over Cassie's shoulder as she shuffled through a handful of cards. "I'd go with that one," he said, and the small woman cringed.

"Ah, I haven't had time to get a new license," she said as she passed it over.

"That's fine." The prickly woman glanced at Jenks, then decided not to ask. Shoulders hunched, she scanned them, and the printer under the counter spit out two passes. Clearly irate, she ripped them free, hesitating as she eyed them, then me, and then the pass again. "You're Rachel . . . Morgan? Er, I'm sorry. I didn't know you were *that* witch."

My flush of pleasure vanished. *That witch?* "Thank you," I said stiffly as I snatched the ID from her grip. Jenks hovered beside me, and Cassie inched closer, the spicy aroma of werefox becoming obvious over the scent of hospital soap.

"I only meant," she fumbled, a bright red creeping up her neck as she set Cassie's ID on the counter. "Your hair is so . . . and you don't look at all—"

Her words cut off as Jenks rasped his wings. "You might want to put the shovel down," he said, and she made a tiny noise.

"Do you need an escort?" she managed.

"Third floor?" I asked, and she nodded. "We know the way," I said, bumping into Cassie as I turned. Crap on toast. We had come out of the closet to save the human species from extinction over forty years ago. It wasn't as if she'd never talked to a witch before.

But I wasn't a witch. I was a witch-born demon, and that was something new.

"Wow," Cassie said as she paced along beside me. "That wasn't uncomfortable at all. Tell me again why we are here? At least when I'm insulted at the I.S. it's not personal."

I came to a halt beside the elevators and hit the up button. "Trust me." I hit the button again, in quick succession to feel like Ivy. "The things the FIB can do are amazing."

Cassie's frown deepened when the doors opened and three people strode out. A hushed "I think that's Edden's witch" made me twitch, and I stepped inside and turned, dead center within the lift.

"I'm Glenn's witch now," I said as Cassie and Jenks joined me, and the three people spun, their faces pale. "Get it right."

The doors dramatically closed, and I slumped against the back of the elevator when Jenks hit the button for the third floor. *Glenn's witch . . .* It would get me places, but it was still irksome.

"Rachel is right," Jenks said. "The FIB isn't the swiftest brick in the stack when it comes to politics, but once they get past the them-and-us, they're like real people."

Arms over her chest, Cassie huffed. "I can marshal the entire city to find Walter and David. I don't need the FIB's help."

*Or a finding amulet, either, apparently.* But an entire city of Weres out for blood was not what I wanted. "The FIB is quieter than the I.S. I don't want to get the city's Weres involved."

"You think you can stop them?"

The doors slid apart, and I strode out into the open floor plan. It was pleasantly noisy with the sound of work, and no one looked up. Glenn's office was at the far end. He didn't have a window, but he did have four walls and a door.

"See you there," Jenks said as he darted high over the desks to find Glenn.

Cassie, though, was still in the elevator, and I caught the door before it shut. "Cassie, we are here," I said, and her angular jaw clenched. "I understand where you're coming from. But if you cruise the city, find Walter, and then attack him, I *guarantee* you there will be five years of fighting lawsuits and paying off people who suffer collateral damage in the process. And that's even saying you can recover David safely. I want the backing of a police force. The I.S. is bogged down in procedure, so the FIB is our best bet. Besides, who would you rather have searching for David? A bored I.S. agent, or a FIB detective who counts David as a friend?"

It was the last, I think, that convinced her, and Cassie slipped past the doors as they began to shut again. "Thank you," I said, feeling nervous and upset.

"I don't know what you think a human can do," she said sourly, but I understood her doubt. The ignorance of the woman downstairs wasn't unique, which made what Edden, and now Glenn, was trying to accomplish all the more precious.

"Give him a chance," I said as we wove our way to Glenn's office. It was his dad's old one, and I could find my way blindfolded. Heads were beginning to turn, and I tried to smile. *Edden's witch,* I thought. But the farther we went, the more convinced I was that it wasn't me but Cassie's stunning features that had caught their interest.

"Besides," I added as we slowed at Glenn's open door, "I don't want the pack getting hurt trying to rescue David. The FIB has tools and skills you will not believe."

"I don't see it," Cassie said softly, and as I knuckle knocked on the doorframe, I winced.

Glenn was an organizer, but he had clearly been overwhelmed. Stacks of half-taped boxes made a shaky tower against one wall. Another box of sundry office supplies sat on a chair, and I sighed at the stuffed rat on top, a reminder of Nick, my ex-boyfriend who had cleverly escaped human justice only to fall to demon reckoning.

The detective's desk wasn't much better, with a desktop computer, a laptop, and a tablet all trying to sync. Or at least, I think that's what he was doing. The old-school landline phone and answering machine were both in the trash, and Glenn's top-of-the-line cell phone was resting on a charging pad as if it was a shrine. Clearly he was having issues reconciling his dad's paper existence with his own, electronic organizing.

"Martie?" Glenn shouted as he and Jenks looked up from his computer, the man's expression shifting to pleasure as he saw us standing there. "Rachel, good," he said as he stood, his chair rolling to hit the wall as he gestured for me. "Come see this."

I inched in past the boxes as Jenks rose up and down, dust slipping from him as he went to perch on Glenn's pencil cup. "Hi, Glenn. Merging your offices?"

"In theory, yes." Glenn nodded to Cassie. She'd laced her hands behind her back, clearly not wanting to shake his hand. "I'm starting to wonder if it would be easier to learn my dad's organization system than refiling everything the way it should be." Glenn's attention returned to Cassie—and lingered, his entire mien shifting as he took in her fatigue and annoyance. "I am sorry about David. We will find him. Please come in."

"Sure," Cassie muttered, and I gave her a nudge to be nice, gaze going to the door at a soft knock.

"Glenn, we have talked about you yelling for me," a tall, uniformed woman said, her obvious annoyance hesitating as she noticed us. "Oh.

Hello." Her dark eyes touched on Cassie and me before lingering on Jenks. "I didn't know Detective Glenn had anyone visiting." Her head tilted, small lips parted. "A little late in the season for a pixy," she added as she touched her tightly curling hair, clearly charmed.

"Martie. Good." Motions fast, Glenn sidestepped out from behind his desk. "I want you to meet two of my favorite people, Rachel Morgan and Jenks. They own and operate Vampiric Charms out of the Hollows."

Jenks spilled an uncomfortable yellow dust as he moved from the pencil cup to my shoulder. "Yo," he said simply, but I extended my hand over the desk, appreciating the tall woman's take-no-prisoners attitude.

"Nice to meet you," I said as we shook hands, and she smiled, her gaze darting to the charms on my shoulder bag as if recognizing them for what they were. "Is it Martie, or Officer Martin?" I asked, seeing her full name on her badge.

"Martie, please," she said, smiling. "My dad is Officer Martin. It's a real pleasure," Martie said, and Cassie quietly fidgeted at the niceties. "Glenn has told me he's worked with you before. Did you really bring in a banshee by yourself?"

"No one brings in a banshee by themselves," I said, stifling a shudder.

"True." Martie glanced at Jenks. "Jenks, can I get you anything? I've got some nuts in my desk."

"Martie is into the paleo diet," Glenn needlessly explained, and Martie's smile widened.

"Thanks. I'm good," Jenks said, his wings a nervous tickle on my neck.

"And this is Cassie Castle." Glenn shifted to include Cassie. "She owns and operates the Hollow's floating casinos."

Immediately Martie came closer, her brow furrowed in sympathy as she practically shoved Glenn out of the way to take Cassie's hand in comfort. "I can't tell you how sorry I am that this happened. We are doing everything we can to locate Mr. Hue. I actually found Glenn asleep at his desk this morning when I came in."

Glenn shrugged, clearly embarrassed. "I got an extra two hours by sleeping here than I would driving home and back. And it paid off. Rachel, your idea about the street cams was a good one," he said. "Martie, you know about cars, right?"

"Some," she said, but her fingers were twitching, and I leaned to check out her shoes. She had a very low heel, and I didn't think it was because she was already pushing six feet tall. The confident woman was in a career family, and I felt a twinge of kinship.

"Good." Glenn rustled about his desk until he found a paper and handed it to her. "I need you to go down to impound and find something that runs but needs work. Oh, and put on street clothes. You have some here, don't you?"

"Always," the woman said as she took two steps backward to the door. "Ms. Castle, Ms. Morgan, I'm looking forward to working with you to recover Mr. Hue."

"Um," I stammered, not sure what was going on, but she was already in the hall, her pace fast as she called out for someone to hold the elevator.

Jenks rose up, wings rasping. "What do you got, Glenn?" he asked. "Rachel has a couple of finding amulets to prime for Walter."

"Great. I'll send one with Martie for confirmation." Mouse in hand, Glenn hooked his foot onto his rolling chair and pulled it forward in a practiced motion. "I've got a pretty good lead. Come and see."

"This is taking too long . . ." Cassie complained, and I looped my arm in hers and dragged her closer. I was pretty sure that Glenn noticed, even if he was focused on his computer, clicking open a folder and finding a video.

"Right. Here. Take a squint at this."

He clicked it to play and dropped away. I inched forward, practically shoving Cassie into the chair right before the desk. Jenks pushed off from my shoulder, landing lightly to watch the fuzzy shot of a city street. The time stamp was this morning, and my pulse quickened as first one, then three figures came running toward it, the last rolling a wheelchair holding an unresisting figure. It was David. It had to be.

"They took him out in a wheelchair?" Cassie whispered. "The foul-bred curs!"

Glenn glanced at her. "I pulled this from the street cams a few minutes before I got Rachel's call." Silent, he watched as David was slung into a big cab and driven off.

"I can't see the plate," Jenks said as he stood before the screen. "Can you sharpen it?"

"Nope." Glenn leaned over me to work the mouse and play it again. The scent of his cologne drifted to me, and I smiled. "But we got it at the next light," the man added, and a picture of a street cam photo came up. "It was reported as stolen the day before. Golden Key Kab. Unfortunately we lost it in a parking garage."

Cassie stared at him. "You didn't track the plates of every car that left?"

"We tracked everything that came out for the next half hour. But this particular garage is attached to the subfloors of the Cincinnatian."

My shoulders slumped. "And from there, they could go anywhere. The Cincinnatian doesn't maintain cameras in their undead areas."

Wings humming, Jenks went to sit on Glenn's shoulder, startling him. "They don't want *anyone* knowing what they do down there."

"Or with who," I added, stymied.

"You lost them." Cassie took control of the mouse, halting the feed and zooming in. "Golden Key Kab." She reached for her phone. "Address . . . I'm going to go talk to their owner."

I stiffened in worry, but Glenn was faster. "Whoa, hold up," Glenn said, and Cassie's silver eyes narrowed in challenge. "Walter is using stolen cabs to cover his tracks, but I don't think the owner is in on it. All the cabs in Cincinnati are equipped with LoJack. The ones Walter lifted were disabled, but he made a mistake."

"Which doesn't mean the cab owner is innocent," Cassie started, but Glenn had already taken control of the mouse to bring up a map.

"Agreed, but all the LoJacks went offline at the same spot. Here."

Cassie leaned forward, finger tapping the screen. "I know that place," she said. "That's a chop shop working out of a legit auto repair. The guy who owns it ran up a thirty-grand tab and offered me a stolen convertible. Thanks for the lead."

Cassie stood, forcing me back a step. "No." I reached for her. "You are not taking the pack out there," I said, and the woman stopped short. She had recently become the pack's alpha female, and I knew she was stronger willed than even me. Needless to say, my gut was in a Gordian knot. "Please," I added as Glenn shuffled his feet.

"Martie is going out to check for suspicious behavior," Glenn said.

"Her?" Cassie blurted, and my eye twitched. "She can't even shift."

"She has two years in undercover, and not being a Were is an asset in this particular situation." Glenn's attention went out the open door and into the noisy offices. "Please. Sit. We will know a lot more in a few hours."

"David might be dead in a few hours," Cassie said, and I wondered if I'd be handling this any better if it had been Trent who was abducted. *Probably not.*

"Cassie, please," I said, and she glared at me. "They know what you look like. If you show up, even with a busted car, they will go deeper into hiding."

"So I go as a fox, or you can magic me into someone else," she said.

"Martie has this," I said, brow furrowed. "Jenks can go, maybe, but not you."

"Oh, sure." Cassie cocked her hip, clearly peeved. "Like *he* won't be recognized?"

"No offense, Rachel," Glenn added, "but she's right. If they see a pixy, they'll get twitchy."

Jenks dusted a peeved orange as he flew to the center of the room. "I've been sneaking around since before you shot your first popgun, Glenn. No one is going to see me, much less recognize me. We all look alike to you lunkers."

Glenn took a breath to protest, then thought better of it, lightly rubbing his neck. He'd gotten on Jenks's bad side once. Once was enough.

Cassie deflated with a startling suddenness, seemingly lost as she leaned against the wall beside the door, arms around her middle. "I can't sit here and do nothin'," she whispered, and I touched her arm in support. I hadn't known the depth of her feelings for David. This was more than a fling, and I forced myself to smile—even if she could tell it was a lie.

"When was the last time you ate?" I said, and her eyes welled. "Let's grab something at Piscary's. Give Glenn and Martie time to work. I want to talk to Pike. Maybe borrow his muscle. I don't want to bring the pack in on this if I don't have to."

"This is a pack matter," Cassie said, and I wondered how the Were registry was handling a werefox being a female alpha of a traditional Were pack. Probably better than when I'd been one. "I can't go back to them and tell them that the FIB and Piscary's vampires are handling it."

Silent, Glenn went to one of his dad's file cabinets, and Jenks joined him as he began to search. "Cassie," I pleaded. "I know you want to help, but Walter has his own rules, and they pull on the worst practices imaginable. I don't want you, or anyone in David's pack, to have those nightmares."

Cassie flushed. "You are actin' like a mongrel bludger. David is my alpha."

I glanced at Jenks, not knowing whether that was an insult or not, and he shrugged. "Yeah? Well he's my friend," I said forcefully. "Don't you *ever* think I don't care. I am more worried about David than you are."

Her brow furrowed. "I beg—"

"No," I interrupted. "I'm more worried about David because I know what Walter is capable of. I'm sure you can find him. Crash down on him with half the Weres of the city. But a large attack will be seen. Walter might kill David before we even get close. Subtlety will save David, and that means few, not more. Smart, not force."

Our argument was beginning to filter into the common room, but I couldn't shut the door. I didn't want to get that close to her at the moment.

"Ah, Cassie?" Glenn said, and the woman jumped, rounding on him.

"What?" she snapped, and he dropped an open folder on his desk.

"Look at this before you marshal your pack into an assault," he added, and I blanched, recognizing the ugly photos. The first was Nick, beaten up and nearly dead. A photo of Brett Markson was under it—not the pretty one in the Were registry that Cassie had probably seen, but him on a cold slab, his wounds pale and gapingly empty. Glenn had a handful of photos of the room they had found him in, too, complete with blood-splattered restraints and walls. Walter had tortured him, counting him as a betrayer.

"This is Vincent's work," Glenn said, his manicured fingernails touching Nick's photo. "What he did to Rachel's thieving boyfriend to find where the focus was."

"Thievin'?" Cassie asked, her complexion somewhat gray.

"Long story," Jenks said, his sparkles a sickly blue and green.

Glenn adjusted Brett's photo, making it lie just so. "And this is what he did to a member of his own pack when he walked away because it had gone too far. Needless to say Markson didn't survive. To live through it wasn't Vincent's intent. I've got several reports of permanent maiming that I'm trying to link to him, but Vincent is skilled enough to know what to conceal and how to do it. That's what scares me. What we haven't found."

My stomach hurt, and I stuffed my fear down deep. "Where did you get these?" I said, wanting to hide them in the folder again. "I didn't even know these existed."

Glenn shrugged. "We were allowed to investigate because Nick was human. This," he added, dropping another folder on his desk, "is Parker's work. I got these from the courts."

"My God," I whispered, appalled at the multiple, court-worthy shots of missing digits, ruined eyes, shredded ears. The damage was so bad that Wereing had made it worse.

"Finding Parker's work is easy," Glenn said, seemingly unaffected by the maulings. "She tends to take trophies. Alpha female is new for her. I'm not sure how long it's going to last. She's been a loner since her last pack turned on her."

Jenks took to the air on a column of bright sparkles. "They did what?" he said, shocked.

Cassie was clearly shaken. "You're right," she whispered. "This is too much for the pack. They aren't fighters." But my relief was short-lived when she added, "I have to go."

*Damn it to the Turn and back. . . .* "Cassie."

"I have to go," she said again. "If I'm not there to stop them, they will start looking."

Jenks's wings hummed as he stared at her. Pixies could tell when people were lying, and he didn't seem convinced.

"I'll go home. Get them calmed down." She hesitated. "Eat something."

"Thank you," I said, relieved.

"But if you go out to that chop shop without me, I will make your life a livin' hell," she added, and Jenks snickered, his cheerful dust telling me she meant it.

"Deal," I said. "We'll be at Piscary's until Martie checks in."

"The vampire bar down at the waterfront?" Cassie eyed Glenn, now filing the folders, hiding them with the rest of the atrocities we commit on one another.

"Mmmm. Sounds good. I haven't had a decent pizza since I left Cincy," Glenn said as the cabinet clicked shut, and Cassie's lips parted.

"You can't . . ." she said as Glenn unlocked a lower drawer and took out his sidearm.

"Yes, ma'am," he said cheerfully as he holstered it. "I can and have. Rachel is right. Bringing in vampiric muscle would be an asset. I can't ask anyone *here* to make an assault, which means I need to coordinate with Pike. Me going to Piscary's is better than Pike coming into the FIB." He touched his chest pocket, eyebrows rising as he remembered something. "Give me a second. I want to make sure Martie knows how to use an amulet." Glenn lurched to the door, then hesitated. "You'll wait for me. Right? Let me hear you say it, Rachel."

My lips curled up in a grin. "Glenn, I would never let you walk into a vampire bar alone. Besides, I have to prime the amulets."

"There it is." Motions fast in anticipation, Glenn strode out into the common area, voice raised for Martie.

"You can't be serious," Cassie said, and Jenks dropped down to that stuffed rat to arrange his whiskers. "He's human. You can't take him into Piscary's."

Hip cocked, I looked down at my phone and texted Ivy to save us a table for three. It got busy around noon. "He'll be fine," I said as I hit send and dropped my phone into my bag. Arm going over her shoulder, I guided her out into the FIB's third floor.

"What about the tomatoes?" she asked, rightly worried.

"Don't tell his dad, but he eats them," I said, and she squinted at me in doubt. "Glenn pushed his way into Piscary's one night with Ivy and me and was forced to try one of Piscary's own creations. When he enjoyed it, everyone in the place sort of took him in. I think Piscary gave him a protected status hoping that Ivy would bind him to her and forget about, ah, me, but Ivy didn't want to, so while they are not platonic friends, they are bloodless." *Probably.*

"Oh."

She was thinking, and I eased us to a halt, waiting for Glenn. "Thanks for getting the pack calmed down. Glenn won't mind me sensitizing an amulet in his office." *I think.* Yes, we knew where they were, but an amulet would be helpful in fine-tuning the assault.

"Great. Thanks. Don't leave for the chop shop without me. Promise."

"Promise," I said, but I frowned as I watched her walk through the open offices.

"You want me to follow her?" Jenks said from my shoulder. "Make sure she doesn't do something brave but stupid?"

"No," I said, deathly worried for her. "I want you to follow Martie."

# CHAPTER

# 7

I HELD MY BREATH AS I EDGED PAST THE LIVING VAMPIRES CLUS-tered inside the door of Piscary's. It wasn't that the surrounding people smelled bad. Quite the opposite. Everyone waiting was chatty and in a good mood, most with a glass of something already in hand, just after noon or not. The scent of vampire incense was heady as it mixed with the intoxicating aroma of hot tomatoes, bacon, peppers, and mushrooms. But mostly tomatoes.

"Excuse me. I need to leave my name," I said, and a slim man in gray shifted to give me access. Glenn was tucked in behind me, oppressively close. He wasn't cowed, but people had begun to notice him, and by the number of raised eyebrows, most didn't know his favored status. I wasn't sure what bothered them most, that he was human, or that he was from the FIB.

The host stand was empty. Impatient—and a little uncomfortable with Glenn breathing down my neck—I scanned the large, open floor for Ivy. The restaurant/bar was mostly dark wood. Tables in the middle, booths against the two walls. I'd accidentally blown out the wall common with the parking lot last July, and Pike had put in three garage doors. They were closed at the moment, but come sundown, the parking in front of them would shift to overflow tables. Bright spotlights showcased the tomato theme, and the red fruit was everywhere.

Ivy was working the art deco bar against the wall, the svelte woman

moving competently as she filled drink orders and took the political tem-
perature of Cincinnati at the same time. Pike's logo of a twined *M* and *W*
was front and center on the mirror behind her, the decorative swoops and
swirls done in a classy gold paint. Ivy's long, enviable straight hair hung in
a black sheet, swinging as she moved before it.

She was trim and tall, and her mix of European and Asian heritages
gave her an almost ethereal look. She could have been a model if her tem-
perament wasn't so . . . Ivy, and my skin tingled as she gave a patron a rare
smile, flashing her small but sharp canines. She was a living vampire and
wouldn't get the extended versions until she died. She didn't need blood to
survive, but like most living vampires, she enjoyed it with her sex.

And with that thought, Ivy's head lifted, finding me through the noise
and commotion as if sensing my ripple of remembrance, the delicious feel
of her teeth sliding cleanly into me, bringing me alive.

"You okay?" Glenn said, and I gave myself a mental slap, even as I made
a "kiss-kiss" gesture across the bar to say hi. Ivy smirked and turned away.
I'd always known when Ivy was in the room, and she me. Sort of a creepy
super-sense sort of thing.

"Fine," I said, then coughed to get my voice out of that whispery, come-
hither lilt. My gaze went across the room to a familiar laugh, and my tension eased at Pike chatting up a mixed table of witches and Weres. The
early-thirties man might have once been classically handsome: tall, good
build, light complexion, dark wavy hair. But years of abuse had left their
mark, and scars covered him—not the fun bedroom kind, but the torture,
trying-to-kill-you variety. Even so, he took no pains to hide them, preferring to wear a lightweight, short-sleeved shirt when the weather allowed.
The truly ugly scars remained hidden.

Pike's nose was lumpy from being broken too many times. His hands
were the same. His hip tended to give him trouble, leaving him with a limp
that he tried to hide. And yet . . . I thought him all the more attractive for
it all. I appreciated the marks of his past struggle. It gave me hope that I
could survive my life.

His voice was low and suggestive, and though clean-shaven most of the time, Pike had a hint of stubble today. One of his canines had been chipped, and a pewter ring glinted dully on his right hand. It was his only bling other than the scars. Needless to say, the man's personal allure went all the way, a much-needed attribute seeing as the living vampire was posing as Constance's scion, working with Ivy to keep the Cincinnati vampires in line.

True, Ivy and Pike were waiting tables and mixing drinks, but the reality was that they were keeping tabs on the city. Gossip, requests, complaints, the right word in the right ear—it was how things got done, and Ivy was all about seeing and settling a problem when it was small. Piscary had been training her from birth to take control of the city when she died her first death, and she had a knack for it.

So it wasn't surprising that Ivy and Pike had been doing a far superior job than most undead city masters. They didn't make the demands on a population that a long undead did, and I think their success was much of the reason why the DC vamps had tried to supplant my rule with one of their own. Maybe if they hadn't sent a psycho to oversee Cincy's vampires, I might have ignored Constance, but regardless, I was clearly making them look bad, or rather, pointing out that there was no reason to put up with sloppy stewardship.

"Good thing you called ahead," Glenn said as he peered over my shoulder to the waiting list.

"Piscary's on a slow day." I waved for Pike's attention. I wasn't here for a pleasant lunch; I was here to rescue David, and the pinch of that was growing in my gut.

Pike lifted his hand in acknowledgment, and I eased down to my heels. The tension in his shoulders wasn't obvious, but that's why he made such a good enforcer.

It was crowded and hot. Nina was downstairs, obviously, seeing as the sun was up, but the scent of her was everywhere, an intentional buzz for the living vamps upstairs, reassurance that they were taken care of and that a voice spoke to their concerns. True to his word, Pike had made the motif tomatoes, and pictures of various varieties adorned the walls like mug shots. There were little tomato lights over the bar, and a basket of them at the front door in recognition of Halloween. Six varieties of ketchup stood at every table because . . . well . . . they could.

A mixed-population license hung over the unlit stone fireplace, and if not for needing an MPL to get a liquor license, I'd say it wasn't required. Most humans became physically ill at the sight of a tomato, a quirk that Pike played on to keep them out. Glenn, though . . .

I smiled through my worry as Glenn eagerly eyed the stand of ketchup beside the bar. "They are for sale," I said, and the man's expression lit with avarice.

"Seriously?" he said, gathering annoyed and then wondering looks as he edged through the crowd to reach them. Glenn was comfortable with what and whom he liked, and I was proud of him as he took one of each variety, juggling them in his arms as if they were liquid gold.

"You want some help?" I asked, and he held them closer, head shaking.

Ivy was clearly trying to get out from behind the bar as she gave some last-minute instructions to a green-haired, lots-of-skin-showing bartender. I followed her pointing finger to Brad Welroe as her lips moved. The living vampire was dressed exactly like Pike, sitting behind the bar as he put olives on sticks. The man in his early forties was Pike's brother, and he seemed a little lost as he chatted with people who obviously knew him but he had no memory of.

A flash of guilt took me. Brad had no short-term memory. Worse, the curse was steadily eating away at his long-term, and he was losing his sense of self, day by day, week by week. The countercurse I'd tried hadn't worked. *Atlantean mirror,* I grumped, a pang of worry taking me. Where in the Turn was I supposed to find one of those? I'd tried substituting a hand-polished mirror just last week. It hadn't worked, and I was running out of ideas.

That Cassie had opted out of lunch was probably a blessing in disguise. Brad was the one responsible for her employees being in long-term coma care, the living vampire having made a deal with Hodin for the ring that had put them there. Some might say that losing his mind was a just penalty, but no one deserved to be eaten alive like that.

Exhaling, I squared my shoulders as Ivy finished her instructions and slipped from behind the bar. Heads inclined and bodies pressed back, getting out of her way. Her attention, though, was on me, and I smiled as I reached for her, pulling her close.

"Rachel," she said as she gave me a hug. "Perfect timing. Your table just cleared."

For a moment, there were no militant Weres, no troublesome I.S. detectives, and I breathed her in, feeling her pheromones go to my core in a wash of relaxation. And then her grip eased and she dropped away. I was glad Ivy had found someone to spend her life with who needed her, but sometimes I wondered what might have happened if I'd said yes to her more than once.

"How is it going?" I asked.

"Better now," she said, the rim of brown around her pupils shrinking as she stood before Glenn, her thoughts lost behind a suddenly placid expression. "Glenn. Moved into your dad's office yet?" she asked as she gave him a quick peck on the cheek. She glanced at the bottles clinking between them. "We have a special bag when you buy all six."

"That'd be great." A flush had crept up Glenn's neck. "You look fabulous."

"I could say the same." Smirking, she put a hand on his shoulder and yanked him closer to give him a real kiss, one she clearly wanted to evolve into something more.

It did not go unnoticed, and a light laughter eased through the waiting people as Glenn was officially claimed and tagged as hands-off. It might sound insulting, but it would make for a much more pleasant experience. And as word got around, Glenn would be safer for it, both here and on the street.

But as the kiss lingered and grew, I began to get uncomfortable. I didn't want to know what my friends did in the dark. "Hey, hey. Come on, guys," I muttered. "No one will bother Glenn now. Can we sit down?"

Glenn took a stumbling step as Ivy let go. Her eyes were pupil black, and if it wasn't noon on a sunny day, Glenn might have had to cash that check immediately. But the woman smirked, her mood good as she adroitly caught one of Glenn's bottles when he dropped it. "I'll get you settled, and then we can talk." Hips swaying, she angled to an empty table.

"Good. I want to bring Pike in on it, too, if you can spare him," I said. "We're waiting on confirmation that Walter is on-site before we go in."

Ivy's brow creased. I knew her thoughts and I appreciated her agreement. Lunch was busy, but Walter was erratic and unpredictable. We couldn't wait until after the lunch crush.

"Drinks," she said as she set Glenn's bottle on a small empty table with a bench at the wall and two chairs opposite it. "Glenn, you want a Bloody Mary?"

The table was tight, but that's how Piscary's was. "Iced tea?" I said as I took the bench. "No lemon." But Ivy would know that.

"Virgin, please," Glenn added, and Ivy made another one of her little smirks.

"Can do," she said, gaze flicking to the rafters. "Tell Jenks if he gets dust in my sauce that I will pluck his wings off."

"He's not here." I shifted to the end of the bench when Glenn sat beside me, both of our backs to the wall. "He's doing recon with the FIB."

Glenn froze, halfway through a little scrunch hop. "H-he . . ." he stammered, ending his move with a grimace. "I thought we agreed Martie would go by herself."

My elbows were on the table, chin on my hands. "You can't keep a pixy from anything."

Glenn's brow pinched ruefully. "And you can't keep anything from a pixy."

Ivy hesitated, flinching at a crash from the kitchen that raised an *ooooh* and claps from the patrons. "Let me check on your pizza," she said, then sauntered away.

The table felt empty without her, and neither Glenn nor I felt like talking. The man was fussing over his ketchup bottles, lining them up like soldiers, squinting to read the fine print. Yes, I'd told Cassie that we needed to plan this, but I was itching to get moving. *Pizza. I should have called a city-powers meeting.*

"David has some time," Glenn said as he saw me fidget. "They won't kill him outright."

"If I thought otherwise, I wouldn't be sitting here," I said, resisting the urge to check my phone. The memory of Nick, beaten and bloodied, tied to a sink in a cruddy one-season cabin on an island in the Straits of Mackinac rose in my thoughts, and I grimaced. Walter didn't play by any rules. Even his own.

An eerily fast motion drew my attention as one of the employees set aside a stack of dirty plates to go after Brad. The forgetful man had finished his task and was heading for the door. Pike had noticed, too, but his reaction was far more casual as he got Brad settled at a table that was apparently kept open for him, seeing as there was a gaming tablet on it.

His voice low and casual, Pike lured Brad into playing it while one of the waitstaff took a break to eat with him. It was all very loving and gentle, with no anger or frustration on either side, and I wondered what it said when the most vicious of our species could also be the most caring. Course, they weren't dead yet.

Pike still wore his stilted smile as he wove through the tables to us. "Hi, Rachel. Glenn," he said as he spun a chair around and gracefully sat where he could see us and his brother. "Ivy getting your drinks?"

Glenn nodded, clearly reluctant to set his ketchup aside. "It's busy."

Pike's gaze traveled over the noisy room. "Yep, but it's a good busy." His expression shifted. "David, eh?" he said, his voice low.

"Soon as Glenn verifies Walter is on-site, Cassie is joining us and we are going out and getting him." I hesitated, eyebrows rising. "You want to come?"

Watching the full room, Pike leaned his chair back on two legs. "Me and Brad both," he said, surprising me. "He needs to blow off some aggression."

"Brad?" I questioned, gaze flicking to the absent-minded man now focused on his game with the intensity of a sixth grader. "Are you sure?"

Pike let his chair return to four legs. "You'd be doing me a favor, actually. He's good in a fight. I'll make sure he knows friend from foe."

"Thank you. He's more than welcome," Glenn said, then started when Ivy was suddenly at his shoulder.

"One iced tea and a tomato smoothie," she said as she set down the drinks, then handed Glenn a fancy cloth bag for the ketchups. "So where is David?" she asked as Glenn began fitting the bottles in the narrow sleeves.

I took a sip of my iced tea as Ivy sat with her own glass of fizzing pop and ice. "We're checking out a chop shop where the LoJacks on the two cabs Walter stole were disconnected."

Pike frowned. "The one on Vine?"

"That's the one." Glenn's ketchup was now all safely ensconced, and after setting the bag square on the table as a centerpiece, he took a sip of his "tomato smoothie," his pleasure obvious. "Martie will give me a call if Rachel's amulet pings," he added. "I doubt Walter is foolish enough to leave a thread that large to pull, but it's a start." Sighing, he took another long draft of his drink. "My compliments to the mixologist."

"Thank you." Ivy leaned away, but her fingers were drumming the table, a sure sign she was thinking. "Maybe I missed something. Why isn't the I.S. running vanguard on this?"

Uneasy, I pushed the ice around in my drink. "Because it takes forever to get a court order for a finding amulet, and when Glenn hit gold on the surveillance cameras, we moved."

"That's a good strategy." Pike leaned his chair back on two legs again to check on his brother, then rocked forward. "David is a big part of your subrosa security structure. I'm not keen on going to the I.S. to recover him. Besides, Walter won't kill him outright. They'll try to pull the focus from him first, and if that doesn't work, then kill him."

That wasn't helping, and I gave him a sour look.

Ivy stood in a sudden movement. Three seconds later, a chime rang from the kitchen. "That's your pizza," she said, excusing herself. Behind her, she left an uncomfortable silence. Ivy had seen what Walter was capable of. That that butcher might be carving into David this very instant did not sit well with either of us.

"How's Brad?" I asked, frustrated, and Pike's brow furrowed. He smoothed it nearly as fast, finding a half smile that I knew hid worry.

"Good days, bad days," he said. "Have you found an Atlantean mirror?"

"Not yet. I'm still trying alternatives." Guilt hunched my shoulders, and I focused on the ketchup bag. It was decorated with an old-timey picture of tomatoes on the vine, and I wondered what Glenn's neighbors would think, gasping in horror as they peeked through their blinds when he brought it in from the car. "Vivian wants to see the original curse. If she doesn't put me in Alcatraz, she might be able to help me find a substitute for it."

My tone had been sourly sarcastic, but Pike was too busy watching his brother to catch it. The forgetful man was flirting with a friendly woman at the nearby table, and the waitstaff was having mixed success at diverting him.

"Good. It's time to untwist it," Pike said. "I know he tried to kill me, but I don't like seeing him this way—even if no one else has tried to take a swing at me in the last three months." Pike's thin lips quirked. "I don't know if it's because of what you did to Brad, or because I'm taking care of him and if they kill me they will have to step up and it's a pain in the ass. It's getting more difficult. The more memory he loses, the harder time he has controlling his bloodlust." Pike lifted one of his shoulders and let it fall. "Today is a good day." He frowned at his brother now calling after the woman. "So far. I appreciate your talking to the coven."

"Sure," I said softly, still not wanting to show Vivian the curse until I had the cure. It was dark, illegal magic. That I had been told it was white was immaterial. I was relying on her to speak for my good character and pattern of hack-assery to keep me out of Alcatraz, and I had a feeling this curse would be her line in the sand.

*Never again,* I thought with a shudder, trying to disguise it with a sip of my iced tea.

"That's pretty gutsy," Glenn said, still arranging his bottles. "Voluntarily showing the head of the coven of moral and ethical standards a dark curse."

*Voluntarily, a pixy's tight ass.* "She trusts me," I said, but I wasn't sure anymore.

Glenn's phone hummed against me—we were sitting that close—and he leaned to wiggle his phone from his pocket.

"Hey, sugar tooth!" Brad shouted at a passing trio. "I gots your table for three right here."

Frowning, Pike got to his feet. "Excuse me."

"Is it Martie?" I asked, trying to see, but the profile pic was one of those empty silhouettes.

"Yep." Shoulders tense, Glenn hit the accept icon. "What did you find out?" he said, not putting her on speaker, and I leaned in to hear.

"That I should have listened to my mom and become a mechanic," Martie said. "Over three thousand to fix a squeak and high-speed clunk?"

Glenn cleared his throat. "And?" he prompted.

I could hear the clicking of heels, and then a soft sigh as they went silent. "I did not see Parker, but the amulet went green, and I'm ninety-five percent sure I saw Walter making a call on the shop's landline. There was a grimy plate of glass between us, but he's the right height, right attitude, wide shoulders, and short buzz cut."

A thrill spiked through me, and the vamps at the next table stiffened, sensing it. If Walter was there, then David was probably with him. Twisting, I found my phone to call Cassie. It went immediately to voice mail, and I grimaced, frustrated.

"I'm on a bus at the moment," Martie was saying. "I left the car in case you wanted to play the angry husband. You want me to hang close, or head to the tower?"

"Tower." Glenn had tensed, and the scent of his cologne became more obvious. "I need you to go to my office and find a folder titled 'Tunnels.' See if there are any in the area that they can escape through. Give me a text on what you find. I'm turning my ringer off. Rachel and I are going out there right now with her vampire enforcers."

"You got it," she said, and I reached for his phone, jerking it right out of Glenn's hand.

"Wait! Martie?" I exclaimed, and Glenn gave me a dry look. "I need to talk to Jenks."

"The pixy?" Martie said. "He's not— Hey!" she yelped, and I felt a wash of relief at the sound of rasping wings. "Where did you come from?"

"I'm here, Rache," Jenks said, then louder, "God, woman! It's dust, not Agent Orange. Hold the Tink-blasted phone still."

"Jenks, is it too cold for you to return to the chop shop?" I asked. "A layout of the place would be helpful. I don't think Ivy has had enough time to print out anything." I'd said the last rather sourly. The woman lived to plan, planned to live.

"Will do," he said, and then the sound of his wings faded.

"Sweet mother of God," Martie whispered. "I had no idea he was there."

Glenn arched his eyebrows at me. "Can I have my phone?"

"Sorry."

Sighing, Glenn put the phone to his ear. "Martie? You good?"

"You'll never know, Detective," she said. "Watch yourself."

Glenn smiled as she ended the call, reaching for his glass as Ivy came forward with a large pizza balanced in one hand. Ivy's attention went from Glenn as he downed his drink to my adrenaline-laced posture. "I take it this is to go, then?"

"I need to pay for these." Glenn stood, his bag of ketchup in hand. He got all of three steps, then made a sliding hop back to grab a slice before pushing his way to the register.

My breath to ask him for some zip strips vanished. *Cassie.* I'd promised I'd wait for her, and she hadn't answered her phone. "Ah, Cassie," I started, and Ivy shrugged.

"Leave her a message. You know what Walter is capable of. She'll thank you."

"I suppose." I stood, resolving to call her again on the way. "You're coming, right?"

"Wouldn't miss it." Turning, she called, "Brad! Road trip! Bring your Band-Aids!"

Clearly eager, Pike slapped his brother across the shoulder as he drew him to his feet. Brad, too, looked ready, excited without knowing why, and I felt a little ill. Atlantean mirror or not, I had to find a way to fix this. Now.

Ivy started for the kitchen to box the pizza. Her bike was probably parked at the rear door, and I followed her, hoping she'd give me a ride. Glenn would have to leave his FIB cruiser three blocks away, but Ivy could ride right up to the front door. "I'm surprised you don't want to plan this," I said as I came even with her, and she stuck a hand in her pocket, handing me a folded printout of the chop shop. The exits, including the windows, were circled, and she had already verified there was no official underground access. If there was one, it wasn't registered.

"I'm good."

"Yes, you are," I said, pulse fast. If Cassie didn't check her messages, it wouldn't be my fault.

# CHAPTER
# 8

A STRAY STRAND OF IVY'S BLACK HAIR WAS HITTING MY FACE AS I rode behind her. My arms were loose about her middle, and the thrum of the bike and the shifting of our weight as we moved reminded me of fish in a stream. Breathing her in along with the faint adrenaline buzz, I couldn't help but wonder again what my life would be like if I had said yes to her. But when you were in a committed relationship with a vampire, even a living one, you belonged to them. Your wishes, your dreams didn't matter anymore. Not a problem if you both had the same goals, but Ivy and me? She wanted to survive her past. I wanted to survive my future.

Even so, I sighed when we idled to a halt outside the converted manufacturing building. Letting go of Ivy, I swung off to leave her to balance the bike. The wind had been chilly, and I was worried about Jenks. I'd left a message on Cassie's voice mail that we were on our way here, but a quick look at my phone said she hadn't gotten back to me.

"It wouldn't have been like that," Ivy said, an empty, almost hurt expression on her face.

"What?" I said, confused as I took my borrowed helmet off.

"I'm not an extension of Nina, and she's not an extension of me. But you're right. You couldn't be who you are if you were tied to me. It was a good decision."

I stared, fumbling for my mental balance. "First of all, how do you do that? And second . . ." My shoulders slumped, and a faint, honest smile quirked her lips. "Never mind."

Clearly feeling as if she had scored points somewhere, Ivy took my helmet and set it behind hers on the long seat. "The best, most frustrating years of my life are those that had you in it. Let's go rescue some were-wolf ass."

Nodding, I faced the long, low building. My arm went around her lower back for a few steps, and then we broke apart, our feet striking the ground at exactly the same pace. Yes, my world might be in turmoil, but she was right, and I felt at peace with it all.

The building was six large bays, able to accommodate buses, by the height of them. Unfamiliar graffiti had been painted over the traditional Were symbols. Atop that was Pike's bracketed diamond logo, glinting as if still wet. He had beaten us here, and I looked in the corners for the telltale hint of pixy dust.

Ivy and I shifted direction when a clang of metal rang out, aiming for the three rough, oil-smeared men working with a car on a lift. What I assumed to be Martie's beater sat in another bay, ignored. A leather cushion lay on the ground beside a low couch, both in the sun by one of the open bays. A chain-link fence around the place made a questionable statement, but the corners were clean and the light on the tool-strewn table was bright. There was a fishbowl of a waiting room with cutouts of ghosts and tomatoes plastered to the walls and windows, but I imagined most of their patrons went to the coffee shop next door, seeing as the enormous trash barrel was full of single-use cups.

"This is very loose for you," I said as the heavily tattooed man under the car came out to stand with the others, wiping his hands on a nasty towel as they ogled us. Clearly he was a Were. They all were. "We don't even have an exit plan. You okay with that?" I squinted at the roof, hoping Jenks had put their cameras on a loop.

Her faint smile was devious. "You'd be surprised how easy I play it now. Pike . . ."

I glanced at her, wondering at the extra sway she had put in her hips.

But we *had* been noticed, and there was nothing like flirtation to buoy up the soul. "What about Pike?"

Her pupils held the faintest hint of widening. "Like you, he's best when he's spontaneous. He says you're cute when you get excited. I told him I'd break his other fang if he ever put a finger or tooth on you."

I snorted, but it was nice to be loved. "I can handle myself."

"*You* are not my worry," she said as we came to a confident halt before the three men. "I need someone to look at my engine," Ivy added, her feet spread wide and hands on her hips. "Maybe grease it. I'm getting too much noise when I grind."

"Good God, Ivy," I muttered, but whereas the first two Weres were grinning appreciatively, the other had gone pale.

*Crap on toast, they know who we are.* Or it could have been Glenn, his fast pace and swinging arms practically screaming FIB as he strode up the sidewalk, nearly a block away.

Ivy turned, lip between her teeth as she followed my gaze. "Maybe we should have waited for him," she whispered.

And then her eyes went black at the metallic ringing of a tire iron against pavement.

"You're in the wrong place," the one hefting the tire iron said, and I drew in my arms and shifted my weight, pivoting where I stood. The impact of my foot into the gut of the nearest man was fast and satisfying. Spinning, I hit his jaw with my other foot, seeing as he had conveniently dropped into my range. It was hard to knock someone unconscious. If you did, it meant you had used enough force that brain damage was a possibility. I'd found out over the years that if you gently smacked them around enough, they often faked being out so you wouldn't hit them again.

Ivy, though, liked to be sure, and she knocked the second man out completely with one front kick, snapping his head back to cut his strings and send him to the ground.

That left the tire-iron guy. "Ivy!" I called in warning as I rolled the man I'd dropped to his front, my knee between his shoulders as I wrenched his arm behind him. He'd have to dislocate it to be free, and with a practiced quickness, I zip-stripped his wrists. His ankles would be next.

*Ooooh, bad idea,* I thought, wincing in sympathy as Ivy ducked the man's first swing, then twisted to grab the iron and yank the man spinning into her. The iron bar was now at his throat, and as he choked, she gave another yank, cutting off his air.

Glenn broke into a run, light-footed and efficient, but if he didn't hurry, he was going to miss everything. I got to my feet as Ivy took a hit to the gut. Her eyes black, she let go of him, teeth clenched as she smacked her elbow into his jaw.

Howling, the man stumbled into Glenn's grip.

"Thanks for waiting," the FIB detective huffed, quickly subduing the squirming, pained Were by zip-stripping his wrists.

"You're the one with the swirly lights on top," Ivy said, her expression bright with adrenaline.

"Pike and Brad?" Glenn asked next, handing me a wad of zip strips.

"Inside," I said as the two men still conscious began to squirm.

"I wouldn't," Ivy said softly, giving one a nudge in the nuggies, and he yelped in surprise, glaring at her with a pressed-lip anger. The other went quiet as well, and I frowned at the clearly defunct cameras. Jenks might be with Pike and Brad, but I didn't like not knowing.

"Okay. Let's get 'em inside," I prompted. The buildings across the street weren't vacant, and we hadn't exactly been quiet.

Ivy clamped a hand on the shoulder of one, then another, easily manhandling them inside, leaving Glenn and me to deal with the deadweight of the last. "We should zip-strip him," I said as we dragged him, heels leaving marks in the dirty grease, and Glenn grunted his agreement. Ivy's strength was no surprise to him, since he'd dated her for almost a year.

A pained *ooof* came from the shadows, and we dumped the unconscious man atop the other two. I crouched down as they squirmed to get him off, and Glenn zip-stripped the last. "You know who I am, right?" I said. Smiling meanly, I waved a hand dramatically, making the glyph sign for beginnings. "I just spelled you," I lied as one of them whimpered, his eyes widening in fear. "If you try to go wolf to get out of your cuffs, you will twist your insides into pretzels. It will wear off in an hour, okay? Nod if you understand."

The two men pushed up against the wall nodded frantically, and I patted the cheek of the nearest. "Good. The oil pit leads into the basement, right?"

They bobbed their heads and I stood. "Thank you."

Glenn bounced on his feet for a moment, then sidled close. "You're going to leave them like that? What if they shout for help?"

I glanced at Ivy, and she smirked. "You're right," I said, patting my bag where my splat gun was. "But until you make my position a paying one, I can't legally use my splat gun apart from self-defense. Three zip-tied Weres against one demon isn't self-defense."

Glenn rubbed his chin. "Time spent and materials."

"Done," I said as we fist-bumped the arrangement into reality.

"No, wait!" one of the Weres protested, but I'd already pulled my cherry-red splat gun. The three puffs of air were extremely satisfying . . . and then they were out. It would take a saltwater bath to wake them.

Ivy jumped into the oil pit and levered the heavy iron floor panel up in a silent whoosh. "You two are sweet. Can we move now?"

She held the heavy iron plate as if it was cardboard, and I sat on the cold cement to drop into the pit. "Your foot imprint in their gut can't be traced back to you as my charms can," I muttered, shifting to give Glenn more room when he landed next to me.

Hand on his holstered sidearm, Glenn peered into the darkness, his nose wrinkling at the smell of wolfsbane, oil, and urine wafting up. "Have you reached Cassie?" he asked, clearly reluctant to commit to the dark stairway and its close poured-cement walls. There was no light, but we could hear a muttered echo of conversation, and my thoughts went to Pike and Jenks.

"No. She isn't answering her phone. I left a message."

"They're here," Glenn said. "Let me call in reinforcements."

"Great. They can meet us in the basement," I said, and he frowned, torn.

"This isn't plywood, people," Ivy complained, and with a deep breath, I pushed past Glenn and started down. He was fast to follow, running into me when I slowed for my eyes to adjust. I reached for a ley line, feeling better when the heady energy rushed in, but I quickly dismissed the thought to make a light. According to both Ivy's and Glenn's layouts, there was a huge two-story basement at the bottom of the short stairway, but why advertise our presence until necessary? And besides, my eyes had adjusted. A faint glow grew with each step, and the muted squabble was argumentative, not combative.

"I have point," Ivy said as she brushed past me. The woman swam in darkness. It was her true element.

"You're not going to shoot that, right?" I said as my gaze touched on the pistol in Glenn's grip. I didn't want anyone shot, especially me.

"Right," he said, and then we both started at the faint thump of flesh on flesh.

"Clear," Ivy whispered from the bottom of the stair, and I crept forward, breath held as I stepped over the downed man to come even with her. Glenn was tight behind, and the three of us looked out onto a surprisingly large, high-ceilinged underground room. The stairway came out at the top balcony that circled the open area below. Lights had been strung below our feet, leaving us safely in shadow.

*Storage?* I wondered, nose wrinkling at the scent of river and wolfsbane. Heavy chains dangled from the ceiling to lift dusty machinery set out in a uniform precision. Storage, yes—not for parts but for machinery, forgotten when the need for tank assemblies and bomber engines shifted to cars and refrigerators. It had been abandoned when the machinery of war moved on and made them obsolete. *I had no idea this was here. . . .*

"There," Ivy whispered.

I stifled a shiver as her words iced over my skin, following her pointing finger to an open space. Four people stood in a loose cluster under a faint light, two in a heated argument. A fifth stood at the outskirts, the woman flipping and catching a knife in utter boredom.

"Is that Walter?" I mused, then started, staring at Glenn. "You brought binoculars?"

"Trying to keep up," he whispered as he handed the tiny pair over. "Behind the woman flipping the knife. West of the group."

*West? Which way is west?* I thought as I lifted the binoculars. My pulse jumped. Walter. His stocky, military build and white buzz cut were unmistakable. Face red, he stood eye to eye with that blond magic user, his shouted words almost audible. The knife-flipping woman was Parker, and she snickered when the magic user shoved Walter back with a pop of unfocused spell. The genetic tinkering to keep the elven species alive had left them all looking basically the same, and the disguised man fronting Walter could be Trent's brother. *I wonder if Walter even knows his magic user is under a doppelganger charm.*

"Cassie is down there," Ivy said, voice cold.

"Oh no," I whispered, binoculars shifting. "How did they . . ." And then my words faltered, my anger a heady flash. She was unfettered, clearly there of her own volition as she pushed out of the shadows and headed for Walter.

"Where are you going?" Ivy practically hissed, and I lowered the binoculars. She was talking to Glenn, the vulnerable human now making his furtive way to the far end of the room, where a stairway snaked down. Pausing, he motioned us to stay, then continued on.

"Can you hear them?" I asked as I turned to the floor. *Son of a bastard, no wonder Cassie isn't answering her phone.* She was with Walter. She'd told me to wait for her, then come here herself. Alone. *Please, God, may she be here alone. . . .*

"She had no intention of waiting for your call," Ivy muttered. "I don't see the rest of the pack. Either she was smart enough to leave them home, or they're locked up."

Because if they were dead, Cassie and I were going to have some major trouble. "I can't believe she went around me like this," I said as I focused the binoculars to the shadowed railing to find Glenn, Pike, or the sparkle of pixy dust.

"David," Ivy whispered, and I jumped as she touched my shoulder, pointing.

"Where?" Breath held, I followed her line of sight, my pulse hammering as I spotted him beaten and bruised, caked blood cracking to ooze in ugly rivulets. He lay in the shadows at Parker's feet in an awkward slump, his torn skin showing where they had ripped his hospital gown. "He's awake!" I added when he moved, eyes bright as they fixed on Cassie with a fevered intensity. "They have the countercurse," I breathed, and my gaze shifted to the blond guy still in his spelling robes.

Until David tried to rise and Parker shoved him down with her foot.

"You little . . ." I started, halting when Ivy grabbed my arm. Cassie exploded into motion, yanked to a stop by two clearly nervous alphas. Parker's laughter echoed against the unseen walls, and I eased deeper into the sheltering darkness, tugging my arm free of Ivy's grip.

"You said you couldn't take the focus out of him if he was cursed," Walter shouted, and I fumbled to get the binoculars focused. "Well, now he isn't," he said, throwing something at the magic user's feet. It was a ring, bouncing once before rolling to a halt in front of the man. "Do your magic and rip it out of him," Walter practically growled. "Or I'll rip something out of you."

The robed figure snatched it up, motions holding anger. "You fool!" he said, his loud voice hollow from a disguise charm. "I can't remake it. You made it useless!"

"My God," I whispered, my relief that David was awake shifting to horror. "They're going to try to take the focus out of him." Pulse fast, I lowered the binoculars. "Where are Pike and Jenks? We have to get David out of there."

"No!" Cassie struggled with the two men holding her. "That wasn't part of the deal!"

"Shut up, you little fox shit!" Smile ugly, Parker slammed a fist into Cassie's ear. Staggering, Cassie went down, a hand to her head.

"That's my ring!"

Everyone froze at Brad's confused shout.

"Let go, Pike. Get off!" Brad snarled. "He's got my fucking ring!"

# CHAPTER
## 9

I STARED, SHOCKED AS BRAD BURST FROM THE SHADOWS, HIS HANDS fisted as he plowed into Walter and the man. *He remembered something?* I thought, and then I lurched to the railing when Cassie tried to get to David only to be yanked back by the two men. Howling, she began to fight in earnest. Parker cackled in delight, fingers crooked to gouge as she yanked David up. Brad yelped as Walter coolly snapped his wrist and the ring went pinging into the dark once more.

"Brad! Over here!" Pike shouted as he slid to a halt in the middle of the fray, and his brother stomach-kicked Walter to him.

*Brad thinks it's the ring he used to curse Cassie's security?* I mused as Brad scrabbled into the shadows after it to leave Pike to fight Walter alone. David was awake, and I thought that ring had broken the curse, the same curse that Cassie's employees still suffered from.

"This is the Federal Inderland Bureau!" Glenn shouted. "Everyone on the floor!"

Ivy's hands on the railing went white-knuckled. "They'll kill him."

"Let go, you crazy bitch!" Cassie shouted, and with an intake of breath, I jerked a wad of ley line energy into me, harnessing it in a spell to knock everyone down.

The magic user looked up, his elven tan going pale when he found me near the ceiling.

*That's right,* I thought, feeling strong up here in my high aerie in the shadows. *Felt that, huh? I found you, you little moss wipe.*

"He's running!" Ivy shouted as the man darted for the shadows, spelling robes furling.

"Damn it back to the Turn!" I shouted, frustrated, then yelped as Jenks was suddenly bobbing in front of me. "Follow him!" I said, pointing, and the pixy zipped off, dust a thin line.

Cassie's shrill anger rang high as Walter grabbed her, using her as a shield to keep Pike off him. Ivy swung a leg over the railing to make the jump, and I tensed. I wasn't a vampire, and a drop that far would break something.

"Ivy," I pleaded, and she smirked, wiggling her fingers for me to hurry up. I got one leg over the railing and she jerked me into her, swinging me up and around as if I was a baby.

My gut dropped and I stifled a gasp as my braid flipped into my face. We hit half a second later, my yelp of pain quickly squelched. I'd bitten my tongue. *Crap on toast, I do not need this.*

And then I hit the floor as Ivy dropped me.

"Hey!" I said, then rolled for cover when gunfire echoed, sounding like a cannon in the tight confines. That was *not* Glenn's handgun. Ivy had gone the other way, and I found her unhurt in the shadows.

"Pike!" Ivy whistled to get his attention, then pointed to the sniper. "You got David!" she shouted to me, her eyes eager as she hunched deeper behind a defunct machine.

*David.* I was closer, and I jumped, invoking a protection circle when another shot rang out. It was the last, though, as Pike had reached the sniper and the Were went screaming over the railing to hit the floor in an ugly, wet sound.

Uneasy, I pulled my splat gun and furtively ran to where I'd last seen David. The magic user was long gone. Parker, too. Walter was still here, though, and I skidded to a halt as I saw Cassie pinned to his chest, his weight-pumping, muscular arm holding her close. The werefox was clearly pissed, signs of a struggle hard on her. David slumped on the floor between us, the blood-caked man in his hospital gown hurting too much to get up.

But he was awake, and my thoughts went to the ring that Walter had thrown down, the ring that Brad thought was his. *I can't remake it. You made it useless,* echoed in my thoughts. Clearly the ring Brad thought was his was actually the countercurse, not the curse itself. But if it had woken David, it would wake Cassie's employees. I didn't have the invocation phrase, but Walter obviously did.

"Let Cassie go," I said, and Walter shook his head.

"Walk away, Morgan," he intoned, teeth bared at me. "Or I'll rip out her throat. Right now. Right in front of you. She'll be dead in thirty seconds."

Pulse fast, I lowered my splat gun. "Go ahead. She doesn't mean anything to me."

Walter's brow lifted as he looked at Cassie. "I think she means it. You have no value."

Cassie's eyes widened. "She's bluffin', you idiot!" she exclaimed, wiggling to no effect.

"Behind you!" Glenn shouted, voice faint, and I spun, adrenaline a quick flash.

It was Parker, and she had a gun. Without a word, the woman pulled the trigger.

*Rhombus,* I thought as I fell on David, yanking on the line so hard it hurt.

Red and gold energy rose up with a sodden crack, and Parker's three shots went pinging into the dark.

"What the hell are you doing!" Walter shouted, his face red as he backed up, dragging Cassie before him. "I'm fucking standing behind her!"

"I. Don't. Miss." The wild-eyed woman stood ten feet from me, feet spread and smoke still drifting from the barrel. "That's an undrawn circle," Parker said as she closed the gap. "Can it hold up under point-blank range?"

I pulled David's deadweight closer to me. "Try it."

And then Ivy slammed into Parker, sending them both sliding across the cement floor and into the darkness. Soft thuds and shrill yells punctuated the shadows as they began to fight even before they found their feet.

The gun, though, was not in Parker's hand anymore. Parker, I mused, was going to lose.

"David?" Safe under my protection bubble, I grasped David's face and turned him to me. "Open your eyes. Open them!" I demanded, relief filling me when he cracked his lids, clearly in pain. The focus was still there, swirling like a chained madness, and I set my splat gun down to snip his zip tie.

"Who broke the curse?" I asked as I freed his hands, and a soft groan slipped from him. "David?" He seemed okay apart from a massive beating, and relief trickled through me. "Who broke the curse that you were under?"

"Help Cassie," he rasped, his gaze fixed to Walter struggling to contain a wildly contorting Cassie. Jaw clenched, I grabbed him under his arms and dragged him to the shelter of a machine. The ley line was a wash of tingles as I broke the plane of my circle and our protection vanished. "Doyle's gonna be pissed," David slurred. "You ruined his run."

*Doyle?* I sat him up with a heave, his back against a slab of cold iron. "Are you telling me that Cassie and Doyle planned this? Without me?" I said, voice rising. No wonder she'd ducked out so easily, not answered her phone, gotten me to promise not to move without her. She'd hung with me for as long as it took to find out where Walter was, then ditched me.

"This is a *sucky* plan, David, even if she did get you uncursed." Ticked, I stood over him, not caring that Cassie was fighting for her freedom. She was a big girl, and apparently she didn't need me. "If I hadn't shown up, Walter might have killed you, cremated you, then kept your bones to possess the focus."

David rubbed his ribs, a rueful expression on his face. "I doubt that. He'd have to cart around my entire skeleton. Easier to have his mage pull it out of me. That guy is whacked." Breath held, he tried to stand only to fall back with a pained grunt. "He looks like an elf, but he swears like a witch."

"Where's the pack?"

"Not here," he said, focus sharpening. "Go help Cassie. She needs your help."

"Yeah?" I barked, listening to her struggle with Walter. Ivy and Pike were gone, but I could hear Brad shouting, and there was still some sporadic gunfire. Staggering, I got David on his feet, but getting him up the stairs would be a real challenge. "Ivy! Glenn! We need to move!"

I had no idea where they were, but Ivy's voice returned in a faint "Get David out!"

"That's what I'm saying!" I shouted, struggling with David's weight. "I need some help!"

But there was no sparkle of pixy dust or rasping of wings, and David wasn't cooperative, brow furrowed as Walter finally got control of Cassie. Her hits were beginning to take their toll, though, and David made a satisfied sound when she broke free again.

Walter had clearly had enough. He wiped his bleeding face as he cut his losses and began stalking away. Cassie, though, wasn't done, and howling in anger, the tiny woman ran at him, jumping on his back and gouging his eyes. His expression murderously angry, Walter tried to pluck Cassie off, failing. Maybe if she hadn't lied to me, I might have felt inclined to do something.

"Oh, thank God," David rasped, and I stiffened. "Doyle is here."

My gaze lifted, and I fought with the twin feelings of relief and annoyance as I.S. agents swarmed in, some from the upper balcony, but others from who knew where, shouting and waving red-sheened flashlights that didn't ruin their night vision. But seeing as everyone except Walter had fled, the I.S. agents were yelling mostly at Ivy and Glenn, both of them now with their hands high and unmoving.

Snarling, Walter slammed his back against a machine to dislodge Cassie. The tenacious woman lost her grip and fell, gasping for air. Free, Walter ran for the darkness.

"*Stabils!*" I shouted, funneling the line energy through my free hand. Breath held, I watched the curse fly, my smile of victory quirking my lips.

Until Cassie flung herself at him again, snagging his heel and bringing Walter down.

"Damn it, Cassie!" I yelled as my curse went spinning into the darkness.

Walter stared at me from the cold floor, then kicked at Cassie until she let go.

"No-o-o-o!" Cassie howled, furious as he scrambled up and was gone.

I knew how she felt, and after easing David to the floor, I found my splat gun and slipped it into my bag before the I.S. confiscated it as spoils of war. "Jenks!" I called, then stared into the darkness. Unless Walter's magic user had sprung for a scent charm, Jenks could identify his species by smell. "David, do you know who that spell caster was?"

"No." Head down, David held his ribs. "Everyone called him the mage."

That was no help at all. I jumped at a soul-shaking thump, and the basement was flooded with an eerie amber glow that slowly brightened as the bulbs warmed.

"Top to bottom!" Doyle shouted from the center of the room. "Hey! Did we bring a witch? We need a general finding charm."

"Please tell me you have a pain amulet," David whispered. "My head is exploding." His gaze was on Cassie slumped against a machine. The small woman looked as if she'd been through a wringer, scraped and holding her ribs, a panicked expression on her narrow face. Clearly she was worried about David, and I watched her lips move as she answered the I.S. agent detaining her.

"Yeah. Hang on a sec," I said as I swung my shoulder bag around and opened it up. "Was Cassie present when they broke the curse?" I asked, fingers tingling as I drew it out. "If she heard the invocation and we got that ring, I might be able to uncurse her security." It wasn't the cure for Brad's curse, but it might buy me a few days to produce it.

David fumbled for the small wooden disk as I held it out, sighing in relief when his fingers clamped about the amulet. "I don't know. You'll have to talk to her," he said pointedly.

*Great.* I glanced over my shoulder as Doyle laughed. The large man was with Ivy and Glenn, watching as his men dragged Brad from the shadows. The confused vampire was trying to fight them off even with his broken wrist. Pike was right behind them, clearly angry as he tried to explain that Brad had no functioning memory from moment to moment and that they needed to stop scaring him.

But it was the faint glow of pixy dust slipping from Ivy's shoulder that I was truly searching for, and I made a sharp whistle. Immediately Jenks rose, his amber-green dust billowing about Ivy for a moment before he darted my way.

"Can you walk?" I asked, and David took a slow breath, his eyes never leaving Cassie.

"I'll try," he said, and I tucked my shoulder under his to help him stand.

"Slow it is," I said as we started, but immediately my gut tightened in worry; he couldn't put any weight on his right foot. Walter was a sadist, but this was probably Parker's work.

"Hey, Rache." Jenks flew a quick circle before landing on David's shoulder. "Dude, they beat you bad," he added. "You okay?"

"Need a hot bath," David said, but I didn't like the wet rattle in his lungs. If one was punctured, he'd need more care than I could give him. I wasn't keen on returning to the hospital.

"Who is Walter's magic user?" I asked as we slowly moved forward. "We got him, right? Is he human, elf, or witch?"

"I lost him," the pixy muttered, his high voice tight in self-recrimination. "Didn't even get a sniff."

"Don't worry about it," I said, my grip on David shifting when he swallowed a groan. "Ah, can you do something for me? I need that ring Brad is obsessing over. I think Walter used it to break David's chakra curse. I might be able to wake Cassie's employees with it."

"You want to *help* Cassie?" Jenks said, and David lifted his beaten and bloodied face. Unrepentant, Jenks took off from his shoulder, his dust a sour green. "She lied to you," he said loudly, hand on his hilt. "Flew behind your back with Doyle to—"

"I know," I interrupted as I concentrated on keeping David moving. "If it had been Trent, I would have done the same thing."

But Jenks looked unmovable as he flew backward before us. "No, you wouldn't. She doesn't trust us. I'm sorry, David, but she doesn't."

David gasped in pain, and I eased him to a halt. Eyes closed, he leaned against a machine. "That's our fault, not hers," I said. "Can you get that ring? Ask Pike to help you."

Jenks hovered for a moment. "I can do that," he said, then darted away.

I slowly exhaled, my weight shifting from foot to foot as I tried to plan my next words to David. I totally got Jenks's opinion to cut her loose to swing. A pixy only lived twenty years or so, and there wasn't much time to recover from mistakes. But alienating Cassie might drive a wedge between David and me, and that was not going to happen.

And besides, I'd probably done far worse before I had smartened up.

"He doesn't mean it," I said as I tucked my shoulder under David's again.

"He does." David's voice was thick with pain. "Please don't be hard on her. She was desperate to get me uncursed, and she trusted Walter to keep his word more than she trusted the FIB. She made a mistake."

"One that almost got you killed." Ivy had noticed us inching forward. Brad was beside her on the floor, looking like Gollum as he held his ring and tried to remember why he was down here. "You okay?" I mouthed to Ivy across the space, and she nodded, her eyes narrowing when she glanced at Cassie. The I.S. agent was finally satisfied, and Cassie had rolled to her feet in one smooth motion.

"David," Cassie whispered, but her rush slowed as she saw my anger. Guilt crossed her, and then it was gone. "Go ahead," she mocked as she yanked David from me to take his weight herself. "'She doesn't mean any-thin' to me.' What is wrong with you? He could have killed me!"

"I called you," I said as David groaned at the sudden shift. "Left a mes-sage." Angry, I pulled David out of her grip. "Why didn't you tell me you got the I.S. to help?"

Cassie took a breath to speak, freezing in apparent indecision.

"Ladies . . ." David groaned, and I staggered as he suddenly became deadweight.

"Doyle, you got an ambulance here?" I said as we struggled, and Doyle's first, sneering comment vanished as he took in David's pain.

"Get him upstairs," he said as he made a quick motion, and two I.S. agents came forward. Worried, I reluctantly released David into their care. They weren't paramedics, but they clearly knew what they were doing as they picked him up in a chair sling and headed to the distant stairway. Cassie followed.

*Oh, we aren't done yet,* I thought, jerking to a halt when Doyle was suddenly in front of me.

"What did you think you were doing, witch?" the impressive man said, and I yelped as he practically pinned me against one of the machines. His eyes were black with anger, his posture stiff. Vampiric power flowed from him, but I was too ticked to let it cow me. "We could have had them all," he added, "but you moved in before we had the exits covered. I could throw you in jail for obstruction."

"Then do it," I said, and the conversation behind him vanished. "But seeing as you won't, why don't you get out of my way? I want David looked at, not admitted to the hospital. Their security isn't up to this."

For one dangerous instant I thought Doyle might try it. Eyebrows high, I stared him down, pulling hard on the nearest ley line until loose strands of my hair began to float.

Doyle's bluster snapped off as if on a switch. I would not be intimidated. If he kept trying, it would only make it more obvious to the watching I.S. personnel that I wasn't scared of him. "You aren't worth it," he grumbled. "Tamwood!" he barked. "How many did we get?"

Ivy glanced up from her conversation with Pike, and Brad slunk into the shadows. "Conscious or total?" she asked casually, and Doyle's mood became positively jovial.

"You have to appreciate her attention to the minutiae," he said, his words so soft that only I could hear, and I wondered if there was a hint of camaraderie in there. At least until he added, "She would have done well in the I.S. You ruined her, too, Morgan."

"I beg your pardon?" I said, but he had already walked away. Ivy gave me an amused shrug. No, not ruined. Ivy had found the courage to be who she wanted. That made her perfect.

"Whatever," I muttered, then made a quick jog to rejoin David before they reached the stairs. There was no way David was going to end his day at the hospital, and especially not with Cassie thinking I would let slide the shit she had dumped on me and my team.

"David? David!" I called, and the two men carrying him halted. "Don't let them check you into the hospital," I said, ignoring Cassie gripping his hand possessively and glaring at me. "They can patch you up enough in the ambulance to get you to Trent's estate. He has an entire medical wing going wanting."

"Where David receives his medical care isn't your decision," Cassie said, and my brow furrowed.

"No, Rachel is right," David rasped, clearly in pain despite the amulet. "But I'm not going anywhere until you two hash this out."

Cassie's gray eyes widened in horror, her grip on his hand spasming. "Davie . . ."

"Fight. Apologize. I don't care," he said, and the two men carrying him gave us a look to hurry this up. "But you will settle this. Now. I mean it."

*He means it,* I mocked sourly. But my clenched jaw eased as I glanced at the ring Trent had given me. The pearl was a stunning, glowing white, and I made a fist as the first hint of forgiveness found me. I would have done the same thing if it had been Trent. Worse, probably.

"I'll be waiting for you both in the ambulance," David said as he wedged Cassie's hand off him. "Officers, can you . . ."

"Davie . . ." Cassie whispered as the two men hustled him up the stairs. Heartache pinched her brow, but it shifted to anger as she turned to me. "He's not going to Kalamack's estate."

*Yes, he is,* I thought as I took a breath to let her have it.

"We have nothin' to talk about," the small woman added bitterly as she walked to the stairs, her back stiff and her shoulders high about her ears. Behind her, Ivy and Pike had Brad against a machine, the bewildered man looking anxious as Ivy soothed and cuddled him.

"Hey!" I tried to ease the tension in my gut, but I was still angry, and I'd never been good at hiding that. "Cassie, I understand why you did what you did, but if you ever do anything like that again—"

Cassie jerked to a stop. Motion smooth, she reversed her course, arms swinging. "You don't own me, Rachel Morgan."

Jenks's wings rasped a warning, and I twitched my fingers to tell him to stay out of it. Ivy's lilting conversation with Brad had gone silent, and I pulled myself straight as Cassie halted before me, the smaller woman glaring up at me, itching for a fight.

"And Cassie Castle owes no one anything, right?" I said, pulse fast. "Especially trust. We were working together to recover David, and you lied to me. I told you I wanted the backing of a police force. If you could have gotten the I.S. to help, you should have said something."

"Yeah?" Cassie retreated a step, glancing at Doyle organizing a top-to-bottom search. "The only way Doyle would lift a finger was if you weren't involved. Get it?"

My eyes narrowed. I was sure the man could hear our argument. He was a vampire after all. "He doesn't like me," I said, thinking it was pretty lame, but this conversation wasn't my idea. "Look. David wants us to hash this out, and I will, for my part in it, because he's important to me in ways that you will never understand. But if you *ever* lie to me again, we are done, and I need to hear you say you understand that, because I am not going to lose my friendship with David over you, so if you got a problem with me, or the FIB in general, you tell me now." I took a breath, lungs empty from the long sentence. "Got it?"

Cassie stared at me with an angry intensity. I could feel her strength, her pride. It was obvious now that she and David were more than casual partners, and something in me seemed to shrivel and die. He was my friend, and I didn't want to lose him because of her.

"But let me be clear," I added when she said nothing. "I am forgiving you for going behind my back to rescue David because I know why you did it. I am not forgiving you for lying to me. That's going to take longer. He's worth both of us combined."

Cassie's posture eased. "On that, we agree," she said. "For David, I will apologize for not taking your call and not telling you what I was doing. I should have trusted you. And the FIB."

That last was grudgingly said, but I let it go. It was as good as the prideful woman could manage with half a dozen people watching. My trust in her was cracked. A few forced words were not going to mend it.

"Ah, I am serious about David not going to the hospital," I said, and Cassie stiffened. "Trent has better security. I wish you would go with him. I need to talk to Al, and I don't want to leave David alone."

Unsure, Cassie glanced over her shoulder as Ivy and Pike started our way. Jenks was with them, his cheerful gold dust telling me they'd gotten the ring. "You couldn't stop me from stayin' with him," she said, clearly not happy.

"Great." I met Ivy's gaze and she smiled, one arm draped over Pike, the other on Brad. Glenn followed at a distance, his head down over his phone.

"Jenks, do you want to go out to Trent's estate with Cassie and me?" I asked when the pixy darted close, and the thrum of his wings eased when he dropped the ring into my palm. I tensed, expecting at least a tingle of magic, but there was nothing. It was dead silver, and my hope faltered. But perhaps it slept until the invocation phrase. If it had uncursed David, it could uncurse the rest. "We won't have to find Walter if Al knows the invocation phrase, and his place is only a few minutes' walk in the ever-after from Trent's ley line." If I could jump the lines, I could have been there in three seconds from even here, but until Bis and I figured it out, the only way I could reach the ever-after was to stand in a ley line and will myself across. It made me feel less like a demon and more like a witch, and I was tired of it. Grumpy, I stuffed the unadorned ring into a pocket. I wasn't about to put it on.

"Naw," the pixy said. "Glenn's offered to drop me at the church. Tell Jumoke I said hey, will you?"

"If I see him." I turned to Cassie. "Just you and me and David. Good. We don't talk enough."

"Great," Cassie said softly. She looked as if she had eaten a slug but was too full of herself to admit it and spit it out. It was likely going to be a cold, silent ride to the hospital.

But that wouldn't be my fault.

# CHAPTER

# 10

TRENT'S FINGERS LACED IN MINE FELT MORE THAN RIGHT, AND I STI-
fled a shiver of libido when the energy he was using to make a globe of light
spilled into me, tingling. He'd taken my hand shortly after we had crossed
into the ever-after from the ley line snaking through his estate, keeping me
steady as I walked with my head craned to the moonlit heavens and giving me the chance to soak in the beauty of the ever-after stars. A light rain
had started in reality, but here the skies were clear, and the great bands of
heated gases marking the Milky Way had to have come from Bis's ancestral
memory, because they certainly hadn't come from mine.

I didn't often have the chance to walk under an ever-after midnight
sky, and Trent had been silent as we made the short trip to Al's wagon in
the woods. We'd long since found the forest and lost the primordial heavens, but Trent still held my hand. And I felt loved.

"Thanks for coming with me," I said as the trees seemed to close in
on us. It was positively dank in the woods, and I held Trent's light higher
as I spotted a glint of glitter on his front. "I see the girls gave you their
cards."

"Mmmm? Oh." Trent looked down, his free hand brushing his coat to
no effect. "Yes. This afternoon. Glitter. I swear, it's got to be demon dan-
druff in disguise."

"I should have given you your present this morning," I whispered, and
he tugged me into him so our feet struck the soft earth together like matched

horses. I could feel the ley line he was using to spell his light into existence, and it warmed me clear through.

"You are all I need," he said, and I smiled, loving him.

"That's beside the point." I hesitated. "I didn't mean to take you from your party prep. Or is that why you're out here?"

Trent chuckled. The medical suite where we'd left Cassie and David had been an oasis in the out-of-control chaos. After verifying that David's ribs were not broken and his lungs were clear, we'd made the five-minute walk to the ley line in Trent's garden in about forty minutes. Some of it had been the girls, now terribly excited about the prospect of the cider mill tomorrow, but most was where to put what, and how many of the other thing did Trent want on hand.

Green eyes black in the magic light, Trent lifted my hand and kissed my knuckles. "The prep I can handle. I want to talk to Al about my books."

"Mmmm." I was quite sure *that* conversation wasn't going to go well, and I lifted Trent's globe of light higher when a moss-covered trunk was suddenly barring the path. It looked as if it had been there for twenty years, but it hadn't been there last week. "You don't know if he was the one who took them," I said as I let go of Trent's hand to step over the log. It was a warning, and I wiped my hand clean on my jeans.

"Right." The word was flat, and Trent's expression was tight as he followed suit. His books had vanished about the same time that the university library lost theirs, and whereas the library had written them off, Trent was tenacious.

"Maybe I should have told Al we were coming," I said as the trees began to thin and the moonlight brightened. Al might be the easiest way to find the invocation phrase. Unfortunately, easy always seemed to bite me on the ass.

"How? He can't use a scrying mirror."

That was kind of mean, but Al *had* tried to sell him one once. "I could have sent Bis," I said as the path suddenly widened and vanished, spilling into a large, perfectly circular opening in the woods a good sixty feet in diameter. One end held three trees forever in pink bloom, tiny petals drifting like snow. A stream ran close to the colorfully painted wagon, the tongue of which was too massive for horses. Big-ass oxen might be able to handle it. Moonlight made a white glow on the flat rocks about the simple fire pit, and the ribbon of smoke rising from the center looked like a forgotten spirit. A new toadstool ring delineated Al's "property" line, and I drew Trent to a halt before it. Anything new was to be distrusted.

I waved when a craggy head lifted from the lump atop the huge wagon. It was Treble, and the ancient gargoyle yawned, wings stretching to look like the devil herself. After giving me a nod, she took to the air, her tail thumping into the wagon with enough force to send it rocking before she flew to a nearby conifer. Her laugh sounded like a rockslide when a faint bellow came from the wagon.

Not surprisingly, the door slammed open, hitting the side with a bang. "Mother pus bucket, what's wrong with you, you reptile reject!" Al shouted as he leaned out over the first step to glare at the now empty roof. "There is tea all over my floor!"

"Ah, hi, Al!" I called, and the demon's head whipped around. The imposing silhouette didn't move, his thick-fingered hand shifting to touch his wildly embroidered vest and plain black slacks. He was not in his usual elegant Victorian crushed green velvet frock coat—and he didn't dissolve into a mist to reappear with it on. Worn shoes instead of his shiny, trendy boots covered his feet. His hair was in disarray, and he ran a hand over it to find order. But it was his expression that tore at me. Embarrassment.

"You're right," Trent said softly. "We should have sent Bis."

"Ah, sorry for barging in on you," I said as Al slowly thumped down the huge wooden steps. The fire was nothing but smoldering ashes, but moonlight made the large clearing bright, and I could see his frown from here.

"You brought a plus-one. Wonderful," he mocked, and I took Trent's elbow before he could step over the toadstool ring. A faint vibration was cramping my toes, undoubtably a spell. New fence, log across the road: I was beginning to wonder how accommodating Al was going to be. Sure, he was my mentor, but that didn't mean he was roses and warm fuzzies.

"Is this ley line magic?" Trent asked as he looked down, and I shrugged, not knowing for sure. It was kind of both earth and ley line, all mixed together. Which, when you parsed it out, was what made demon magic demon.

Trent turned to Al, his stance finding a formal stiffness as his toes edged the toadstools, now throwing off a faint haze of sparkles. "May we come in?" he said, his musical voice amid the crickets bringing a shiver through me.

"A Kalamack elf," Al grumped. "I never thought I'd see the day that I *invited* you in. Yes. Come in. Both of you."

"Thank you." Trent gingerly stepped over the ring. One might think a chalk-drawn circle would be stronger, but the mushrooms were an interlaced mass of mycelium under the ground, and the living tissue pulled in the power of the ley line without Al needing to do a thing. It was a marvel, really. Even without the ley lines, Al was a master of magic.

My hair lifted as I crossed the ring, and I hustled to catch up with Trent. Al's mood was closed as he pulled a pin on a ley line charm and dropped it into the middle of the smoldering fire. Blue flame rose up with a whoosh. Eyes averted, Al put more wood on, stacking it carefully as if unsure how long the starter amulet would last.

"It's nice tonight," I said as I settled on a flat rock before the fire, my feet on the bare, slow-baked earth.

"Give it time," Al grumped. The flames were already beginning to subside, and I added a piece of split wood before I shifted closer to Al and out of the smoke. Seeing him using premade charms and wearing clothes he'd washed himself was disheartening, and I reached for the poker to fix the fire just to have something to do.

But I hesitated as I took the length of metal in hand, stopped first by its exquisite balance, and then the pure beauty of the thing. It was clearly well used, with a slow deepening of black ash toward the tip, but it had been crafted with such care and art that it felt like a crime to consign it to the flames. The twisted metal hinted at birds and squirrels. Oak leaves decorated a secure handle, and a fanciful fish made a hook near the end. It must mean a great deal to him if he had made the effort to rescue it when the original ever-after collapsed.

"A thing of beauty has no purpose if it is not used," Al said as he saw my study. "It's from a time long spent," he added, taking the poker from me and rearranging the fire. "Once you live as long I have, you'll realize only things that survive are those that don't break easily."

Trent had settled to my left, and his brow furrowed at the reminder of how old Al was, the war he had fought, and for how long—and against whom.

"That's a good charm," I said as Al shifted a piece of smoldering wood and a new flame flickered up. "To light the fire? How long did it take to make?"

Al gave me a sidelong look, clearly uncomfortable with Trent sitting there. "I gave Dali an hour of my time for a box of them."

"Al . . ."

But my words cut off as he glanced at Trent. "My skills will return," he said bluntly. "Hodin will not. Let this go, Rachel. It's not your burden." The demon resettled himself, turning to face Trent more fully. "Rachel is obviously in trouble," he said bluntly. "Why are you here?"

Trent's attention came back from the hazy moonlight now filling with fireflies. Yes, it was too late in the season for them, but as Al liked to point out, the new ever-after was still linked to my psyche, and it changed itself to suit me. Or, put shortly, it rained here when I was unhappy. "Um, about the books you borrowed from my mother's library . . ." Trent started.

"I believe the word you mean is *recovered*," Al drawled, his goat-slitted eyes glowing red from over his blue-tinted glasses.

"They were not yours to take," Trent said boldly. "If they were in my mother's possession, she got them from you legally. I've been through her last requests and she did not will them to you upon her death. I want them back."

Al jabbed the fire with his poker. "Prove it."

"You want to see her will?" Trent said incredulously, and Al flung the exquisite poker to the ground.

"I want to see the paperwork where she legally acquired them," Al said. "He who has the most data wins, and you have none because I didn't give your mother any."

Trent slumped on the stone, stymied.

"You don't give your prize possibility a piece of paper that might land her in Alcatraz," Al said, his good mood restored. "No . . ." He practically sighed the word. "Your mother was too smart for me. But they say intelligence skips a generation, like hair loss. Lucy is very clever. She hides it behind her prattle. How did she learn to do that so quickly? Surely not her mother."

Annoyed, I gave Al a soft nudge in the ribs. "Now you're being mean."

"I am being a demon." Al pulled himself straighter. "It's all I have left. Ah, the coals have relit. S'mores, anyone?"

Clearly frustrated, Trent frowned as Al stretched, sighing happily as he reached for a carefully wrapped bundle tucked behind a rock. With an overdone flourish, he unrolled the rough silk to show a bag of Piggly Wiggly marshmallows and a set of roasting sticks more elaborate than his poker. The incongruity between the two was striking, and as Al fussed and worried over the marshmallows, I bumped my knee against Trent's.

"Wait until you have something he wants," I suggested, and Al made a low, knowing chuckle.

"I shouldn't have to bargain to get my own books back," Trent complained, and I set my hand atop his. Our matching pearl rings glowed pink and orange in the firelight . . . and then faded. Brow furrowed, Trent pulled away, his focus distant as he mentally went through his artifact vault for something the demon might want. Agreeing to stop seeing me would do it, but that wasn't going to happen.

Clearly feeling as if he'd scored points, Al jammed a marshmallow on a stick and handed it to me. "You're here concerning David and that would-be alpha Were you tricked into believing the focus was destroyed. Walter Vincent."

"Yep," I said, glad that someone finally got it right.

A rumble escaped Al. "I am sorry, Rachel. David was downed by a chakra curse. There is no cure. It's not like melting ice to water and refreezing it. Stilled chakras can't be set into motion again. I apologize for leaving you at the time, but Hodin is the only one of us who knew how to craft such an abomination, and I feared he had escaped."

My reach to show him the ring faltered. "Has he . . ."

"No. Hodin still abides in his prison. I'm guessing he passed the ring on to someone before we caught him." Al hesitated. "Someone is doing demon magic in Cincinnati, someone other than you. Have you considered . . . your roommate, Stephanie?"

"It isn't her," I said as Trent's attention snapped back to our conversation. "It's some guy calling himself the mage. He's under a disguise, but David said he swore like a witch and he invoked the Goddess in one of his spells, so . . . who knows?"

Al's grip on his roasting stick tightened. "Hodin's reach extends to you even from his prison. Rachel, your future is more important than your present. If you are here for my advice, it is to retreat to the ever-after to pursue your studies."

"Ah," Trent started, and I took his hand and gave it a squeeze.

"Leave Cincinnati to Walter?" I said tartly. "Not happening."

Al shrugged, his teeth gleaming in his not-nice smile. "Walter Vincent's goal is assuredly the focus, but that's not my concern. Hodin's student is. He is after you. You will be safe here."

I doubted that. The ever-after had its own set of dangers, and if I was here, Al's kin would take a stronger interest in me. "Then he is going to fail," I said, stiffening when my marshmallow caught fire. I jerked it free of the flames, accidentally flinging the burning wad right off the tip. Arching dramatically through the air, it hit the flattened grass with a splat. *Ruined.*

Al nonchalantly grasped my stick, angling it toward himself as he stuck another marshmallow on it. "I'm not so sure," he said as he let go. "David is a pillar of your three-prong power base. Hodin tried and failed to bring you down through the vampires. Now his student is trying the same with

David. I'm betting he manages it, seeing as he has both grudge and aim. Congratulations, itchy witch. You are no one until you have a nemesis."

Trent snorted his rueful agreement, and my mood soured.

"Gee, thanks," I muttered as I bobbed my marshmallow in and out of the flame, daring it to catch fire. Which it did. I quickly blew the flame out, but the puff was too black for my liking.

Al's eyebrows rose at my slumping sigh. "If by some miracle you *do* maintain control of the Weres, I imagine he will try to use the elves next," Al said. "Seeing as he's likely an elf. The witches, though, might be a better choice. The witches never liked you. Odd, that." Al's expression became introspective. "Perhaps because they can see what they might be if they had the courage, and are pissed that they are afraid."

It was the same vibe I was getting from Vivian, and I sat before the fire, my ruined marshmallow hanging high over the flames. "Jenks never got close enough for even a sniff," I said, wanting to show him the ring in my pocket. "I think he knew me, though."

"The mage? Everyone knows you," Al said lightly. "Are you going to eat that?"

He was eyeing my charred marshmallow, and I handed him the stick. "No wonder you're all reclaiming your books," I said as Al delicately nibbled the burnt marshmallow, his eyes closing in bliss. "Ever since you regained your ability to cross into reality, everyone seems to think they can do your magic. And who gets blamed? Me."

Al popped the marshmallow into his mouth and licked his fingers clean, apparently satisfied with the entire world. "Yes. It's a problem. What do you intend to do about it?"

Worried, I took the ring from my pocket and rolled it between my thumb and finger. "Will you look at this and tell me what it is? Walter used it to uncurse David."

Al's gaze flicked from me to Trent and back again. "He's awake? David is okay?"

"*Okay* being a relative term," Trent said.

"They beat him near to death before uncursing him," I said as my hand dropped, the ring heavy in it. "They wouldn't have bothered to uncurse him at all, except the mage thought they couldn't peel the focus off him if he was spelled." *Thank God I was there to stop that.*

"David can't be awake," Al said, sounding affronted. "I saw what happened at Eden Park." And then Al sort of froze. "I made a mistake. David was not downed by a chakra curse."

Trent's gaze flicked to me, the slant of his eyes telling me he'd heard the unusual tightness in Al's voice as well. *He made a mistake?* "Fine," I said. "Then tell me what this is."

I extended the ring again, and again Al didn't take it, the very way he stared at it chilling me. "I am sure I don't know," he said as he focused on his marshmallow, now a perfect tan. "If David is awake, it wasn't a chakra curse that downed him. There is no cure."

But his words were too fast and his voice too low. Trent shook his head, confirming it. Al was lying. To me.

My jaw tightened as Al set his marshmallow aside and reached for the Piggly Wiggly bag, taking out a box of graham crackers and a chocolate bar. He really was making s'mores. "The hospital verified it," I said, fishing.

"The hospital is mistaken."

I made a fist around the ring. "I bet Hodin knows what it is."

It was an empty threat, but Al finally looked at me. "You are not talking to Hodin."

"That's right," I said in a huff. "I'm talking to you. Will you look at the stupid ring?"

Eyes narrowed to slits, he put out his hand and I dropped the ring into it. His focus went distant as he held it, but it wasn't until he gazed at the moon through the battered circle that he exhaled. "Hodin indeed crafted this," he said, worried. "I know his aura as well as my own, and it clings to his work like a disease."

Al blew through the circle to hear it ring, and my gut tightened. "What does it do?" I asked.

"I don't know," Al said. "I should keep it."

Annoyed, I held out my hand, not liking his hesitation before he dropped it into my palm. *Doesn't know what it is, my lily-white ass.* I'd seen David's chart. He had been under a chakra curse, same as Cassie's employees, and now he wasn't. Walter had clearly used the ring to break the curse. Brad thought the ring was his, and seeing as Brad would be doubly stupid to buy a curse without the cure, he was probably right.

"I'd help if I could," Al said, and my eyes narrowed in suspicion. *He's offering to help?*

"Promise?" I said sarcastically, and he grimaced as he unwrapped the chocolate bar and broke it into four pieces with a disturbing reverence. He gave the first to me, ate the second himself, and squished the remaining two pieces into two thick, gooey sandwiches. Nothing for Trent, but that was par for the course, and Trent shook his head when I divided my piece in two and offered him half.

"Rachel, I know you will not listen . . ." Al started.

"Brad thinks it's the ring he cursed Cassie's employees with, not the cure for it," I muttered, wondering what Al was trying to distract me from as the chocolate dissolved on my tongue. "The mage was furious, almost as if Walter had broken the ring itself, not just its hold on David. Said he made it useless." Which sounded right if he had been Hodin's student. Hodin had a nasty habit of leaving things out to keep himself above those he deemed a threat. That was how I had ended up cursing Pike's brother in the first place.

My head snapped up, a new thought trickling through me. "Unless the curse and countercurse are within the same ring?"

"Ah . . ." Al's posture stiffened.

"Is that possible?" Trent said in excitement, and a soft groan slipped from Al.

"Is that it?" I said, knowing I was right. "The ring is both the cure and curse? I didn't think you could do that."

"That's because we don't," Al said, his expression pained in the come-and-go firelight.

"Because you can't, or because you won't?" I asked, and his breath escaped him in a worried sound. *Crap on toast, there's more to this than he's telling me.*

"Won't." Al glanced at Trent as if reluctant to divulge demon secrets. "It would have to be crafted on a Möbius strip to hold both the cure and curse."

This was new. I was familiar with the twisted strip of paper that turned three dimensions into one, but had never heard of it being used to spell with. "A Möbius strip?" I questioned, and Al glared at Trent as if all the woes of the world were his fault. "You may as well tell us both. I'm going to tell him anyway."

"You would, wouldn't you." Mood bad, Al flung a log on the fire and the sparks flew.

I jumped when Trent touched my shoulder. "It's okay," he said as he rose. "I don't mind stepping away. I do this all the time to protect trade secrets."

"Sit," I said coldly, my eyes narrowed on Al. If he didn't want Trent to know, he shouldn't tell me. If he didn't tell me, I was going to find out some other way, probably hurting myself—and Al knew it. Most days Al probably wouldn't care if I hurt myself, but lately I'd become a convenient buffer between him and his kin. "Well?" I added as Trent slowly sat.

"You try me, itchy witch," Al grumped. "If either of you use the knowledge, you are too stupid to live and therefore deserve to die." He took a breath as he drew himself into a dignified stiffness. "A spell utilizing a Möbius strip base creates a self-renewing magic. Back and forth like the tide. Never-ending and therefore dangerous."

I'd always felt that love was a self-renewing magic. But then again, love *was* dangerous. "So, one side is the curse, and the other is the cure?" I guessed, and Al nodded.

"Because of its never-ending capacity, a Möbius curse exacts a correspondingly high price for its construction." Lip curled, Al glared at Trent. "Which is why the elves were the only people desperate enough to practice their creation," he accused. "What you hold is experimental elven war magic. Something they tried to make work and couldn't. Otherwise, they would have used it on us and there'd be a record of it. The only reason Hodin knows of it is because they tried it on him. Tried and failed."

"Well, it worked on David." I nudged the ring across my palm with a finger. "What does it cost to make it?"

"The life of the one who twists it."

Trent jerked, his foot hitting mine with a tingling surge of energy. Suddenly the ring felt foul, heavy as it lay in my palm. It was dark magic, not just a curse, and I curved my fingers around it, hiding it. "Why would anyone . . ." My voice faltered. "You'd have to trick someone into doing it. Someone with enough skill to perform it and foolish enough to trust you. One death for a lifetime of magic."

Trent touched his chin. It was one of his tells that he was worried, and I didn't see it often. "Hodin wouldn't have a problem with that," he whispered.

"Mmmm." Al tugged a colorful scarf from his sleeve and carefully wrapped the two s'mores. "Don't tell Vivian. She might overlook spelling a vampire into forgetting his name, but not this."

Crap on toast, I didn't have the cure for the chakra curse, I had the Turn-blasted curse itself. The former was legal; the second, not so much. "But a Möbius strip has only one side," I said, wondering if this might be the mythos behind the coven using a Möbius strip as their emblem. "It's safe, right? As long as we don't say the phrase to invoke the curse?"

"I don't know," Al whispered, the three words sending a chill through me. Shoulders hunched, he fell into a memory. "Möbius curses don't expire, but flip from curse to cure and back again, and I don't know what initiates that. My concern is that if the mage was upset that Walter turned it to uncurse David, it's more than likely that it requires another death to flip it back to curse mode. Be glad that it's presently set to cure and mourn its last victims."

He said it as if it was over. But it wasn't, not with four of Cassie's people still in a coma and the cure phrase out there somewhere. I stood, my knees wobbly as I looked down at Trent's ashen complexion. I had to go. If the ring was set to cure, I could wake Cassie's employees. I only had to find the right invocation phrase. Locating Walter was one option, but if Hodin had made the ring, the book and invocation phrase might be in his old room.

Trent stood as well. "If it's Hodin's magic, then perhaps we should talk—"

"Stop!" I said before Al could do more than take a breath. "Hodin would only lie. Getting into his room is a hindsight easier than finding Walter and beating what we need out of him. I bet Walter is kicking himself for uncursing David at all, but he clearly wasn't planning on us interrupting his mage's magic to pull the focus out."

"Mmmm." Al peered up at us, a hand extended. "Perhaps I should hold the ring for you. You're lucky that Walter knows David needs to be alive to pull the focus out, or they would simply shoot him."

My fist tightened, and I stuffed the ring into a pocket. "No," I said, and Al's eyes narrowed. "Tell you what. You can have it after I uncurse Cassie's employees if you give Trent his books." Head lifting, I peered into the firefly-filled night. "We have to go." I stepped over the flat stones, eager to make the trek home—or at least get to reality, where I could call Glenn. He still had that finding charm sensitized to Walter. I'd have some time tomorrow after I watched the girls. Jenks and I could tour the city. Find him. Beat the cure's invocation phrase out of him.

But Trent's hand pulled from mine as I moved away, his expression blank as he stood beside Al's fire. "What?"

"Ah . . . about tomorrow with the girls," Trent said. "That mage might want that ring back, flipped or not. It's the only thing that slows the focus down enough to best David."

"The ring he said was useless? That he couldn't remake?" I said, quashing a twinge of worry as I recalled how the mage had thrown himself after it. "Go do your drug-lord golf outing. We'll be fine." It was the first time I'd have the girls alone, and I wanted to try out my mom skills—such as they were.

"Mmmm." Clearly unsure, Trent took my elbows. "I'm going to cancel."

My smile faltered. "I said we'll be fine," I insisted, eye twitching when Al nudged the fire with his foot to send more sparks flying. He was listening. "The mage is not about to crash a cider mill filled with kids for a ring he can't use. If he wants it that bad, he'll wait until I'm alone."

Trent's grip on my elbow tightened. "Perhaps you should stay at the estate tonight."

I leaned in to give him a kiss, the small smack of lips turning awkward when I began to smile at Al's annoyed growl. "I'll be fine," I whispered, loving them both. "I need to go home and see if I can get into Hodin's room. The sooner I can find the phrase to cure Cassie's people, the better. I'll see you tomorrow at eight thirty at Junior's with the girls." I could give him his present then, too.

"Here." Al handed me the silk-wrapped s'mores. "For the girls," he said, and Trent sighed. "Rachel is right," he added. "The ring is set to cure, and if the mage can't turn it, it has no worth."

*No worth for him*, I thought. "So we're good?" I said brightly. Get Walter's finding amulet from Glenn, break into Hodin's room for the cure's phrase. Uncurse Cassie's employees. Al gets the ring. Destroys it. Cincy's power balance course corrects. Walter and his mage go home.

Piece of cake.

# CHAPTER

# 11

THE LIGHT FROM THE CHURCH SPILLED OUT ONTO THE COLD ground to make confusing shadows on the street as I pulled into my carport and cut the engine. Stef's electric car was not at the plug. She was at work, and I smiled, glad the woman had gotten her hospital job back. Smutty auras had traditionally meant illegal behavior, and I was pleased to see that inaccurate prejudice beginning to correct itself. Or maybe they simply really needed the help.

"Tomorrow is going to be a killer," I whispered as I stared at the car's dash clock. It was almost two a.m., and though that wasn't unusually late for a witch, I'd been trying to crash closer to midnight, when Trent went down. I could have gotten a few extra hours of sleep if I'd stayed at Trent's— at least in theory—but I wanted a crack at Hodin's door. Not to mention that Glenn had promised to drop off the finding amulet. Martie had been wearing it all day to no avail.

I felt the late hour all the way to my bones as I dragged my shoulder bag across the seat, but before I could get out, my phone hummed. Vivian.

For three rings, I debated letting it go to voice mail as I got out of the car, and then, reluctantly, I hit the accept icon. "Hi, Vivian," I said, heart in my throat.

"Where have you been?" she said, clearly tense. "I've been trying to reach you all night."

"The ever-after," I said, not liking her tone. "Finding out all sorts of things about the ring that cursed David. It's the same thing that hit Cassie Castle's employees, and I'm *this* close to finding the cure. When I do, do you want to meet me at the hospital and see how it works?"

"You were in the ever-after?" she said, voice tight. "Rachel, I can't express how important it is you remain in Cincinnati."

My bootheels were a soft thump on the cement walk, and I tugged my jacket closer against the chill and waved to Bis. The cat-size gargoyle was perched on the roof, an eerie sentry with his red eyes glowing. He took to the air, his huge bat-like wings cutting a threatening shadow across the night sky as he dropped to me.

"Why?" I said as Bis landed on my shoulder, his white-tufted tail wrapping securely behind my back to help cut his momentum. A faint rise in energy lifted through me at his touch. It was an echo of the nearest ley lines, and though it was only a hint of what I should be feeling through him, even that little was appreciated. "Am I a person of interest?"

Bis's red eyes met mine when Vivian didn't answer. Worried, I stopped on the stairs, not eager to take this inside, where Jenks would complicate things. "Vivian?" I prompted, and she sighed. "Hey, I was there trying to find out how to untwist the curse, not skip town," I said, feeling miffed. "Isn't that a good thing? Finding the cure? Walter already used it to uncurse David. He's going to be okay, by the way," I finished tartly. She hadn't even asked after him.

"I'm pleased to hear that," she said faintly. "I know how important he is to you. I agree that on the surface, you finding a countercurse seems positive. But it also links you to the initial chakra curse that much stronger."

Knowing how to twist a curse wasn't the same as using it, and I felt myself warm. "You can't put someone in jail for the ability to do something," I said in my own defense. "They have to knowingly do it." *And get caught. They have to get caught, too.* "Whatever happened to innocent until proven guilty?"

"You are not being reasonable, Rachel . . ." she coaxed. "The coven is not happy about me asking them to wait on filing a formal complaint concerning Brad. If they find out you went to the ever-after . . . don't make me regret this."

She was worried about me skipping town? "Hey, Vivian? I gotta go," I said bitterly. "My goats just came in from the farm, and I have to get them into the basement." Mood bad, I hit the end icon and stuffed the phone into a pocket. I wasn't ready to go in yet and deal with Jenks, and Bis's wings flashed open, beating once to keep his balance as I sat down. Knees up and chin on my cupped hands, I stared into the peaceful, chill night.

"Jeez Louise," I muttered. "I thought Vivian was my friend."

"She is," Bis said. "But you put her in a hard spot. Ms. Vivian has her coven responsibilities and her friendship with you." His tail tightened across my back, almost in a hug. "I think she's afraid."

"Of what? Me?" Depressed, I fiddled with my bootlaces. Two friendships on the skids. I had to do something about that.

"What you might cost her, maybe?" Bis's brow furrowed. "You're asking a lot. She's had to smack too many dark magic users around to find the truth. And now you aren't talking to her."

*Vivian doesn't trust me?* I thought as I reached to touch a gnarled foot planted firmly on my shoulder. True, I hadn't been very forthcoming, but she knew me. *Doesn't she?* "I shouldn't have hung up on her," I said. Bis was right. She was afraid to trust me. But then again, I was afraid to trust her. Depressed, I put my chin on my knees and listened to the night. Vivian thought my silence hid dark magic, and I was too scared to trust her to keep the rest of the coven off my back. I had to do better.

My head lifted and I waved to a neighbor as he drove slowly past, headlights gleaming. "I'm going to show her the curse I used on Pike's brother," I said, my gut tightening. "It doesn't matter if I was tricked into using it or not, I did it. I'm scared to death that she won't be able to keep the rest of them from putting me in Alcatraz. It's an illicit curse. They only need the proof." I forced my jaw to unclench. "And I'm going to give it to them." Because I was not going to be afraid of the coven. And I was not going to be afraid to trust that Vivian could protect me. *Saturday. She is coming on Saturday.*

"Stef is the one who added the ingredients that made the curse illegal," Bis said.

"She made a mistake," I said. "No one deserves Alcatraz for a dumb mistake." Vivian might be the only witch who could bring me in. There was a reason neither one of us used magic when arguing. I had to trust that she would speak for me, keep me from Alcatraz. But as I stood, slowly to keep Bis from losing his balance, I felt a little ill.

"I'm glad you're telling her," Bis said. "Is David okay? Jenks told me he took a beating."

"He's on the mend. Trent's on-call physicians are university grade." I looked up at our sign, my worry easing as I read VAMPIRIC CHARMS, LLC. TAMWOOD, JENKS, AND MORGAN. "I would have stayed the night, but I want to try to get past Hodin's door."

"That would be wizard if the invocation phrase was in Hodin's room," he said, surprising me until I realized Jenks would have told him.

"Easier than trying to beat the information from Walter or that mage guy." I hesitated, hand on the handle. "Ah, Al says the ring we got today is both the cure and curse. If I can't get into Hodin's room, I'm going out tomorrow to look for Walter after Trent takes the girls back," I said, and Bis made a low, gravelly sound.

"Glenn told me. He dropped the finding amulet off about an hour ago. It's inside." His grip on my shoulder tightened. "If Walter is smart, he is long gone."

"Maybe," I said. But though Walter was wickedly smart, he was far more determined, and another flicker of worry rose and fell. "You on sentry duty?"

"Yep." He flushed a warm pink, his entire pebbly skin glowing. "Cassie put the pack a block out. No one will bother you tonight. Yell if you need me," Bis said, sounding like Jenks as he pushed off to leave the stray strands of my hair swirling.

"Thanks, Bis," I called after him, feeling good at the faint snap of disconnection as he left me. *Someday,* I thought as I opened one of the wooden doors and went in and soaked in the sounds of home.

"Hey, it's me!" I said as I leaned into the door to shut it. The foyer was dark, but the sanctuary beyond was bright with light and noisy with a nature documentary. We might spring for blinds at some point, but until then, the stained glass worked.

"Hi, Rache." Jenks rose up from an end table before the TV. Getty was with him, and the smaller, dark-haired, dusky pixy dusted cheerfully. She was surrounded by colorful paper, ribbon, and cutout snowflakes. I had no clue what she was doing, but the woman was always busy. "Glenn dropped off that finding amulet."

"Great. Thanks," I said as I saw it on the end table. I shrugged out of my jacket and took it in hand. The simple wooden disk briefly flared green as it connected to my aura, and then it went dark. *Tomorrow,* I thought as I dropped it in my bag and left both on the end of the couch.

"How is David?" Getty asked as she scrolled through Jenks's phone, needing to use her entire hand to shift from picture to picture of grainy black-and-white gangster photos.

I sat down and put my heels on the low, slate table. "He'll be okay. Cassie, too."

Jenks dropped to the remote and stomped David Attenborough into silence. "Like anyone cares about Cassie," he said, the image of Peter Pan with his hands at his waist.

"Jenks," I said with a sigh. "Look me in the eye and tell me you wouldn't go behind my back to save me. Better yet, tell me you *haven't* gone behind my back to save me."

His wings drooped, and Getty smirked. "I don't trust her," Jenks said.

"Me either." Exhaling, I bent double to take my boots off. "But I understand her." I eyed Getty's paper and glue in curiosity. "Halloween decorations?"

"Not exactly." Jenks frowned, an odd blush to his dust. "She's, ah, making a costume out of craft paper and glue."

"At least I'm trying," the dark pixy said with a sigh. "*Someone* thinks it's *silly*."

She scowled at Jenks, and the pixy flushed. "It's paper," he said, gesturing.

"It only needs to hold together for one night," I offered as I kicked off my boots and sank into the couch. "What are you going as?"

Getty fussed with the cutout of a lacy ballroom-like dress. "A snowflake," she said, sounding unhappy. "Jenks wants to be a forties gangster, but he won't let me fit it to him. Come and stand here," she said as she got to her feet and took a measuring tape from a fold of her dress. "Let me measure your shoulders at least."

"I need to check on Bis," Jenks said sullenly as he took to the air.

"It's only a paper costume!" Getty yelled as he darted out. "It's not a real suit!" Angry, the fiery pixy threw her tape measure after him. "You are impossible, you gutless slug!"

The tiny clink of her tape hitting the floor seemed loud, and I winced as she flew to get it, a dark dust spilling from her. "Um, it's not you," I said, and she landed on the coffee table beside my socked feet and slumped into a depressed lump. She'd been working incessantly at the loom Jenks had rigged up for her, and her torn tights and patchwork dress had slowly been replaced with a black dress and stockings that glinted in the light. It wasn't Matalina's impressive embroidery, but the fabric was sturdy and strong and, perhaps more important, warm.

"Yes, it is," she said, sniffing through the tears. "I thought if he accepted a paper suit for Halloween that he might let me make him something real." She played with the hem of her dress. "Maybe it's not appropriate for me to make him clothes. It's not as if we're married."

But they weren't simply friends, either, and I scooted to the edge of the couch, wishing I could give her a hug. "I think you making him a costume is more than appropriate." A small movement at the archway to the hall caught my attention. It was Jenks, his young face holding a torn expression.

"I was going to use it as a pattern," Getty admitted. "Make him something splendid. I owe him for letting me stay rent-free. I'd be doing security no matter where I was."

I shot Jenks a dark look to get in here. "I think it's a great idea. You're both seeing to the security of this place, like partners. Partners do stuff for each other all the time." I hesitated. "Don't they, Jenks."

The pixy started, then flew in, pointedly avoiding Getty. "Bis is fine," he said as he landed atop the lampshade and gently moved his wings as if warming them up. I doubted he had ever left the church. "Did Al have the invocation phrase for that ring?"

"Ah, yeah. About that . . ." I took the ring from my pocket and set it on the table next to the small bowl full of Getty's scraps. "Apparently it holds both the curse and cure. The mage said he can't turn it back, so it's stuck in cure mode. If I can find the phrase, I can uncurse Cassie's people."

Jenks dropped to poke at the ring with his sword. "I didn't think you could do that."

"Not without killing someone," I said sourly. "It's failed ancient-elven war research, twisted on a Möbius strip." I sighed at the bad blood between the elves and demons. "I'm hoping if I can get into Hodin's room, I might find out how to invoke the cure half."

Jenks smirked. "Hence you not spending the night at Trent's." His back was to Getty, but his wings were an odd color, and I knew he was dying to take a closer look at her paper cutout.

"Hence me not spending the night at Trent's," I agreed, tired. Behind Jenks, Getty held up a six-inch-long ribbon of black paper. She'd painted silver lines on it to mimic pinstripes, and I hoped Jenks would wear it at least once. I wanted to see this.

"And Trent is still cool with you taking the girls tomorrow?" Jenks asked. "You saw how hot that mage was to get the ring back, right?"

"He's fine with it," I said, nervous now for an entirely new reason. "Hey, ah, don't let me forget to make a reservation for the pony rides. They don't take them early. I have to do it when they open."

"Pony rides. Got it."

My attention went to a tiny movement at the top of the hall leading to the kitchen. It was Constance, her little furry ass on the old wood floor and her tail arched beautifully over her back. A diamond ring hung around her throat like a necklace, and her ears glittered with tiny studs. The scarf that Getty had given her was draped over her narrow shoulders like a shawl to make her look like a character from a children's book. "Who pierced your ears?" I said, and Jenks spun, darting up in surprise.

"You!" he shouted, his hand going to the hilt of his garden sword. "I have a right to know where you have been parking your dead carcass. It's my property. You're in the garden, right?"

Constance's black eyes went darker yet, the vampiric mouse bristling as she started in with a squeaking harangue, wobbling on two hind feet as she came forward.

"Pearls. Right." I stood, and Jenks's dust went a hot red. "Wait here. I'll get them."

The little mouse pulled up short, looking vulnerable as she sat on her haunches in the middle of the sanctuary. Her squeaking ended with a tiny chirp of a huff, and her little white paws tugged her new scarf back up her almost nonexistent shoulders.

"It looks great on you," Getty said. "Very chic."

"Squeak, squeak," Constance said, her pink nose in the air and her fangs catching the light.

I eyed the mouse, then the ring on the table. With a casual slowness, I dragged the ring across the smooth slate and dropped it into my pocket again. "Be right back." I inched out past the low table, careful to move slow and not bump anything. I knew what it was like to be that small, and it wasn't very fun. Which begged the question as to why she was still a mouse in my garden. I had been careful, but it wasn't that hard to find a vat of salt water. *She doesn't actually like it here, does she?*

I headed for the foyer, surprised when Getty was suddenly in front of me, flying backward as I'd seen Jenks do. "Can I talk to you?" she said, her tiny features pinched, and I glanced over my shoulder to see that the mouse had crept closer to the low table and was looking up at Jenks, sharp fangs bared.

"Sure." Jenks would be okay. He'd fought full-size vampires before, and I watched the pixy take to the air when Constance climbed to the top of the table. "It's going to be a great costume, Getty," I said loudly as we hit the dark foyer. "I can't wait to see it."

"It's not that." Getty's glow lit the handle to the stairway as I reached for it. "I mean, I hope he likes it, but . . ."

Her words faltered into silence as I went up the stairs to my room and flicked on the light. My blinds were open, and as Getty settled herself on the marble-top dresser, I made the rounds to close them. The antique monstrosity had been here when we'd moved in and was too cumbersome to even think about taking down the narrow stairs. Besides, I needed somewhere to stash my socks.

"What's up?" I prompted as I pulled one of the tiny top drawers open and the loose pearls rattled from the back to the front. I'd broken the strand to use one of the pearls to spell Rex into not clawing the furniture. It was no loss to me. The necklace had once belonged to Constance. I wasn't about to wear it even as spoils of war, seeing as I'd found it draped around Nash's neck, stained red with his blood in some perverted mental game of hers. That the elf had died protecting Zack still bothered me.

But my shudder of remembrance vanished when I realized Getty was crying.

"What did Jenks do?" I said, half the pearls in my pocket, half still in the drawer.

"It's not him," she sobbed as she wrung her skirt. "It's me. I try and I try, but I can't get anything to grow!"

My shoulders slumped in relief, and I took the time to gather the last of the pearls before I knelt before her. The pixy had never had a garden before, and though Jenks was attempting to teach her a lifetime of skills in half a season, she still couldn't sense when a seed would grow and when it was infertile. To say she was frustrated was an understatement. "You haven't had a real chance yet, Getty. Wait until spring," I coaxed.

"Spring won't help." Getty sniffed, gaze averted. "I've planted things before. Nothing ever grows. And Jenks . . . he can make a dust bunny grow into a mop."

I scooted up onto the fainting couch. "I know this is important, but you're good at some amazing things. You can sew, and knit, and weave. You braid hair better than he does, and cook a meal from nothing at all. I know he's impressed with the way you organize the fairies and string security lines in the garden." But the fairies were gone now, down in Mexico until spring.

"A pixy who can't grow food is useless," she burbled. "When he finds out, he'll *hate* me."

I doubted that very much. Her failure probably stemmed from never having had a scrap of dirt to call her own. Nothing cultivated grows well if you aren't there to tend it. But she needed proof, not my hollow words, and I thought for a moment before standing up and going to the corner of the octagonal room that I arbitrarily called my closet.

"I have an idea," I said as I rattled around in a large bag on the floor until I came out with a small paper sack smelling faintly of onions and dirt. "Here," I said as I took out a small bulb.

"It's too late." Getty wiped her eyes. "The ground is hard. I know that much at least."

Smiling, I rolled the bag closed and shoved it away. "This isn't to plant outside. It's a paper-white, sort of a daffodil. You grow them inside during the winter. I got them to give to Ivy for the solstice, but I bought like a dozen. You can have one. Check it out. Make sure it's firm and viable. All you need to do is fill a vase with water and set the bulb so the bottom barely touches it. It doesn't even need to be in the sun."

Getty wiped her nose with a scrap of cloth, her eyes on the bulb. "I don't understand."

"It will grow," I insisted. "In the dead of winter."

She blinked back her tears, hope making her beautiful. "You think?"

"It's guaranteed. Says so right on the package."

I set the bulb before her and she picked it up, the papery bundle as big as a load of laundry in her arms. "Thank you, Rachel," she said, her wing pitch shifting higher as she struggled to find the air. "Jenks means the world to me. I don't want him to think I'm stupid."

"You're welcome," I said, but she'd already darted out the open door and down the stairwell. "And Jenks would never think you were stupid," I whispered.

A happy sigh shifted me, and after a quick check to make sure that I'd gotten all the pearls, I thump-bumped down the stairs in my socks. Getty was not in the sanctuary, and Jenks looked up from where he and Constance were standing over his phone. The screen was lit, and she was apparently using it to swear at him, if the poop emojis were any indication.

"What's up with Getty?" Jenks said, his dust an embarrassed red. "She flew through here as if the devil herself were after her."

"She was bored," I lied, not wanting to tell him she was suffering from feelings of inadequacy. "So I gave her one of the bulbs I bought for Ivy. She probably wants to get it going."

"Oh." His feet left the table, and then he sank back down, clearly torn between watching Constance and busting in on Getty and her new bulb.

Constance sat on her haunches beside the glowing phone, patting it for my attention. It was open to a notes app, and from Jenks's bad mood, she was getting her point across. Whatever her point was.

"I appreciate you not messing with my stuff anymore, Constance," I said as I took out a handful of pearls, then hesitated. I had nowhere to put them. "Ah, you want me to take them into the garden? There's a lot here."

Constance shook her head, pointing for me to set them in the bowl with Getty's scraps.

"Bloody Whiskers here thinks you're doing a piss-poor job of running Cincy," Jenks said, his arms over his chest as he kicked his phone to make Constance chitter at him.

A handful of pearls went pinging into the bowl, and I sat down. Constance began squeaking, gesturing at the screen with a white paw. The bowl was too small, and I began stacking the pearls, frowning as I read, She's a bad leader. Her wolf is hurt because of it and now she has to do his job too. The witch is in over her head.

"Don't listen to her, Rache," Jenks scoffed. "Like she could have done any better."

"Yeah," I breathed, but a feeling of guilt flickered as Constance began patting at the phone's pop-up keyboard.

Five minutes with me and Vincent would be my puppy or he'd be dead. You let him live. Fatal mistake.

The mouse pointed at the screen, her beady black vampire eyes fixed on mine. It was probably a good thing she was so small, or her angry-vampire pheromones would be hitting me hard. She was pissed. I wasn't sure why. I didn't think she had ever cared about the city's residents, only that she was in charge of them.

"Killing Walter Vincent won't solve my problem," I said, my rising justification faltering when the mouse adroitly switched the keyboard to the emoji menu and hammered at the poop symbol three times.

"Says you," Jenks muttered.

"The only reason Walter could down David was because of the mage's magic," I said as Constance began picking words again. "And I have that now."

The mouse rocked back and gestured at the screen. Jenks leaned over it. "You're still doing the dog's job," he read, bristling. "Killing Vincent sends a message. Not killing him says, 'Take advantage of me.'"

I squirmed, feeling the rebuke. "If I kill Walter, I go to jail."

Constance pulled her lips from her teeth in a weird grin, patting out, That's what I'm saying. You are ineffective. You have to kill to rule.

"No. No, I don't," I said. "The mage is my responsibility, and I will take care of him."

But she was at the keyboard again, and I leaned over to read, The next time you are challenged, David will die. You are a bad ruler, sacrificing your people to keep your soul clean. Learn the art of killing, or let someone else do it.

And with that, the guilt hit me hard. She was right. David was hurt because I wasn't doing my job.

"Rache, the furry blood bag don't know anything," Jenks said, and Constance gave him a pink-pawed one-finger salute.

"No, she's right." Guilt made my chest hurt. Head down, I stacked the last few pearls in the bowl. But they were round and I was distracted. One rolled off to send the rest into a rattling cascade over the table.

Frantic, Constance scurried after them, catching and stuffing two in her cheek pouches before four more bounced off the table.

"If you kill Walter, you go to jail," Jenks said, ignoring Constance as she crawled from the table and began chasing down the four pearls rolling noisily across the oak floor. "You aren't a vampire living above the law. She don't know pixy piss."

"Maybe that's her point." Sighing, I put my elbows on my knees and cupped my chin in my hands. "The only reason David is hurt is because he's supporting me."

"That's not how I see it." Jenks's gaze flicked to Getty as the pixy flew into the sanctuary from the kitchen, clearly concerned about the noise.

But as I stared at Hodin's door, doubt took a stronger hold on me. Constance might be cruel and half-crazy. Her bedroom tastes might cross the border into the sadistic. But she was also right, and I wasn't sure if I could keep putting my friends in danger anymore.

And then my lips parted when Constance followed a rolling pearl right under Hodin's door.

"She's in Hodin's room." I stood. My knee hit the table and it jumped. Pearls went everywhere. "She went right under the door."

"Yeah?" Jenks rose up, clearly not impressed. "She's been doing that for months."

"Yeah, but how come she can go under it and we can't even touch the door? What's the difference? It's not her size. You can't touch the door, either."

Jenks's next words faltered, and his eyebrows went high in thought. Two pearls slowly rolled out from Hodin's room, and then Constance followed, squeezing out and sitting up beside them to arrange her fur. "Her aura," he said, and I nodded. Her aura. The undead never had much of one, and when they did, it was borrowed from whoever they had fed on. *Maybe . . .*

"Hey, fang girl!" the pixy shouted. "How long has it been since you ate? You don't have much of an aura."

Constance flipped him off, then gathered her pearls and scampered into the kitchen.

"It doesn't cost anything to be kind," Getty said in rebuke as she swooped down to take up two more pearls from the floor.

"Where are you going?" Jenks said brusquely.

"To help Constance," the pixy said. "She can't carry all of these by herself." Rising high, she flew into the hall. "Constance? Let me help."

"Outside? Getty, it's too cold out there!" Jenks shouted, stymied as the sound of her wings faded. "She's going to throw herself into hibernation if she's not careful," he added as he hovered in the middle of the sanctuary.

"Her pixy winter wear is better than yours," I said idly, and Jenks rasped his wings. Motions slow in thought, I gathered the pearls on the table and dropped them in the bowl again before setting the bowl on the floor. "If the door lock is triggered by auras, maybe I can get around it by pushing my aura off my hand."

"I thought removing your aura was a bad thing." Jenks fingered his jacket, frowning in thought.

"It is. But temporarily peeling it away from my hand long enough to touch something is okay. I've done it before." *But never when I was trying to get around a warded lock.* "I'm going to try it," I said as I got to my feet and strode to Hodin's door. *Easy-peasy,* I thought, nervous as I forced myself to completely let go of the ley line in the garden. My head began to hurt, and I ignored it. Concentrating, I set my left hand over my right. All I had to do was pull my aura up to my elbow, but to do that, I had to put a thin layer of nothing between me and my aura, sort of puff it up. "Tell me the instant you sense anything coming from the door, okay?"

"That's why I'm here," Jenks said, hovering at the ceiling and out of the way.

I slowly exhaled, left hand atop the right. Using only the power in my chi, I forced a wad of energy into my right hand, letting it simmer for a moment, thickening it until my hand began to cramp as my aura lifted free. Dizzy, I stroked my right hand to peel the aura away. I couldn't see it, but Jenks could, and at his nod, I reached for the door, fighting to keep my aura from flowing back into place. Breath held, inch by inch . . .

"Rache!" Jenks shrilled, and I yanked my hand back, yelping at the flash of pain cramping up my elbow.

"Crap on toast, I'm never going to get past this door!" I shouted, more angry than hurt.

"Rachel?" Getty called from the kitchen. "You okay?"

I flushed, embarrassed. "Fine!" I shouted, and then softer, "Son of a moss wipe." I wrung my stinging hand, Constance's rebuke soaking in to knot my gut. But if she could get into Hodin's room, so could I. I just needed to find out how.

# CHAPTER

# 12

"QUEN ISN'T HERE," JENKS SAID, PLASTERED AGAINST THE WINDOW of Trent's big-ass SUV parked in front of Junior's coffee shop. "He always has the seat pushed back."

"Maybe he went ahead." I shut the door to my red MINI. Leaning against it, I checked my bag to make sure I had everything—phone, splat gun, pain amulets, Walter's finding amulet, gummy bears. I lurched forward, yawning.

Last night had left me tired, like walking-in-to-take-a-test-after-cramming-all-night tired, and the sun hurt my eyes. At least I'd found a parking spot right beside Trent's SUV. Moving the car seats would be easier.

"Morning isn't your time, is it," Jenks said as I pushed open the door and winced at the clunking chimes. They were glowing in response to the lethal-magic-detection amulet on my key ring. It was either that, or the "help, I'm dead and can't get up" ring Trent had given me last fall.

I didn't answer, figuring Jenks's question was rhetorical. I'd been up less than an hour and felt it, having figured I'd get my coffee here. Big mistake. I'd forgotten Trent's present, too.

"Hey, Rachel," Mark said from behind the counter, and I gave the witch a listless wave. He'd gotten the coffeehouse cheap after some nasties and I had trashed it. I think it had been the third time in as many years. "I've got your usual in the queue. Mr. Kalamack is in the back."

"Thank you," I managed, but he was already talking to the next person in line. The shop was busy, noisy and warm with conversation and the scent of coffee. It was all tables in the middle, booths against the window, and tables with benches and chairs at the rear. The counter took up one entire wall, and the bathrooms and archway to the storeroom were tucked to the side. Mark had recently restaffed, and now he had Weres helping out in the morning, witches after noon, and even a living vampire crew after dark, when things really switched over.

"Go. Sit," Jenks said when I saw Trent with the girls. "I'll get your coffee."

"Thank you," I said again, my smile widening as Trent half stood, Lucy in his arms. Ray was in the kid's chair drawn up to the table. He looked good in his golfing outfit, clean-shaven and sharp, and I wondered how I could have been so lucky.

"Hi, Trent." I gave him a kiss, taking Lucy almost in self-defense when the little girl flung herself at me. "Where's Quen?" Lucy gave me a loud, little-girl kiss on the cheek, and I bent to give Ray a cuddle before settling across from Trent.

"Hi, Aunt Rachel!" Lucy crowed, dramatically stretching to reach a cookie.

"Quen is on the course doing his pre-event security check," Trent said as he pushed the cookie closer, and Lucy took it with a sweet "Thank you, Daddy."

"Jenks?" Trent questioned, and I shrugged, slumping into the hard chair.

"Scamming some honey from Mark?" I guessed as I set my purse beside me. "Do you want me to take your car? It's easier to move your clubs than the car seats."

Lost in a sip of caramel latte, Trent bobbed his head. "Good idea," he said when he came up for air, hand already searching a pocket for his key fob. His lips quirked, probably at the thought of arriving at the swanky club in my unassuming MINI. "I ordered a skinny demon for you. Venti. Good?"

"Bless you," I said, wondering how he had gotten his sooner than mine . . . but he might have told Mark to wait until I got here to make it.

"How was your night?" he asked, his tone concerned. "Quiet?"

"Very," I said, seeing no need to tell him about burning my hand trying to get past Hodin's door. "You?"

He lifted a shoulder and let it drop. "I got through a handful of books looking for any mention of Möbius strips." He hesitated. "Nothing. Rachel, if you have any doubt about the mage—"

"Lucy, do you want a big pumpkin or a little one?" I said as I took Trent's key fob.

"Pony," Ray said, her high voice utterly charming.

"Big!" Lucy practically shouted, which I thought was funny. She had no idea what we were going to do with it, but she did know the value of big.

"Pony," Ray insisted, and I nodded, brushing the crumbs from her.

"Big pumpkin and pony rides. Check."

Trent's eyebrows rose. "You got a reservation? They were booked when I called."

Content, I slumped into my chair. Lucy had settled, and it was like holding love. "Jenks made them. He was up at the crack of dawn." I cuddled Lucy as she ate her cookie. "So we get to ride the ponies," I said, voice higher. "We have all morning before your dads meet us with a bucket of chicken at Eden Park." I turned to Trent. "Right?"

Lips quirked, Trent glanced at his watch. "I promise I will not get roped into lunch at the club." Then he winced. "Unless it will clinch the deal," he added faintly.

I resettled Lucy before me, delighted when she laced her fingers to match mine. "Fair enough," I said. "I've got your car. If you take too long, I'm taking them to the church for lunch and naps."

"No naps," Lucy whined, and I hugged her closer.

"Not now, silly. When the sun is high in the sky and you get tired. You want to dream about ponies, don't you?"

She had to think about that, her brow furrowed until she spotted Jenks coming over with Mark. "Jenks!" Lucy shouted, and Ray threw her cookie at her in disgust. Lucy began screaming and I grinned as Trent sighed. It went without saying that I was awake, coffee or not.

"You two newlings better shut your pollen holes," Jenks said as he hovered over the table. "Or I'm going to make you itch for a week. Ray, I saw what you did. Apologize."

Lucy caught her next outburst, tears spilling from her. "Ray?" she warbled, and the little dark-haired girl actually sighed.

"Sorry," Ray said, her arms spread wide, and Lucy scrambled over the table to get a hug, peace restored.

"You're going to have a great morning," Trent said, but I couldn't tell if he was being sarcastic or not.

"Yep." I beamed at Jenks, glad he was here. "Jenks is a great dad. He's going to teach me a couple things if I'm not careful."

Jenks went a bright scarlet, the dust spilling from him heavy and thick.

Still smiling, Trent turned to Mark as the kid set an envelope of cookies down along with my coffee. "Thank you, Mark. Much appreciated," Trent added as he stood, cookies in hand.

"Anytime, sir." Mark sort of bobbed his head, then retreated to his register. I'd say it was subservient, but he knew Trent had more money than God. Or at least, he once had. Now he only had more than Oprah, which was nearly the same thing.

"Daddy?" Lucy almost whined, her arms wide and hands opening and closing. I thought it was for a cookie, but she wanted a hug and kiss, which he obliged, giving me one as well.

"Good-bye, my wise and kind ladies," he said as Ray got a kiss and hug, too, the small girl bouncing in her elevated child seat for attention. "Enjoy the cider mill." Expression soft, he touched my chin. "I can't thank you enough for watching them this morning. Sometimes, I think Ellasbeth wants me to fail so she can drag the girls back to Seattle."

"That will be the day," Jenks muttered, his wing pitch rising as he sipped his coffee and the caffeine hit him.

"Go make deals," I said as I handed him my keys. "Save the world."

"Just my corner will be enough." His fingers trailing from me left tingles. And then he was walking away.

I felt loved as he wove through the tables, and I took a sip of sweet cinnamon coffee, practically moaning as it slipped into me, bringing me awake in a way that little-girl voices at full volume couldn't. My arms around Lucy, I watched Trent shift his clubs to my car. He must have felt my stare, because he turned, waving once before getting in and driving off. Yes, it was golf, but it was with Lee, and the man had once broken Trent's hand to win a canoe race. I was sure Lee still hadn't forgiven me for falling into their lives and convincing Trent to stop taking shit from Lee and to stand up for himself.

Though they'd been inseparable at camp, I doubted that Trent and Lee had ever been true friends. Lee was too aggressive, his drive to be the best easy to see. Their parents had insisted on the relationship, probably thinking that interaction early and often might help keep an open dialogue between the two crime families.

It had worked . . . sort of, but I'd never trusted the witch who clearly had a problem with being alive thanks to Trent's dad. Lee, too, had been born with the Rosewood syndrome. Unlike me, though, he couldn't pass the cure on to his children. The repair had been engineered into our mitochondria, and since a baby got that from their mom, it was a final, surreptitious dig, or perhaps insurance, from Trent's father.

*Be careful, Trent. I love you. Desperately.*

"Hey, short stuff." Standing on the centerpiece, Jenks stared at Lucy, hands on his hips. "Think you could lower it a few decibels? Your aunt Rachel has to finish her coffee."

"Diceuhbulls?" Lucy questioned, the word clearly new to her.

"He means make your voice softer," I said. "Supersecret whisper."

"Shhhhhhh," Lucy said, green eyes dramatically wide. Ray wasn't impressed, quietly eating her cookies, her gaze taking everything in.

Until it stopped at the door and didn't move.

Jenks's wing pitch changed as well, and I followed his attention to the six heavily tattooed Weres coming in, moving too slowly for this to be their usual hangout. They were studying the ceilings, the floor, the way to the storage room. My grip on my coffee tightened.

*Are you freakin' kidding me?* I thought. It couldn't be Walter's people, but I didn't recognize their tattoos, and I began gathering the girls' things. "Body count, Jenks?" I prompted.

"On it," he said, and both girls silently watched him fly off.

But it wasn't until I saw a black van take the spot where my MINI had been that a flicker of fear hit me. Worse, another car with four silhouettes inside had parked on the other side of Trent's SUV. There was no way I would make myself and the girls vulnerable by trying to get them in their car seats—not with unknowns to either side. I didn't see Walter or the mage, but it was obvious these weren't Cincy Weres.

"Ray!" Lucy suddenly shouted, and I jumped. "Aunt Rachel, Ray's made an uh-oh!"

She'd spilled her juice. Flustered, I reached for the napkins as the six Weres at the register placed their orders. "It's okay," I said as I gave a napkin to Ray and both of us worked to mop it up. "We will get more at the cider mill."

But I wasn't sure we were going to get to Andie's Apples anymore.

"Lucy, sit still. Let me think," I said as she wiggled under the table. I yanked her up, wishing Jenks would return. For all his diminutive size, he was better with the girls than I was.

"Lucy, stay put," I said, voice harsh, and she did, shoving to the bench's back and thumping her feet. God, what had I been thinking, offering to watch them when I was in the middle of something?

"Six here, two times that outside, Rache."

It was Jenks, and I looked up, exhaling. "Okay. I can't get them into the car. We make a stand here." Was it the ring? Had the mage figured out how to flip it, or did he just want me out of the way? *Damn it back to the Turn. Trent is never going to trust me with them again.*

"Mark has a good circle behind the register," I said as I gathered Lucy in my arms, and she clung to my neck, clearly scared. "Let me know if you see the mage or Walter."

Jenks nodded, worried. Lucy had quit fidgeting, and Ray was gripping her cookie so tightly that her fingers were white. "Will do." In a rasping of wings, Jenks flew away.

"Aunt Rachel?" Lucy warbled, whisper soft as I unbuckled Ray, and the little dark-haired girl practically jumped into my other arm. An odd sensation was tripping through me. I had always been hard on bullies, standing up for the nerd or shy girl at school, often ending up sitting in the principal's office with a busted lip. The anger coursing through me wasn't unfamiliar. But the overwhelming need to protect the two people clinging to me in fear was. I was in full mama-bear mode, and it was utterly terrifying what I'd do for them.

A child on each hip and two bags over my shoulder, I boldly walked past the tattooed alphas scattered over the store as they pretended to sip their coffee.

"I know you're scared," I said, talking to both of them. "It might get even more scary. But I will not let anyone hurt you. Okay? The less afraid you are, the faster I can fix this." And I was going to fix this. Hard.

"Aunt Rachel?" Ray whispered, watching Weres. "They're scared, too."

"Are they?" I stood at the counter waiting for Mark to realize what was going on. People were leaving. It had become that obvious. "But *you* don't have to be. Mark will be with you. He's a witch. He can make a superstrong circle. Stay in it for me while I talk to them. Okay?"

"So they won't be scared?" Ray asked, and I managed a smile.

"Something like that. Can you both be very quiet while I take care of this?"

"Supersecret hide-and-seek?" Lucy whispered.

My heart hurt that they knew how to hide and be quiet. "Just like supersecret hide-and-seek," I said, not a hint of play in my voice. This was how Quen had taught the girls to stay safe, and by Ray's worried eyes and Lucy's pinched brow, they knew it wasn't a game.

"Hey, Rachel . . ." Mark's cheerful voice faltered as he saw my anger and the girls' fear.

"Can you hold them for a moment?" I said, shifting so Lucy's feet hit the counter.

"Uh, yeah?" His voice was high, but his reach was sure as Lucy edged to him, her eyes never leaving me. "Ah . . . should I call Mr. Kalamack?"

*You have his number?* I thought as the door chimes clunked behind me, but I couldn't turn until Ray let go. Hot and sticky, her fingers left my neck. Loss spilled through me, followed by more anger—anger that anyone would put the girls in danger for their petty issues and city-domination plans. "I don't know yet," I said. "I can tell you in about thirty seconds. I'm so sorry about this, Mark. Trent will cover any damages."

"I'm not worried about the damages," he said weakly, and then my heart gave a thump when he invoked his circle and the girls were safe behind a shimmering wall of energy.

Jenks at my shoulder, I spun. All the Weres had stood, some still sipping their coffee, but most eagerly staring at me.

*Their confidence will be the first thing to go,* I thought, still not seeing Walter or the mage. "You are making a mistake," I said, and then my attention shifted as the chimes clunked dully. It was Parker, dressed in jeans and a tee, a new, raw gash under her eye.

"Surrounding yourself with children to protect yourself?" Parker halted, an entire pack of alphas behind her. "Lame, lame, lame, lame, lame," she practically sang, her fingers playing with a metallic amulet about her neck.

"Seriously?" I took my splat gun out of my shoulder bag before tossing it behind the counter. The girls' bag was next. "I'm standing in front of them, not behind. Look, I already have my morning planned, and you aren't in it. Tell me what you want so I can say no and get on with my life. I've got a pony ride scheduled at ten forty-five, and if you don't use it, you lose it."

A lopsided, mean smile quirked her lips. Holding up a finger for me to wait, Parker grasped the hem of her shirt and pulled it over her head to leave her in a thin camisole. *She is going to Were? Great,* I thought as she kicked off her shoes.

"Parker, why are you here? That ring is useless, and if it isn't, that's more reason to not let you have it."

"I don't give a flea's tit about that ring," the woman said. "But the mage doesn't want you to have it, and seeing as we both felt a change needed to be made, here I am." Stretching, Parker bent at the waist to do a perfect A, palms on the floor and butt in the air. She wasn't the bling type, and I studied the amulet dangling under her chin. It was an unknown, but I was sure she'd enlighten me soon.

"Limber little minx, isn't she," Jenks scoffed, and Parker came up, her expression seriously empty.

"You irritate me," she said. "But what I can't stand is Walter's insistence that we could down David without getting rid of you first. You have to take the bitch out to get the dog to move, but most alpha males have an over-inflated opinion of their sex. Until you are gone, the focus is safe with David, ring or not. I'm going to fix that." Her attention flicked over my shoulder to the girls. "Give me the ring and I will walk out of here." She hesitated. "For now. Don't, and I'm going to rip you into strips so small I can feed you to my Pekingese. Either way, I win."

Jenks's wings hummed, and I checked the hopper as if unconcerned. Walter, it seemed, was no longer in charge, and looking at Parker, the gash over her eye open and bleeding, I wondered if he was even alive. "You think I have the ring with me?" I said, feeling it heavy in my jeans pocket.

"I know you do," she said. "The mage wants it back. I want you dead. I don't care what order it happens."

"You talk too much," I said, splat gun lifting, and Parker jumped. Right at me.

Braced against the counter, I fired, getting three shots off before I had to block her swing. Every. Single. Shot. Missed.

"Hey!" I yelped as the thump of impact shook me. Arm smarting, I ducked, jerking away from her elbow and slipping on spilled coffee to go down right under her.

Sitting where I was, I spun to knock her feet out from her. I had an instant of thought that my gun was gone . . . and then she landed on me, elbow in the gut.

My breath exploded from me in an *oof*, but she'd missed my ribs, and

I rolled to my hands and knees, struggling to breathe. The surrounding Weres hung back, treating it as an alpha challenge, jeering and making bets on how long I'd last.

"Incoming!" Jenks shouted, and I clenched my gut, still not having found my breath.

Parker's foot struck me, lifting me from the floor. I grabbed it even as the pain made my eyes water. Still holding her, I rolled. Either she'd go down or I'd break it.

She went down, landing on me and trying to spin me into a choke hold.

It was one move too far, and, grabbing the woman's face, I stared into her half-mad delirium and dumped a load of ley line energy into her. Elated, I felt the line course through me. *You brought a knife to a gunfight, babe,* I thought smugly—and then my hold on the ley line sort of hiccuped and died.

*Son of a moss wipe!* I thought in panic as I scrambled for the ley line. The amulet about her neck was glowing. It had to be an NMZ amulet. I'd brought a gun with no bullets. *Crap on toast, where did she get a no-magic-zone amulet?* But it was obvious. The mage.

Howling in success, Parker slammed her head into mine.

*What the hell?* Reeling, I pushed away and into a stand.

"Get her!" Jenks shrilled, but I was struggling to stay upright as I leaned against a table.

Laughing, the woman stood before me, confident and sure. That amulet about her neck was pulsating. Yep. It was an NMZ. I was up a creek.

I put a hand out, asking for a moment as I caught my breath and reassessed. The chairs and tables had been pushed to the outskirts. Alphas cheered and shouted, urging us on. My hair was a snarled mess, and Mark stood behind the counter with the girls, all three of them terrified that I was going to lose.

I wasn't going to lose. I was a freaking demon.

"Rache," Jenks said, his sword pulled. "Do something. She's Wereing."

"She's what?" I blurted, then went pale as I saw Parker curled into a pained ball, silver hair grotesquely sprouting on her elongating face. Her legs went thin, and her center thickened. Not only was she Wereing, she was almost done.

"You can't fight a wolf without magic," Jenks said again, hovering at my ear as if he was a personal trainer. "And you won't survive a mauling. You got a Wereing curse. Use it!"

I risked a glance behind me at the girls, scared as they watched. Parker was getting to her feet as a wolf, a ripple shifting her coat as she settled into her new skin. That gouge on her eye was worse. If she stayed a wolf, she was going to lose it. Seeing me watching her, Parker lifted her lip in a soft threat of a growl.

"Do something, Rache," Jenks begged, and I held up a hand for her to wait. My abilities were there, but the closer she got with that amulet, the less sure they were.

"Mark?" I wedged off my shoes, my gaze fixed on Parker. "Call Trent if I lose."

"Okay," he warbled.

"Jenks, I need three seconds."

"You got four," he said, then flew at her.

Every strand of me wanted to watch Jenks, but I backed out of the reach of that NMZ amulet and felt for the ley line, sinking deep into myself as I heard her jaw snap and the pixy laugh, taunting her. *Lupis,* I thought fiercely, pulling the curse into me with a savage quickness. Pain was a bright lance, and I fell, gut wrenching as I coughed. The sound exploded from me, and when I tried to push the pain away, I no longer had hands. Red, silky fur softer than silk brushed my sensitive nose.

"Incoming!" Jenks shrilled.

I yelped as something heavy smashed into me and I slid, crashing into the counter.

But I was a wolf now, and I snarled, twisting to close my teeth on whatever they could find. I bit down, and a thin, furred leg slipped through my mouth. I caught a rasping nail, and then it was gone. Twisting, I flipped myself upright and shook my black panties off my foot.

"You and me, Parker!" I shouted, hearing it come out as a bark. The larger Were stood well back, a paw lifted to show where I'd scored. Haunches bunching, I launched myself at her, ears pinned, mouth open. We hit, jaws snapping. She went for my feet and I knelt, finding an ear and ripping a bloody tear. Wiggling, I skittered from her, the taste of her blood in my mouth.

I got two pants in, and then her weight slammed me to the floor. I twisted clear, then darted around a table and jumped onto the next, my nails scrabbling for purchase.

"She's on your six!" Jenks shrilled. "Now!"

I spun, jaws wide. Parker slammed into me, and we slid off the table. But I was ready for it, and I twisted to land on her. My teeth found her foot, and she yelped and pulled free.

"Get her, Rache!" Jenks shouted. "Pull her troll turd of an ear off!"

Parker huffed, her body contorting to pin me. The NMZ amulet dangled almost within my reach. I lunged for it, teeth scraping. Barking like a mad thing, Parker went for my throat, cutting off my air. My eyes bulged, and I kicked at her. *Get off!* I thought, my hind paws gouging her soft underside.

With a yelp she was gone.

I flipped upright, panting. Parker stood eight feet away, tail drooping as she realized it wasn't going to be as easy as she thought.

"That's right!" I barked. "You're looking at the only person who ever took down Aunty Lenore. You're *nothing* compared to an Alcatraz queen! Come here." I stepped forward. *"Here!"*

And even though it was all barks and yaps, I think Parker got the message.

Parker lifted her bleeding paw. Her eye was oozing again, the new scab open and dripping into her sight. Her lip lifted from her wicked canines ... and then she lunged.

I went with it, rolled and tumbled by fur and sinew as I fought to stay clear of her teeth, my tail tucked and my ears pinned. *You are one crazy-ass cur,* I thought as I wiggled free . . . then jumped her.

My teeth grazed her sore foot, and she dropped. It was exactly what I wanted, and with a twist and flip, I found the amulet and pulled it right over her head.

Parker felt it leave, howling as I backed up and tossed it into the air for Jenks to catch. The pixy was ready, and in a flash of dust and rasping wings, he had it and was gone.

*Stabils!* I thought triumphantly as my hold on the ley line became sure again.

Parker yipped, her lips pulled back from her teeth as she fell over, barking as she suddenly couldn't move.

"*Stabils, stabils, stabils!*" I barked, and the three closest alphas were down, too. With a sudden rush, the rest scattered.

"Get 'em, Rache!" Jenks shouted. "Pin those sorry-ass excuses for Were pups!"

I stood, shaking as I pulled in line energy so fast that my fur stood on end. They were all scrambling for the door in an elbow-jabbing, shoving stampede, slowed by their frozen kin. Tail waving, I watched them run. But my satisfaction paled as I turned to the girls.

White-faced and scared, they clung to Mark.

"You let them watch?" I barked, but he didn't understand a word I was saying.

"They're gone," Mark said, and the shimmering energy protecting him dropped. "Jenks, they are gone, right?"

"Yep." Hovering with his hands on his hips, Jenks dusted a happy gold. "Hey, they dragged Parker into that van. You want me to tail them?"

I suddenly realized that the shop was empty except for us and a faint scent of wolfsbane. I shook my head, exhausted as I sat on my haunches, my crushed paw raised to my chest. "Why did you let them watch?" I barked again as the van's tires spun, squeaking to make my ears pin as it bounced into the street. Two more cars were right behind. Obviously it had been an arranged hit, but seeing as I wasn't the one bleeding on the floor of the van, I was going to call it a win.

*A win-win,* I thought, wincing as I held my bruised paw high. It took me a moment, but I awkwardly figured out the three-legged-dog walk as I went to the girls. Rising up, I put my face on the counter to reassure them that I was okay.

"Aunt Rachel?" Lucy warbled, and I nosed her fingers when Mark set her on the counter.

"It's okay, short stack," Jenks said as he alighted on the bananas. "Your aunt Rachel got 'em."

It was embarrassing, but I stood with one paw on the counter and wagged my tail. No wonder Ray was still pale. There had been snapping and barking and biting, and in a sudden need to reassure them, I dropped down. I needed my clothes, my voice, and a couple of arms to tell the girls that everything was okay.

*Non sum quails eram,* I thought once I had my jeans and shirt, and with a tweak on my thoughts and a flash of pain in my gut, I was sitting on the coffee shop floor—utterly naked.

"Aunt Rachel!" Ray cried out, as if only now sure it was me.

"Hi, sweet pea." Jeans held to my chest, I smiled up at her. Fortunately, unlike witch transformation spells, demon curses reset everything, and my crushed hand was again whole. Mark had averted his gaze, but as Jenks snickered, I snatched up my camisole.

"Aunt Rachel, you're naked," Lucy said, and I felt myself warm. A crowd was growing outside. I had no idea where the rest of my clothes were, but relief filled me when I found the ring where I'd left it in my jeans pocket.

"Um, are you okay?" Mark asked, his neck red as he sat both girls on the counter.

"Yes, thanks," I said as I held my clothes to myself.

And then I stiffened when I felt a pull on the ley lines.

"Where are my godchildren!" a cringeworthy, familiar voice boomed, and I spun to the jump-in/out circle Mark kept roped off. It was to give demons a safe place to arrive and depart, and I slumped when I saw Al standing there in black pants and a long-sleeved shirt, an exquisitely embroidered vest flashing with metallic silk.

*How?* I wondered, but then my hope died when he tucked an amulet into his inner vest pocket, an embarrassed press to his lips. He'd bought a jump from someone. Dali, probably.

"Streaker Saturday isn't until tomorrow, love," Al said, eyeing my hairy legs and bony feet from over his blue-smoked glasses. "You're a day early."

"Hi, Al," I said sourly, awkwardly leaning to drag a sock closer. He'd seen down to the bottom of my soul countless times, but it was still uncomfortable.

"Uncle Al?" Ray warbled, and his attention snapped to the girls.

"Excuse me," I muttered, head high as I stood and pushed past the demon to find a sliver of privacy in the storeroom. I could hear people talking in the parking lot, and my face warmed. *Underwear is optional, right?* I thought as I tugged my jeans on. I was going to be rocking the orangutan look all morning. *Yuck . . .*

"Why did you Were? Did you singe yourself trying to get into Hodin's room?" Al asked, and I looked up from zipping my pants to see him holding both girls. Jenks sat above him on a broken light fixture, Parker's NMZ amulet beside him.

"No," I said, my voice muffled as I pulled my camisole on. "Parker was after the ring or me dead, or both. The mage gave her an NMZ. You don't happen to have a Nair curse, do you?"

Al grinned like a fool, a girl on each hip. "I have always appreciated the natural look."

"TMI, Al." I could stop at a spell shop on the way. It would take like five minutes.

"Rache." Jenks dropped down from the fixture to leave the NMZ amulet where it was. "Your phone is ringing. Want me to get it?"

"Please," I said, wondering how long it would take before the videos hit the internet.

"I got it," Mark said, his head down over my bag now on the counter. Jenks hovered over his shoulder as he found my phone and hit the connect icon. "Rachel's phone," Mark said in a professional voice, then added, "She's nearly dressed. Hang on."

"Really?" I said as I padded barefoot out of the storeroom. "Nearly dressed?"

Jenks grinned as he sat on Mark's shoulder. "It's Glenn."

"I hate social media," I said as I took the phone. *Where are my shoes?* And yet, even as Mark hustled to the door to put up the CLOSED sign before the first of the gawkers began to inch closer, I felt invigorated. There was something fulfilling about kicking ass when in fur. That is, until I saw Al with the girls. He had set them both atop a table, brow furrowed in sympathy as he listened to their tearful testimony. Trent wasn't going to be happy. Hell, I wasn't happy.

Worry pinched my brow as I wedged a shoe on. I had no idea where the other one was. "How on earth did you find out so fast?" I said to Glenn as Jenks hovered close to listen in.

"Fast?" Glenn's voice was tight in confusion. "He's been in the hospital all morning."

"Who?" A flash of panic took me as I looked at my pinky ring, but the pearl was a pristine white. Trent was okay. *Relax, Rachel. He just left you.*

"Walter," Glenn said, and I parted my lips in understanding. "A jogger found him under Twin Lakes Bridge this morning."

"Parker," Jenks said, and I nodded. *That bitch doesn't fool around.*

"Let me guess." Phone to my ear, I went to stand under the busted light. Jenks shoved the NMZ amulet off, and it landed in my hand with a soft pop. "Multiple bites and bruises?" I said, my hold on the ley lines faltering as I fingered the silver amulet. *God, I hate these things. . . .*

"Mauled within an inch of his life," Glenn said. "If it had been anyone else, I don't think he would have survived. It's still touch and go."

"Mmmm." Tired, I hooked my foot on a chair leg and pulled the seat out. "That explains why I just slugged it out with Parker," I said as I sat down.

"Ahhh. Aggressive takeover." Glenn hesitated, then, "Oh. There you are," he said, clearly having pulled it up online. I could hear faint shouts and engines revving, and Glenn added, "Damn, girl! You fight naked?"

Al smiled to show his flat, blocky teeth. I put a hand to my forehead, eyes closed as I gathered my strength. *I should probably text my mom. . . .* "I didn't want to tear my jeans," I said. "Hey, I appreciate the update on Walter, but I have the girls and I need to call Trent before he freaks."

"Go," Glenn said. "I wanted to let you know that David is on his way in to question Walter. You want me to have him ask how to work the ring?"

A sudden need to be somewhere else hit me. Constance's claim that I was forcing my friends to do my job was tight behind. With the strength of the focus, David could compel Walter to talk. Of course I wanted to be there, but the girls came first. "How to work the ring, if the mage figured out how to switch it back to curse mode, and who the mage is," I said. "Could you text me if you get anything? I've got the girls until noon." I was *not* about to take them to the hospital. They were upset enough as it was.

"Will do," Glenn said, and then the connection ended.

Jenks was dusting heavily over my other shoe, and I shuffled over to it as I dropped my phone into my pocket, where I'd feel it vibrate. The need to question Walter dug at me, but as I saw the girls with Al, I knew there was no way. *Constance, you suck. Me not killing people is not putting my friends in danger.*

"Rachel, you want another coffee? To go?" Mark said pointedly, and I nodded.

"Me too," Jenks said loudly. "Someone spilled mine."

Lips crooked, I went to sit with Lucy and Ray, taking the first girl who reached for me. "That bad wolf bit you," Lucy said, her little fingers carefully playing over my curse-fixed hand as I sat her on my lap. Ray abandoned Al, and I suddenly had them both.

"She did, but turning back fixed it," I said, feeling their weight and trust. "I'd never let anything hurt you. You know that, right?"

Both girls bobbed their heads, and I let them slide to the floor, where I tugged their clothes straight, one at a time. "Go pick out a juice box for the cider mill," I said to distract them. Al had listened and reassured them, but I could see their fear. Trent had taken great pains to hide the ugly side of their security even as he made sure they knew that steps were being taken. He was not going to be happy that they'd witnessed this, but I'd always felt that seeing a threat resolved was less traumatic than the threat your mind could invent and magnify.

"Come on, short stacks," Jenks said, his dust a cheerful yellow. "You like fruit, right?"

Lucy took Ray's hand, and with that extra security, they crossed the room. Even with Jenks there, the ten feet felt too far, and Ray looked back once to be sure I wasn't going anywhere.

"Trent's going to kill me," I said, and Al smirked. "How did you know I was in trouble?"

"When are you *not* in trouble?" Al tugged the hem of his vest, flicking a foul glance at the people lingering in the parking lot. "Truth is, I didn't. I was crashing your morning in the hopes of spending time with the girls. An NMZ, eh? Hence you going wolf. Clever thinking. Do you still have the ring?"

"It was Jenks's idea," I said, but there hadn't been much thinking going on. I was lucky that the rest of the pack had stayed on the outskirts, treating it as an alpha challenge. Tradition had saved me. If they'd been thinking, I would've been wolf chow.

Clearly the mage wanted the ring back. Being a target I could handle— that I had told Trent I had everything under control and put the girls in danger was another story, and embarrassment warred with anger.

"Aunt Rachel was a wolf," Lucy said, still holding Ray's hand as they returned, Mark behind them with a bag in hand. "She bit that bad wolf. *Hooooowl!*"

Beaming, Al lifted the little girl up. "It's only proper to bite people when you are both wearing fur. Now that she is wearing clothes, your aunt

Rachel would curse them with a spell instead." Al gave me a sidelong glance. "Even if she is still sort of wearing fur."

Annoyed, I pulled Ray to me. A stop at a spell shop was in order—soon as I got my coffee. "Parker put Walter in the hospital. Glenn and David are going down to see if he can talk. Find out who the mage is and if he found out how to turn the ring."

"That seems appropriate." Al reached for the NMZ amulet, making a *tsk-tsk* when Lucy tried to take it. Her little brow furrowed, Lucy drew away, clearly frustrated.

"Hey, ah, could you hang on to that for me for a while," I said. Holding it meant I couldn't tap a line, and seeing as Al couldn't . . . Grimacing, I quashed a rising wave of guilt.

"Of course." Mood reserved, Al coiled the NMZ lanyard into his palm and delicately tucked it in a vest pocket. "Perhaps you should go to the hospital to question Walter while he lives?" he added. "I can mind the girls for an hour."

"Ah, thanks, but Glenn has it," I said, admittedly torn. I took out my phone at the reminder, shooting off a quick text to Trent that we were on our way to the cider mill and that the girls were fine. If I was lucky, he would assume I was giving him a worried-dad update. And if he did see the news, my casual text might convince him it hadn't been a big deal. If I was really lucky, he'd be in a dead zone.

"I am not helpless, Rachel," Al said, the implication clearly grating on him.

"I know," I said. True, he was resorting to buying charms from other demons, but if he offered, he had enough of them to keep the girls safe. Al's reputation, too, would keep trouble at bay.

But I really wanted to be there when David questioned Walter, and, seeing my indecision, Jenks lifted off the table, wings a blur. "Parker wanted you, not the girls. You go. I'll stay with Lucy and Ray."

"Yes, go." Al gestured flamboyantly. "Spend an hour with that cur of a Were. I am their demon godfather. Trent would not have made me such if he didn't trust me with them." He hesitated. "Besides, they are safer with me than you . . . at the moment."

He was right, and, not happy, I turned to the girls. "Is that okay? It was supposed to be our time."

"Pony?" Ray asked Al, and the demon grinned wickedly.

"As many times as you like, my little ever-after sparkle," he said, and a knot of worry eased in me as the little girl reached for Al. Sure, I could have felt slighted, but it was Al. Who wouldn't want to ride the ponies with a demon?

"How about you, Lucy?" Al arranged Lucy's dress, his expression serious. "Will you come with me, Jenks, and Ray while your aunt Rachel discovers why the Weres are scared?"

Nodding, Lucy put her arm around his neck and gave him a noisy, little-girl kiss.

"Aww, that is sweeter than pixy pi—ah, sweat," Jenks said as he hovered, hands on his hips. "Go on, Rache. We got this."

"Okay. Thanks." Somewhat relieved, I pushed myself up and went to get the girls' bag next to the register. There was a tall cup of coffee beside it, and, taking both, I shuffled back. "You need Trent's keys," I added as I dropped everything on the table and began to rummage. "Make sure you get them in their car seats properly."

Jenks was a tight hum by my ear. "I know how a car seat works."

Head down, I pushed past Walter's finding amulet, the adrenaline beginning to trickle through me again. I was going to see Walter, and if he didn't tell me what I wanted to know, I would pinch off his morphine feed. *The mage wants the ring back, my ass.*

"Jenks booked two ponies for ten forty-five. I'll try to meet you there."

Al's eyebrows rose as I set Trent's key fob and credit card in his hand. "Ten forty-five," he drawled, looking charmingly domestic with the girls.

"Aunt Rachel?"

It was Lucy, and I jerked to a halt, shoulder bag swinging. Her arms were out, hands opening and closing. She wanted a kiss, and I leaned down, bringing the scent of snickerdoodles and the tang of the ley lines into me.

Ray was next, and as I gave her a hug, I thanked Al with my eyes. He was not helpless. He was not worthless. He was healing. I had to believe it.

"Thanks, Jenks," I whispered, and his hand touched the hilt of his garden sword.

"No prob. Go pinch Walter's ass, er, assets," he said, his dust red as he glanced at the girls.

Uneasy, I turned and walked out, thanking Mark for the coffee in passing. I could get a cab at the corner, and from there, the hospital.

# CHAPTER

# 13

"HERE IS FINE," I SAID AS I RAN MY CARD BEFORE GATHERING MY BAG and reaching for the door. "Thanks for the ride."

"You got it," the man said, already having forgotten me, and I stepped out, scanning the hospital's drop-off area with people on phones, catching a smoke, sitting in their wheelchairs while waiting for their family to bring the car around.

An odd sort of quashed panic began to tickle the folds of my brain as I walked to the oversize revolving doors. Too many late-night runs into pediatric emergency had left their mark, and I stiffened as I boldly strode into the muffled quiet.

My mother had once told me that when she was a little girl, you could come and go at the hospital as if you were walking into a grocery store, but homegrown terrorist attacks during the Turn had resulted in more security than it took to get on a plane. Things had eased forty years later, but the eight-foot-wide arch of a spell detector still remained, and, as I had expected, something I was carrying triggered it—probably the charms in my splat gun.

"Here," I said when the security guard glanced up from his phone, flashing him my runner's license. He beeped it with his scanner, checked the screen, and waved me through.

"Yeah, that's nice," I whispered as I skirted the faded white box taped to the floor. Glenn had texted me where Walter was, and I headed for the elevators. C wing, fifth floor. Room 526. I had a pretty good idea where that was, but I slowed as I was passing the display of Underground Railroad quilts. My phone was ringing, and my gut twisted. *Trent?*

Grimacing, I hit connect. "Hi," I said cheerfully, phone to my ear. "You got my text?"

"Let me talk to Lucy."

His voice was terse. It reminded me of when he was ticked at Ellasbeth, and my anger flared. "She is fine," I said, walking right past the elevators. I could get to C wing on the ground floor and then go up. "Ray, too. Al is watching them while I stop in at the hospital."

"You're hurt?" he gasped, and I felt a headache start.

"No. Parker mauled Walter, and I want to talk to him. Find out who the mage is."

"Oh." He paused, but his voice was still angry when he added, "I saw the video of you tearing it up with Walter at Junior's. You left the girls behind a counter with a barista."

"Then you saw them safe in a circle that would hold a demon," I said, tensing. Yeah, they were his kids, but I had handled it. "Mark is not a barista. He's a self-made entrepreneur who worked with Dali for over six months. You don't think he picked up a few things? And it wasn't Walter, it was Parker. I was wrong. The mage wants the ring back. Either he figured out how to turn it, or he thinks I will. I took care of it, and I'm going to meet up with the girls at the cider mill in about an hour." *Damn it all to the Turn and back. Is Constance right?*

"Then why are you at the hospital?" he said, and I took a slow breath.

"Because I want to talk to Walter," I said again. "He knows both the invocation phrase for that stupid ring and who the mage is."

"You left Ray and Lucy with a demon incapable of doing magic?"

My jaw clenched. *My God. Are we having our first fight?* "Hey!" I said loudly, my shoes pounding the hard floor. Either he was going to trust my judgment, or we were done. A pang of fear hit me. "Al loves them more than he loves himself, and if he offered to take them, then he can keep them safe even if the moon should fall down. Jenks is with them." I hesitated.

"They are probably safer away from me," I added, hating myself, my world, everything.

Trent's silence hung there, making me wonder why he had ever agreed to let me watch the girls in the first place.

"David is meeting me here," I said when the silence became too hard to bear. I had reached C wing. The corridor had become smaller and the people more numerous, and I lowered my voice. "This is my best, safest chance to find out who the mage is."

Trent still hadn't said anything, and I stopped before the elevators, not wanting to lose signal. The residue of powerful medicinal spells was making my skin tingle, and I was uncomfortable. "I was wrong about how important the ring was. Trent, I am so sorry," I finally said.

"This isn't just about the ring . . ." Trent began, and a misplaced anger flared.

"Look," I said, immediately wishing I'd used another word. "Walter is here. I am here. I'm going to talk to him. The girls are fine."

"You left them with Al. Rachel, this was supposed to be your time with them."

Jaw tight, I stared down the busy hallway. "I'm in the elevator," I lied as the one across from me opened to let two people out. "I think I'm losing you."

I hung up, anger and guilt rising from his last words. "They will be safe with Al," I whispered as I stepped into the elevator and hit the button for the fifth floor. Arms over my middle, I slumped into a corner. My mother had put her entire career on hold while she raised first Robbie and then me while my birth father had let his best friend step in and play dad. I knew Takata regretted his choice—even as his guilt and regret had been the dross that he spun into music gold. Ray and Lucy weren't my children, and yet I felt as if I was standing in the same place.

I was the only one in the elevator, and I pushed from the wall when it dinged. Maybe me playing mother wasn't a good idea. I was so self-absorbed that I couldn't even remember if Jenks's cat was a boy or girl.

Frustrated, I walked past the unattended nurses' desk, counting down the room numbers. It was easy to see where I was going; there was a FIB officer stationed outside his door. "I'm going in," I said as I scuffed to a halt, a hand on a hip and begging for trouble. "Rachel Morgan."

"Yes, ma'am." The officer opened the door. "Detective Glenn said you were coming. He'll be here shortly. He left to escort Mr. Hue up."

*Alone with Walter? Nice.* "Thanks." I stepped inside and pulled the door shut behind me.

But my misplaced anger only grew as I saw Walter on one of those ugly, narrow beds, one hand cuffed to a bedrail, the other sporting a pulse monitor. The window looked out onto a courtyard, and I set my bag on a chair to close the blinds. His eyes were shut, but he was awake; his pulse had quickened when I had entered the room.

Thick bandages covered his head, and his already close-cut hair had been shaved off. A medical-grade pain amulet was taped to his upper chest, the holographic label showing through the thin, lightly patterned hospital gown. I'd be ripping that off shortly—the amulet, not the gown—and I took his patient tablet from the wall. "Hey, Walter," I said as I halted at the end of his bed. "Acknowledge that I'm here, or I will shove you onto the floor."

His eyes opened, brilliant with pain despite the amulet. His lip curled, and the cuff clinked when he moved.

"Yeah, I'm happy to see you, too," I said, and he grunted when I shoved his legs over to make room for my ass. "I'm supposed to be babysitting Trent's and Quen's girls right now," I added, one hip on the bed as I scrolled thorough his stats. "That I have to come down here and beat some information out of you really pisses me off. I don't get much one-on-one with them." My eyebrows rose as I looked at him over the tablet. "And here I am with you."

Walter silently stared at me, perhaps hoping that Glenn would walk in, as that was the only way he was going to remain pain-free.

"Mmmm," I said as I read his chart. "Multiple internal injuries, nicked jugular, crushed wrist. Your ear is gone." I tossed the tablet to the narrow, rolling table, the clatter loud in the small room. "Wow. Parker is a bitch." I slid from the bed. "She take you by surprise? Bet she did. Five minutes, and she ripped away everything you built. Left you for dead. I know how that feels. Want to get back at her? Here I am. Talk to me."

Walter's pulse quickened, his lips pressed tight.

"Okay. I don't mind going first." Standing, I pinned his free arm to the bed, my other arm heavy across his chest as I drummed my fingers atop that pain amulet. "Who's the mage?"

"Go turn yourself," Walter rasped, and I pushed off him, hard enough to leave him gasping for breath.

"Manners," I said, not liking who I was at the moment, even as I imagined worse things.

Smiling, I reached for a ley line, inhaling as I drew it in and then flicked a tiny wad of it at the ceiling monitor. With a puff of electronic smoke, the little red light went out. Not as clean as if Jenks had done it, but I wasn't fussy. "What's the invocation phrase to break that chakra curse?" I asked, and his eye twitched when I pulled the pulse monitor off his finger and put it on mine. "Did the mage figure out how to flip the ring? Is that why he wants it back? Or does he think I will figure it out." Walter was silent, and I leaned in, whispering, "What did you give him for helping you? Not your kidney, I hope. You're probably going to lose one."

His chin lifted, scraped and bloodied. "Kill me or get the fuck out of here," he rasped.

"Let's not get ahead of ourselves." I pulled the other rail up and leaned the flat of my arms on it. "I'd think you'd be happy to see her fail after what she did to you, because, Walter, you're out of the game." The pulse at his neck was fast, but the machine made a steady *beep, beep*, reading mine, not his. "Tell me about that ring. Did the mage figure out how to flip it?"

"What ring?" he practically growled.

"Maybe I can jiggle your memory. Sometimes these pain amulets are too strong."

I reached for his amulet. Walter grunted as he lifted his bandaged arm to stop me, but I hesitated as the door opened and the noise from the hallway spilled in.

Relief crossed Walter's face. But I leaned closer, having recognized the scent of Glenn's aftershave. "Glenn won't help you," I whispered, then ripped the amulet clean off him.

"Oh . . . God . . ." Walter moaned, clenching in on himself.

My pity faded fast. Dizzy from the powerful spell, I tossed the amulet to Glenn.

"Walter's overmedicated," I said as Glenn caught it, juggling it from hand to hand like a hot potato until Cassie made a grab for it and sent it thumping into David's lap. Though dressed in his usual jeans and button-down shirt, the Were was in one of the hospital-supplied wheelchairs, and his focus blurred as the magic took hold. "He can't seem to string two words together and tell me how to uncurse your people, Cassie," I added.

"He's awake?" Glenn came forward, his attention going from the slow beep of the pulse monitor on my finger to Walter, curled up and gasping as if it was his last. "Seriously, Rachel?" he said as he took the amulet and handed it to Walter. Walter grasped it with his good hand, his breath rasping in with relief.

"You stunted little whore of a bitch," Walter gasped, and Glenn's expression hardened.

"You want the pulse monitor back on him, too?" I said sweetly.

"No, you can keep that."

"Thought so." I was glad Glenn was content to let me be the bad guy, and I eyed the monitor on my finger as if it was a new manicure, smiling. "I'm simply trying to move my day along. David, you look better."

The Were rolled himself closer, Cassie tight to his side. "At least I don't forget to take my clothes off before I Were," he said.

"You saw that?" I said, embarrassed, and Cassie smirked.

"It's trending," she said as she moved my shoulder bag off the chair and sat down.

Yes, I was still angry with Cassie, but seeing as Cassie was sore and David was in a wheelchair, I figured she knew it had been a bad idea to romance David's location from me and then give Doyle the last dance.

"You want me to make him talk?" David said, and Walter slowly uncurled.

"Yep." Extra sass in me, I bent over Walter and arranged his sheet. "So if you have any hope of coming out of this alive, you should tell me who the mage is before Parker kills you to shut you up. Now. Did you meet him before or after I put Hodin away?"

"I want a lawyer," he wheezed, and Cassie snickered.

"You don't get a lawyer," I said. "You get me. I want to know who the mage is, or Detective Glenn from the FIB is going to take the agent off your door and walk away."

David pulled Cassie down and whispered in her ear. I didn't hear what he said, but I think Walter did, as his brow furrowed.

"See, Walter," I said, hips swaying as I went to peek past the blinds. "I know what it's like to have a lot of power. You tend to piss people off, and if you don't make amends, they remember it. One day, you lose your power. And then all those people you made angry or afraid come back. Real fast. Real ugly."

I turned, probably nothing more than a dark silhouette against the sun-bright blinds.

"Okay, ease up, Rachel," Glenn said softly. "You're starting to scare me."

But he hadn't been the one responsible for two little girls, terrified as Parker and I fought.

"Let me try," David said, and I gestured for him to have at it.

David turned his attention to Walter and went still. Slowly his pupils widened until his eyes were nothing but black orbs. His face became gaunt, and a wild, feral tension took over his stance. Breath by breath, his mien changed until it wasn't David sitting there. It was the focus. I stifled a shudder. It was always there, but David rarely gave the sentient curse so much freedom.

David had taken the living curse into himself to save my sanity when

I had stupidly tried to control it. Even now I wasn't sure I understood what the curse did to give him sway over the multitude of packs that Cincinnati boasted. I'd never heard him make one decree, or promise, or threat, and still what he wanted seemed to get done, whether it was helping to quell a vampiric uprising or finding a parking space. He might seem to be living a charmed life. But watching the raw, wild power surge through him, I realized it was more of a burden than he ever let on. To control this was not easy.

"Rachel needs to know what you know," he said, and I glanced at Cassie. She'd gone pale, clearly shaken. *She hadn't seen the depth of it,* I realized, hoping this wasn't going to change things between them. "What's the invocation phrase to break the chakra curse?"

"You can . . . stuff your tail up your ass," Walter rasped, his expression drawn as he fixed his gaze on David's. My lips parted. He was afraid. I'd never seen that in him before, not even when his wife lay dying in his arms.

"Walter," David all but whispered, and I started. His voice had changed, becoming wispy and cunning. I recognized it from how my own voice had sounded when I held the focus. Madness drifted through my memory, and I retreated until I bumped into Glenn.

"You've been leading others alone for too long," David said, and Walter's eyes bulged as he clenched his jaw. "Breathe easy. Run smooth. I know. I am. See me. I am. Let go. Set your burden down and live."

Walter groaned, expression twisted. "You were supposed to be mine. Mine!"

David shuddered, and when his face settled, I wasn't sure the man was still in there. "I was never yours," he said, and I knew it was the curse that was speaking. "You feed the worst of us instead of starving it. I am what makes us worth being, and you will acknowledge that. Speak what the demon wants to know."

"I . . . can't," he gasped, and David—or maybe it was the focus now—reached out, grasping his wrist in demand.

"Speak it," David insisted.

Glenn's grip on my shoulders tightened, and I stiffened as a tickling sensation of building energy seemed to trip along my spine. "Who is the mage?" I asked, and Walter's lip twitched, a name, perhaps, struggling to remain unsaid.

"You already . . . know," he choked out. He took a sudden breath, and I started at a surge in the ley lines. Walter's body shook, his pulse pounded at his neck, and veins stood out upon his forehead. Something was happening, something other than David pushing Walter. I could sense magic gathering, but there was no one in the room but us.

"Is anyone else feeling that?" I said, and Cassie gave me a blank look.

Walter grasped David's hand almost in desperation. "You can make us more powerful than even the vampires. Why do you stay with him? He is nothing. I can make you a king."

David pulled away, his lip curled in distaste. "The wolf does not crave dominion. The wolf craves clear nights, open fields, and the security of the pack. You are the worst of us, not the best, and I will not lend my strength to you. I will drive you out. The lone wolf will perish."

Walter's expression suddenly went riven, as if God himself had told him he was shunned.

Glenn bumped into me, intent as he inched closer. "Where is your safe house?" he asked, and Walter stiffened, eyes bright. "Where is Parker? Is the mage with her?"

"Ah, guys?" I said, stifling a shudder as the power in the room prickled down my spine. "Hey, ah, we need to slow down," I added, but Walter was grinning, a wild look finding him.

*He's seeing around corners*, I thought, recognizing his wish to be dead. I'd seen it before in hospital friends who had suffered more pain than any child should. He wanted out. The one thing he most coveted had spurned him. He was going to kill himself.

"David, wait!" I exclaimed, but Walter had choked down a cough, his gaze fixed on me.

"You want to know who the mage is?" he said. "I'll tell you. The mage—"

"No!" I exclaimed, surging forward to put my hands over his mouth.

But I was too late, and with the name unsaid, Walter spasmed. Stiffening, he groaned. Behind him, the machinery pegged their readouts, and a faint alarm began to sound.

"What did you do! He was goin' to tell us!" Cassie exclaimed.

"No he wasn't. He's trying to kill himself," I said, backing off as three nurses burst in.

"Out!" one of them demanded. "Crash cart! Now!" he shouted, turning to me even as he began chest compressions. "What did you do to him?"

"It wasn't me." Arms over my middle, I retreated to the covered window, the trapped heat beating my shoulders. "I tried to stop him." My attention went to Glenn, then David. The Were was slumped, hands to his face as he tried to push the focus to the bottom of his psyche. Cassie's hand was on his arm, her touch a mix of possessive protection. "I tried to stop him," I said again, but no one was listening. The crash cart had been wheeled in, and they were getting ready to shock his heart.

"He's got a no-divulge spell on him," I said, and the lead nurse's head rose. "I felt it gather as we questioned him. He triggered it intentionally. I didn't do this."

The lead nurse went still. He gave me a quick study, assessing in an instant that I might know what I was talking about. "This isn't going to help," he said even as he yanked the cords from the walls. "Emergency decurse. Move him out! Let's go, people. We've got three minutes!"

Cassie rolled David clear as the three nurses suddenly became five. In a heartbeat, Walter was in the hall. "Empty that elevator!" came a loud voice, and then they were gone.

Slowly the door arced shut.

There was a big hole in the room where Walter had once been. I stood against the window, afraid to cross into the space. It felt chancy, like walking over a new grave.

"Where are they taking him?" Cassie said, and I jumped.

"A lead-lined room deep underground. It will cut off his access to the ley lines. Possibly reset the curse." I winced, shoulders high. "It might save him, but we won't ever get the name of the mage."

Cassie inched forward. I didn't understand the light of hope in her eyes. "Can we do that to my people?" she asked, and I stared, not under-standing for a moment.

"Oh. No," I said, finally figuring out her mental gymnastics. "The curse on Walter was a no-divulge curse. The chakra curse works differently. Um, I have to go," I added, shaken by the empty room. I'd seen it before, the sudden commotion followed by a long quiet. A place where someone had been, had talked, had laughed, had cried, was suddenly empty. They never came back.

"I need to go," I said again, softer. Fear I had thought long vanquished was twining about my heart. It was old, and dark, dirty with cobwebs and neglect. "The girls are waiting for me."

"I'll stay," Glenn said. His expression was closed, and I wondered if he had seen an empty room, too, or if he'd been hustled into the hallway, kept apart while his mother died.

"Rachel, you mind if I come with you?" David asked, and I reached for my bag and held it close as if it was one of the stuffed animals from my childhood. *I hate hospitals.*

"Um, sure." I glanced at Cassie, seeing this was a surprise to her, too.

"I want to make sure Lucy and Ray aren't afraid of Weres," he added, and Cassie bent to give him a kiss, her hand tracing his jawline as she searched his face. She was looking for the focus. It was still there but again hidden.

"I'll stay with Detective Glenn," she said. "I'll let you know if he pulls through."

Head tilting up, David reached for her, and they kissed again, long and lingering, full of promise and connection. "See you tonight," he whispered as they parted.

I moved behind him and made sure the wheels were unlocked. "Let me know, too, 'kay?"

Glenn nodded, his head bowed in a needless guilt. There was no way he could have guessed Walter had been under a no-divulge spell. Besides, Walter had intentionally triggered it.

I shoved the door open with my foot, taking a deep, cleansing breath as we found the hall. The air was cooler and my pace fast. Three interns were gossiping at the desk, their attention following us as we came to the elevators and stopped. Tense, I smacked the down button. *Ow* . . .

David took a deep breath and lurched upright, shocking me as I scrambled to keep the chair from rolling. "What are you doing?" I said as he put a steadying hand against the wall.

"Ditching the chair. I was only in it so Cassie would stop bitching at me."

"No, you aren't. Sit. You're too heavy for me to catch."

David frowned, and I shrugged, pointing until he sat back down. I didn't like wheelchairs, either, but I liked hitting the floor less. *Get a grip, Rachel. You aren't a frightened little girl anymore. Walter is not your friend, and if he dies, your life will be easier.* "Can we take your car? I came in a cab," I said, trying to change where my thoughts were going.

The elevator pinged, and I rolled him in.

"Sure." David tapped the button from his chair and the doors closed. "But I'm driving."

"Yeah?" I questioned, even as I felt that flicker of fear quiver and grow: sudden change, empty space, a loss you couldn't replace. Grimacing, I shoved the sensation down as I always did.

But the fear was not going out. Not this time.

# CHAPTER

# 14

DAVID'S GRAY SPORTS CAR BUMPED OVER THE FLATTENED GRASS, slow because of the ruts. The sleek icon was out of place amid the SUVs and vans, and that along with the wheelchair hanging out of the open trunk had gotten us into the front lot instead of the back forty of Andie's Apples. We were surprisingly close to the main building, and I eased the car to a halt, appalled at the pandemonium of the cider mill on a beautiful Friday afternoon a week before Halloween.

"Bartholomew's balls," David whispered over the hush of his seat belt sliding away. "You *wanted* to come here?"

Wincing, I peered out the front window at the kids running free and in the wild. Moms and dads oblivious or immune to the chaos pushed strollers over the grassy ruts, their children kicking chubby legs and waving juice cups on the way in, sticky and pumpkin laden on the way out. More often than not, there was a toddler or two in tow.

"I don't remember it being like this," I said as I opened my door and the noise rose.

"Wow." David took a steadying breath as he got out. "More effective than a box of prophylactics," he said as he found his balance.

My door thumped shut, and I hesitated, the flat of my arms on the roof of David's car as I studied the main building, the cider press hut, and finally the pumpkin fields. The tangy scent of cider and hot doughnuts made my mouth water. "Sticky," I whispered. "Al doesn't have a cell phone anymore. Let's try the pumpkin patch. You want to ride out there on the hay wagon?"

David took a careful step, then another, his motions quickly easing. "No. As long as we go slow, the walk will do me good."

Still, I hooked my arm in his, hitching my shoulder bag higher as we angled to the cider press building and the smell of cooking dough. David and I were like slugs amid the noise and movement of too many kids hopped up on baby goats and pumpkins. The day was sunny and warm, not a given in Cincy this late in October. I had the city's most eligible Were bachelor on my arm, and I breathed him in, letting the complex scent of Were relax me as we made our very slow way over the flattened grass.

"How you doing?" I asked as we found a dusty two-track.

"Me? I'm fine. It's you I'm worried about."

Surprised, I tucked a stray strand of hair behind an ear. "Me?"

"At the hospital?" he prompted, and I winced. "I've never seen you mean before."

"Yeah, well . . ." I hedged, wondering if misplaced aggression was to blame. I was still mad at Trent. Or my life, maybe. I couldn't take two girls out for a morning without having a fight with a wannabe city power. "I'm okay," I said, knowing I wasn't.

"That was okay?" David's grip tightened on my arm as three kids ran by, nearly knocking into him. "Remind me never to get on your bad side."

"I'm a little on edge," I admitted, then started when a warm, sticky hand grabbed my fingers. "Ray!" I said as she beamed up at me, Jenks sitting cockily on her shoulder. "You're sneaky."

Jenks took to the air, a satisfied smirk on his angular face. "She's going to be the queen of sneak," he predicted. "Hey, Mr. Peabody. You look like a cat barfed you up."

"Nice to see you, too," David said, his eyebrows high at the irksome moniker.

I picked Ray up, content as her weight settled nicely on my hip. "Where are Al and your sister?" I asked, and she pointed to the picnic area, where Al and Lucy sat surrounded by a ring of conspicuously empty tables. Three

Dixie cups of cider and an open bag of doughnuts were before them, and the demon in his black pants and a colorful vest didn't seem as out of place as he might, having a wealthy-uncle-taking-his-nieces-out vibe. Eyebrows high, he gave me a mocking look. Despite the distance, he'd clearly known where Ray was the entire time.

*He's good at this,* I thought, making a little jiggle to set Ray more firmly. Not like me, dragging my life into everything where it stained even the most simple pleasures. But then again, those goat-slitted eyes of his tended to keep people away, especially when they were half-hidden behind a pair of blue-smoked glasses.

"Have you picked out a pumpkin yet?" I asked Ray, and she shook her head, her attention fixed on David. There was a hint of fear in her grip, and guilt clenched my heart. "This is Mr. Hue," I said, and David smiled at her. "He's one of my most important friends."

"Hello, Ray," David said, his voice gentle. "I know both your daddies."

"He's a good guy," Jenks added, but it wasn't until the pixy alighted on David's shoulder that Ray began to relax.

"Were?" she asked, her high, clear voice sounding small.

His expression serious, David nodded. "Yes, I am."

But we had reached the tables, and the ever-bubbly Lucy was now standing on the bench, working hard to keep Al from cleaning her hand. "Aunt Rachel?" the little girl shouted. "Caramel apple, caramel apple, caramel apple!"

I winced at the memory of my brother, Robbie, sticking mine in my hair, but then Lucy lost her fire as she saw David. Eyes widening, she tucked in behind Al. That she was afraid of him bothered me. *Trent is not going to be happy. . . .*

Al finally got Lucy's hand and cleaned it with a packaged wipe from the girls' bag. "Busy morning?" he asked, his gaze lingering on David's bruises.

"I was going to ask you the same thing." I eyed the ring of empty tables surrounded by an even wider ring of overly full ones.

"Bunch of dewdrop milksops never seen a demon before," Jenks said.

Al's smile became positively . . . demonic. "We are *marvelous*." Al encouraged Lucy to sit, her pinky lifted high as she delicately took up her half-eaten doughnut. "I have spent the morning fielding many questions concerning Weres. Together, we have learned how to gather the pack."

"Owwuuwl!" Lucy shouted, and from across the orchard, three high-pitched howls returned to make the little girl bounce in excitement.

"That is a most excellent call, Lucy," David said. "You could run with the pack and not get lost. I'm Mr. Hue, one of Rachel's friends."

Lucy slumped against Al again, her green eyes going from me to Ray and back to David. I could almost see her thoughts; if Ray wasn't afraid of him, she wouldn't be, either.

"Wolf Sa'han," Ray said boldly, and Jenks snickered.

"Well, not exactly," David admitted. "Weres don't have a Sa'han."

I stepped over the bench with Ray to sit down across from Al. The doughnuts smelled delicious and were still warm from the fryer. Breaking one in two, I handed half to Ray and then broke my part again to share with Jenks.

Lucy, though, hadn't taken her attention off David, her doughnut forgotten as she studied him in mistrust. "Do you bite people?" she finally asked, voice high and clear.

David grinned, and I passed him the doughnut bag. "Only when I'm in fur," he said as he carefully eased himself down. "And only if I have to."

Lucy's chin lifted. "My daddy can turn into a wolf. But he doesn't bite people."

"Your daddies know how to do magic," Jenks said as he brushed the sugar from his front.

David nodded, his dark expression serious. "Magic is more dangerous than biting."

The little girl frowned, distracted when a hornet landed on her cup of apple cider. "Ray!" she shrieked, and I jumped, startled when I felt a tug on the lines and the hornet fell over, dead.

My lips parted at Ray's smug satisfaction. She'd killed it. With magic. "Ah, Al?" I questioned, and the demon turned to me with a dark look.

"Do you think for one instant I would give either of those children anything they can harm themselves or another with?"

"No," I admitted. "You cleared it with Trent and Quen, right?"

Smirking, Al used a tattered corn husk to flick the dead insect off the table, where it landed on a veritable morgue of them. "We've been practicing our spells," he said in pride, not answering my question, and Ray scrambled up, doughnut forgotten in her effort to reach him. "You did very well, little elf," he added as he took her on his hip, and she giggled.

I sighed, knowing that somehow this was going to be my fault. "Hey, ah, you mind if we talk shop for a moment?" I said, and Al's eye twitched.

David stood, motions slow as he maneuvered his sore and battered body out of the picnic table. "Ray? Lucy?" he said, half-eaten doughnut in hand. "Let's find the best two pumpkins for you and your daddies to carve."

"I'm in." Jenks rose up, clearly intending to serve as a second pair of eyes.

"Thank you," I whispered, and Jenks gave me a pixy salute before landing on David's shoulder. Seeing him there, first Ray and then Lucy fit their hands into David's, and they wove their way through the tables to the nearby field. They got about ten feet before Lucy let go, hair flying as she ran ahead, Jenks in hot pursuit.

"Ah, how the elves have fallen," Al said with a sigh. "Perhaps enough that we might survive them," he added. "There's no harm in giving Ray something to protect her sister with. Perhaps if she was equipped with the proper tools, the girl might stop acting like a forty-year-old security guard and enjoy her childhood."

"You said it couldn't hurt anyone."

"And so it does not." Al stood, turning to sit atop the table, where he could watch them better. "Its reach will grow as does her understanding. For now, it kills bugs."

Trent was going to be ticked—if he found out. "They love you. You know that, right?"

"They are my godchildren."

I felt a hint of a smile find me. "Elven godchildren. I bet Dali is . . ."

"Frustrated," Al finished for me. "Incensed at me, outraged at you, and perturbed at the world, yes, but we have all cared for elven children before. He thinks it's a step back. I say it's a step forward. Everything circles back unto itself. There are no straight lines in nature."

My attention lingered on David as he lifted a white pumpkin for Ray to inspect. It was easy to forget that the elves had once enslaved the demons as domestics. "When you were . . ."

"Yes." Al's expression was lost in thought. "Strange. It feels much the same. Perhaps it is because children are also much the same, whether now or thousands of years in the past." He looked askance at me. "Who is Hodin's student? I would like a word with him or her."

I scooted myself up on the table beside him. My worn shoes seemed rather plain beside his new derby boots, the leather gleaming and the stitching still white. "Yeah. About that . . . Walter had a spell-induced cardiac arrest. He triggered it to keep from talking."

"Mother pus bucket," he muttered, surprising me.

"Parker might know who the mage is," I offered. "If we're lucky, she won't have the same no-divulge curse on her." But I doubted it. The mage seemed too clever for that.

Out in the field, David had a large pumpkin in his arms. It was clearly Lucy's, as Ray was still going from pumpkin to pumpkin, Jenks dusting each one to help her decide. I suddenly regretted that I wasn't the one out there, but they'd lost their fear of David, and that was more important.

"You are being uncommonly stupid," Al said, his eyes lost behind his blue-tinted glasses as I fumbled for my phone, now humming from my pocket. "Give me the ring and be done with it. Trying to save four werefoxes paints an unneeded target on you. If the mage wants the ring back, it's because he can flip it. Or he thinks you can."

"I know," I said with a sigh. It was Trent. I didn't answer it, instead shooting off a quick text that we were at the pumpkin patch. If we were going to argue, we were going to do it properly in person, not through the phone.

Almost immediately a new text came in. He was in the parking lot.

Great. I exhaled, my attention rising to the girls half a field away. "If I can uncurse Cassie's employees, the coven might trust me a little concerning Brad's curse. It's worth the risk," I said, then slid off the table to join Lucy and Ray. They were fine where they were, but Trent would have kittens if he saw them with no one but Jenks and David beside them.

"Ray! Lucy!" Al pushed off to follow me, and the conversation from the nearest table went silent in alarm as we passed it. "Come here, my darlings. Bring your pumpkins for your aunt Rachel to carry. It's time for caramel apples!"

*Yay! Caramel-sticky everything!* But I smiled, dropping to a knee when Lucy careened into me, bright-eyed and excited for the chance to do something different. "Your daddies are on the way," I said as I stood with her on my hip, thinking it had been an awfully short round of golf. "Did you find a pumpkin?"

"Big, big, big!" Lucy said, and David came up alongside, a pumpkin large enough to need two arms in his grip. Ray still was undecided, and I let Lucy slip to the ground so I could take it.

"I've got it," I said as I took the pumpkin from him, and he exhaled in relief. "Ray, you have to choose by the time we get back to the tables, or you will be stuck with whatever Jonathan brings home from the store."

Brow furrowed, Ray looked about in frustration.

"I'll help you, Ray," Jenks said as he made circles around the little girl. "I can tell which one has the most seeds."

"The most seeds?" Al said importantly. "You want color and depth, not seeds. Only a demon can find the most perfect, most sincere pumpkin." He extended his hand, and Ray fit hers within its enormity. "I suggest we try over there," he added, and a wash of feeling took me.

"Me too!" Lucy shouted, hair flying as she jumped in circles.

I shifted the sun-warmed, heavy pumpkin to my hip, and David and I slowly followed the girls as they wove their circuitous way to the table.

"He wants to destroy the ring," David said, his chin lifting to indicate Al, and my shoulders shifted in a silent sigh. "He's right. The possibility of bringing back four lives is minuscule compared to the chaos that will ensue if Parker uses the ring to get the focus."

"Then we have to ensure she doesn't," I said firmly, and the tired man took a breath as if to protest. "David, Hodin had to have written the curse down. The mage wouldn't be trying to recover the ring unless he knew that the cure's invocation phrase or a way to flip the ring to curse mode was in Hodin's room."

But David wasn't listening, a confused wonder on him. "Al really cares for them, doesn't he."

Startled, I followed David's gaze to where Al was bent over a small pumpkin, turning it so Ray could see all sides. Jenks hovered over them, his dust a bright silver in the heat of the day. A fond softness filled me— until a stilted, fast pace drew my attention. It was Trent, striding over the dying vines as if he was treading over his vanquished foes. Quen was some distance back, clearly content to let Trent handle it—seeing as he was the one with the issue.

"He looks upset," David said, and my smile dribbled away.

"He doesn't trust me with them," I said, feeling panicked as I spoke the words aloud. "I had one shot to prove I could handle them—"

"And you did."

David's confidence wasn't catching, and I held that stupid pumpkin closer. "He won't see it like that," I whispered as Trent called out to the girls and they spun.

"Daddies!" Lucy shouted in delight, and both she and Ray ran to them, leaving Al and Jenks standing alone, both irate, and a sour green dust sifting from the pixy.

"Hello, my ladies!" Trent's musical voice rang out as he dropped to a knee to come up with them. Quen closed the gap, and after a mishmash of confusion and shrill demands, Quen ended up with a wildly chatting Lucy, and Ray remained with Trent.

"Did you have fun with Uncle Al?" Trent asked the solemn girl, and my pulse quickened, hearing a rebuke in his soft question.

"Aunt Rachel bit a wolf!" Lucy exclaimed. "But she was a wolf. You don't bite anyone unless you are both in fur. Use magic instead."

Trent blinked, his surprise quickly hidden. "I'm sorry you had to see that, Lucy," he said as they began walking to David and me, and with that, my temper snapped.

"I'm not," I said loudly, and David sort of ducked his head and rocked away. "Now they know I can keep them safe." *Do you?*

David lifted a hand in greeting, clearly uncomfortable. Al, though, was two hot comments from laughing at me. Jenks already was.

Trent frowned, clearly not wanting to argue in front of a dozen picnic tables full of people, and not with Ray on his hip. Me? I had no problem yelling in mixed company. I was a Midwest girl.

"Ah, hey," David offered hesitantly. "We were on our way to make caramel apples. Perhaps Quen, Jenks, and I should take the girls and get in line."

"Good idea." Al settled his dress shoes firmly in the dirt. "We'll catch you up."

"You too," I said shortly, huffing because of that pumpkin. "I mean it," I added, then smiled so the girls wouldn't think I was mad. But it was kind of obvious.

"She means it," Al grumped cheerfully as he held his arms out to Ray and the little girl went willingly to him. "Ray, did you know you can get sprinkles on your caramel apple?"

But Ray was having second thoughts, thumping her feet into Al to get him to stop.

"Daddy? Daddy!" the little girl demanded, and, grimacing, Al turned around.

Lips a thin line, Trent took Ray's hand, clearly distracted. "Yes. What is it?"

Ray had a surprisingly big vocabulary, even if she was content to let Lucy do most of the talking. Still, she didn't always use her words right, and my anger flared at Trent's impatience.

"Lucy and me supersecreted hide-and-seek," she said, the worry in her high voice obvious. "Aunt Rachel was brave. A Were bit Aunt Rachel, but we were supersecret hide-and-seek."

I blinked fast to keep my tears away, and I held that big pumpkin wishing I was holding her. It wasn't fair that she'd had to see that, but she had, and it was my fault.

Jenks's wings rasped as he sat on David's shoulder, and Trent's expression eased as he glanced between Ray and Lucy. "I don't want you to be scared, Ray. Ever."

Ray's brow furrowed as she tried to find the words, and then she pushed off from Al to get to me. Panicked, I dropped the pumpkin as I scrambled to catch her.

"My pumpkin!" Lucy shrieked. "Uncle Al, fix it?"

My arms found Ray with the surety of the sun rising, and the scent of snickerdoodles and cinnamon filled my world as her arms went around my neck and she clung to me. Lucy's pumpkin, though . . . The top had snapped off. Al was crouched before it, trying to console the little girl, but seeing him unable to do the magic, I got only more mad.

Glaring at Trent, I patted Ray's back as Lucy wailed. "Ray?" I said, trying to help her find the words. "You're not scared now, right?"

She blinked at me, her face holding a very real worry. Not about Weres or fighting but about Trent being mad at me. "No."

"Good." I set her feet on the earth as her sister wailed in Quen's arms, Jenks grinning at Lucy's heartache. "I don't want you to be scared. Go get your apple. I'll be right there."

Hesitant, Ray put her hand into Al's, and the demon harrumphed in satisfaction. Jenks darted down, and he led the way, blue and green sparkles falling from him.

"Wait until they can't hear us," I muttered to Trent as David, Quen, and Al beat a hasty retreat with Lucy still wailing about her broken pumpkin. Ray trusted me. So did Lucy.

Frustrated, I picked up the busted pumpkin. They had charms at the front to stick the tops back on. "I've got it," I snapped when Trent tried to take the pumpkin, and he retreated a step, his green eyes cross. I wasn't simply talking about the pumpkin, and he knew it.

"Please don't make this into something it isn't," he said, and my pulse quickened, my steps hitting the earth hard as we found the beaten pathway to the main building.

"Don't you dare try to gaslight me into thinking I didn't hear the anger in your voice when you called me earlier," I said, and his fingers twitched. "I know you're mad that I had the girls for one morning and managed to expose them to violence."

For a moment, Trent seemed as if he was going to pretend everything was normal. But it wasn't. "I said the mage might want the ring, flipped or not," he said, his eyes narrowed.

*And so it begins.* . . . "I agree that I made a mistake—"

"You can't make mistakes when it comes to them," he interrupted, and my jaw clenched.

"Trent. I made a mistake. And I took care of it. There is not a scratch on them," I protested, even as the guilt tightened around my heart.

"Not that you can see."

I took a breath, then let it out slowly. The girls were halfway to the apple hut, a demon, a pixy, and a Were as their awkward guards. A part of me agreed with Trent, but another part, the part that kept me going when the world seemed dead set on bringing me down, knew better, and I pulled my gaze from Lucy and Ray.

"They are not flowers," I said softly, and his attention flicked back to me. "They are elves, and they are girls, and they will someday be young women. If they never see anyone kicking ass to protect them, they will not have the guts to kick ass to protect themselves."

Hesitating, Trent took a breath and let it out. "You're right. I was angry."

But there was no flash of vindication at his admission, and my shoulders slumped. "I am so sorry," I said as we began to follow them, our pace slow. "This was not how I wanted my morning to go. I wanted . . ." My head drooped, and then I started as he touched my hand. Only then did I let him take the pumpkin.

"They are fine," he said, and I sighed. The weight of the pumpkin was gone, but that of my guilt lingered.

"That doesn't change that I had them for one morning and I exposed them to violence."

"Perhaps." Trent managed a smile. "But as you say, they saw you keeping them safe, and they obviously feel comfortable around David. It's possible that I might have overreacted."

"It's also possible letting me ever watch them again is a bad idea," I said.

Trent's gaze went sharp on mine. "I was never angry at you. I was scared for them, and it came out as anger."

And yet, I still felt as if he didn't trust me with them. Maybe I didn't trust myself.

"Rachel." Trent pulled me to a stop. "I'm not used to relying on anyone for their safety apart from Quen and Jonathan. They are just so damn vulnerable. You protected them in a very trying circumstance. That's all anyone can ask."

Finally the tightness in my chest eased, and my hand hesitantly found his. "I was so scared," I whispered, feeling my eyes well up, and Trent set the pumpkin down, pulling me into a hug right there in the middle of the field. "I'm glad I didn't have to do anything worse than knock out a Were, because, Trent, I would have."

"Welcome to my world," he whispered as he tucked a strand of hair behind my ear.

"I don't want them to be afraid of Weres," I said, never wanting to let him go.

"They aren't." Turning, he picked up the pumpkin and handed me the stem. "Is that why you asked David to come?"

"It was his idea." I was starting to feel better. "Ray called him the Wolf Sa'han."

"She's very perceptive."

"Hey, ah, just so you know, Parker was after the ring. I was a convenient bonus," I said, touching my pocket to tell him it was in there. "Either the mage knows how to flip it, or he thinks I do. It's probably the only thing that can slow David down." I bit my lip. There was always the option to just kill David and possess his bones, but as David had said, who would want to cart them around? David had to be alive to draw the focus from him, and I shuddered, glad I had been unconscious when Ceri had peeled the curse out of me.

"Um, I'm going to try to get into Hodin's room again tonight. That's probably where the spell book on the ring is." I hesitated. "You want to stick around after Lee leaves?"

He nodded, but his silence worried me. "Yes," he finally said, almost to himself. "I'd like to help you get into Hodin's room. I'd like that very much. Thank you."

Trent smiled as his hand found mine, and for a moment, the world felt right.

Except for the lingering worry that he wouldn't trust me with the girls ever again.

# CHAPTER
# 15

MY HEAD RESTED UP ON THE ARM OF THE INDOOR/OUTDOOR couch as I lay on my back with my knees bent and my toes tucked under Trent's leg. Rain was threatening, and a damp chill had taken the back porch. The book I'd bought this afternoon on auratic locks was not holding my attention. I fidgeted until Trent shifted his weight and hunched deeper over his knees, engrossed in the demon-cookie cookbook I'd given him for his birthday. The mix of cookies and magic was hitting him on all sorts of levels, and it made me feel good that I knew him so well.

"Lee is going to be late," I said, flipping pages back until I got to something I remembered reading. "I've got stuff to do." Stuff like find an Atlantean mirror to break Brad's curse and get the coven off my case, and figure out who was dumb enough to hitch their wagon to Hodin's world-domination train.

Trent frowned at a recipe. "He's a busy man, and busy men are seldom late." His lips quirked. "Usually."

Warning lifted through me. "You didn't tell him a different day, did you?"

Trent straightened, sighing as he cracked his spine. "Not this time."

I gave Trent a sidelong look, then shifted to sit properly beside him. I swear, the two men still acted as if they were at camp trying to get each other into trouble.

"Hey, Trent?" I said as I dropped the textbook on the table. "I know it's last minute, but I don't mind coming out with you and Lee to the festival tomorrow as extra security."

"Really? I didn't want to ask, seeing as how early it is." Trent leaned deeper into the couch, and I snuggled up against him, appreciating his warmth in the autumn chill rolling in over the wide steps. It had taken lunch at Eden Park followed by a book-buying spree downtown with the girls, but every hint of our argument was gone. "I know Quen wasn't looking forward to it. You sure you can handle eight?"

I nodded, but he had already lost himself, intent on a shortbread cookie that used lavender to carry a spell to give the person who ate it pleasant dreams. My thoughts on exotic coffee and tiny tasting cups, I focused on the dark garden. The faint silver light flitting about the damp graveyard was probably Getty. The bulb I'd given her had already sprouted tiny rootlets, galvanizing her into a new intensity as she ransacked the garden for anything remotely edible.

Between the pixies in the garden and Bis on the steeple, I was not worried about Parker—at the moment. She'd taken a beating this morning, and most bullies needed at least a day to convince themselves that it had been a fluke and to come at you again. I wasn't happy that she'd attacked me at all. My belief that the girls would be safe with me had unraveled like an exploded baseball.

Uneasy, I took the ring out of my pocket, cradling it in my fingertips to stare through the hole at the empty fireplace. "Is this a mistake?"

"Is what a mistake?" Trent asked as he flipped a page.

"Asking for Lee's help with a ward?"

Immediately Trent broke from his book. "No. Of course not." His expressive eyes pinched. "You aren't still worried about having tricked him into being Al's familiar, are you? He was trying to sell you to Al. And you did free Lee. Eventually."

"I'm not worried about that as much as our three years at camp," I said as I shoved the ring into my pocket. "Three years that I think he remembers more than both of us combined."

"Oh." But his wicked, fond smile faded as he flexed his right hand in a remembered hurt.

I put my arches on the edge of the coffee table, jerking when it slid two inches. "Sometimes I wonder if you two hung out together not because you were friends, but because Lee knew you and he were the only paying customers. Everyone else was a charity case."

Trent snapped the book closed. "You weren't a charity case."

"You're right. My dad paid for my treatment with his life," I said, unable to look at him.

"Rachel . . ."

I shrugged, my gaze fixed on the dark garden. My dad and Trent's dad had been friends, but it had been an unequal situation. I'd long suspected that Trent's dad hadn't saved my and Lee's lives for anything less than the hope that one of us might be able to infiltrate the demons' genetic vault and steal a pre-curse sample of elven DNA. Which I had, leading to the genetic health of the elven race and saving them from extinction. That I had also saved the demons probably had Trent Senior rolling in his grave.

Both Lee and I were witch-born demons, but only I could pass the corrected genes on to any possible children. I refused to believe that little item had been an accident. Elves did nothing without purpose.

"Trent?" I played with a curl of my hair, hoping I wasn't opening a can of worms. "Do you think that your dad intentionally put the cure to the Rosewood syndrome into the mitochondria so that Lee couldn't pass the cure on? So that if he had any kids, they might need your help to survive, and thereby ensure that the Saladans maintain good relations with you?"

Trent's reach for the open bag of beet chips hesitated. "My God. I never thought of it that way. That might explain a lot."

"Yeah. That would put sand in my Cheez Whiz, too," I whispered.

"No." Trent turned to face me. "I wasn't going to mention it unless he brought it up in front of you, but I found out yesterday that his wife left him after their baby girl died."

"Oh no." My shoulders slumped as I took Trent's hands. "I didn't know."

He rolled the bag closed, a fistful of chips in hand. "It was Rosewood."

"Why didn't he . . ." My brow furrowed. "Why didn't you—"

"I did." Trent grimaced. "I told him treatment was available even before I knew his wife was pregnant. I asked if he wanted her screened, which he didn't. I was unaware that the child had it until she died. The only reason I can fathom why he ignored the possibility was that he would rather mourn his child than be beholden to me for saving her life."

"Oh." The small word slipped from me, unbottling my childhood pain at the hands of Trent Kalamack Sr. Still, it had been worth it, obviously.

"Perhaps he regrets his decision," Trent said. "I've often wondered if half of Lee's issues stem from the belief that his father regretted becoming indebted to my father for saving his life."

"A father would never regret that," I whispered. "I had no idea. He must be devastated."

"Clearly." Trent pulled me closer. "I'm thinking it might be better if you don't bring it up unless he does. He didn't tell me not to say anything, but . . ."

"Yeah, I got it." My brow furrowed in sympathy, and then I stiffened as someone's phone hummed. "It's me," I said as I reached for it. "I bet he's not coming," I added as I glanced at the screen, my eyebrows rising when I saw who it was. Vivian.

"Um, I should probably take this." I stood, missing Trent's warmth already. "I hung up on her yesterday."

Trent wasted no time reaching for his new book as I went into the nearby kitchen. "Hey. Hi, Vivian," I said when I hit connect. "Sorry about the goat thing yesterday. We're still on for tomorrow, right?"

"Rachel," she said, and I winced at the wary tone in her voice as I eased the door between Trent and me closed. "Were you by chance at the hospital this morning?"

The kitchen was silent and dim, and I grabbed a cookie from the nearby plate. "Ah, yeah." I bit down, my mouth coming alive with the taste of chocolate and almonds. *Damn, Trent doesn't need a demon-cookie book. These are magical all on their own.* "I was helping Detective Glenn interview Walter Vincent. I had no idea he had a no-divulge curse on him. I was trying to get the invocation for the chakra curse cure." *That, and find out who the mage is.*

Vivian sighed, and I could almost see her petite features bunching up. "Were you in the room when Walter Vincent went into cardiac arrest?"

*Ah, crap on toast.* Hand to my forehead, I leaned against the counter. Maybe I shouldn't have busted the camera. This looked bad, and if she was asking, she probably already knew the answer. "Um, yes, but he triggered the curse himself."

"He passed this afternoon," she said, and I slumped.

"Glenn was supposed to call," I said, arm wrapped around my middle.

"He is under a gag order," Vivian said. "The only reason I'm allowed to tell you is because . . . Actually, I'm not. But I'm calling because the tests have come in and the curse that took Walter down requires demon blood. That's why they couldn't break it."

"That doesn't mean it was me," I said, pulse quickening. "I'm not the only source of it. Walter is working with Hodin's student. Walter could have been under that no-divulge curse before he even *got* to Cincinnati."

"Yes," she interrupted. "We're investigating that, but until then, I'm asking you to not leave Cincinnati. You are more than a person of interest and half a step from being charged."

*Charged?* "Hey, I did not curse Walter," I said, but even I had to agree that I had the motive and the means. Sure, Glenn had been standing right there, but FIB or not, he was also human. His testimony would be dismissed because unless they had a degree they couldn't use, humans generally didn't know a spell from a dance step.

"Vivian . . ." I slumped against the counter. My chest hurt. "You know I didn't do this. I wanted answers, not his death. I've never killed anyone in my life." Well, I had, but Peter had wanted to die, begged for it, and afterward, he thanked me.

"What I know doesn't mean anything. I have to prove it," she said.

"You're still coming over tomorrow, right?" My voice sounded hollow, as if coming from somewhere else.

"Yes."

And after that, I'd be in Alcatraz. That cookie had gone tasteless, and I threw it away.

"I know you are a good person, but I also know how easy it is to be misled. Unfortunately I'm not the only one here who needs convincing. I'll be bringing another coven member with me. I'm giving you this chance, so don't squander it. We need to see everything. Everything, Rachel. You have to come clean if you want any hope of beating this."

Clean. That was funny, when what she wanted to see was a dark curse. "I understand," I said, my gaze going to the French doors as Trent quietly opened them, his brow furrowed in concern. "I'll be here with the curse that Brad Welroe is under."

"Thank you, Rachel. I'll see you then," she said, and then the connection ended.

Trent's sigh went to my core, and my stomach knotted. "I'm sorry you're dealing with this. She is on your side," he said as he gave me a hug. "She knows you're a good person."

"The rest of them don't," I whispered, my face buried against his shoulder. "She's bringing a plus-one. Can you be here? Two o'clock?"

"Absolutely," he said as his hand traced the outline of my hair. The compassion and love in his eyes hit me hard. "Quen can act as security at the festival if you want more prep time."

"No. I want to go." My arms tightened around his neck, and I gave him a lingering kiss. "I don't entirely trust you and Lee together," I whispered into his ear, and he chuckled. "He's very good at leading you to the top of a bad path, then leaving you to walk it alone."

"He is, isn't he." Trent's voice was a soothing rumble, and I let go.

"If I should cancel on anyone, it should be Lee." I glanced at the clock over the sink. "I have to find something that says I didn't spell Walter into a cardiac arrest. Something that links Walter to Hodin or the mage," I said, my eyes going to Jenks as he flew in from the porch.

"What about that ring?" Jenks said, his arms full of damp brown maple seeds. "Al said Hodin made it. They can match its aura resonance to the curse that took Walter out. Hey, Trent? Be a pal. Open the trash for me? Getty is trying to store these things, and they aren't any good."

"He's right," Trent said as he opened the lower cupboard and Jenks darted inside.

"About the maple seeds?" I said, and he grinned.

"No, about linking the ring to the mage and Walter."

"I'd have to give it to them," I said, unsure. "Parker or the mage might try to take it."

"Which makes it an even better idea." Trent made a little hitch with his shoulder, his smile mischievous. "Let Parker harass Vivian, not you. I'd be willing to bet one of my best yearlings that if Parker tries to take the ring from Vivian that the coven's focus will shift dramatically."

Jenks came out from under the counter and landed atop the faucet. "Sounds easier than trying to get past a demon's ward," he said as he brushed his gardening jacket clean.

"Mmmm." The memory of being thrown into the wall, smoke coming from my nose as I tried to dump a crapload of line energy, wasn't that old. And I hadn't even touched the door. Sighing, I checked my phone for the time. *Too late to cancel on Lee.* But then I paused, and Jenks's wing hum got louder as he saw my expression blank.

"She got an idea," the pixy warned, and I spun to Trent, excited.

"The lock on Hodin's door is a ward, right? Maybe Lee can break it."

"Whoa, hold up," Trent said, and I felt a quickening of hope. "Yes, Lee is an expert, but it's demon twisted."

"He can at least look at it," I said.

"Mmmm." Trent took one of his cookies and chewed in thought. "I wouldn't mind seeing him try and fail. I wouldn't mind that at all."

"So we convince him," I said, and Jenks abruptly darted out into the hallway, his dust a bright silver. "It's not as if we don't know what buttons to push."

"True," Trent said, a rueful smile gracing him.

"He's here," the pixy shouted from the sanctuary, and my adrenaline jumped. It was a sign, damn it, and as Trent crammed his half-eaten cookie into his mouth, I paced to the front door, my steps unheard under a faint pounding.

"Lee!" I exclaimed as I yanked the door open and the hush of rain washed over me. Light glinting on the wet street spilled into the dark foyer, and Jenks swore, quickly retreating to the warmer rafters. The thought of Lee's daughter lifted through me, and I pushed it aside. "Thanks so much for coming over. I know you're busy."

Lee was little more than a silhouette, but I drew him in, the scent of damp redwood almost a physical assault. He'd been spelling lately. A lot. A car waited at the curb, wipers on and still running as his driver/security watched me. "Your guy can come in," I added.

Lee half turned to the curb and gave the man a curt hand gesture. "No, I'm good." He smiled, his dark eyes taking in what he could see of the sanctuary. "Hey, Kallie," he added as Trent's presence eased up behind me. "I didn't know you'd be here."

"You think I'd leave you alone with Rachel?" His pleasure obvious, Trent pulled Lee deeper into the sanctuary. "Right on time," he added, and then to me, "Told you."

"Yeah, whatever," I muttered as Lee stood in the sanctuary and spun a slow circle.

"Wow," he said as he unwound his black scarf and unbuttoned his coat spotted with rain. "This is nice. Back porch, right?"

My pulse quickened. "Yes, but I have a favor to ask."

Lee ran a hand over his damp hair, slicking it back as he glanced from Trent to me. "What?"

"Rachel, don't ask. It's too dangerous," Trent said, immediately piquing Lee's interest.

"He can say no." I touched Lee's elbow, feeling somewhat breathless. "Um, I have a door I can't open. A demon put a ward on it. And you're so good with them . . ."

From the rafters, Jenks snickered. "It blew her into the wall when she tried to touch it."

"Hey, Jenks." Lee craned his neck. "I didn't see you up there. Damn, that must have been misery. Sure, I'll take a look."

"Great! Thanks!" I said, overly cheerful as I looped my arm in his. A dart of energy tried to jump between us to equalize our internal balances, and I shoved my personal chi down. "It's the one on the left," I said as we passed the bathrooms.

"I'm sure Hodin emptied his room," Trent said from behind us, and Lee jerked to a halt.

"Hodin? Isn't that the demon who . . . You want me to . . . ah . . ."

"See, I told you he couldn't do it," Trent said.

Lee's eye twitched. It was the one with the tiny scar, and I fought to keep from smirking. "I never said I couldn't do it," Lee countered, wary as he stopped before the door.

I took a long step to put Jenks and me on one side, Trent and Lee on the other. "Well?"

Lee's thin lips pressed together, his dark eyes squinting as he raised his hand. Mien distant, he felt the ether. His hand was a good eight inches from the battered, scratched, hollow-core door, and I still felt a slight rise in the ambient power responding to him.

Jenks's wings rasped as he hovered over my shoulder. "Constance goes in and out all the time. I'd say it was her size, but I can't even get close without it trying to fry my dust."

"Constance?" Lee backed up. "Then it's true? You really . . ." Words faltering, he looked at Trent.

"Turned her into a mouse," Trent said, clearly proud of me. I wasn't surprised Lee knew. Everyone did.

"Damn," Lee whispered as he reached for the door, only to let his hand fall. "If an undead doesn't trigger it, it's probably aura based. Complex."

"That's what I thought," I said, pressing close. "I tried pushing my aura off my hand, but that didn't work."

"Just forget it," Trent said. "You came over to help put in a ward, not take one down."

"He won't do anything dangerous," I said to egg Lee on, and the man predictably frowned. Lee had gotten me into so much trouble at camp, but I'd given as good as I got, and seeing Lee fail here would make my day.

As if knowing it, Lee's focus broke and he jerked his hand from the door as if stung.

"Okay. We're done," Trent said as Lee shook his hand as if to get rid of tingles.

"I can at least show it to you," Lee muttered. "I need a dandelion gone to seed or a flower with lots of pollen. And salt water."

"The late dandelions are closed for the night," Jenks said. "How about pixy dust?"

Lee's thin eyebrows rose. "The spell needs to adhere to something light and dispersible, so yes, that should work. Sure."

"How much salt water?" I asked as I walked backward toward the kitchen. "Standard concentration? Does it need to be in anything special? Walnut bowl or copper?"

A wide smile blossomed on Lee's usually placid face. "Damn, I love working with professionals. Do you have anything clear? It doesn't need to be big. Hold about a cup."

I paused, half in the kitchen. "I've got a translucent marble crucible or a Srandford bowl."

"You have a Srandford?" Lee said, and I nodded, feeling sassy as I went into the kitchen.

"Yes, I have a Srandford," I mused aloud as I found it at the back of a cupboard. It was only the third time I'd needed to use the usually expensive, meticulously crafted bowl. I had bought it last year at a yard sale for a quarter, but I was sure that's what it was; no one would dare make a knock-off, and the double-ax and raven stamp on the bottom was distinctive.

My bag had a couple of vials of salt water, and I grabbed them before I returned to the hall to find Trent and Lee still standing before the door, their conversation becoming suspiciously silent as my silhouette eclipsed the light from the kitchen. "You need a counter?" I prompted, and Lee shook his head, rolling his shoulders as if preparing to do the spell right there.

"Trent can hold the bowl," Lee said as I came forward. "It doesn't get that hot. Wow, I haven't seen a Srandford since college," he added as he took it, flipping it over to see the raven and double-ax emblem and the date of manufacture. "Nineteen sixty-five? That's pre-Turn."

"Yup." Smirking, I popped the tops of the two vials and poured them in.

Lee hesitated until Trent cleared his throat, goading him. "Ah, usually the dandelion is dunked in the salt water, so, Jenks, would you?" He held out the bowl, and Jenks flew closer.

"Standard dust okay?" the pixy asked, and when Lee shrugged, Jenks sneezed, sifting a veritable haze of silver sparkles into the bowl. For an instant it sheened atop the water, and then it broke the viscous layer, pooling at the bottom to look like trapped air.

"Cool," I said, and Lee grinned, clearly pleased when Trent inched closer.

"The dust has been cleansed," Lee said, and Jenks glowered, wings rasping as he darted away muttering about Tink and daisies.

"I didn't know you could cleanse pixy dust," I said, and then I stifled a shudder as I felt Lee reach a thought to my ley line and pull in the energy until my aura prickled.

"*Adsimulo calefacio,*" Lee said, and I jumped at the massive draw on the line, my eyes going to Trent's as the water in the Srandford bowl began to steam, the rising mist carrying the pixy dust with it. It was a singularly beautiful sight, but what bothered me was that that was a demon's curse, and my breath caught in suspicion.

"Where did you learn that?" I accused, and then warmed when Lee glared at me. "Never mind." My gaze dropped. Yeah. I had convinced Al to take Lee as a familiar instead of me, and the demon had used him, teaching him a few things in the process. Who was I to talk? "Sorry," I added, and Lee seemed to settle himself in an affronted huff.

"*Obscurum per obscurius,*" Lee intoned, and the sparkling mist rising from the bowl took on a haze of purple-tinted ley line energy, colored by his aura. Exhaling, Lee blew it at the door.

"That is amazing," Trent said as the haze condensed upon hitting the ward, spreading out into first one, then a slightly deeper second band, and finally a third hovering a breath above the door. It wasn't one ward, but three, each one delineated by a slightly thicker band of pixy dust.

"Huh." Trent's pale eyebrows were high. "He made a tri-ward. Three interwoven layers."

"Yep." Lee took the bowl from Trent and set it at the door's threshold, where it continued to steam, replacing the pixy glow as it faded. "I'm going to guess the first is to detect, the second to respond, and that final one is to excite or amplify the middle layer until it's lethal. You probably only triggered the outer two or you wouldn't have survived."

"Sure," I said breathily, reminded how dangerous a mistake could be.

"Can you break it?" Jenks asked. "I can't rent out a room no one can get into."

"Maybe." Careful to keep clear of the wards, Lee took off his coat and handed it to me. The thing weighed a ton, making me think he must have added a spell-resistant liner. It smelled like wool, and I brought it to my nose, breathing deeply.

"I'll hold it," Trent muttered as he took it from me, and Lee smirked.

"Wards are simply two-dimensional circles," Lee said as he studied the door with its three hazed bands. "Designed to let some things through and block others. If your vampiric mouse, who lacks a natural aura, is passing with impunity, then the first ward is probably keyed to blocking everything but the owner's aura. You're not getting through this."

Trent's breath slipped from him in a silent sigh. I, though, wasn't so pleased. "Well, crap on my toast and call it breakfast," I said as Jenks's wings rasped for attention.

"What about Bis?" Jenks said, and Lee's expression went empty. "He knows Hodin's aura. He can coach you on shifting your aura to Hodin's. That's what you do to go in and out of a ley line, isn't it?"

"Hot damn!" I said, eager again. "He's right. What do you think, Lee? An aura is a lot less complex than a ley line, and Bis can do that standing on his head. If the trigger is aura based, there has to be some built-in flexibility. Everyone's aura changes from day to day, year to year. It would have to be attuned to, say, the first two or three outer shells only."

"I thought gargoyles could only teach the people they bonded to," Lee said, confused.

"To line jump, sure. This is way less complex." I took a deep breath, then shouted, "Bis!"

"Here he comes," Jenks said, making a dive for my shoulder.

"Mmmm, Rachel?" Trent inched past Lee. "Have you considered the possible outcomes here? That ward is potentially lethal."

Trent's brow was furrowed in worry, but I barely had time to give his hand a squeeze of confidence before the light from the sanctuary was eclipsed and Bis barreled into the hall, his leathery wings brushing the walls in a soft, eerie hush.

"Sweet mother of God," Lee swore softly, ducking as the small, cat-size gargoyle neatly back winged to land on my shoulder, his long, lionlike tail curving across my shoulders and under my arm for balance. "You got big."

"Hi, Mr. Saladan," the kid said, red eyes sparkling in fun as Lee rose from his crouch.

"I thought you lost the ability—" Lee started, desisting when Trent cleared his throat.

"Bis, you remember Lee," I said, reaching to touch Bis's toes clamped upon my shoulder when the sensitive kid drooped his ears. That Bis and I had lost our connection hurt both of us, but Bis took it personally, and I didn't like that Lee had brought it up. "We went to camp together. Trent and I left him in a well once for three days because he's a rich, entitled—"

Lee's eyebrows rose. "You want help with this or not?"

"West Coast drug lord," I finished as Trent hid a chuckle behind a cough. "There's a chance we can get past the ward if I can change my outer aura shells to match Hodin's."

"Whoa, whoa, whoa." Trent bumped my shoulder as he pushed forward. "I'm doing it."

"Ah, it's my door," I began to protest, and Trent took my elbow.

That fast, Bis, Jenks, Lee, and I were all looking at his hand on me.

"Can you excuse us for a moment?" Trent said, fake smile in place as he dragged all three of us toward the kitchen—seeing as Bis was on one shoulder and Jenks the other.

Jenks snickered. "Guys, technically, it's my door."

I yanked myself from Trent's grip, surprised he was doing this, but he'd been really worried when I'd nearly knocked myself out. "Can you change your aura?" I asked, then waved my hand. "I mean, more than you need to jump in and out of a ley line? How about spindling an overload of line energy in your head? You any good at that?"

Trent winced and glanced down the hall at Lee. I didn't care that he was listening. The refresher on what I could do might help. "Bis is more attuned to me than you," I said. "I know what to expect, and Bis can help if I make a mistake. Right, Bis?"

"Right," Bis said from my shoulder, and my lips parted when his gravelly voice cracked.

"Holy mother pus bucket!" Jenks exclaimed, rising up. "Bis, did your voice break?"

"Not another word, Jenks," I said as Bis's tail tightened. The kid was suddenly throwing off heat like a furnace. Fifty years old, and he was only now beginning to hit adolescence. "Trent, this is our best chance of getting in there, and you know it."

Moody, Trent glanced down the hall to Lee. "If you kill yourself, it's not my fault."

"We doing this?" Lee said loudly, and I nodded, arms swinging as I returned to the door.

Bis hadn't left my shoulder, and I flicked my earring until Jenks moved to Trent. "I'm not going to kill myself, Bis," I said, and the little guy sighed.

"Not with me around, anyway," he grumbled. "Do you remember Hodin's aura?"

I licked my lips, nervous. What had I been thinking? If I screwed this up, Lee would never let me live it down. "Yellow green," I said, shifting my outer shell from gold to green.

"Too much red," Bis suggested, and I toned it down. "More yellow," he added, and my pulse quickened. We had lots of practice shifting my aura, but most times it ended with me getting singed. That was the last thing I needed right now, but if we got into Hodin's room, it would be worth it.

"Better?" I asked, and his tail tightened.

"Little more brown, and put some gold at your hands."

Lee stood there and watched, a little envious maybe, as I did something he couldn't. You needed a gargoyle. That's why the demons created them.

"Careful," Trent whispered as I reached out, hesitating at a warning thrum as I found the first ward.

"You good, Rache?" Jenks asked.

"So far," I said, nervous. The first ward prickled through me like an ice cream headache, and as I inched forward, the second ward seemed to gather, sending darts of promise into me.

"More purple," Bis said, and with a soft exhale, I sent a tinge of pride through me, exhaling in relief when I felt the ward drop, dissolving into the third.

"We're in," I said, the cool feel of the knob almost a shock as I gave it a twist and pushed open the door.

# CHAPTER
# 16

"DAMN, THAT ACTUALLY WORKED!" LEE LURCHED FORWARD TO BE the first into the room.

Liquidly fast, Trent gave him a quick shove to keep him in the hall. "I'll be right there, Rachel," Trent said as he stood before Lee. "Jenks, go with her."

"I won't let her spell herself dead, Cookie Man." Laughing, Jenks made a circle around the both of them before darting into Ivy's old room.

"Right," I said, uneasy as both men stared at each other. They were too powerful now for these stupid games. Someone was going to end up in emergency.

I flicked the switch, but the light didn't turn on, and my nose wrinkled at the faint scent of burnt amber. Whirls of pixy-lit dust rose where Jenks hovered, and Bis's grip on my shoulder tightened. I could smell the rain even though the window was closed.

"We are not kids anymore," Trent was saying from the hallway. "Don't ever endanger her like that again. Understand?"

"Knock it off, Kallie." Lee hit the hated nickname hard. "Your *girlfriend* had it covered."

"The more things change, the more they stay the same," I muttered as the two of them faced off. I'd overheard a similar conversation at camp over a sensory burn and busted fence, but I think Trent had been worried about Jasmine, not me. At least, I think her name was Jasmine. *Stupid memory blockers . . .*

"Hey, Rache. How about some light?" Jenks asked, and I sent a ribbon of awareness out to the ley line in the garden, pulling the living sunshine deep into me. My sock-footed feet tingled, flat on Hodin's glyph-entrenched floor. *He's not getting his security deposit back.*

*"Lenio cinis,"* I whispered, gesturing toward the cluttered workbench set in the middle of the room, and a globe of light blossomed atop it. Unlike most charms, this one required me to maintain a hold on the ley line, and I shifted my shoulders, feeling the energy coming in to settle into well-used channels where I could let it flow for hours without strain. Bis's eyes slitted, his grip on my shoulder easing as the line ran through us both.

"Always said a demon was more handy than a jar of Vaseline." Jenks's wings thrummed as he darted from one corner of the room to the other. Hodin had covered the walls and ceiling with a metallic silver. Three interlacing circles took up much of the floor, one incorporating the neatly made bed, another the freestanding workbench, and a third around the illegal open-fire hearth under the window. There was no hood to funnel out the fumes, definitely not to code.

"Nice lair," I said as I went to the cluttered workbench. A circular, blemish-free mirror was propped against the wall, the nearby oil pencil telling me he used it like a dry-erase board. "Hey, that's mine!" I exclaimed as I found a sock wadded up beside a used pentagram, and Bis's tail tightened about me. I'd thought I'd lost that sock.

"Don't touch anything." Trent pushed into the room, Lee fast behind him.

He was right, and I drew my hand away, frowning at the book open to a doppelganger curse beside it. It wasn't one of the nice ones you could buy for Halloween. This one was as illegal and dangerous as a left turn onto the expressway. *Son of a troll turd. So that's where the socks in the dryer go. Off to a demon's doppelganger curse.*

Lee took my globe of light and raised it to the ceiling. "Hold this, will you, Trent?" He shoved the light at him. "I want a picture of these glyphs. I've never seen anything like them."

"It's as if he lined his walls with tinfoil," Trent whispered, his unease obvious.

"*Abundans cautela non nocet,*" I said as Lee craned his neck, phone clicking. Bis rumbled at the surge of line energy through us as a lethal-magic detection spell hazed the workbench and then dissolved to nothing. The area was clean, and when Bis hopped from my shoulder to the table, I stuffed my sock into a pocket and flipped the spell book closed before Lee could see it.

A handwritten theme book was under it. If Hodin had written down any experimental spells, that might be where they were, and I took it in hand, curious.

"Thank you, Rachel," Trent said, and Lee huffed in annoyance when Trent dropped to his knees and angled the light under the cot. "That is a handy charm."

"If you trust it," Lee said sourly. "Any glyphs under there?" he added as Bis wrestled a leather-bound book open. It was almost as big as he was.

"Yes, and I always trust Rachel's charms."

"Mee, mee, *mee*, mee, mee," Lee mocked, phone at the ready when Trent set my light on the desk and pulled the bed aside to show another, smaller pentagram under it.

"Guys?" I flipped through the theme book as Lee's phone clicked. The handwritten notes were all about Stef, and I set it aside to give to her later. "Can we focus? I'm looking for a really old spell book or anything that will link the chakra curse to the mage."

Lee looked up from helping Trent shift the bed back into place. "Who's the mage?"

Jenks came out from under the cot, hands slapping the cobwebs from his jacket. "That's what we're trying to figure out, dust for brains."

"Hodin's former student." Trent teased a palm-size book out from under Hodin's pillow. It was old, leather-bound, and falling apart—and my interest grew. "We think he's working with the incoming alpha pack to try to take control of Cincy's Weres," he added.

*Or was,* I thought, appreciating Trent's tact. I wasn't supposed to know Walter was dead. Trent, either, but like I wasn't going to tell him?

Bis immediately dropped his large book, shocking Trent from his study when his wings opened and he half flew, half jumped to the elf's shoulder. The kid gave him a wing-rising shrug, then leaned to study the tattered book Trent had splayed open in his hands. My eyebrows rose. The pages were glowing.

"Rachel? Take a look at this," Trent said, his head down as he came closer. "I'm pretty sure it's the last curse Hodin did before you put him in a tulpa. The pentagram on the hearth is the one pictured here."

"You can't put people in a tulpa," Lee said.

Bis smiled, his black teeth catching the chancy light. "Rachel can."

My shoulder bumped Trent's, and with Bis's head between us, I studied the unfamiliar script. "I don't recognize that language," I said, my fingers covering Trent's to turn the book over to see the cover and spine. There was no title, which would, by logic, make it demon. But as the faint warning tingle in my hand began to hint at stabs of pain, I wasn't sure. My almost hold on the book was kindling an as-yet-uninvoked spell, and I pulled away as the glow shifted to red. The book didn't like me.

*But it likes Trent,* I mused as the pages resumed a welcoming, pure white. "Is it elven?"

"Ancient elven," Trent said, and Lee quit taking pictures and came to look. "It's hard to read, but I'm thinking . . ." Trent carefully shifted a tattered page, his focus going from a pentagram to the one on the floor. "Well, it's the right book," he said, now focused on a line of text. "This is the invocation phrase you gave the hospital. Al was right." Guilt pinched his brow. "The chakra curse is elven. I didn't want to believe him."

*As if the book glowing at his touch isn't enough of a clue?* "Does it have the cure phrase?" Impatient, I reached for the book, yelping when a dart of mystic-powered energy shot through me. My globe of light on the bench went out with a pop. Bis chuckled in the sudden darkness, the gravelly, low rumble sending a shiver through me.

"Way to hold the line, Carrots," Lee muttered . . . and then three globes of light burst into existence: mine, Trent's, and Lee's.

"You need to grow up," Trent said, and Bis's white-tufted ears went flat in annoyance.

Flustered, I let my new light go out. "Turn to the end of the curse," I said, ignoring Lee. If I could wake Cassie's people, Vivian might cut me some slack.

Trent eased the old page over, and I held my breath as I studied the hand-drawn pictures of a complicated-looking lens and a Möbius strip. I couldn't tell if it was a continuation of the curse or we had moved on to the cure, and Bis leaned precariously lower to study them.

Again I reached for the book, drawing away when it shot a warning zap of blue-tinted sparkles at me. "Is that the cure?" I asked, my fisted hand behind my back.

"Give me a minute." Trent's brow furrowed as he struggled through the unfamiliar text.

The book clearly did not like me this close. Then again, it might be responding to Lee, seeing as he was tight to Trent's other shoulder, hand reaching. "Lee, perhaps—" Trent started, and then Lee yelped when a bolt of mystic-blue energy darted from the book and struck him.

Lee's light went out with a pop to leave only Trent's. Jenks darted up, clearly startled. Bis, though, steadfastly held position on Trent's shoulder, his red eyes hard as he glared at Lee. The man had backed up and was rubbing his fingers against his thumb, clearly smarting.

"Hey, I found the lens," Jenks said, his dust glowing as he kicked at an elaborately cut chunk of glass the size of a walnut sitting upon the workbench.

"Ah, I wouldn't knock that around if I were only four inches tall." Looking odd with Bis on his shoulder, Trent shifted the book in his hand and tapped the illustration. "It focuses mystics into a dangerously high concentration within the engraved Möbius strip." He licked his lips, a little pale.

"That's how it works. It shoots out a blast of mystics to stop the chakras' spin."

"Except the heart chakra," I said. "No wonder their auras are that greenish yellow."

Trent nodded. The light of discovery in his gaze was heady even if he seemed a little ill, and I felt a pang of love for him. "I've never seen anything like this," he added, and Lee cautiously leaned in, sullen and bad-tempered that Trent could hold the book with impunity and he couldn't. "Look." Trent jiggled the book so we all could see. "The lens focuses the mystics, and the pentagram traps them in the engraved Möbius strip before remolding it into a ring." His brow furrowed. "It remains connected to the ley line even after the curse has been twisted. Odd."

*Hence the person doing it dying of mystic overload.*

Trent didn't notice Lee reach for the book, only to draw away in a frustrated anger—but I did. "If I'm understanding this correctly," Trent mused, "when invoked, the concentrated mystics burst out, jolting the intended chakras into a state of immobility. If chakras don't spin, they don't allow a smooth energy flow."

"And the victim passes out," I whispered.

"To die a slow death." Lee took a picture of the page. "That sounds elven to me."

"And the cure?" I hid my hand behind my back as the book redoubled its glow.

"Hang on a second," Trent said, and I dropped to my heels. Jenks was grinning at me, and it was all I could do not to flick his wing. "Rachel, you know Hodin's handwriting. Are they his notes in the margin?"

"Yep," I said, frustrated when Trent flipped the pages back and forth, but never to the page I wanted.

"That lens looks old," Bis said. "There can't be many people who can make it."

"Like zero," Lee said as he moved to the workbench. "Where do you think Hodin got it? It's almost like a reverse Fresnel lens."

Trent's head rose at Jenks's warning wing rasp. "Put it down, Lee,"

Jenks said, and then I was scrambling, juggling the tiny book when Trent dropped it into my hands to confront Lee.

Bis was suddenly in the air, and I yelped, freezing in indecision. I didn't want to drop something that old and falling apart, but I didn't want to be burned, either. I held my breath—only to realize that I wasn't writhing in pain. The spell protecting the book hadn't engaged. Wondering, I glanced at Bis as he alighted on my shoulder.

"It likes you now," Bis said as he peered down at it splayed open in my hand.

*Maybe because Trent gave it to me?*

"If that belongs to anyone, it belongs to Rachel. Put it down," Trent said, and I turned to see him facing a belligerent Lee, Jenks hovering over Trent's shoulder like an avenging angel.

Lee peered through the lens, goading him. "Why? You going to twist the curse?"

"Don't be stupid. All we need to know is how to break it. Anything else is a really bad idea." Smug, I turned to the last page, looking for the cure. If the invocation for the curse was in Latin, maybe the countercurse would be, too. "Lee, put the lens down before you break it."

"I'm not going to break it." Lee set the lens down with a small click. "Sorry, Trent, I know you're dying to try it, but this is out of your league, ancient elven or not."

"Will you grow up?" I said, glad we hadn't told Lee we had a curse ring already.

"It's a lens and a strip of metal." Lee gestured at the workbench. "What's the problem? Scared of a little smut?"

Sure enough, Trent's ears reddened. I jiggled the open book, uncomfortable with the darts of sensation prickling my fingers. A memory flashed through me of them getting me into trouble at camp. Or Lee, rather, because Trent would do anything that Lee dared him. Course, Lee would do anything Trent dared him to do, so they were both kind of stupid.

Lee took another picture of the pentagram on the hearth. "You don't have to *use* the ring," he said. "Just make it. I've never seen a spell that uses a Möbius strip."

I went to shut the book, but Bis flicked his tail into the pages, stopping me. "Not happening," I said. My voice was calm, but I felt sick as I imagined a stream of mystics too powerful for a demon to handle, much less a witch or elf. No need to tell Lee that twisting the curse requires the death of the spell caster. My reputation was bad enough already.

"Mmmm." Bis's focus darted over the page. "Severing the connection to the ley lines is what turns the ring from curse to cure. Reconnecting to the line again flips it back to curse. You need the lens to do it, not just the invocation phrase."

*Which probably means flipping the ring from curse to cure will likely kill the person doing it as well,* I thought, knowing I was right when Bis nodded at my sick look.

"You can read ancient elven?" Trent asked, clearly surprised, and Bis blushed a deep red.

"A little," Bis said, then frowned at Jenks when he dropped down onto the page, where his dust set Hodin's notes to glow.

"Hodin's notes say he was grooming someone with the initial *S* to make a ring," Bis said, his pebbly brow pinched as he studied the book in my hand. "Stephanie? It's a good thing you put him away."

"The Turn take him," I whispered as I recalled the theme book full of notes regarding her. Having put Hodin into a tulpa suddenly seemed way too good for him.

Jenks's dust went a thin yellow. "I bet Glenn could find out if there have been any missing high-magic users in the last six months," he said, and my gaze went to the pentagram before the hearth. The spilled wax looked like melted flesh, and I stifled a shudder.

Trent's finger tracing a line of print made the book glow. "Bis, what's your opinion here? Could this be the phrase to invoke the cure?"

Hope lit through me when Bis nodded. "This? This is it?" I said as I found the Latin amid the elven gibberish. *Humus, fluenta, accenderaet,* I mused, translating the first three words into earth, water, and sun. *Aer, aether, lucem,* and *spatium* were the last four, which loosely meant air, ether, light, and the-nothing-that-was-all. They were the seven main chakras and, in hindsight, obvious. A thrill of anticipation raced through me. I had the cure.

"The words, together with the ring, summon and direct mystics to get stilled chakras spinning again," Trent said, and then he hesitated, taking the book from me and flipping the pages back and forth. "Bis, double-check me. A simple circle will protect the person summoning them, right? We're not going to bring the Goddess into this, are we?"

"I don't think so," Bis said, and Jenks snickered when his voice cracked. "But I'm going to go with you anyway," he added, his tail tightening across my shoulders.

I stared at Trent for an entire three seconds, a wealth of possibilities making my fingers itch. *I have the cure. See, Vivian? I am a good person.* "Sorry, guys. Bis and I have to go."

"Count me in." Jenks's dust was a cheerful gold. "How about you, Cookie Man? You got time to spot Rachel while she does some spelling?"

"Let me call Quen." Clearly pleased, Trent reached for his phone. "Five minutes."

"Wait, you've actually *got* one of these rings?" Lee said, eyes wide. "You're kidding, right? Can I see it? Where did you get it?"

Bis was practically humming with anticipation, and I touched his foot. "Al has it," I lied, not knowing why. "And no way in hell," I said, jumping when Trent snapped the tiny book in his hand closed and handed it to me again. I froze, startled out of my next thought as the book seemed to warm and settle, accepting my touch now that Trent had made it obvious I was to be trusted. *Like a demon servant shelving books? Ancient indeed.* "I have to go uncurse Cassie's friends."

"What about your porch ward?" Lee asked as he headed for the hall— only to jerk to a halt when Trent stopped him.

"Give me the lens," Trent said, and Lee smirked.

"You little moss wipe!" Furious, Jenks hovered between them. "You tried to lift it?"

"Jenks, relax," Trent said as Lee pulled from his grip. "He's just being a jerk-wad."

The mild epithet made Lee laugh, somehow turning his potential theft into a kid's game. Not at all embarrassed, Lee took the lens out of his pocket and tossed it to Jenks.

"Hey!" the pixy shouted, barely getting under it before it hit the floor. Wings laboring, he managed to drag it back atop the workbench.

"Not funny," I said as Bis rumbled low and deep on my shoulder.

"Can't blame me for trying," Lee said with a chuckle. Hands in his pockets, he went into the hallway.

"He doesn't have anything else," Bis whispered in my ear. "I was watching him."

"Thanks, Bis," I said. Trent had followed Lee out, Jenks hot behind him as he swore, bringing Disney, Tink, and troll turds together in an unholy trinity. I took one last look at Hodin's room as I picked up the lens and dropped it into the pocket with the ring. A weird feeling passed through me as I hit the hall. The last time they were together like this, Hodin was twisting a dark curse, killing someone.

Hodin's door was still open, and I shifted the Srandford bowl between the door and jamb so it wouldn't shut. "Hey, Lee? You're still a jerk, but thanks for your help," I said as I joined Lee and Trent in the sanctuary, a dark elven magic book in one hand and a gargoyle on my shoulder. Lee already had his coat on, but his tight frown eased at my words.

"Sure. No problem." Lee paused as if lost, motions slow as he draped his scarf around his neck. "I'll say one thing. Your life is not predictable."

"No, it's not," I said, and Bis chuckled, giving my shoulder a quick pinch before flying up into the rafters.

I set Hodin's elven-magic book on the end table and sat on the couch to put my boots on. Despite it all, we were still okay, the pattern of irritation and forgiveness ingrained from three years of camp, and my lips curved up as one heel went thumping into my boot. "You're coming to Trent's Halloween bash, right?"

Lee nodded, his eyes on Jenks as the pixy went to sit with Bis. "Wouldn't miss it."

"Yeah?" Wouldn't miss it? He had never come before. "You do know it's a costume party. You got a costume yet? The only thing left now is sexy witch."

The man's eyes dropped down, flicking between Trent and me. "You'll see," he said mysteriously.

Which meant he hadn't gotten a costume yet and would probably come as a hippie. I stood, eager for him to leave so I could get going. "Seriously, thanks for your help getting into Hodin's room. I could not have done it without you."

"Clearly." Lee faced Trent, his expression open and honest. Trent, though, was obviously not ready to let it go even as he reached for Lee's proffered hand. "We still on for the festival?"

"Absolutely." Trent took his hand back, a professional smile gracing his face. "You want to bump it out to ten?"

Lee exhaled in relief as he nodded, made an insulting shooting gesture to Jenks, then smiled at me. "Ten sounds great. See you then." Turning, he walked to the door, opened it, and stepped into the rainy night.

*Finally.* "I'm going to stash the lens and the book in my room," I said, boots thumping as I strode to the foyer. "Jenks, you okay with the temps? It's wet out there."

"I got this!" Jenks said, voice faint behind me as I took the stairs two at a time. "Give me a second to find Getty and tell her where I'm going."

"Coat," I said as I stomped up the stairs and blew into my room, making a satisfied *mmmm* as I plucked it from my makeshift closet. I loved jacket weather. *I can move downstairs,* I thought, but the idea immediately soured. Al had put wards and spells of protection on my belfry room, and the thought of sleeping in the same room where Hodin had? Not happening.

Rain jacket rasping, I turned to my growing collection of books. After

I gained four of Newt's demon tomes, Trent had given me a lockable, glass-faced cabinet for my birthday. It was down in the kitchen, where I did all my spelling, but I had yet to move anything into it apart from a few ley line gadgets. I hadn't liked seeing the yellowed glass in Lee's hand, and my books felt safer up here on the shelf where they had always been. "There you go," I said as I wedged the tattered elven tome between two demon texts and set the lens in front of it.

And then I hesitated, pulse quickening. Vivian was going to be there. I could show her Brad's curse tonight, and not only free up my day tomorrow, but maybe earn some trust from the rest of the coven members. The chance that she might confiscate it right then and there would be less if I had just uncursed Cassie's employees. Right?

Wanting to believe, I cast about my room for something to protect the book from the rain. The plastic bag that Ivy's paper-whites had been in was perfect, and I shook out the papery bulbs, sending them thumping and rolling onto the marble-top dresser before dropping the book in. Hesitating, I carefully added the elven spell book with the chakra curse. I hadn't twisted it, so showing it to her was far less risky despite its obvious dark status—a reminder that there were far more ugly curses than the one I'd hit Brad with.

Tucking them under my arm, I sighed at the mirror and my wild hair before flicking off the belfry light. Out at the curb, I heard Lee roar off. My boots a cheerful *thump-thump, thump-thump, thump-thump* on the stairs, I careened down, shoulders bumping as I scrolled through my phone for Vivian's number. "Hey, Trent? I'm going to show Vivian Brad's curse tonight so I don't have to break up my day tomorrow!" I shouted before I reached the bottom, and my attention flicked to the phone when it connected.

"Hi, this is Vi. Leave a message."

*Short and sweet,* I thought. Not unlike the woman herself. "Hi, Vivian. It's Rachel. I have the invocation phrase to untwist the chakra curse. I'm on my way to the hospital now to wake them up. I've got the book that was used to twist Brad's curse, too. If we find a quiet corner, you can look at it."

*And maybe let me off the hook,* I thought, my words unsaid. "Ah, see you there?"

I closed the phone down, smiling as I swung into the foyer to find Trent ready and waiting.

"Good?" he asked, and I nodded, barring the church's front door and turning to go out the back. It was an unusual precaution, but I hadn't liked Lee trying to steal from me.

Something told me he had once . . . in our shared past.

# CHAPTER
# 17

"STILL CAN'T REACH HER?" TRENT ASKED, AND I SET MY PHONE IN MY lap. The *swish-thump, swish-thump* of the wipers was pleasant in the warmth of the car, and, frustrated, I dropped my phone into my shoulder bag. We'd taken the side streets to avoid the bridge traffic, and now that we were in Cincy, we were hitting every light wrong. It was taking forever to get to the hospital.

"I can't tell if she's ignoring me or having a conference call with someone on the West Coast." Because if she was talking with the coven of moral and ethical standards, she would not hang up to take another call, even if she was the lead member now.

Bis shifted his wings in a nervous tell, the sound of them sliding obvious in the well-insulated sports car. Trent's attention flicked to the dark back seat where the kid was, his thoughts clearly on what Bis's claws might be doing to his upholstery.

"Relax, Rache." The pixy was in his usual spot on the rearview mirror, heels thumping the glass. Though the rain had yet to let up, his dust making a slow, steady stream to the cup holders was as dry as ever, the pixy having made the trip to the car under Trent's hat. "Vivian is busier than a pixy mother with twelve newlings. You left her a voice mail. She'll show."

My grip on my bag tightened, and I dragged it farther up onto my lap. The two spell books made it heavier than usual, and now that I had them with me, I was having second thoughts. "I've left three," I whispered, squinting as the bright lights of the hospital entrance fell over us to shift midnight to noon. A shiver rippled over me, drawn into existence by the memory of pulling up under the lights as a kid, struggling to breathe, my mother scared to death as she carried me in, her stream-of-consciousness babbling an effort to hide her fear.

But that was ages ago.

"Ah, the front might not be a good idea," I said as the parking attendant glanced up, and Trent gave the man a short wave and continued through the turnaround. "I've got two dark magic books with me, and the coven is already thinking about charging me with Walter's death."

Trent's hands clenched the wheel and then eased. "It's easier to blame the demon you know than find the one you don't," he said, and I winced, glad when the comforting, rainy darkness found us again.

"I don't want to spend thirty minutes in the security office trying to explain," I said. "Take a right there. We can go through radiology, where they don't have spell detectors."

"Radiology it is." Trent obediently turned the car, and I caught a glimpse of Bis rolling his big red eyes. "I didn't know they *had* entrances that lack spell detectors," Trent added, slowing as we entered a narrow drive. Experience told me it wound around behind the main building to a small parking lot that few people knew about.

"My mom used to sneak all kinds of contraband in through radiology," I said, a smile finding me as the streetlights became even fewer and the darkness deepened.

"I think I would've liked knowing you when you were young," Trent said, and I touched his knee, easy in the tight confines of his sports car.

"You did."

"I guess I should have said 'remembering you,'" Trent amended, and, loving him, I leaned across the car to give him a quick kiss. He unexpectedly shifted his head, and our lips met, sending a snap of ley line energy through me as our internal balances equalized. The surprise sent a quiver of need rising in me. But me getting randy and us sneaking in to avoid security sort of went hand in hand.

"Oh, for Tink's titties," Jenks complained. "Do you have to sift dust right in front of us?"

Bis giggled, sounding like rocks in a blender, and I pushed deeper into my seat. Trent was right there, a hint of power lifting his fair hair to make him smell of wine and snickerdoodles. The need to fix what Hodin had done to Cassie's employees was riding high in me, and the anxiety of that was an easy spill into other, more earthy releases.

Trent made a tight turn into the space by the door, the car easing to a soft halt before he put it in park and pocketed the key fob. The rain pattered down, louder now that the car was off. "So we go in and wait for Vivian?"

I nodded. "Convincing the nurses that we have a viable cure will be easier than the pencil pushers up front who are more concerned about lawsuits." I hesitated as Trent lifted his hat and Jenks tucked in under it. "Maybe Vivian will take a call if it comes from the hospital."

I got out, hugging my shoulder bag with the books close as I breathed in the damp air trapped in the small cul-de-sac at the end of the narrow drive. No one came back here except radiation patients and the people who treated them. There wasn't enough room for the large delivery vans, and the light above the small, one-door entrance didn't do much.

The door was predictably open, and Trent gestured for me to go first. "Yellow line leads to the main hospital," I said as I went in. Empty hallway . . . good. "Ah, Jenks, if you want to—"

"On it." Wings a soft hum, Jenks darted down the hallway, flying high where the conventional security cameras wouldn't see. Bis went with him, little drops of water spotting the floor as he crawled along the ceiling like a bat. Trent shuddered at the eerie sight, and I slipped my hand in his.

"Trent, can I ask you something? I'm not surprised Lee tried to take the lens, but how come we both gave him a free pass for it? Is it because we've known him so long? Or maybe it's something from camp we don't remember?"

Trent's damp grip on my fingers tightened. "That he put you in a place where you could have hurt yourself bothers me more than some trinket he tried to swipe."

It wasn't a trinket, but that wasn't the point. "Regardless, why do we keep forgiving him for the crap he dishes out?" I said. "Why is it he does the same for us?" I added. "He could have really hurt himself breaking that ward. I think Lee remembers more than we do."

"Possibly." Trent's pace remained even and unaltered as we passed doors and empty lobbies, the scent of disinfectant becoming stronger the closer we got to the regular hospital. "I took a look at our camp records a few years ago when I tried to lure you into working for me."

"Lure?" I said, chuckling. "You practically extorted me."

His hand gave mine a squeeze. "And you extorted me right back. Anyway, I don't remember most of what we did, and it was, mmmm, interesting reading. I had to extrapolate for most of it, but you were clearly good with ley lines even then."

"Until I threw you into a tree." I smirked. "I didn't touch a ley line again until college."

"You must have scared yourself silly," Trent said softly.

"I scared my dad." I went quiet at the memory of his pinched and frightened face as he earnestly tried to convince me to never use the lines to harm anyone ever again. To my younger self, that meant never use the lines, period. And then they kicked me out of the Make-A-Wish camp.

"I've been racking my brains," I added as we wove deeper into the building, my voice low as we began to see people. "Trying to figure out why we let everything roll off and he does the same. My God, Trent. I practically sold him to Al in exchange for my freedom. Do you think it's because we felt as if we were in a club, saved by your dad's illegal medicines when he let others simply . . . die?"

"Mmmm."

"Perhaps that's what keeps us together, forgiving each other," I said, brow furrowed.

"Not the billion-dollar drug cartel?" Trent asked slyly.

"Well, there is that, too," I said, perking up when a familiar rasping of dragonfly-like wings drew my attention. "Find them?" I said to Jenks as he came to a dust-laden hover.

"Yeah," he said, and my smile faded at his worried blue dust. "You might want to hurry. Their auras are thinner than troll shit."

The pixy spun in the air, darting down the corridor the way he'd come. Trent quickened his pace, taking my elbow to guide me when I swung my book-heavy bag around to find my phone. Head down, I texted Vivian that I was at the hospital. The thought that she might be in trouble rose and fell, immediately dismissed. Sure, she'd done a three-hour stint as Dali's strip-girl, but Hodin, the demon who had sold her to him, was gone, and the rest didn't dare try.

The nurses' desk was empty as we passed it, a cooling cup of coffee and half-eaten sub sandwich beside the keyboard; Jenks must have tripped an-other patient's alarm to clear the hallway. We weren't doing anything wrong—yet—but I appreciated Jenks's discretion. It was always easier to get forgiveness than permission. Pulse fast, I followed Jenks's faint dust trail to the last door at the end of the hall.

Immediately I made a light knuckle knock and went in. Trent glanced up and down the hall before drawing the door shut behind us.

"Rachel." Cassie rose from the indulgent chair set beside the black, rain-spotted window. Bis was hunched atop a tall cupboard, and he shifted his skin from a camouflage white to his usual pebbly gray when he saw me. "Thank God. Jenks said you were on your way."

My damp boots squeaked as I gazed at the four narrow cots, and then I jumped, startled when Cassie practically fell into me. "I, ah, didn't know you were here," I said, gingerly patting her back. "Are you okay?"

The woman blinked fast as if to ward off the tears. "Jenks said you found the countercurse?" she said, her tear-wet eyes following him as he went to sit beside Bis. "I don't care what it costs. I'll pay for it. Anythin'. They're my family."

"Um, I have it," I said as Trent studied a patient tablet. "We're waiting for Vivian."

"The coven member?" Cassie asked, still flustered. "I come here to read to them when it gets quiet. Everyone keeps telling me they're doing okay, but they're dyin'." She gestured listlessly at the four beds against the two walls. "I can't see auras, and even I can tell that."

Trent set the tablet down, his brow furrowed. "We can invoke it when Vivian gets here."

"Vivian, hell. Do it now," Cassie demanded, reminding me of a hospital mom, desperate for her miracle cure. "Look at them!" she shouted, pointing. "They can't wait!"

"Cassie might be right," Trent said, his focus distant as if seeing through walls. Jenks, too, was nodding. "I've never seen that before," Trent added, his worry obvious.

I didn't like using my second sight at night when the ever-after was easier to see layered over everything—even if the demon's reality was pleasant now. Using it in the hospital was even worse as the faint images of what people used to call ghosts seemed to flit about within my blind spot. But Cassie's hand-wringing worry and Jenks's pale dust lured me into willing it forth.

Gut tight, I ignored the image of wide spaces and starry skies spreading around and over me as the walls and floor became misty and indistinct. As expected, Trent's aura was a cheerful golden yellow that nearly matched mine, right down to the streaks of red. Jenks's aura was his usual rainbow. It was somewhat shallow in blue, but he was currently dusting that color, and my suspicion was confirmed when the blue returned and the yellow became sparse when his dust shifted color as well. *Interesting.* Bis's aura, which I'd never paid much attention to, was his usual violet and blue, a warming of orange at his chest, and Cassie's was a pleasant greenish blue, almost violet at her fingertips.

But the four men . . .

I blanched as I found the expected sickly green—only, it was fading, flickering about the edges and missing entirely from their legs and heads. "When was the last time they had their chakras balanced?" I asked, trying to hide my alarm. Holy crap on toast, they were more naked than a half-starved undead vampire.

"Two hours," Cassie whispered, her almost terrified expression fixed on them.

*Two hours?* Shocked, I swung my bag around and let it drop heavily on the nearby counter. "I'm calling Vivian again," I said as I reached for the landline phone by one of the nightstands. "Maybe she'll answer if I use a hospital phone."

"Rachel?" Bis warbled, and I turned at Cassie's gasp.

"Oh no," Trent said, and I followed his gaze to one of the men. He was in convulsions.

"Kylie!" Cassie shouted, lurching to his side. "Don't you dare. Don't you dare leave me! Rachel, do somethin'!"

A soft buzzing alarm rose from the nearby machinery, a louder version of it echoing in from the hall. Jenks took to the air as the door slammed open and three nurses raced in. Bis went white, not in fear, but to blend in with the walls, his wings tightly wrapped around himself to become nearly invisible. My second sight vanished. I needed to be in the here and now.

"Who are you?" the largest aide said as the other two registered our presence and shoved us out of their thoughts to focus on Kylie.

Trent inched closer to me, a silent presence as I fumbled for words. "He just went into convulsions," I said. "His last chakra is almost still," I added, stating the obvious.

"Out," the nurse said, pointing, but I was riveted to the spot as the other two did a quick triage, one taking samples and readings, calling them out as the other recorded them.

Until they both stopped and backed up.

"What are you doing? Save him!" Cassie demanded, but the oldest nurse with gray hair and a calm acceptance shook her head, putting her arm over Cassie to draw her away.

"I'm sorry," she said as the last nurse, young and trying not to show it, took Kylie's hand.

"Sorry?" I echoed, shocked. Were they going to let him die?

Trent stepped forward, his brow furrowed. "If it's a matter of insurance—"

The nurse who had asked us to leave looked insulted, but it was the old one still trying to get Cassie to move who answered. "Mr. Kylie has a no-heroic-efforts request."

"Well, fuck that!" Cassie exclaimed. "Kylie, don't you dare," she said, shoving the nurse's arm off her and giving him a shake. "Kylie!"

Sighing, the older nurse pulled the white curtain around Kylie's bed to hide Cassie shouting at him. "I'm sorry, but you need to leave," she said to us, her eyes narrowing upon Jenks as if we had brought in a pet. "Immediate family only."

Lips set, I stuffed my hand in my pocket for the ring. *Sorry, Vivian. . . .*

"If you could move to the hall?" the nurse said, her large size firmly between us and Kylie.

"I'm not waiting for Vivian," I said. "Trent, could you get everyone in a corner? I don't know how this works, and I want everyone in a circle."

"You need to leave," the large nurse said again, and Trent stepped forward, his most coaxing smile in place.

"Cassie?" I took the ring in hand. *Tap a line. Say the words,* I thought. "I can't break the curse with you beside him. Ma'am?" I added as the older nurse frowned at me. "If you could?"

Cassie shoved the curtain aside, wild with hope as she took the nurse's arm and tried to drag her away. "Come on," she said, tugging at her. "We have to get out of the way so Rachel can uncurse them. She found the cure. Move!"

The young nurse beside Trent paled. "You're Rachel Morgan," she said, and the large nurse trying to herd us out hesitated. "You did this?" she added, clearly frightened. "You froze their chakras?"

"What are you, an idiot?" Hands on his hips, Jenks dusted an annoyed orange. "She's trying to fix it. Move so she doesn't have to make such a big protection circle."

But the lead nurse seemed to panic, lurching to the nearest monitor to hit an icon. "Security!" she shouted, as if the new alarm ringing in the hallway wasn't enough.

*Oh, for God's sake,* I thought as the young nurse totally lost it. At the ceiling, Bis put his hands to his ears, clearly in pain.

"Rachel, down!" Trent shouted, and I dropped, hands stinging as they met the hard floor. Rolling, I watched the thrown spell whizz through the air where my chest would have been.

"Hey!" I shouted, still on the floor, and my anger shifted to alarm when the old nurse, clearly a witch, threw another. I rolled again, and it hit the wall with a thump hard enough to shake the air. What the Turn was she packing?

"You idiot!" Cassie shoved the old woman off-balance, and I rolled to a stand. "She can help them."

But the lead nurse made a grab for me, and I danced away. Trent was in a corner with Bis, and Jenks was everywhere, dusting a bright orange I was pretty sure would make anyone it touched itch for a week.

"What's going on in here?" a new voice called out, and I clenched my teeth. It was hospital security: blue uniform, spell-laden belt, little badge that looked as if he found it in a box of cereal. *Why do they always give the insecure man the spell belt?* I wondered as my attention shifted from him to the three nurses and back again.

"Escort them out," the head nurse said, pale and shaking. But at least she wasn't throwing spells anymore. "Better yet, take them to holding."

"Are you kidding me?" Jenks said. "We haven't thrown one spell!"

Cassie inched her way to Kylie, her face wet with tears. He wasn't moving anymore, but his pulse monitor said he was still alive. Maybe they had given him something after all. Something to ease his passage.

"Into the hall. Now," the man demanded. But his hand was hovering near his spell belt, and it ticked me off.

"Please, Rachel," Cassie whispered, and my pulse quickened.

"Kylie won't last ten more minutes," Jenks said. "Stun them."

"Good idea," I said, and Trent smirked, his intake of breath racing through me as I felt him pull on the nearest ley line.

The nurses felt it, too. Their eyes widened, and they foolishly did nothing, relying on the security guard as I smiled and touched the ley line.

"*Stabils!*" I said, throwing the demon's joke curse right at the guard.

"Hey!" he shouted, then slowly fell over, crying out in fear as he hit the floor, blood spurting as he broke his nose. Frantic, the young nurse pulled him deeper into the room, the exact opposite of the way I wanted her to go.

"You killed him!" she exclaimed, terrified.

*Seriously?* I thought. The guard was still shouting bloody murder.

"Stop it! All of you!" Cassie shouted, hunched over Kylie in protection as the free energy in the room began to grow, rocking between the walls like waves in a bathtub. "I'm going to get you all fired for this. I asked Rachel here to help, and you're actin' like asses!"

"*Stabils!*" I shouted again to drop the young nurse, which it did. Yes, it was a joke curse, but it was effective—until you figured out how to get around it.

"Incoming!" Jenks called, and then I yelped, shocked when a crapload of ley line energy hit me square on the back. For half an instant, force vibrated through me until I balled it up, forcing it to my hands, where it dripped in shades of gold and red.

Shoulders hunched, I spun to the old nurse, now pale as I had taken everything she'd thrown at me, a force which had probably downed everyone else she'd used it on. Jenks grinned, knowing what was going to happen next.

"You. Over there," I said, pointing to where Trent had dragged the last nurse, out cold with an elven spell on her. "Bis, the door," I directed, and he shook himself, making the lead nurse, the only one not spelled, gasp. Apparently she hadn't known he was in the room.

"Got it!" Bis called as the door slammed shut.

"Hey, Trent!" Jenks called as he hovered beside Bis. "This thing doesn't have a lock."

"On it." Trent double-checked the nurse he had downed, then strode forward, a muttered curse flaring through my awareness as he spelled the door.

"Cassie, we need to get them clear," I said as I grabbed the security guard's shoulders and dragged him across the small room. "I'm not sure how the countercurse works on unprotected people," I explained as she touched Kylie's shoulder and lurched to help. "Everyone needs to be in a circle."

"Please don't hurt me. Please!" the young nurse begged. "I have a little girl. Please!"

"Good God, I'm trying to help you," I muttered, feeling guilty as the security guard began to threaten me in one-syllable words.

"Rache?" Jenks called out, hovering before the door as someone began violently thumping on it.

Pulse fast, I dropped the security guard beside the two nurses. Turning, I dug the ring from my pocket, and, after a heartbeat of hesitation, I stuck it on my finger. Immediately the ring's dead feeling vanished, and my breath came fast at the sudden tingling warmth. "Jenks?" I called to draw him back.

"Here!"

"Cassie?" I said next.

"Good," she said as she tugged a straying leg clear of the circle Trent had drawn. "Will you shut up!" she added, giving the security guard a nudge in the ribs.

"Bis," I whispered, feeling him before I saw him, and he flew to me, tail wrapping firmly across my back and under my arm. They were safe, but that door wouldn't stay shut much longer. It was now or never. *Sorry, Vivian.* "Trent, you got 'em?"

"Secure!" he said, and I felt him set a circle holding everyone but Bis and me.

"Here we go." *Rhombus,* I thought, encasing us in our own protection circle, strong from my uncertainty. Breath held, I extended my arm, hand fisted as I angled the ring toward the four unconscious men. The line poured into me, and the ring on my finger became warm—glowing white-hot with the tingling heat of magic.

*It's gathering mystics,* I suddenly realized.

"Now!" Bis said. "Rachel, you have enough. Now!"

"*Humus, fluenta, accenderaet,*" I said, arm shaking as my aura flashed into the visible spectrum. I watched it, somewhat horrified as it turned from red to orange to yellow. Vertigo hit me, and I staggered.

"Rachel?" Trent shouted, and I waved him off with my free hand, almost knocking myself down. Bis's wings beat the air, and I again stood tall.

"*Aer, aether, lucem . . .*" I whispered, my aura spinning from green to blue to indigo. "*Spatium!*"

I had an instant of clarity as the world flashed into a translucent violet black, and then a blinding flash of light exploded from the ring. A sodden thump of thunder slammed into me, and I stumbled as I felt the power of the ring blow through my circle, taking it down.

*No!* I thought as it collapsed, and then I staggered as Trent made a new circle, larger than his first, to hold me as well.

But I wasn't the only thing his circle entrapped, and I was suddenly choking, unable to see as mystics swamped us in a humming thrum of power.

"Holy crap, Rache!" Jenks exclaimed, and I squinted past Trent's circle. Outside of it, it was even worse—as if the sun itself was imprisoned by frail walls. "Your hair!" he added, and I reached up, finding it a halo of red.

*Mystics,* I thought, not surprised. They were so thick in the room that I couldn't see the walls. I felt overly full, overwhelmed by something I couldn't name. Tears spilled from me, and Trent wiped them away, his touch painful. The room past the bubble was a blur. The cries in the hall were frantic, and I hoped everyone was okay.

"Are you singed?" Trent asked, his brow pinched in concern, and I shook my head.

"I think I'm okay." The hospital personnel were slumped around us. Someone was crying. Other than that, it was silent. Even the alarms had been stunned by the brilliant light.

Cassie got up, her gaze fixed to the hazy images on the bed. "Did it work? I can't see."

We were in a muffling cocoon, but the glare was fading, or maybe I was simply getting used to it. "Wait," I said when she tried to touch the barrier. "Is it safe, Bis?"

His eyes were shut, wings clamped as if he was breathing in acid. But he nodded, and with a little sigh, Trent broke his circle.

More mystics poured over us in a cascading of pinpricks. I slumped, squinting as I fumbled for the nightstand. Cassie surged forward, arms waving as if to feel her way to Kylie's bed. I didn't feel so good, breathing in magic, choking out power.

"Rache?" Jenks said, voice high and squeaky.

"She's okay," Bis said, hunched in pain as he sat on my shoulder.

I wasn't the only one having issues. Jenks looked as if he'd slammed three energy drinks, a silver dust spilling from him and his wings an invisible blur. Trent was hunched, standing bent over with his hands on his knees as if he'd run a three-minute mile. The nurses, too, were coughing, and the security guard was reciting the Lord's Prayer as if he was about to die.

"Hey, it's over," I said, pushing myself upright. "You're all fine."

"Kylie? Kylie!" Cassie shouted, elated as she began to cry. "You're okay! Look at me. Focus, man. I'm here. Oh, God, you're going to be all right."

And though I still couldn't stand up straight, I found I could smile. It had worked.

Trent's head lifted, and with a slow, pained motion, he gingerly pulled me closer as startling pinpricks of energy jumped between us. "You did it," he said, pushing Bis off my shoulder as he gave me a careful hug. "I'm so proud of you," he whispered, but even his breath was almost too much to bear in the highly charged air, and he reluctantly let go.

The pounding started up at the door again, and the pinch to get moving pricked through me. "I think I'm going to be sick," I said, wondering if it was getting easier to see. My hands shook, and I looked at the ring on my finger, wondering how something so small could control so much power.

Bis had moved to the back of a chair, wings clamped and clearly miserable. "Why aren't they leaving?"

"They are." Jenks finally alighted on a piece of machinery. "There's only like one percent of them left. Damn, girl!" he said, his sparkles so white they could set the floor on fire. "We'd be dead if Trent hadn't put us in a circle."

"Mmmm." Trent glanced at the nurses. "Perhaps we should . . ."

Nodding, I turned to them. "Hey, um, I'm sorry I spelled you. But Kylie was dying. I had to get you into a circle before I uncursed them, and you weren't listening."

"Let us go," the older nurse said, and having to trust that, I broke the *stabils* curse. Sagging, the guard and the nurse began to pick themselves up. Immediately the older nurse went to the last bed, and a smile found me again. Kylie was okay.

"Cassie?" a raspy voice said. "What happened? My throat hurts. I can hardly move."

"You've been in a coma for the last three months," Cassie said, her tears glittering like diamonds in the rarefied air. "Rachel got you out."

"Morgan?" Kylie rasped. "Pike's boss?"

Trent touched my arm before going to help the nurses. The mystics were finally clearing. Cassie was sitting on Kylie's bed, hugging him, rocking him exuberantly, but as the other three began to wake, the elated woman went from one to the other, her voice high as she answered their questions and demanded the nurses get up and do their job.

"We should go," Trent said, his hand on my elbow as the security man began to complain, a wad of tissue at his nose. The youngest nurse was leading him to the door, a flash of fright finding her when she couldn't open it.

"You think?" I found my book-heavy bag and looped it over a shoulder. My hair was still in a halo, and as Trent whispered a word to unlock the door, Bis made the jump to my shoulder, fighting my staticky hair to carve out enough room for himself. Laughing, Jenks dusted my curls, but it didn't help. *Not enough product in the world,* I thought, flashing back to the eighties when I caught sight of myself in the mirror. All I needed was some glittery suede shoes and a friendship pin.

"They're awake!" the young nurse exclaimed when the door opened and people swarmed in. Cassie was in seventh heaven, flushed and as proud as if they had fought the devil themselves to return, and maybe they had.

"I have you," Trent whispered as we pushed through the press of people, forgotten. I felt icky, overly full. Letting go of the ley line only made it worse, though, and I let a stray thought linger in it to give the mystics clinging to me a path to the ley lines.

I felt good at Cassie's elated cry: "They are awake! She woke them up! See? They are awake! Rachel, thank you. Thank you so much!"

"Jenks?" Trent said as he led me into the hallway. "We need a quick way out of here."

"On it," he said, and then even his sparkles were gone.

It was easier to breathe in the hall, and after a few steps, my head came up. Trent was still holding my elbow, and I looked at him, seeing he was as dragged out and weary as I was. It hadn't been the fight. It was the mystics. They sort of . . . drained everything.

"You okay, Bis?" I said as I touched his feet, and he gave my shoulder a squeeze in return. The kid was half asleep, his feet clamped securely as his eyes closed.

"Maybe this will show the coven that I'm not a threat," I said as we rounded a corner and the noise diminished.

"I hope so." Trent's pace quickened, and I found I could keep up. "I'm taking you home."

"Good idea. I could use a soak in the tub," I said, and Trent's hold on me shifted.

"Um, how about a glass of wine in front of the fire?"

A fire sounded great, but it would take at least half an hour to get it going, and I didn't have any wood, much less the wine. "Sure," I said reluctantly. "We'll have to stop somewhere on the way."

Trent pulled me closer until our hips touched. "Not your house. My house. We can call up for wine, or anything else, from the restaurant."

*Eat in? From Carew Tower's revolving restaurant?* I was all over that, and we didn't look back at a sudden commotion in the hall. "I thought you were still waiting on the drywall."

"I am." We followed Jenks's fading dust around a corner, the noise going faint behind us. "But the fireplace works, and some of the plumbing. I, ah, think we should be hard to find for a few hours until we know how the world is going to react to this."

"All I did was wake them up," I said, and Bis sighed in his sleep. Poor guy was tuckered out.

"And downed hospital security," Trent added. "And a nurse. Fled the scene."

My shoulders slumped. "Right."

*Damn it, Vivian, why didn't you answer your phone?*

# CHAPTER
# 18

HANDS CLASPED, I STOOD IN THE SMALL LIFT, BIS ON ONE SHOULder, Jenks on the other. Trent was beside me checking something on his phone until he lost connection and put it in a pocket. "I'm going to have to do something about that," he muttered, and I gave him a thin smile. The elevator was dirty in the corners and smelled like two-by-fours. Which was odd, seeing as it wasn't big enough for freight.

This was actually the second elevator needed to get up here, the first stopping at the tenth floor, where Trent had moved his legal business affairs, and then this one, a private lift from his new downstairs office to what would eventually be his two-story flat under the Carew Tower restaurant. "Did you have this put in?" I asked, and Trent's attention dropped from the instrumental eighties music whispering from the speakers.

"Ah, no. But I did have the call buttons removed from the floors between my office and my new place."

*New place.* There'd been a hint of anticipation in his voice, and I realized it was his *first* place, the first time he had chosen where to live. College dorms didn't count. Loving him all the more, I linked my arm in his.

Now that the mystics were gone, I was feeling pretty good. From nowhere, the memory of the kiss that Kisten and I shared when I thought I was going to die at Piscary's teeth rose through me, making me stifle a shiver.

"Cold?" Trent's arm slipped over my shoulders to pull me close.

"Nah, she ain't cold." Jenks's wings tickled my neck as he darted clear of Trent's arm. "She's randy as a goat. Rache has a thing about elevators."

"Jenks, will you shut up," I said, but Trent grinned, tugging me tighter to him to make Bis shift his wings for balance. Thankfully the doors opened, and the light from the elevator spilled onto a plaster-spattered plywood floor. Immediately Jenks and Bis flew out.

"You up for the tour?" Trent said as he drew me forward. "I have a spot where I've been catching my noon nap if you just want to eat."

"Tour first," I said, and he beamed as he pulled me into the plaster-scented dark.

"Lights full!" he said loudly, and I squinted as big, heavy lights in the ceiling thumped on, bathing the area in a noon glow and reflecting off black windows streaked with rain.

"Ow," Bis complained as he landed on a sawhorse, his eyes clamped shut.

"Wow." My gaze followed Jenks's fading dust trail now spreading the length and breadth of the large space. "Better than a spell."

We'd come up about in the middle of a work zone, sixty by maybe a hundred and twenty feet, the ceilings stretching two stories up. The original art deco windows showed a slice of Cincinnati, the river, and the Hollows beyond. I'd seen the view before from the restaurant, but now it was as if it was for me alone, and I felt pulled to the windows.

"The plywood floor is temporary to protect the original parquet," Trent said as I went to the windows, boots thumping. "This area was actually four apartments, but most of the original flooring was intact, and we can replace the damaged portions and where the walls used to be with large sections where we don't need it, like the kitchen."

"It's beautiful." I scuffed to a halt, a hand rising to touch the nicked, ornate molding.

"The woodwork? It is." Trent hovered beside me, clearly anxious to show me the rest. "I've got over seven thousand square feet on this level, with the private living quarters and a small pool and patio area upstairs.

Or at least I will when it's done." He hesitated. "We tapped into the upstairs here to give us the higher ceiling."

"It's going to be amazing." My fingers slipped from the window. It wasn't often that I felt the differences between us, but seeing him rightfully excited about things that I would never be able to afford . . . Yeah, it was a reminder that we came from two different worlds.

"Hey, I can see the church!" Jenks sang out, and I took Trent's hand in mine.

"Show me," I said, a feeling of foreboding taking root.

"Well, this will be the new great room," he said, gesturing. "Now that they have the walls out and the floor removed from some of the upstairs, it's got that fabulous view and wow factor when you step out of the elevator. There's plenty of space behind it for several conference rooms, and over there is where the prep kitchen goes. Just big enough to stage the food for parties and meetings. The restaurant will supply everything, but I will have to expand the existing dumbwaiters into something more efficient."

"Nice."

"I'm thinking the library and perhaps a study down here as well," he said, leading me to an expansive cardboard-covered stairway going to a second floor. "The outside balcony needs better safety measures before we use it for parties, and I'm getting the permits to move the wall in about twenty feet to make the area out there less acrophobic."

"Wow."

"The girls and I and Quen will be staying on the second floor." Still holding my hand, he drew me up the stairs. "We retained the integrity of one of the original flats for Quen and Ray, but the remainder of the upper floors and patio areas will be combined into one space. Well-appointed kitchen, private study, spelling lab, a walk-in book vault. The upper patio area is quite large once you combine them. There are a few trees from the previous tenants that I'm keeping."

"Sounds amazing," I said, feeling awkward as we reached the top of the stairs to find a blank wall with a big X on it.

"We're removing that once we decide how to work it. It's structural," Trent said, leading me around it. "The views from up here are even better. Come see the private patio."

The ceilings here were lower, more homey, and he took me through the proposed kitchen, where I oohed at the dumbwaiters and marveled at the view where the breakfast nook was going to be. The room he'd been napping in had a fireplace and would eventually be a casual office, and his eager pleasure was charming as he lit the gas logs before taking me to the upper patio. The construction crew had been focused on buttoning the flat up, and the new sliders leading outside still had their protective film.

"You have to see the view," Trent said as he eagerly pulled me into the wind.

"Oh my God," I whispered, my wave of vertigo vanishing as fast as it had come. It had finally stopped raining, and the damp scent of the city was heady. We were up so high, and yet there were small trees and a generous plot of grass. A fountain tinkled to drown out the sound of traffic. Raised redwood beds lined one railing—no soil yet but full of promise. A clearly new trio of tiered beds was set to catch the sun on the other side, and an empty lap pool waited to be filled. I could almost smell the hot dogs cooking.

"Trent, this is fabulous," I said as I pulled my jacket tighter against the damp wind.

"I'm glad you like it. Next year, the girls can grow their own pumpkins. I don't know why I didn't set aside a plot for them this year out by the stables."

"You've been busy." But I wondered if this was what he wanted, or if he was trying to outcompete Ellasbeth's flat across the river in the Hollows. If he was, he'd gone above and beyond. It was more than nice up here, but even so, my unsettled feeling began to grow. I felt as if I wasn't just standing nearly fifty stories up on a plot of grass but was perhaps at a crossroads.

I knew part of this move was Trent making space for me, finding my needs and making adjustments to his. He was setting aside his beloved gardens and stables because I could not work from there. It was obvious with the raised beds and dwarf trees that he was trying to meet me halfway. The secluded, window-rich spelling lab downstairs was twice as big as it needed to be, and a walk-in book vault? They spoke to and lured me.

Still . . . it wasn't my home in the church with its secluded graveyard, surrounded by everything I loved and needed. And it made me feel selfish.

"It's beautiful, Trent . . ." I began, then hesitated at the sound of pixy wings.

"Hey, Rach," Jenks said, and Trent's hand fell from mine. "Can I use your phone? I want to check on Getty."

"Sure." I swung my bag around, head down as I pushed past my books to find it. "You want it inside?"

"Yup," he said, clearly struggling with the wind, and Trent reached for the sliders.

"I should probably get an order in," Trent said. "Jenks, you want something?"

"Honey?" The pixy darted inside. "Hey, Bis! Trent's buying. You want a quail?"

"Oh, please don't," I said, and Trent chuckled as the wind cut out. "But he might appreciate a chicken sandwich. Uncooked if they'll do it."

"Chicken sandwich, raw," Trent said. "Honey for Jenks. And for you?"

I shrugged as Trent shut the door. "Something starchy, or maybe some cheese."

"Flight of cheese and artisan bread." Nodding sharply, Trent strode into the sporadically lit darkness. "Back in a second. Jenks, you want to use my phone? It gets better reception in the kitchen. Something about the skylights."

"Of course it does," I whispered as I put my phone away. I felt alone as I listened to Trent's and Jenks's voices become indistinct, and my boots ground the plaster-spotted floor as I made my way to the orange-lit future study. The fire had already warmed the space, and I set my bag beside the dusty leather recliner. There was only the one chair, but a small table sat nearby with a TV remote and a copy of *Orchid Digest*. Trent was on the cover with his latest development, and my eyebrows rose. Clearly he'd been spending more time here than I thought. The delivery address on the front was for Carew Tower.

"Food is on the way," Trent said, and I turned, surprised to see a thick fleece draped over his arm. "Ah, we can eat on the balcony if you want, but I thought the fire . . ."

"Would be perfect," I finished, then helped him arrange the fleece before the table and chair. "This is nice," I said as I took off my boots and settled in. "You bring all your ladies up here?"

Trent chuckled, his balance perfect as he wedged his dress shoes off and stepped onto the fleece. "Only the ones who have the guts to throw me into a tree."

"Then I'm the only one." Beaming, I pulled him down and gave him a kiss, the length of which promised more. "How long until the food gets here?"

Trent took his phone from his pocket and set it on the table. "Ten minutes?"

"Wow. Fast. Thanks for getting rid of Jenks," I mused lightly, but my reach for him faltered when the sound of Jenks's wings intruded.

"Hey, guys? Whoa! Can't you even wait until after you eat?" he said, and I rocked back with a sigh.

"If the church isn't on fire, it can wait," I said, and Jenks bobbed up and down.

"How about an I.S. car out in front? Getty says they're talking about you."

"Swell." Mood souring, I dug my phone out and saw that Vivian had finally returned my text. Apparently she'd been waiting for us at the front lobby. Oops.

"You should call her," Trent said, and I reluctantly tapped the icon. Trent turned on the TV over the fireplace, flipping through the channels until he found the local news. Sure enough, it was an outside shot of the hospital, a newscaster with one hand holding the mic, the other trying to keep her hair from flipping wildly in the misty gusts. No wonder there was a car at my curb. Trent had the captions on, sound off, and their conversation wasn't only about the mystics in the hospital, but also the magic misfires that had plagued the city more than a year ago.

*Summon an elven goddess, and they never forget,* I thought, unhappy as the hospital room flashed onto the screen. Fortunately the footage only showed Trent and me pulling everyone to a corner, and then the screen going white when I invoked the ring. The part where Trent and I had downed everyone was probably being withheld and studied for possible prosecution.

"Rachel? I am so pissed at you!" Vivian said as she answered her phone, and I felt myself warm. God help me, was my hair really that wild? *Damn mystics.*

"Ah, hi?" I said, and Trent touched my shoulder as he set the remote down and quietly left, hopefully to check on our dinner. Or maybe he just didn't want to listen to me getting reamed out by a hundred-and-twenty-pound, five-foot-two blonde with the backing of an entire demographic of people. "I suppose I should have been more specific about where I was."

"You think?" Her voice was tense, full of anger. "I waited twenty minutes. I should have known it was you when the All-Call alarm went out."

"I'm really sorry," I said, eyes on the TV, praying that the news focused only on those last five seconds. "I was going to wait, but Kylie flatlined, and seriously, Vivian, they wouldn't listen. I wasn't going to let him die."

"Rachel, I don't know what I can do now," she said as if Kylie's life didn't mean goose slip. "I have no idea what you did to revive them."

I gestured to the TV, the footage now on an ugly loop in the background as two reporters talked about it. "I found the countercurse in Hodin's old room. Tap a line, aim the ring, say the words. Not a big deal. Vivian, I brought the book to show you. You have to believe me."

"No, I don't," she said coldly, and my pulse quickened. "But I do. It's ring based? I want to see it."

I glanced worriedly at my shoulder bag beside Trent's recliner. "Ah, yes. Sure. Is tomorrow still okay?" I'd thought uncursing Cassie's people would help, not make things worse. The coven was apparently interested in process, not results.

"Tomorrow," she said, and I exhaled, glad I had that much. The news coverage had shifted, showing the same room, but now it had all four of Cassie's employees sitting up in bed, trays of soup and pudding before them. Vivian was there, too, her brow furrowed as she talked to the security guy holding a towel to his bleeding nose. She was clearly angry but capable in her white coat and perfect hair.

"I'm watching you on TV," I said, and Vivian made a small huff. "You look upset."

"I am," she said. "You agreed to keep me in the loop and you cut me out. Again."

"I brought the book—" I started, eyes going to my bag.

"The intent," she interrupted, "was an exchange of information. The rest of the coven doesn't give a spotted dog's dick about results."

From the mantel, Jenks snickered.

"They want to know what you are doing and how you're doing it. Rachel. I can't express how deep in the shitter you are. Give me a shovel to dig you out."

"I know," I said as I turned from the TV. "I've got everything. You can see it all," I added, feeling a flush of fear. "Tomorrow. My church. Two o'clock. I'd do it sooner, but I'm working Trent's security at the coffee festival."

"Two o'clock," she affirmed.

"Okay," I said faintly, glad Lee had gotten me into Hodin's room. "But, Vivian, you have to believe me. I didn't know what went into Brad's curse when I performed it. Hodin lied to me." Technically Stef had put the illegal ingredients in without my knowledge, but I wasn't going to throw her under the bus. I had wanted the curse. I had used the curse. It was my curse.

"Intent matters," the woman said, making me feel better. "But if the rest of the coven doesn't believe you, it won't mean anything." The woman sighed. "Shunning only needs a two-thirds vote, and that second nay is turning out to be hard to find. Where are you now?"

"Hiding from the I.S.," I said bluntly, and Jenks tittered.

"Probably a good idea," Vivian said. "Doyle wants to bring you in for questioning."

"Are you advocating I stay hidden?" I said, getting a neutral "mmmm" in return.

The background noise grew muted, and the distinctive *click, click, click* of Vivian's heels became obvious. "Stay where you are. You can't show me anything if you're in I.S. lockup. Maybe we should meet somewhere other than your church."

"You can meet here," Trent said as he came in, a tray with silver-covered plates in his hand, and I quickly moved his *Orchid Digest* to the chair.

"Um, how about Carew Tower restaurant?" I offered, and Vivian made a happy noise.

"Done," she said. "I'll make the reservations."

The phone clicked with a startling suddenness, and I exhaled, my request that she add in a seat for Trent remaining unsaid. "This is going to be a sucky Halloween," I muttered, and Trent glanced up from removing the silver covers.

"You're okay. Vivian likes you." Rising up, Jenks rubbed his wings together to make a piercing whistle. "Bis! Chow is here!"

Unhappy, I dug my fingers into the fleece. "She has a funny way of showing it."

Bis winged in with the sound of sliding leather, startling Trent when he landed on the man's shoulder. "Thank you," Bis said shyly, his handlike foot taking the sandwich that Trent extended to him. "Jenks, get your stuff. I've got a place out of the wind we can eat. I bet you a week's worth of sentry duty that I can hit the roof across the street with my spit."

Jenks rose up with a packet of honey, dusting heavily. "You're on," he said, and the two flew out again, but not before Bis gave me a soft, knowing smile.

"Thanks, Bis," I whispered, depressed as I resettled myself and stared blankly at the fire.

Trent's sigh as he sat beside me was familiar. He set the cheese and a basket of bread before us, silent as he poured hot cider from a carafe into two oversize mugs sporting the Cincinnatian logo.

"For you," he said as he handed me the fuller one.

"Thanks." I took it, a soft groan of pleasure slipping from me at my first sip. It was warm and sweet, reminding me of fall evenings when my dad would drive us out to the cider mill to buy a dozen fried doughnuts and a gallon of cider. We'd take it up to Eden Park to watch the sunset, and my dad would tell us of the people he helped that week. "This isn't that processed, thin stuff they serve in the Cincinnatian. This is real cider," I said in appreciation.

"I had the mill drop some off at the kitchen this afternoon."

*Of course you did,* I thought, slumping at the reminder of how different we were.

"Rachel, it's going to be okay," Trent said, misreading my mood.

But I wasn't about to tell him I was worried about us, and I took a piece of cheese, avoiding him. My gaze landed on my pearl pinky ring, glowing a pale pink in the orangey light of the fire. "I don't like it when Vivian is mad at me." Which wasn't exactly a lie . . .

"Who would." He set his cider down and shifted behind me. "Okay, sit up," he directed as he rose to a kneel, his hands finding my shoulders and giving them a firm pinch. "You are tense enough to crack eggs on."

"Oh, God. That feels wonderful," I groaned as he dug his thumb into my scapula to find the knot and work it. "Thank you. How did you know that was there?"

"That's where I store my tension, too," he said. "Ah, I'm sorry for getting upset with you about the girls. I know there is nowhere truly safe. I'm not used to—"

His words cut off, but his pressure on my shoulders never faltered. "Trusting them to me?" I said. "I should have brought them to you immediately."

"To the golf course?" he said, his motions deepening. "Leaving them with Al was not an issue. He is their demon godparent."

"What, then?" I said, and his hands fell from me as I shifted to look at him. I'd already figured it out, but I wanted to hear him say it. I had said the girls would be safe with me despite being in the middle of something, that my life wasn't going to crash over them with violence—and I had been wrong. And it could have cost him everything.

"Trent, I am so sorry this happened," I said suddenly. "I'm sorry I was wrong, not just about the mage. I lied to myself that I could live a normal life for a few hours because I wanted to spend a morning with the girls, and because of that, I put them in danger. I don't know if there will ever be a time when I don't have vampires, witches, or whatever ugly thing comes slithering out of the Ohio River crashing into my life. I'm kind of angry about it."

"I know," he said, his motions on my shoulders resuming. "And I don't want them to be raised as I was, secluded and coddled. I've been thinking about it, and I'm sorry I let my knee-jerk reaction hit you. I'm not happy they saw such violence, but I'm glad that it happened with you. They will always be safe if you are there. I should have remembered that."

But I wasn't so sure, and I turned to him, the scent of wine and cookies filling me as his lips found my neck. "Really?" Crap on toast, I thought I was going to cry.

"Right down to the last mystic," he said, giving me a kiss. "I'm sorry I got so angry. It's just that . . ." He shifted back, his fingers resuming their motion. "Childhood is so fleeting. Three, five, ten years, and then they stop looking to you for guidance and you're lucky if they ask your opinion or will sit and watch a movie with you. I want to share the joy of them with you while it lasts. And I will. I just wish they weren't so vulnerable."

I took a breath, feeling my throat close, feeling understood. Feeling loved. "Thank you," I said, but when did I ever have an afternoon where my life might not intrude?

The silence began to grow, but it wasn't uncomfortable, and I smiled as I heard Bis's distant crow of excitement. Apparently he'd won the bet. "I like what you're doing to the apartment," I said. *And my back, and neck, and everything.* With a sigh, I felt myself relax.

"There it is," Trent said softly, his strong grip pinching my shoulder easing as my muscles let go. "Much better." Leaning, he gave me another kiss before moving to sit beside me. "I'm glad you like the changes. I wish you could move in with me."

My lips quirked wryly as he settled himself more certainly, not sprawled out on the fleece so much as stretched, enjoying the warmth of the fire. *Can't move in with him?* "Reverse psychology doesn't work when it's that obvious," I said, and he arched his eyebrows as he took a piece of bread and dipped it into the dish of honey.

"Oh, no," he said, his tone confusing me. "I'm serious. I wasn't kidding when I said my insurance won't cover you. Demon damage is no longer considered an act of God. And having you up here?" He sighed, decidedly sexy as he ate his bread and honey. "You are too high-risk for even me, my love. Can you imagine your chaos at the top of the tower?"

"I'm glad we had this talk," I said, disgruntled as I ate a piece of cheese. "I don't want to move up here into your overgrown apartment with no tombstones or vampiric mice."

"Maybe I need to talk to Jenks," he said, his lips quirked as he scooted closer and put his head in my lap. "See about renting out Hodin's room."

"Yeah?" I huffed as he reached up and played with my hair, smoothing it. "You wouldn't last a week in the church. There's nowhere to park your cars, for one."

"Mmmm." He sat up, his gaze on my hair as he arranged it. "I can do small living. I spent four years in a tiny condo with two witches and a Were when I was at school. I can handle anything you and your pixy can dish out."

His touch in my hair had shifted my thoughts in a decidedly different direction. Eyebrows high, I looked him up and down, then finished my cheese. "You think so, eh?" I reached out, running my fingers across his stubble, enjoying it. I leaned in, and he met me halfway. Our lips met, and my breath caught at the haze of energy trying to equalize, tingling where we touched.

He was beautiful before me, his thoughts on how we could spend the next half hour obvious. "You roomed with a Were in college? Why wasn't he with his pack?"

Trent pulled me closer, and I snuggled in, the warmth of our bodies touching familiar. "He said he was a loner, but I think my dad was paying him to watch me. All our classes were the same."

"Nice," I said, remembering getting beat up for being different—until I was strong enough to beat them back.

"Nice? No. Hart was a big pain in the ass." Focus distant in memory, he tucked a strand of hair behind my ear. "Lights off," he said, and then, when nothing happened, "Lights off!"

The room went dark but for the glow of the fire, and I blinked, waiting for my eyes to adjust. Trent's smile was loving, and his touch held an obvious question.

"Oh, I like this," I said, answering him, and a certain something seemed to drop to the pit of my soul, making my pulse fast with a coming need. "Ah, how sure are you that an inspector isn't going to come through here?"

"It's Friday." Trent tucked his head beside mine and breathed, his fingers gripping my waist sending a delicious shudder through me. "I'll be lucky to see anyone by Tuesday. Besides, why do you think Bis and Jenks are out there spitting across the street?" Love was in his gaze as his hand brushed through my hair. "You still have mystics clinging to you."

"Yeah, they're like that. They tend to hang around things they think will amuse them."

But a shiver took me when they pulled away under his touch, the tiny draws of energy cutting through me like ice. My eyes closed, and I reached to find his ear and tugged on it, my lips gentle. "You got a working three-piece bathroom up here?" I whispered.

"Check," he said, amusement in his voice. "Anything else?"

"Nope." My hands went around his neck, and I nibbled on his ear. "That's good for me." Relaxing, I sent a ribbon of ley line energy through him, delighting at his new tension. Head on his shoulder, I undid one, then two of his shirt buttons to send my hand across his chest.

"Mmmm," Trent whispered, and my pulse quickened in anticipation when he tugged my shirt up and off, tossing it to the chair behind us.

*Buttons* . . . I wanted to pop the damn things and rip his shirt right off, but I wasn't sure he had another shirt, and I struggled to concentrate, to get them through the holes as he lifted me up onto his lap and nuzzled my breasts, tugging, pulling . . . demanding.

My legs wrapped around him, ankles crossed, and when I squeezed him, he pinched me hard, sending a spasm of desire through me as sharp as a whipcrack.

"Crap on toast, I can't get this off . . ." I muttered, and then I gave up, shoving him over to trap him between me and the fleece. He grinned at me, and I reached for his zipper.

That, I could manage, even when his touch continued to play over me, rising to my back, tracing down my spine, curving suggestively to my front. I quivered, my lips finding his when he reached my zipper and clicked it down one agonizing tooth at a time.

*Bet I can get him to quicken this up,* I thought as I dipped a hand under his tighty-whities and found him. My lips quirked devilishly at his intake of breath, and then I gasped as he grasped my shoulder and rolled me over, pinning me between the soft fleece and his demanding presence. Imprisoned.

It was where I wanted to be. My fingers played with his hair, my pants loose at my hips and his half-undone as he hesitated, love and passion in his gaze.

"How did I get so lucky," he said, and I pulled him close, relishing his weight.

"Perseverance," I whispered, and we kissed as he covered me, one hand supporting his weight, his other lingering at my side, caressing it, shifting lower, finding my curves.

I reached to find him taut. His breath caught, the sound going to the pit of my soul and alighting through me. I pushed his pants free with my foot and accidentally knocked aside the cheese board.

But neither of us cared as he found my breast with his lips, bringing me to a hip-moving tension. My grip on him tightened, and I arched up, trying to find him.

He moved against me, teasingly out of reach, his lips driving me mad as they explored until I was frantic with desire. My pants had come off somewhere, and I wrapped my legs around him, demanding he do something as I pulled the thinnest trace of ley line energy from him as my fingers touched his inner thigh.

He groaned, eyes closing, his lips tantalizing as they found mine.

Trills of ley line energy sparked, diving from my lips to my groin. Unable to wait, I reached for him, guiding him to me. I shuddered, almost climaxing right then as he entered me, and we moved together. I could not think, lost in the all, my body responding to him, driving my passions higher.

His body was full upon me, and a wild response rose as he drew a tentative pull of line energy from my core, the lingering mystics an unexpected burst of energy everywhere our bodies touched. I gasped as his motion became more demanding, pushing me to fulfillment.

Wanting it all, I reached for the energy between us, drawing it through him in time with his motions. His masculine energy swirled in me, and he groaned, almost a growl as he yanked his energy back, taking more than what belonged to him and leaving me gasping.

My hands spasmed on him with a wild need. He bent low, still inside me as his teeth found my neck. "Mine," he whispered, and I shuddered as he found my old vampire scar and worked it. I trembled, my entire body alight with passion.

Feeling it, Trent stiffened, climaxing with a shuddering breath. His teeth fastened on me in a new demand. Sensation rippled through me, and I climaxed as well, moaning as our energies pooled into one. Together we went still, hanging in a haze of fulfillment, nothing but sensation wrapping us into one.

Breath fast, I lay under him, feeing little jolts of pleasure, knowing it wouldn't last.

Then Trent's head lifted and he gazed at me, his weight shifting as he propped himself up on the flat of his arm. "Don't go," I breathed, and he smiled, fingers playing with the hair about my ears.

"Never," he said, and his head dropped again, tucking in beside mine. Spent.

My fingers traced spelling glyphs along his shoulder, and I felt him relax against me. "You okay?" I asked, seeing as he was usually invigorated by our lovemaking, and he seemed so . . . relaxed.

"Yes," he said, voice husky and somewhat rueful. "I wanted this to last longer." Sighing, he looked at the scattered cheese tray and spilled basket of bread. "You drive me crazy, Rachel." Leaning in, he gave me a kiss, sweaty and sweet.

I stretched to stay with him as he pulled away, and he lingered, drawing the kiss out.

But eventually our lips parted, and I fell into the fleece. "Happy belated birthday. Hope you like your second present, 'cause I can't return it," I said, and his chuckle turned into a grunt when he tried to lift from me and realized he couldn't. Not yet. My body refused to let go. And where once I found it an unending embarrassment, I now reached to pull him down to me. I wasn't going to let go. Not for anything. He was making an extraordinary effort to blend our lives, and that meant more to me than just about anything.

I could feel him smiling as he gripped me tight and shifted us so we lay side by side, still joined, twined in the glow of the gas fire. Little pinpricks of energy darted between us where we touched, and as he caressed my shoulder, I felt my muscles finally let go.

Sighing, Trent shifted his weight, his arm going still across me as he tucked closer. Slowly his breath evened out.

"Trent?" I whispered, wondering. "Are you asleep?" I suppose I could find the bathroom myself. It couldn't be too far.

"No," he said, eyes closed.

My shower could wait, and I stayed where I was, my hand moving against his shoulder. The light from the fire on the ceiling was mesmerizing, and I sent my senses out, finding Bis, and hopefully Jenks, at the balcony. A wave of satisfaction crossed me; Bis's emotions were joyful and content. He loved being up here, perched where he could see everything.

Jenks, too, didn't need a full garden anymore if he was not raising a family. Getty was used to finding what she needed outside the traditional garden. I was the only one dragging her feet, Trent's claim that he couldn't afford to insure me aside.

And for a moment, I felt my pulse quicken at the idea of helping Trent fill the empty space I could feel spreading around us, seeing it come alive with his plans and the girls' needs, and maybe a little of myself.

Until the reality of the past four years crashed over me, four years of destruction and large swaths of collateral damage. If I was to be here, seeing the girls become who they would be, I would have to let go of everything I had not only worked for but taken into my circle to protect. Ivy, Pike, David, and even Vivian.

My eyes flicked to Trent as he sighed in his sleep, and a wave of determination swept me.

*I will find a way to make this work.*

# CHAPTER

# 19

"I FORGOT ABOUT THE SPELL CHECKER," TRENT SAID, HIS RAIN-DAMP fingers touching his jacket's breast pocket as we waited in line to enter the coffee festival.

"You want me to fly something over it?" Jenks said from my big hoop earring, and Trent's worried expression cleared.

"No. Thank you."

But even as he said it, he was glancing behind us and out the tiny lobby of Cincinnati Music Hall's ballroom to where he'd parked across the street.

"Jenks, would you do a quick recon?" I asked as I took off my jacket and gave it a good shake. It was raining again. Still. Whatever. Halloween was going to be a soggy mess.

"You got it, Rache," he said, my earring swinging as he darted off to survey the practice rooms and other areas currently off-limits.

Three flights up, the small festival was already in full swing, and the rich, welcoming scent of freshly brewed coffee poured down the steps as we inched forward. I'd been here lots of times. The ballroom was basically a large, long, high-ceilinged room, the venue perfect for wedding receptions, elaborate city functions—and the Cincinnati Coffee Festival.

Behind us, a buzz was starting, and I inched closer to Trent, possessively looping my arm in his. It wasn't often that Trent mingled so freely with Cincy's down-to-earth citizens, but he'd lost a lot of notoriety along with his councilman position, and it was only the gossip tabloids that kept him in the news now. Still, it made me nervous, as he had removed his usual first layer of security—separation.

"I'm surprised you wanted to come to this," I said as he scrolled through his phone to find the tickets, then showed them to security to be scanned.

"I like coffee," he said, smiling at the attendant as he boldly stepped through the detector. It didn't even blip, and it was my turn to be nervous as I followed him. But I, too, got a clean screen, even with the chakra ring in my pocket. I'd left the spell books in Trent's study under his *Orchid Digest* magazine, but the ring was too dangerous to leave unattended. It would stay in my pocket until Vivian saw it and I gave it to Al in return for Trent's books.

"Yes," I said, resuming our conversation as I joined him on the stairs and looped my arm in his again. "But you're rubbing shoulders with the common folk."

"I like common folk nearly as much as coffee," he said, and I pulled him to a stop at the top of the stair, wanting a moment to study the room before we entered. Inside were three aisles of vendors selling everything from coffee to tea to pastries, and my stomach rumbled. Waking up on the floor of an unfinished flat in Trent's arms had made for a hurried morning. I'd skipped breakfast in order to take a shower and hopefully tame my hair. It hadn't worked. My hair was in its usual braid, but there was only so much pixy dust could do, and with no product . . . yeah. It didn't help that I was in yesterday's clothes, either.

"They had a VIP party last night where you could have gotten your coffee fix," I said as I scanned the crowded floor. "Don't tell me you didn't know about it."

Trent's head bowed, and I stifled a shiver when his arm went behind me and we stepped forward. "I'm tired of VIPs," he said, lips close to my ear so I could hear. "Of having to flirt with women wearing too much perfume and agree with men who don't know what they are talking about. I simply want to hang with two of my best friends and try some new coffees."

"Well, you can do that here," I said, wondering how long it would take to get to the front of one of the booths.

"Besides." Trent hesitated, his hand touching his pocket as he scanned the room. "Lee is less likely to try anything with this many people around."

I chuckled, remembering the practical jokes they used to plague each other with, then started when Trent made a beeline to the front corner. "Ooooh, a silent auction!" he enthused, dragging me along as he reached for his pen.

The festival was more than coffee, and as Trent went from basket to basket jotting down the occasional bid, I read the pamphlet to find out that the festival's purpose beyond coffee was to promote the fragility of the Ohio watershed, inform people about the wildlife that supported it and was in turn supported, and why it was important not to dump pollutants from oil to medicines that might end up in someone's faucet. Trent, though, clearly already knew this, seeing as he dropped a big bill into the contributions basket.

"Tax-deductible," he said. "I want to check my bid on that coffee maker before we go."

I glanced at the twin-bulb, glass-and-copper contraption, immediately seeing how it worked. A Bunsen burner heated the water up in the lower bulb, forcing it through a tube into the higher bulb, where it soaked the beans like a percolator. That's where any similarity ended, though, and once the heat was removed, the water that had been forced up all drained back, giving you a nicely brewed cup.

"That's not a coffee maker," I said, envious. "That's an earth-magic implement to make an infusion." *A really nice one,* I thought, though I wouldn't ever use it but maybe twice a year. There were easier ways to make an infusion other than a two-hundred-dollar toy that would take up cupboard space.

Trent's head cocked as he eyed it. "It looks like a coffee maker."

Looping my arm in his, I bumped my hip into him to get him moving again. "What do you think coffee is? It's an infusion. So is tea."

"Mmmm."

We got all of five feet before he jerked to a halt, riveted to the next booth with its tiny cups of coffee arrayed for tasting in the front, bags of coffee for buying behind. "Do you mind?" he murmured, and I grinned, gesturing for him to have at it.

Immediately Trent struck up a conversation, leaving me to watch the crowd as I felt my security hat go on. There were a lot of Weres here, but Weres had a tendency to be snobby about their morning brew.

The rasp of pixy wings sounded as Jenks dropped down, his dust a warm yellow when he landed on the back rim of the hat in front of me. "Downstairs is good," he said. "I'm heading for the attic." His tiny features bunched. "There are a lot of Weres here."

"I noticed," I said, and then Jenks rose, hovering as his unknowing perch walked off. "Have you seen Lee?"

But Jenks was gone, and I frowned at his dust trail leading to the ornate light fixtures. "Trent?" I put a hand on his shoulder and inched closer. "Where are we supposed to meet Lee?"

"Oh, I see what you mean," Trent said to the vendor, nodding as he studied the bottom of his tasting cup. "Do you have a pound of this in a bag? Beans, not the ground."

"Trent?" I said as he reached for his wallet. "I know the space isn't that big, but did you have a place to meet?"

Trent tapped his card and tucked it away. "I assumed we'd meet at the bar," he said dryly.

I looked at the blond-wood bar against the wall, a feeling of concern rising at the number of people between us and it. "Jenks says we're good, but I'd feel better if we were all together."

Trent sighed as he took his bag. "Lee doesn't like to shop," he muttered, and I smirked as his free arm went over my shoulder and we ambled forward. We got three steps before a stroller nearly ran over our toes and I jerked us to a halt.

"Ah, I can carry that bag," I said, and Trent tugged me closer.

"Stop being my security. I like you better as my girlfriend. No one is going to bother us."

Unsure, I eyed the press of people. They were not scary or threatening, but there was nowhere to go if there was a problem. Sardines had more exit opportunities. *How long does it take to check out an attic?*

"At the bar. As expected," Trent said. He raised a hand in greeting, and I followed his line of sight to Lee, one foot on the rail, a glass of something in his hand. He had the air of a secret service agent in his black slacks and matching jacket. *Shaken, not stirred.*

Trent's pace increased, and I smiled, remembering how attractive Lee had been in a tux, teaching me how to shoot craps. And then Kisten blew up his boat and I pulled Trent to safety. At the time, I hadn't even remembered Lee from camp. It was complicated.

"Lee!" Trent called as we closed the gap, beaming as he smacked the man on the back a shade too hard. "What do you think of the coffee festival?"

Lee tore his gaze from my hastily woven braid. "It's, ah . . ." He hesitated, his attention on my hair again. "It's nice."

*Nice?* "Hi, Lee." I leaned in to give him a professional hug, pulling away when our internal energies tried to equalize. He was holding a lot of power, and I drew in an additional load from the nearest ley line to match it. My braid snapped and popped, a veritable halo of escaped hairs rising as I ran a hand over it apologetically. "It's not Seattle," I agreed, having heard a slight in his hesitation. "But we do what we can."

"It's really to bring in funds to keep the water clean," Trent added. "And have some fun."

"And try new coffees and teas," I added, overly cheerful, not sure why we were both trying to prove to him that we weren't a hick town on the edge of a river. But then all thoughts seemed to vanish when I saw the Breadsmith booth. A round of their pull-apart bread and some chili would make a hellacious dinner.

I started, shaken from my thoughts of Skyline chili and hot cider when I realized Lee was staring at me. Or my hair, rather.

"I'm sorry?" I said, deciding he had asked me something.

Lee chuckled, and I felt myself warm. "I said, have you seen Trent's new flat? He took me on a tour yesterday."

"Oh!" My flush deepened. I was in the same clothes I'd been wearing yesterday when he got past Hodin's warded door, clean, if a little wrinkled. Trent, too. Lee must have noticed. "Yes. Last night. It's going to be amazing."

Lee lifted his drink, drained it, then set the small cup on the bar with a click. "If you ask me, he's overcompensating for something."

Trent chuckled, drawing me closer. "As a matter of fact, I am trying to outdo my almost-wife's skill at upper-class snobbery."

The conversation was going in a dangerous direction, and smiling at them both, I looped my free arm in Lee's and moved to stand between them. It felt as if I'd been there a long time. "Shall we sample Cincy's brewhouses?"

"Lead on," Lee said, and we stepped out as one. I glanced behind us once to spot Lee's security, but it seemed as if he didn't have any. Nevertheless, I still couldn't shake the feeling that someone was watching us.

"You have to try one of these, Lee," Trent said, angling us to a busy vendor. "These are the people who are doing the Halloween cookies for the party. I'm glad you decided to come this year. It's the last at the estate, and we have an amazing lineup of entertainment."

I tuned them out, my initial scrutiny of the friendly, talkative people behind the counter lifting to the rest of the room. I was sensing tension at the outskirts that couldn't all be blamed on Trent's unexpected presence. As Jenks had said, there seemed to be a lot of Weres leaning against the walls, holding empty tasting cups.

It was too tight in here, and I jumped when Jenks practically fell out of the air to hover in front of me. "Whoa, Jenks!" I exclaimed, but my surprise shifted to worry at the sickly green dust spilling from him. "You okay?"

"The attic isn't heated," he muttered, clearly cold, and I shifted my hair so he could land on my shoulder instead of my big hoop earring. Icy wings pressed my neck, and I heard him sigh as he began to warm up. "It's also empty, but this place is so packed it would take an entire garden of pixies to patrol it."

"We'll play it tight, then," I said, my tension rising when I realized Lee was watching us, his wallet open as he bought a bag of cookies.

"Hi, Jenks," the witch said cautiously. "I didn't know you were here."

"That means I'm doing my job," Jenks said as he hummed into the air. "Excuse me. I'm going to go sit on a lamp. Let me know before you leave, and I'll sweep the stairs."

"Thanks, Jenks," I said, and then he darted away.

"You're going to share those, right?" Trent said as Lee opened the cookie bag, took one out, and rolled it back down again.

"Wasn't planning on it," Lee said, and when Trent huffed, Lee's thin lips curved up into a smile as he extended the bag to me. "Rachel?" Lee offered, and I took one, giving half to Trent when Lee predictably did not offer it to Trent in turn.

"Always ganging up on me," Lee said with a sigh, and I laughed.

"Only when you were trying to make my and Jamie's life hell."

"Jamie?" Lee's brow furrowed, and Trent looked up from the tea vendor. "Oh, Jasmine!"

"That's her name," I said, embarrassed. "I can never remember it when I want to."

Lee's head bobbed. "Whatever happened to her, anyway?"

"I don't know," Trent said, his face sort of empty. "My father's records are often full of gaps."

That she'd died seemed more than likely, and Lee's lip twitched before he forced a smile. "So, Rachel. I saw you on the news. I guess the counter-curse you found worked."

I practically choked on the cookie, eyes watering as I took the little tasting cup of coffee that Trent shoved at me. *Lavender? Who puts lavender in their coffee? Yuck!*

"Yes. Vivian wants to see everything, and then I'm giving the ring to Al," I said, not wanting to tell him the ring was in my pocket. I wasn't sure why, other than that misdirection was better than any protection curse invented.

Lee's eyebrows rose. "Not the book, too? Or are you giving that to Trent? It is elven."

"It's also not my book." Trent's hand found mine, and we started in a slow amble down the center of the aisle. "Besides, who is going to steal from Cincinnati's resident demon?"

I grinned. "That would be me."

"I suppose," Lee said, chuckling. "Sooo, you're keeping the book?"

"I'll probably give it to Al, too. For safekeeping." I looked past Trent at Lee, wondering what his game was. "You saw what it takes to twist. That thing is elven nasty and has no place this side of the ley lines. What, you think I'm going to save it to give to my children?"

"Elven nasty?" Trent questioned.

"You know what I mean," I said, then halted, surprised at Lee's empty expression.

"Would you excuse me," Lee said distantly. "Too much coffee."

Trent nodded, his eyes holding sympathy. "Want me to hold your bag?"

Lee hesitated, then handed it over. "I'll be right back."

"Take your time," Trent said, and Lee took two toe-to-heel steps before turning and striding to the far end of the hall. His posture was hunched as he vanished around the floor-to-ceiling partition that separated the ballroom from the small rear lobby that serviced the restrooms—and then he was gone.

"That was weird," I said, seeing as his departure had been rather abrupt, and then I winced, getting it. His daughter. He had no one to pass his legacy on to and probably never would. "Oh, man. I suck," I said softly.

"Don't worry about it," Trent said. "You want to do some shopping?" he suggested, but I was focused on two plainclothes pushing their way through the ballroom. Their faces were grim, and I stiffened when they stepped around the partition. Lee was back there.

"Ah . . . Trent?" I said, then whistled for Jenks.

Trent spun at a shout cutting through the live music. "That was Lee," he said, and then we both jumped at the abrupt and sure tug on the ley line.

We stepped forward together. "Jenks!" I shouted, then flinched at a sudden bang. The floor trembled and the music cut out. Everyone looked up at the disco ball in the ceiling, now pulsating a gentle warning red.

I pushed in front of Trent. The room was suddenly full of a nervous mutter as vendors began pulling their wares and parents with strollers turned to the main exit. "Trent, stay here. Jenks and I will take care of this."

But Trent was already gone, running to the rear as everyone else pushed to the front.

"Jenks!" I called again, shoving past someone when I felt another tug on the line.

Jenks darted up, sword pulled, wings a tight hum. "It's Parker."

"She's here?" I jumped at an angry shout from behind the partition. "Trent?" Lurching forward, I finally caught up with him as he swung around the partition.

Together we slid to a halt, and I felt my expression empty. A threatening wall of scruffy, tattooed Weres stood before us. Lee was behind them, under a protection circle and on the floor. Two plainclothes sprawled before him, unmoving. Pulse fast, I filled my hand with raw power, fist tightening to squeeze gold and red from me. "Move."

"Lee!" Trent called, and the downed witch shuddered. He was alive.

"I said, move!" I shouted, recognizing the lead Were's attitude, if not the Were himself. It was Walter's alpha pack.

The heavily tattooed man shook his head, gold chains jingling.

He reached for me, and I shoved the raw energy in my hand right at him.

It hit with a sodden thump. Arms pinwheeling, the Were rocked back to be caught by the man beside him. The tiny opening was all I needed. Trent and I pushed through as he whispered a word in Latin and a sudden pop of energy widened the hole.

"Trent, help Lee!" I yelled as I dropped to check the two downed officers. They were breathing. Relieved, I looked up, blanching at a low, rumbling growl.

Trent was facing a snarling wolf. Torn ear, ripped eye: Parker had gone to fur.

"*Stabils!*" I shouted, and the enormous wolf darted clear. My magic slammed into the woman behind her instead, and she collapsed, crying out in fear.

Parker's malevolent eyes fastened on me. Again a low growl rose—until Trent's spell hit her and she skittered sideways, fur smoldering.

"Behind you!" Jenks shouted from the ceiling, and I dropped.

*Rhombus!* I thought, my palms finding the matted carpet as a thunderous boom shook the dust from the ceiling.

It had been Lee. He was down but conscious, and Parker slammed into the wall, thrown by Lee's spell. Stunned, she staggered to all fours and shook, clearly trying to see straight. Her pack was scattering, and I rose, pulse quickening as I hit my circle and its energy flowed into me.

"We good?" I called. Trent had finally reached Lee, and the witch lifted a hand in acknowledgment as Trent helped him sit up against the wall. Lee had clamped a hand to his shoulder, the blood turning his black jacket shiny. Parker had bitten him. Savagely.

"Dust won't hold that together for long," Jenks said, and I noticed the odd matte dust coating Lee's fingers.

"Get back here!" Parker shouted, and my head whipped around. She'd returned to her human shift, utterly naked as she gestured for her pack. "I'm not leaving without him!"

*Trent?* I wondered in a pulse of fear. Did she think that I had given the ring to Trent? No wonder Lee had intervened. "Both of you stay down," I said as a siren's wail rose in the street below. Standing, I settled before them both, feet spread wide, the power of the ley line snarling my lifting hair. Jenks hovered beside me, making me feel invincible. "You got a problem with me, Parker? Deal with me, not my friends."

"Back off," Parker intoned as the few remaining pack members filed in beside her. "That mangy cur of a bastard is mine."

"Try it," Lee rasped, pale as he sat against the wall and held his shoulder.

"Ma'am," someone said, touching me, and I jumped, landing a spinning kick in his gut before I realized it was building security.

"Oh, crap on toast. I'm so sorry," I said as I helped him up, and he glared at me.

"Ma'am, leave the area. Let us do our job," he said.

"You bet. Give me a second to wrap things up," I said as I looked from the emergency exit to Trent and Lee. They'd be safe once past it, but for how long? Parker knew who the mage was. She wasn't leaving here unless it was in cuffs, and my gaze caught Trent's. "In three," I said, and Trent nodded.

"Two!" I continued, and Trent's wicked smile turned him into an elven warlord.

"One!" I shouted, yanking the building's security behind me.

*"Dilatare!"* I called, flinging an exuberant hand out as the energy flowing through me found direction, exploding in a wave of red-tinted force to spin the remaining Weres into the walls.

*"Elerodic!"* Trent shouted, and the overhead lights burst in a blinding flash. The building's security cowered with a yelp, but Lee watched, slumped against the wall with an odd expression of pain and satisfaction on his face. I thought it wonderful that even though we argued and messed with one another, if you hurt one, you hurt us all. *Lee tried to protect us,* I thought, all the more determined to bring Parker down.

"Parker!" I shouted across the narrow expanse as the last of her pack began to flee before the sound of I.S. sirens. Parker turned at my voice, hunched and angry.

Trent moved forward to stand beside me, unmoved and unafraid. Energy flicked about his fingers, sparks of it rubbing against my aura like a dangerous caress. His lips pressed into a line, and his green eyes fixed on her; he was clearly capable of defending himself.

"You sure you want to do this, Parker?" I said, power dripping from my hands to smolder against the matted carpet. *It needs to be replaced anyway.* But I wasn't going to throw the first punch. The building's security was watching, and I'd learned the hard way to take my licks before dishing them out. It kept me relatively free of lawsuits, and Trent appreciated that.

"Hands up!" an authoritative voice thundered. "You too, Morgan. Drop the ley line!"

*Crap on toast, it's the I.S.* I never took my gaze from Parker as the I.S. agents spilled in the fire exit and around the partition from the front room.

"Tink's a Disney whore," Jenks swore. "How did they get here so fast?"

"Grab her!" I yelped when Parker made a dive for the exit, and three I.S. agents scrambled to catch her, their motions too gentle because she was naked.

"Don't let her get away!" I exclaimed as she fought them off, her intent obvious: the rear balcony and its three-story drop. My breath caught as she wiggled free, and I threw myself at her, catching a heel as the naked woman found the balcony.

Outraged, Parker hit the floor and kicked at me. "Who gave you that ring? Who is the mage?!" I shouted as I struggled to get a hold on her.

"Stand down, Morgan!" someone bellowed as a heavy grip found my shoulder, and I let loose a blast of unfocused energy. The hand fell away, and Parker lurched to her feet.

"You are so stupid," Parker said with a sneer, and then she was gone, vaulting over the railing as if a soft pillow waited for her, not a three-story drop to the pavement.

"No!" Teeth clenched, I scrambled up as a metallic thump sounded, followed by a loud screech of a bus's brakes and hiss of air. Breathless, I lurched outside and to the railing.

"You think she meant to do that?" Jenks said as he hovered at my ear and gazed down.

Parker was flat on the pavement, a bus beside her. There was a telling dent in the roof where she'd hit, and the driver was getting out, clearly upset as he raced to her. Cars had stopped, and a few I.S. personnel were running over.

"Don't let her go!" I shouted, elbowing someone as they tried to drag me inside. "Cuff her!"

And then two big men spun me around.

"Get down there. Retain her for questioning," I said, ticked when neither of them moved. "I need to talk to her."

"Ma'am," one said, and my jaw clenched. One was a Were, the other a living vamp.

"He called you ma'am." Jenks snickered, then dropped into the street in case Parker regained consciousness before the I.S. could reach her.

"Don't ma'am me," I said in a huff. "I am Rachel Morgan. Get someone down there to apprehend Parker or get out of my way so I can."

Then I jumped when the vamp slapped a band of charmed silver on me and every ounce of ley line energy tingling through me vanished. "Hey!" I yelped, ticked. "Son of a troll turd, did you hear me identify myself?" I said, my bitchy hat firmly on my head. "I am Mr. Kalamack's security, and as such, I have not only the legal right, but the corresponding paperwork to do what I deem appropriate in a security situation. Take this off." I held out my arm. "Now."

"Yes, ma'am," the vamp said, and I stumbled when he shoved me inside and into an informal corral of detainees. It held mostly unhappy Weres, and I looked for Trent and Lee, finding them on the other side of the long lobby amid the paramedics and flustered staff.

"Excuse me," I said as I tried to get around the man barring my way, and he showed me his teeth, thinking it would cow me, but after having lived with Ivy, I was unimpressed. "Find someone who knows who I am. Is Doyle here?" Exasperated, I rose to my tiptoes. "Trent!" I shouted, then added, "You need to move," as I used one finger to try to push the I.S. agent out of my way. It didn't work.

Crap on toast, I had to trust that the I.S. was not going to let Parker get away, regardless if she was naked and knocked out. But Trent had heard me, and after giving Lee's shoulder a pat, he left him with the paramedics and went to talk to the I.S. agent in charge. Trent at least was being recognized, and after a word, the agent with him gave me a toothy grin.

"Hey! Mr. Kalamack says that's his security. Let her out of the pen."

I dropped down to my heels in relief. "I would have had her if not for you," I muttered as I held out my wrist and the I.S. agent before me clipped the zip strip off, but realistically? I wasn't about to jump three stories down.

"They got her," Trent said as he joined me, and I fought the urge to run downstairs and make sure of it. Jenks, too, seemed to think everything was under control, his dust a contented gold as he rose up to the ceiling to keep an eye on everything.

"Thanks. Are you okay?" I said as Trent's fingers laced in mine, stilling their tremors. "How is Lee?" I added, suddenly feeling as if I were twelve and had accidentally gone too far. Again.

"She *bit* me," Lee said in disgust as I knelt beside him. But he went pale when the tech cut his shirt free and the blood gushed.

"Okay, we're taking this one in," the man said to his partner, and they eased Lee down before one left to get the stretcher.

"Where's my bag?" I said, a sick feeling in the pit of my stomach. Lee was staring at the ceiling, breathing slow. "Where is my bag!"

"Ma'am?"

It was that same I.S. agent, and I took my bag, head down as I searched for a pain amulet.

"Lee?" I extended the already invoked amulet, and the tech tending him frowned. "It's just a pain amulet," I encouraged, more for the tech than him. "They won't give you anything stronger than an aspirin until you get to the hospital."

Ignoring the tech's grimace, Lee took it, fingers shaking. "Thank you," he said, his expression easing immediately. "You carry invoked pain amulets around with you?"

"Carry them?" Trent's light voice did a poor job of hiding his worry. "She makes them by the gross."

"Laugh it up," I said, my anxiety growing as the two paramedics loaded Lee onto the stretcher and raised it in an ugly, familiar sound. He was leaving, and I touched Lee's arm. "Lee, thank you. There aren't many people who would step between me and danger."

"You're welcome." Lee's grimace was pained as he held his shoulder. "Sorry I wasn't good enough."

"Your mistake was trying to take her on yourself," I said. "I think we could have done it together."

"Yeah," he rasped, looking all the more ill. "Sure thing."

"Rachel . . ." Trent said, his want to stay with Lee obvious.

Worried, I gave Trent an earnest hug. "Go," I said, feeling his loss already. "Give me your keys. I'll bring your car. I have Jenks with me. I'll be fine."

Trent's posture relaxed. "Thank you," he whispered as he drew his key fob from his pocket and handed it to me, distracted. "I'll text you when he's moved out of emergency."

"I'll try to find your coffee before I leave," I said as his hold on me tightened . . . eased . . . and fell away.

Without even a glance back, Trent broke into an enviable smooth jog to catch up to Lee. Doyle was doing his detective thing at the stairs, and he waved Trent through without having to see his ID. I probably wouldn't be as lucky. Though Doyle had helped me in the past, he was not above making my life difficult just for the fun of it. Sighing, I pulled my bag higher up my shoulder and started over. After a fall like that, they'd have to take Parker to the hospital before putting her into custody. Doyle would know where Parker was.

Which sort of begged the question, How had Parker known where I was?

# CHAPTER

# 20

IT WAS THE FOURTH TIME I'D BEEN AT THE HOSPITAL IN ONLY THREE days, but at least I was visiting, not a patient.

"Thank you," I said to the emergency room attendant as I took my bag from the belt and headed for the ID station, boots clunking.

"Relax, Rache," Jenks said, his small tugs on my hair annoying as he fought the snarls. "They're scanning for illicit medicinal spells, not high-density plastic."

"Yeah? Well the sleepy-time charms in the hopper aren't exactly innocuous." Sneaking in sleeping potions to avoid the "hospital tax" on the ones they provided was not uncommon, but it was the chakra curse ring that had me worried. But either the ring had pinged as uninvoked or the woman manning the spell check had recognized me.

Either way, I was past the first hurdle unchallenged, and I walked a little taller as I gave the man behind the counter my driver's license and smiled at the camera to get my temporary, time-and-date-stamped visitor tag. I'd half expected to be detained by some stiff, pencil-pushing accountant wanting to talk to me about what I'd done yesterday, but as a frustrated murmur grew the closer I got to the emergency waiting room, I decided they had more to worry about than four coma patients regaining consciousness under questionable circumstances.

"Wow." I halted just inside the large, multi-partitioned room with its people-filled chairs. TVs flickered soundlessly at the ceiling, and as I watched, an orderly wheeled a pained-looking man in street clothes out from triage and into the waiting room, parking him almost in the walkway. There wasn't anywhere else to put him.

"Minimal security," Jenks offered, and I sidestepped to get out of the wide doorway. It was the hospital's usual complement of two, one officer by the twin sliding doors leading to emergency drop-off and another standing almost next to me. The sound of the rain came and went as the wide doors opened and two more people came in, leaving wet footprints as they made a beeline to the reception desk. It was warm, and the damp air was beginning to smell like wet wolfsbane. Not surprisingly, seeing as the yellow chairs were full of heavily tattooed people carrying bags with the festival's logo.

I felt bad for the woman holding her blood-soaked arm, her husband coddling their fussy baby. Clearly she'd gashed her arm open in her panic to get out. A man at the triage overflow was complaining of ankle pain after tripping on the stairs. A third man was in the corner, his probable panic attack getting him whisked away to be checked for a serious heart problem.

The two nurses manning the admittance desk were busy handing out forms and directing the worst to immediate triage. I didn't see Trent, meaning he was likely already in a room with Lee here or the hospital itself, and, head down, I dug in my bag for my phone.

"Hi, Rachel," a familiar voice called before I could find it, and I turned to see Stef, looking capable in her red hospital scrubs. "Please tell me you aren't responsible for this?"

"Not this time." Jenks took to the air now that his wings were dry again.

"I thought you were working downstairs," I said as I leaned in to give her a quick hug. I was going to miss her when she left the church, but I totally understood. There was nothing there for her. Not really.

She shrugged, clearly pleased with herself as she eyed the chaos in the emergency waiting room. "I am," she said, then pulled me aside as an empty gurney came in. "But they ask me to help out up here when it gets busy. I heard you were bitten."

"Me? No," I said immediately. "It was someone else. I'm looking for Trent. He's okay, but he came in with a man named Lee Saladan."

"Let's find him." Stef rocked into motion, and both Jenks and I followed her to a smaller desk set to the side. The man behind it glanced at the OTHER WINDOW placard, then relaxed when Stef walked behind the counter and found a hospital tablet. "S-A-L-A-D-A-N . . ." she murmured, tapping the pop-up keyboard. "Got him. Mr. Saladan was treated for a severe Were bite, but he's got some movement issues so they took him in for a deeper scan." She set the tablet back on its charger. "Trent's probably still with him. Were bite, huh? Good thing you can't turn from that."

"Parker is a mean bitch," Jenks said, his dust now a bright silver.

"She doesn't fight fair, either," I added, grateful that Lee had tried to stop her. "Ah, speaking of which, the I.S. brought her here for treatment after she fled the scene and landed on a bus from a third-story balcony. Any chance you can get me in to see her?"

"The other half of this nightmare Oreo cookie?" Stef smirked. "I don't see why not. She's downstairs. I'll take you. We don't have a line painted on the floor for that."

"Downstairs?" I questioned, pushing forward to meet the woman's fast pace as she gave the security by the door a little wave. I lifted my hospital ID for him to see, but he didn't care, more concerned about the Weres collecting in a corner. "The undead's emergency facility? How bad was she hurt?"

"It's not how bad she's hurt. It's because she's the reason most of these people are here."

"Right." I reached for my phone, then thought better of it. "Jenks, could you find Trent and tell him I'm downstairs checking on Parker?"

"You got it, Rache." The pixy darted away, clearly glad for the excuse to snoop around.

"Oh, and tell him where I left his car!" I added loudly, since he was already halfway down the hall. I'd left the fob atop the visor, seeing as his car locked with a code, not a key.

"Yeah, yeah, yeah!" the pixy shouted, garnering surprised looks from those he passed.

"I've never been down to the undead's emergency department," I said as Stef and I started forward again. "I've seen their morgue, though. Is it nice?"

"It is, actually, and quiet right now." Stef stopped at an oversize elevator, the multitude of rings on the arch of her ear swinging as she hit the down button. "They have better security, not to mention a separate entrance/exit bay that isn't in use while the sun is up. Doyle insisted. Soon as they rule out a concussion, he's moving her to the I.S."

True, I'd hidden from the I.S. last night at Trent's, but Doyle hadn't given me any trouble at the festival, so why would he here? He wanted this settled as much as I did and would probably let me talk to Parker despite what his superiors wanted. I think. I had to find out who the mage was.

"Sorry for the wait. It's a dedicated elevator, but they keep it at the bottom," Stef said as she stared at the closed doors. I wasn't surprised. Most undead vampires were compliant, but if you got an ugly one and had to vacate the area, you didn't want to have to wait for the elevator.

Finally it dinged and opened, and we filed in. There was only one button, and Stef hit it. "So," I said as the doors closed and the faint scent of undead vampire tickled my nose. "You like working down here?"

"I do," she said immediately. "The regulars don't appreciate me, though."

"Your smut?" I questioned, and she shook her head.

"No. I'm not as fast as everyone else with casting spells, but I can hold tons more line energy than them, and management thinks I'll pick up what I need." A faint smile quirked her lips. "They call me baby witch."

Not exactly a nickname I would have appreciated, but she seemed happy as the big sliders opened and she strode confidently into a low-ceilinged walkway that smelled faintly of vampire and redwood.

Someone was shouting in the distance. Parker, probably. Other than that, it was calm down here, relaxed, and a little chilly. The walls were a warm taupe instead of white, and there was no scent of antiseptic. The hum of the fans exchanging the air was obvious, and everyone we met wore the same red scrubs that Stef had on. *The better to hide the blood, my dear. . . .*

It was clearly their slow time, as most undead accidents happened just after sunset. Still, I was impressed by the competency everyone showed as they prepped for the coming night.

"I need to clear you," she said as she angled us to a small counter, visibly shuddering as she stared at the classically handsome man behind it. He was an undead, and if he was working daylight hours, he had died young without the enormous fortune needed to "retire" comfortably.

"You okay?" I asked as her breath quickened.

Stef grinned. "There's not a word for what I am. That ID only works upstairs. Hang on a sec."

Clearly she wanted to talk to the man alone, and I went to sit at one of the indulgent waiting chairs. Stef greeted the man familiarly, the flat of her arms on the counter as she flirted. Yeah, I'd put up with a lot of hazing to work here, too.

"Hello," a soft voice said, and I whipped my head around to see a pleasant-looking woman in red scrubs standing before me. "Are you ready to go back?"

"Ah, sure," I said, standing up, my bag held tight to my middle. Stef was still busy with her conversation, but I could hear Parker screaming in the background. "Don't I need an ID?"

The woman glanced at her tablet. "Not for this."

*She's a witch,* I decided. And a damn fine one by the scent of redwood lifting from her. My aura was thickening as if in protection, and I stifled a shudder as our balances tried to equalize and I yanked my chi's energy where it belonged. Not only a witch, but a ley line specialist.

She must have felt it, because she sort of stiffened. "This way," she said warily, and I frowned at Stef, reluctant. But, deciding she might be a while, I took a large step to come even with the woman.

"Thanks," I said, feeling our energies rub each other wrong. "I appreciate you bending the rules like this."

"No, it's me who should be thanking you," she said, relaxing now that we were moving. "Speaking for the hospital, we really appreciate you coming in." The nurse made an abrupt left turn into a small room, and I slid to a halt, surprised. Parker was clearly a few doors down. "Have a seat," the nurse encouraged, her back to me as she rummaged in a drawer.

I cautiously went in, scanning what seemed to be a remote nurses' station. "Ah . . . I think there's been a mistake," I said as I saw the rows of bottles. They held auras. Not souls, but auras. I didn't even know you could do that.

"Your first time down here?" she said casually, and I stayed where I was, eyeing the comfortable chair with its ankle and wrist straps. As I watched, she lit a candle and spilled wax in an enviable smooth pentagram atop a small scrying mirror.

"Yes. Are those auras?"

Her head came up from her spell prep, and she nodded. "Pretty, aren't they. Go ahead and have a seat. It takes about five minutes. But we'd like you to stay for an additional fifteen to make sure your body reacts positively. Most people experience a slight dizziness is all. Is there someone who you'd like to credit your donation to?"

My lips parted. "Donation? You mean my aura?" I said as she took an empty bottle from a cabinet. "I'm not here to donate my aura. I didn't even know you could do that. I'm here to talk to Parker. That nutjob of a Were yelling at the end of the hall."

The woman—I wasn't going to call her a nurse anymore—seemed to hesitate. "You're with the I.S.?" she said, making me wonder if what she was doing was even legal.

"Not exactly," I said as Stef slid to a halt in the hall, her cheeks red in embarrassment.

"There you are," she said as she grabbed my arm and pulled me into the corridor. "I am so sorry, Dr. Ophees. She's not down here to donate. Rachel, here's your ID."

I took the more substantial card and looped the lanyard over my neck. Dr. Ophees put the bottle away, then used a huge knife to scrape the wax from the mirror. She looked peeved.

"Jeez, Rachel. I turned my back for five minutes," Stef said as we walked off.

I glanced over my shoulder at a sudden crash. *A little upset, are we?* "Is that legal?"

Stef's hold on me vanished. "Yes. Technically. Because it's voluntary. I'm so sorry. Ophees is kind of a jerk. More of a vampire than some vampires. But she's good at what she does. She was part of the group who pioneered the process to distill auras from blood. The blood goes upstairs for general use, the auras stay here for the undead, seeing as that's what they are really taking in when they drain a person. Ophees's spell is just about ready to go into clinical trials. If it clears the Federal Charm and Spell Association, we will have an amazing new tool to avoid unwanted early transitions to an undead existence, but we're looking at years right now."

*In a hospital setting? Does Vivian know about this?* "The only way I know how to take someone's aura is with illicit magic."

Stef winced. "Which is why it's experimental? She makes the spell, stores the auras, administers them. If not for her, Cincinnati would probably lose its A1 status of preventing accidental, unwanted transitions. She's saved countless lives."

*Unwanted transitions,* I thought sourly, peeking into an empty room being cleaned as we went past. That was polite speak for when a master vampire decided the law didn't pertain to him or her and drained someone. But I couldn't help but wonder if I could have saved Kisten if I had gotten him here fast enough.

"Get your bloody hell paws off me!" Parker shouted, and Stef stopped at a door. The color-coded placard to indicate the level of danger inside the room was green, but considering what they typically dealt with, green was probably appropriate.

"I'll stay with you," Stef said as she knocked and pushed open the door.

"Sure." I jerked to a halt, surprised when I nearly ran into a huge barrel of a man just inside the room. He glanced at my ID and lost interest. Stef barely got a sniff.

"You have no cause. I'm the victim!" Parker shouted, and I closed the door behind me as I took in the dim lighting, soothing colors, and the enormous soft chair they'd put her in. The straps were heavily padded to not leave any marks, but the Were was trying her damnedest to get free, her hair in her face and her hospital gown spotted with spittle.

"Hey, Doyle," I said, and the man's attention rose to me. "Thanks for bringing her in."

"Shut up! I want to talk to Morgan!" Doyle shouted at Parker, and the woman glowered, her bruised and road-rashed face ugly as she went silent.

Doyle smirked, his black eyes finding a rim of brown as he approached me. "It's easier subduing the badasses after they fall three stories onto a bus." His attention went to Stef, then me. "I'm surprised you're down here. Aren't you wanted for something?"

Nodding ruefully, I inched closer, hissing in sympathy as I looked Parker over. Her right arm was in a breakaway cast, and the tight wrapping peeping past her robe said her ribs had taken damage. The road rash went from her jawbone to her shoulder and beyond. In short, she was a mess. But she was not only alive but fighting, and that said a lot.

"I need to ask her a couple of things," I said, and Doyle's brow furrowed.

"So about that stunt of yours yesterday in the coma ward . . ."

I focused on Parker, pulse quickening. "Here I am. Ask me."

Doyle's arms went over his chest to make his biceps bulge. "It doesn't work like that."

I chuckled, thankful he wasn't trying to drag me into the I.S. I still had my late lunch appointment with Vivian. "I appreciate your discretion. Do you mind . . ."

I gestured at Parker, and the woman jerked against her bonds. "You are dead, Morgan!" she raged, and I sighed. "Dead! They can't hold me for assault, and when I get out of here, I'm going to shred you. Then I'm going to shred everyone you care about, starting with that elf!"

A twinge of worry rose, and I quashed it. "She can't shift, can she?" I asked, eyeing the breakaway cast. It was popular with the shape-shifting set in case of emergency.

Stef reached for Parker's chart. "Not at the moment. They pumped her full of hexabane."

"That bitch killed Walter!" Parker shouted. "Why are you detaining me? Arrest her!"

"I said, *shut up!*" Doyle bellowed, and Parker flung herself back into the cushions. "We're moving her out as soon as a van gets here," he added, softer. "Her finer muscle and bone tissues were still in flux from her last shift when she jumped, which evened out a lot of the damage. She's got a couple of bruised ribs, broken wrist, cracked collarbone." He sucked on his teeth, a faint hint of vamp pheromones rising. "Nothing that needs a hospital."

Parker sneered. "Your line ends with you, Morgan. You will have never existed."

"Probably," I said, having given up on the idea of children when I'd found out I was a demon. "But not at your teeth, and not today."

Frustrated, Parker spit at me. It fell short, and I took a breath to say something, changing my mind at the familiar sound of pixy wings.

"Hey, Rache," Jenks said as he came in, garnering suspicious looks from I.S. and hospital staff alike. "Lee's stuck in a hallway until they finish their tests. They aren't giving him a room. I'll take you to Trent when you're ready." Hands on his hips, he hovered before Parker, the angry woman watching him around her stringy hair. "You going to beat some information out of this scrotum sack of a Were first?"

"Try it," Parker taunted, and I turned to Doyle.

"Can I talk to her?" I asked. "She knows who has been spelling for Walter." But whether she would tell me hinged not only on her attitude but on whether she was under a no-divulge spell.

"Be my guest." Doyle gestured at Parker, the woman thrashing as Jenks dusted her. "But can I give you some advice? David Hue has this piece of work in a doggie bag already. You need to be more worried about the coven of moral and ethical standards."

Jenks's wing hum went silent. I glanced up, surprised at the concern in Doyle's eyes. "Tell me about it," I muttered. "I've got a meeting with Vivian

today, so if you could put off arresting me until after two, I'd appreciate it."
*Crap on toast, Trent won't be able to make it. . . .*

Doyle laughed at that, startling Parker into silence. But yeah, I'd stop
raving to hear his low voice rumbling about, too. "Well, Parker?" I said,
careful to not step in the wad of phlegm she'd spit out as I came closer.
"You want to make your I.S. stay easier? Get into a communal room with
a TV instead of a standard six by ten? Tell me who you've been getting your
illicit magic from. I might be able to convince Doyle that you're the victim.
The worst of the charges will fall to the practitioner, but I have to know
who it is for you to even have a chance."

"Seriously?" Parker laughed, the sound choking off as her ribs hurt,
and I looked at Stef.

"Is that the hexabane?" I asked, and Stef shook her head. *Why do they
always have to be dicks about it?* I wondered as Parker chortled as if I was
wearing a pink tutu on the bus. She might have the same no-divulge spell
on her, but I was willing to take that risk.

"Doyle, you want some coffee?" Jenks suggested, and Parker's expression emptied.

"Don't hurt me! Let go!" she suddenly shrilled, though I hadn't even
touched her. Shocked, I backed up as the door opened and a tight-lipped
nurse came in, his no-nonsense posture reminding me of my days in the
children's ward. "They're hurting me!" Parker screamed, dissolving into
sobs.

"Oh, that's as lame as a troll condom!" Jenks exclaimed, and Stef hid a
smirk.

*Damn, she's got to be hopped up on something,* I thought, my hands
high to prove I'd done nothing. But clearly Parker knew how to work the
system as the nurse pushed me to the edge of the room, his eyes pupil black
in threat.

"She's killing me," Parker sobbed as two more nurses came in, drawn
by the woman's distress where they had ignored her angry threats before.
"Please don't let her kill me!"

It must have been a trigger phrase, because they all fell into full mama-bear mode, two nurses making a living wall between us as a third soothed Parker, bathing her face with damp cloth. *Oh, for sweet troll turds on a stick,* I mused when Parker winked at me.

"Honey, I haven't even started killing you," I said, and the nurses between us bristled.

"We don't do that here," one said, and Doyle rubbed his temple.

"Accidents happen," I offered, but they had no humor, and one pointed at the door.

"She's right," Doyle said as he took my elbow. "They don't hurt people *here.*"

Jenks snickered at where he'd put the emphasis. Parker, too, heard it, and her confidence faltered. A garbled conversation on a handheld told me her van had arrived. "Hey, can Jenks and I bum a ride to the I.S.?" I asked, and Doyle's grin widened. "I can't stay because I'm meeting Vivian, but I can do a lot on the way in." The thought to stand Vivian up was fleeting. I wouldn't give the coven the fuel to burn me at the stake.

"What an intriguing idea." Doyle's chin lifted to acknowledge the I.S. crew coming in, bulky in their anti-charm gear. "I'd appreciate the chance to ask her a few questions in a more informal setting as well." He hesitated. "I'll drive you to your appointment with Ms. Smith myself."

"Don't let them take me!" Parker shouted as new cuffs were attached and the gentle, padded bindings were taken off. "They'll kill me! Please. No!"

"Dumbass," Jenks said, once again safely on my shoulder as a doctor came in.

The woman was a living vampire, and she stood toe-to-toe with Doyle, her lips in a hard line. "I am not releasing her if you are going to hurt her."

"Asylum!" Parker shouted as if it was a real thing. It wasn't. "I claim asylum!"

"Doctor, the last thing you want is Parker in your care," Doyle said as his men began to strap her into a wheelchair. "She is the probable cause of the misery upstairs, but as she is only a suspect, she will be treated with the utmost care. That's why we brought her here—to make sure she was okay. Is she fit for travel?"

Jenks's wings tickled my neck as the doctor on call turned to Parker. The woman had finally shut up, her eyes holding hope.

But the doctor was used to dealing with the undead, who lie, and cheat, and manipulate more than they need blood, and finally she reached for the tablet to sign Parker over. "She's yours," she said, and Parker began shouting again.

"You think you could sedate her a little?" Doyle asked, and after a dismissive glance, the doctor nodded, pissing Parker off even more. "Not heavy. I need her to be able to talk."

Satisfied, I leaned against a wall as one of the nurses went to a drawer and filled a syringe. Stef came forward, her eyes wide. "Wow," she said as too many people fought to get Parker locked into a wheelchair. "You had me scared. I half believed you'd really hurt her."

"Right," I said, and Jenks made an odd snort from my shoulder, making me wonder if he had begun to rub off on me. Three years ago, I'd never think of hurting someone for information, but now? I'd found out it was far easier to live with the knowledge that I'd hurt someone than to live with the pain of someone dying because I hadn't.

Doyle took control of Parker and pushed her out into the hall. Her swearing began to go faint, and as the room emptied, I lingered, wanting to call Vivian.

"I should get back to work," Stef said as I found my phone at the bottom of my shoulder bag. "See you both at home?"

"Absolutely," I said, and she gave me a little grin before pacing to the front desk, her arms swinging confidently.

Parker was already in the elevator, not the one that went up to the mundane emergency floor, but the other at the far end of the hall that serviced the undead's emergency drop-off. It would be empty this time of the day, and they could whisk Parker to the I.S. before the news van even knew she was moving. The infuriated woman was still shouting through the sedative, and Doyle stuck a hand out and stopped the doors from closing. "Coming?"

I waved for him to go ahead. "Have to make a call," I said, and he let the doors shut.

"Trent?" Jenks guessed, and I shook my head.

"Vivian," I answered, and the pixy's wings went still. Vivian, though, wasn't answering, and I sighed when her voice told me to leave a message.

"Hi, Vivian." I decided to take the stairs. Less chance of dropping her call. *Probably.* "Ah, I had an issue at the festival," I said as I yanked the door open and started up. "I might be a few minutes late. Um, I'm really sorry about this," I added, my voice echoing. As busy as I was, she had a tighter schedule than me. "Go ahead and order the BLT for me. Trent won't be joining us, but I'll have Jenks. I'll call if we're going to be any later than a few minutes."

"Yeah, she won't mind waiting," Jenks said, and I felt myself warm.

"Not a word," I said as I closed my phone out and pushed the fire door open. But my quick pace faltered when two big orderlies ran past, almost knocking me into the wall.

"Close that bay door!" Doyle shouted from the undead's emergency drop-off, and I bolted forward. "Get down! Get down!"

*Son of a pup,* I thought, remembering the number of Weres lurking in the emergency waiting room. "Move!" I shouted, pulling heavily on the ley line as I shoved through the fleeing people. Alarms were going off, and I tripped, barely catching myself before hitting the floor. Jenks took to the air, and, flustered, I staggered forward.

A group of ragtag Weres was rolling Parker across the huge underground garage to the steep exit ramp. The rain had finally quit, and the sun pouring in through the opening was almost blinding as the wet pavement scattered the light. I squinted, trying to see. Doyle was picking himself up off the pavement, but three other I.S. agents were down and not moving.

"They got a van outside!" Jenks shrilled, and I ran forward. "She's getting away!"

"Not this time," I whispered, and, pulling hard on the lines, I imagined an enormous protection circle, one that would encase the fleeing Weres. *"Rhombus!"* I exclaimed, setting the rim of it just in front of Parker.

The Weres ran right into it, yelping in fear. Parker's chair tipped, spilling the shrieking Were onto the pavement. One of her ankles was still strapped to the chair, and she fought to be free of it.

"Hey! You!" I shouted as I let the circle drop, and both Doyle and Parker turned, one in hope, the other, hate.

"Stay out of it, Morgan!" Doyle yelled, gesturing for me to retreat, but I stomped forward, intent on bringing the grinning woman in. She was absolutely crazy, shoving at the people trying to uncuff her, nothing but the thin fabric of a hospital gown between her and the filthy pavement.

But my expression emptied and I slid to a halt when the woman raised her arm, aiming her shaking fist at me. "She's got a ring!" Jenks shrilled.

*"In articulo mortis!"* Parker shouted, and I dove to the side as a green bolt shot from the ring on her Jupiter finger. For one glorious moment I thought she had missed, but as I hit the ground, a sharp pain cramped my foot.

"No!" I exclaimed, butt on the cold concrete as I panicked, staring at the green haze enveloping my foot. But I hadn't fallen unconscious, and I sat there, not believing it as the spell spent itself and the captive mystics found release.

*"In articulo mortis!"* Parker shouted again, and I jerked, my skin tingling as another bolt of green shot from her to thump into an advancing I.S. agent. He went down, not even shaking.

I looked at my tingling foot, pulse hammering. Clearly the second ring worked, so why hadn't it worked on me?

*It's because I'm holding its twin,* I thought as my side cramped with cold and I took out the old ring, my hand shaking. *Oh, you're in trouble now. Rhombus,* I added as I put the ring on and stood, filled with a new purpose.

And then I freaked as my circle didn't form. I slid to a frightened halt, scrambling for cover as Parker laughed and took out two more I.S. agents. I felt betrayed—the ley line was gone—and then I realized what had happened. It wasn't the ring or Parker's spell. My first, multiple-story circle had tripped the hospital's security system.

"Jenks, I got no line!" I shouted as I yanked my bag around to find my splat gun. The charms were earth-magic based, not ley line. They'd still work. That I couldn't be downed by that damn ring had given me strength. The mage must have tricked someone into making a new ring. Clearly the rescuing Weres must have given it to Parker, as Doyle would have had her searched, naked or not. That someone had died making it made me feel sick.

"Stop! You can't fight this! Jenks, tell them to stand down," I called, and Jenks made a swooping arch over to Doyle hiding behind an over-turned gurney.

Parker was still laughing hysterically, whatever sedative they had given her making her more erratic than she already was. Shaken, I gazed across the nearly empty drop-off garage to Doyle. The man was clearly pissed, but he was listening to Jenks. His head swiveled to me, and I frantically waved him to stay put.

"I need backup in here. Now!" he bellowed, and frustration filled me as more I.S. agents began darting in from all sides, organizing as Parker was dragged to her feet by two Weres.

"I want Morgan dead," Parker snarled as more Weres converged on her, all of them trying to get her to the van at the top of the ramp. "The one who kills her becomes my second."

*Great.* I gave Doyle a disgusted look. So much for I.S. efficiency. I had my splat gun, but she had a chakra curse and clearly knew how to use it.

*"Now!"* Doyle exclaimed as he launched himself from behind the crash cart.

"No, wait. Doyle!" I watched in horror as eight agents rushed Parker. But their vampiric speed and outright cheek stunned the Weres struggling with her, and she only got one curse off before the rest slammed into the tight knot about her.

Like a Titan among lesser men, Doyle waded into the fray, flinging the Weres aside as if they were rugs to be shaken. A cry of success left him as he snagged Parker's heel and dragged the woman out from under two other agents. His face alight, he practically sat on her, holding her fisted hand in his so she couldn't use the ring.

Jenks's wings rasped as he hovered beside me. "I told him you had the cure. She can't curse them all at once, and he thought the risk was good."

"That doesn't mean the coven will allow me to use it," I said, and his satisfaction dulled. "Doyle?" I came out from behind the ambulance, figuring it was probably over.

But Parker's loud shouts hadn't gone unheard, and more Weres were coming in from the parking lot, their silhouettes sharp in the bright patch of sun at the top of the ramp. Doyle might have her, but he was badly outnumbered. *You are not slipping me again,* I thought as I jogged forward, jerking at the pop of a conventional gun.

*Oh, come on!* I thought as I slipped and went down. Again a gun fired, and I rolled under a second ambulance, squinting when the chipped pavement peppered me. "Doyle?" I shouted, hearing him yelling. "Jenks, stay clear!"

"Like hell I will," the pixy said, and my hand went to my mouth. The incoming Weres had Doyle down, but he was still fighting. Eyes narrowed, I rolled out from under the ambulance and strode forward, shooting my spell pistol at anything that moved.

"She's got a splat gun!" someone yelled, and I took him out. Arms stiff, I continued to pick them off as I advanced. I was vulnerable without the ley line, but I was so pissed I didn't care. The scruffy Weres predictably scattered, dragging Parker away amid her demands they turn and fight.

"Get her," Doyle groaned from the pavement as the Weres ran for the entrance.

There was nothing left to shoot at but vanishing heels, and I dropped to Doyle as the van's engine turned over, sounding like thunder in the low-ceilinged garage.

"Three o'clock!" Jenks shrilled, and I spun, still crouched, picking off two more Weres before they could reach the van. Parker, though, was already in it, and I knelt beside Doyle as the van raced for the street, tires squeaking on the wet crosswalk paint as it bounced free.

I.S. agents were picking themselves up, assessing their failure. "You okay?" I said as Doyle groaned and rolled to his hands and knees, his hands in a fisted frustration.

"Rache, he don't look so good," Jenks said.

"Detective?" I said, hand extended as Doyle collapsed to roll over onto his back, one hand tight about his middle. His eyes were closed and blood was leaking past his fingers.

"You've been knifed!" I said, and his eyes opened, utterly black and glazed with pain.

"Put that circle up, Morgan!" he demanded, clearly in agony.

Pulse fast, I swung my bag around and searched for an amulet. His ability to change pain to pleasure had been overwhelmed. He was in trouble. "She's gone, and I can't," I said as I looped the amulet's lanyard around his neck. "Hospital security shut me down. How bad is it?"

Doyle was silent, and, brow furrowed, I pulled his hand from his middle to see. Blood gushed, and I felt myself go white. "Holy shit," Jenks whispered, then darted away.

"Man down!" I shouted, pressing my hand atop Doyle's in panic. "I've got a deep knife wound. I need some help! Now!"

I looked up, my hands slippery and warm. People were beginning to filter in, and I pressed harder, not liking how still he had become. "Doyle? Stay with me. Jenks went for help. Don't you dare close your eyes!" I threatened, and his eyes flashed open, black and scary.

"What are you doing?" he said, voice flat. "Go after her."

*Oh, shit. He didn't just die, did he?* I wondered. "She's gone, and I'm not leaving you until someone gets here," I said, and then I was pushed away by two paramedics. I stumbled to my feet, hair in my eyes as my hands went cold in the breeze from the entrance. They were red, and I stared at them as the two women began a fast triage, voices terse.

"Is he going to be okay?" Jenks asked. Doyle was trying to sit up even as the paramedics were forcing him down, and my worry grew.

"Rachel?" Doyle called, a slight quaver to his voice giving me hope he was still alive. Arm shaking, he raised his hand as the paramedics tried to get him to lie still. There was a bloody wad of something in it. "Find her," he said, and I realized he was holding a mass of bloodied hair. "Time and materials," he added, and I leaned forward to take Parker's hair, ripped from her skull.

"Deal," I said as I held the ugly mess up in my hand, and he grinned—until his expression went slack and he fell unconscious.

"Is he alive?" I asked, and one of the paramedics nodded. "Good." Finding my feet, I looked at my bloodied hands . . . and smiled. Vivian wanted a peek at my life? That was exactly what she was going to get.

But maybe I should clean up first.

# CHAPTER

# 21

"I DON'T THINK MORE DUST WILL HELP," I SAID AS I CAUGHT SIGHT OF my blurry image in the walls of the elevator, and the pixy hovered, his expression serious in scrutiny.

"Meh," he said noncommittally, then darted forward, dusting me anyway.

Trent's apartment was a scant two stories down from the world-class restaurant that spun at the top of Carew Tower, but unless I wanted to make the trip in the dumbwaiter, I needed to go down to the tenth floor and grab a public elevator to reach it. It was something I was sure that Trent would put some thought, if not money, into.

But the up and down elevators aside, even I had to admit that the ten-minute walk from the I.S. tower to Trent's unfinished apartment had been far easier than taking a cab across the river to the church and back. I was lucky, really, that I'd left both books in Trent's unfinished study this morning.

Unfortunately, not going to the church meant I was *still* in the same clothes I had on yesterday. Two showers without product or charms had left my hair totally out of control. I could undo the new, flyaway-ridden braid Jenks had put it in and let the thing halo, or leave it as it was, staticky and falling apart. I went for falling apart, as the alternative would be really scary.

"This isn't going to go well," I whispered as I hoisted my book-heavy shoulder bag higher up my shoulder.

"Rache, ain't no one up there that is going to know what's in your bag."

"It's not the books I'm worried about," I muttered as I glanced at the curse ring on my finger. Now that I knew it blocked the curse, I wasn't going to take it off until I recovered its twin. Either Vivian would believe me when I said it was set for the cure, or she wouldn't. I was betting she would, but there'd be another coven member with her, a complete unknown, seeing as Vivian was the only member left from the original group. You couldn't retire from the coven of moral and ethical standards, but you could take disability. Apart from Vivian, the few members who had survived trying to best the demon Ku'Sox had done just that.

"I don't know why you're worried," Jenks said, wings humming as he came to rest on my shoulder. "It's not as if you dress like a hooker anymore."

"It's not my clothes," I said, and Jenks made a scoffing snort. "Okay, maybe some, but how smart is it bringing two demon tomes into Carew Tower's restaurant?" Exhaling in resignation, I glanced at my phone for the time as the doors slid open and the soft, peppy eighties-gone-classical spilled in. *Five minutes late. Not bad.*

That Parker was on the loose with a new chakra curse ring was more than worrisome, and I was going to ask Vivian if she had the time to come with me once I primed the finding amulet to Parker's blood. *You want transparency, here it is,* I thought as the elevator dinged and the doors opened.

Taking a deep breath, I strode out of the small elevator and into a disappointingly dull afternoon, the skies heavy with clouds. The host stand decorated in autumnal shades of silk was at the unmoving center, as was the bar, and I scanned the ring of empty tables with their tiny pumpkins and fake oak leaves, slightly queasy though they were hardly moving. The bar was unstaffed at this hour, and I didn't see Vivian. Cincinnati was a short arc past the daily cleaned windows. But the Ohio River and the Hollows beyond were the real view, beautiful this time of year with the yellows and oranges of the surrounding hills despite the rain.

"Do you see them?" I asked, and Jenks made a noncommittal "mmmm."

I checked my phone for an incoming message. Nothing. I'd texted Trent before I'd jumped into the shower, warning him that Parker had a new ring and asking him to alert Ellasbeth and Quen. For once, I was glad he was with Lee, safely out of harm's way, and I twisted my pearl ring once around my finger, my worry easing at its warm, pale glow.

Glenn, too, had gotten a call. I'd had to leave a message, as he'd been out. Not surprising, since he was working nights. He could tell me if any high-end magic users had been reported as missing, possibly tricked into killing themselves to make that second chakra ring.

David, at least, had responded to my warning, sending me a cool-shades icon. Cool shades. He was being overly confident, but that's what an alpha was. Yes, Parker was pretty well beat up after falling onto a bus, and then whatever damage she sustained at the parking garage, but she was vicious. I had to find out who the mage was. Until I did, David had a big target on his tail.

The woman polishing silverware finally noticed me, wiping her hands on the hem of her black, somewhat skimpy uniform as she came forward with a bland smile. They weren't busy at this hour, and I was messing with her groove.

"Do you have a reservation?" she said pleasantly enough, but I felt myself warm as she eyed my jeans and casual top. And then her expression went positively frozen when she noticed Jenks. *Crap on toast, they know it's me.*

"Ah, it's under Vivian Smith. We're a little late," I said, shifting to hide my books.

Jenks lifted from my shoulder, clearly not liking how she'd looked at him. "We had to kick some fool Were's butt first," he said, making what was probably a Herculean effort to clean up his language.

"We have you over here." The woman hesitated briefly before taking three menus and stepping onto the revolving ring.

I followed, wincing at Jenks's heavy dust. The view was stunning and the colors vivid with the cold, gray river cutting through them, but I was more interested in the people, and I looked for spies amid the well-dressed men and women here for the view as much as the food.

"Is this suitable?" the woman said as she gestured at a small round table for four, and I nodded. Vivian wasn't here yet.

"Fine, thanks," I said as I settled myself so that I'd be moving forward, not back. The host was lingering, and, realizing she was serving double duty, I added, "Ah, can I have a coffee? Oh, and some distilled water."

"Distilled?" she questioned as Jenks settled himself on an overturned coffee cup.

"No added anything for flavor. Jenks, do you want a honey stick or peanuts?"

"Coffee. Black," he said, and the woman nodded, not bothering to write anything down. "And one of those lavender-infused honey sticks," he added.

"Coffee for two, distilled water, and a honey stick," she said as she began to gather the redundant place setting, startled when I grabbed the water glass right out from under her reach.

"I'm going to need that," I said, and to her credit, her expression never shifted as she turned and walked away, stepping up to the bar as soon as she could.

Jenks immediately abandoned his perch, flitting over the table to check everything out before landing beside the unlit candle. "You warm enough?" I asked, and his wings rasped.

"Don't turn into my mother, Rache," he said as he tugged a corner of the linen napkin up and used it to polish his sword.

My lips quirked, and with a small thought, I lit the candle with a whispered word. We were right next to the window, and it was drafty.

"Thanks," he said, dragging the napkin over to it and sitting with his back to the warming glass. He looked like a gang member in his working black silk and red bandana, his focus distant on the view to make me wonder if he had something on his mind. Getty, maybe?

"It's not like Vivian to be late," I said as I found my phone and texted her that I was at the restaurant and asked her if she wanted me to order for them. Setting my phone on the table, I bowed my head over my bag, pushing past the demon books for the zippy bag I'd gotten out of the trash at Trent's apartment. Parker's bloody hair was in it, rinsed but not spellworthy clean. I'd been in a hurry, and the only salt in his apartment had been in tiny takeout envelopes.

I had everything I needed to make a second finding charm, and I found the package of unprimed amulets, glad now that I'd left them in there. *Glows green when near subject. For use with blood, hair, sputum, or urine,* I read, satisfied the DNA-based charm would work with what I had. I'd have to remove every evidence of Doyle's blood from it first, though.

"Would you like cream or milk with your coffee?" the host asked, startling me.

My attention snapped up, and Jenks snickered when I drew my bag shut, hiding everything. "Ah, no thank you." The clatter of porcelain and the scent of rich coffee were soothing. She'd brought the entire carafe and a tiny espresso cup for Jenks. It was a nice gesture, even if it was still too heavy for him to lift. But my smile fell when I realized my mug had the same emblem as the one I'd drank hot cider out of last night. Trent was safe. I had to believe it.

The woman set down an unopened bottle of water. "Can I get you anything else?"

My phone dinged, and I glanced at it before setting it facedown on the table. "Ah, the rest of our party is on their way. Can I put in an order for two BLTs, a large Cobb salad, and a plate of fries?" I asked, and she nodded.

"I'll let your server know," she said, and then she was gone, her pace fast as she made a beeline to the bartender prepping for tonight.

"Jenks?" I hesitated as I poured myself a cup of dark brew. "I want you to stay home tonight when I go out to find Parker."

The pixy looked up from his honey stick. He'd already stabbed it with his garden sword, and the chopsticks he'd taken from his back pocket were unmoving. "It's not that cold."

I hid behind the cup, taking a quick sip. "Did you see the forecasted lows?"

Angular face tight, Jenks pulled a strand of honey from the punctured stick, spinning it madly until he had a wad. "I know how to take care of myself."

"Obviously." I flipped my phone over, checked the time, and then flipped it back. I had so much to do today, and here I was, cooling my heels waiting for Vivian. "I don't want to put you in a place where you have to choose between safety and your job," I added, and he seemed to lose some of his annoyance.

"I'll be fine," he said, giving me a grimace before licking the honey off the sticks. "Tink's titties, dis is good stuff," he slurred. That quick, he was halfway to being honey drunk, but it would vanish as fast as it hit him, and my fingers drummed on the table. Vivian was at least ten minutes out. I could do a lot in ten minutes.

Eyebrows high, I took the package of unprimed amulets from my bag and smoothed out the printed instructions. It was pretty basic stuff. "Yeah, I have time," I whispered, and, deciding to have at it, I cracked the bottle of water and poured it all into my extra water glass. The top to the salt-shaker ground as I took it off, and I heard a gasp from the bar as I dumped it into the water.

Wings high, Jenks slumped against the candle, giggling at the shadows his feet made on his tiny cup. "Whatcha doing?" he slurred.

"Using my day to its best advantage," I said, glad now that Doyle had agreed to time and materials. I wouldn't be able to get lunch past him, but with a post-use warrant, the finding charm would be legal now. I dipped my pinky in to taste my makeshift bath, then snagged the shaker from the nearest table and emptied that one, too. A third shaker I kept, warming at the buzz of muffled outrage from the bar as convention warred with the-customer-is-always-right.

*It's not as if you're busy,* I thought as I stirred it with a spoon, bringing the salinity up to that of the ocean and taking the anti-tarnish spell off the silver flatware at the same time. It was perfect, or perfect enough, and I warmed in embarrassment as I teased a wad of black, tap-rinsed hair out of the zippy bag and dropped it into the makeshift salt bath. A tiny rill of red spilled down to stain the water, and I gave the ugly mass a quick swirl to speed things up.

Ignoring the conversation at the bar, I dribbled the last of the salt into a pentagram and set the unprimed amulet into its center cave.

Jenks had begun to snore as I drew the black hair out of the salt bath, coiling it into a thimble-size wad before drying it between the folds of a bleached linen napkin. This was a little loose for me, but prepackaged charms were known to be forgiving. Pulse fast, I set the cleaned hair on the de-spelled spoon and set it over the candle flame, then tipped it to let a strand catch fire.

With a whoosh, the entire wad went up.

"Rhombus," I whispered to snare the foul smoke. The comments from the bar were getting louder, and I hoped that Vivian's reputation would keep them back.

The hair burned too slowly for my liking, and I finally had to use a napkin to insulate my fingers holding the spoon before the hair in my makeshift crucible sputtered and went out.

"Ma'am."

I glanced up, beaming at the woman facing me. She had to be the manager, her black jacket and long pants decidedly more professional than the catch-a-mate outfits everyone else was wearing. "It's for Vivian Smith," I lied. "I was supposed to have this done before our meeting. You know, the coven of moral and ethical standards?"

"I know who Ms. Smith is, and I know who you are," the woman said, her gaze touching on Jenks as he rolled over into a tiny ball, snoring. "I'm not going to have a repeat of what happened last year. Put out the spell, or leave."

"Oh, God. Please don't ban me," I said as I tapped the ash onto the amulet. "Trent will never forgive me."

The woman pressed her lips together. "I'm well aware Mr. Kalamack bought the building, but he didn't buy us. Put it out."

"Yes, ma'am." Smiling, I snapped open a finger stick and jabbed myself.

"Morgan," the woman intoned as I quickly squeezed three drops of blood atop the ash.

"Absolutely. Putting it out," I said, tightening my grip on the ley lines.

She felt it, and as she stupidly reached for the amulet, I finished the spell. *"Inveniet quod quisque velit,"* I whispered, and she jerked her hand away as the amulet flared a startling green, immediately fading to a steady, neutral red. *It worked!*

"Morgan," she protested, and I snatched the amulet up, feeling the magic grow and strengthen as it came within my aura.

"I'm done," I said as I stuffed it in my bag and out of sight. *Each shall find what he desires,* the invocation phrase promised, and I quickly dropped the spoon in the water glass. It was a sooty black, and the manager frowned. "I'll pay for the damages," I added, one hand brushing the salt from the pentagram into my other. "But really, it only needs a good polish, and maybe renew the anti-tarnish spell."

Her eyebrows high, the woman took the candle and water glass with the spoon. "This is a restaurant," she said, lips tight as Jenks woke up, his protesting words an unrecognizable slurring. "Not a spell lab."

She clearly wanted to replace the setting, and I nodded, taking up first Jenks and then my phone as the woman behind her pulled up the corners of the tablecloth and, in a clattering of dishes, walked off as if she was Father Christmas in reverse. *Huh,* I mused as I saw the bare wood and the anti-spill hex engraved on the top. *The things you learn.* "Sorry," I said with Jenks squirming in my hand. "I won't do it again."

The manager's up-and-down gaze over my casual clothes made me cringe. "Rush her order. I want them out ASAP," she said as two of the staff descended on the table to cover the hex and quickly reset the plates and silverware. A third brought me new coffee, and as I sat and held a sleeping pixy in my hand, I snuck a peek at the finding amulet.

It was a faint red, not a hint of green. I'd have to drive it around the city and hope it pinged on Parker before she did something stupid.

"What am I doing in your hand?" Jenks said, his voice steady, and I shifted my hand to the table and opened it. The pixy eyed me, wings sifting an odd, almost clear dust as he jumped to the table. "Tink's a Disney whore, did I throw up?" he added, noticing the candle was not the one he had fallen asleep against.

"No, they caught me stirring a spell," I admitted, and Jenks sat cross-legged by my warm mug. Together we silently looked out onto Cincinnati and the Hollows beyond.

Vivian should be here by now, and, nervous, I resettled my bag on my lap. If I was lucky, a quick show-and-tell and a formal statement that I had been used by Hodin might be enough. I was actively trying to make reparations, ensuring the victim's care in the interim. It had to count for something that I'd broken the chakra curse. Didn't it?

"Who am I kidding?" I whispered. Vivian had been angry that I'd broken it without her present, but for little green apples, what was I supposed to do? Let the man die?

"Your phone is going to ring," Jenks said, his gaze fixed upon the distant spire of our church, and I reached for it as it hummed.

"You know that's as creepy as all hell, right?" I said, and he shrugged, his wings sifting a melancholy blue dust.

But it wasn't Vivian. It was David. "Hi, David," I said, not putting him on speaker. The staff thought I was uncouth as it was. "I'm glad you called. Soon as I finish with Vivian, you want to drive me and Jenks around to find Parker? I've got an amulet primed for her. Doyle pulled a mess of hair—"

"It's me," Cassie said, and my smile vanished. *Why is Cassie using David's phone?*

"Cassie? Is David okay?" I asked, and Jenks was suddenly wide-awake.

"I don't know!" the clearly frustrated woman shouted. "We got word of a pack mob forming at Eden Park Overlook, and when I went to get my gun from his safe, he left. Took the car and *left me*. I am *not* a glass doll!"

"How long ago?" I said, stiffening. "Cassie, how long ago!"

"Five minutes, maybe," the distracted woman said. "I'm waiting for my ride. Rachel, it's Parker. I know it. And if she's got another one of those rings . . ."

*Damn it, did I just get myself banned from the tower restaurant for no reason?* "Cassie, I'm like ten minutes from Eden Park," I said, wishing I could line jump. "Maybe five if I can find a Were cabdriver."

"Thank you," she whispered, voice distant. "He won't ask for help."

A rueful smile quirked my lips. "He wouldn't be an alpha if he did. I'll be right there. If you get there before me, tell him not to do anything stupid."

The call clicked off, and I quickly flipped to Vivian's icon, my thumbs hitting the wrong keys as I typed. "Had to go. David in trouble. I'll show you the books when I get done."

"Two BLTs, a Cobb salad, and a plate of fries," a dry voice said, and I looked up into the forced-pleasant face of the manager.

"Ah, I'm going to need one of those BLTs and fries to go."

# CHAPTER
# 22

"AS CLOSE AS YOU CAN, THANKS," I SAID, MY HEAD DOWN OVER THE finding amulet showing the first signs of green as I sat in the back of the cab. We were almost there, and I could hear the bullhorns already. "Jenks, if it gets cold, you're in the bag," I added.

"Yeah, yeah, yeah." Jenks spilled a bright silver dust as he sat in his usual spot on the rearview mirror, holding the stem for balance. The cabdriver had been sneaking glances at him from the moment we'd gotten in, silent as Jenks checked his sword, took off his red bandana, turned his jacket inside out to protect the embroidery, and generally got ready to work.

"I'm not kidding," I said. "Give me some indication that you agree, or I'm going to spell you and put you in there now."

Jenks's dust went red, and it made the speakers hiss when it hit the dash. "You do, and I'll pee in your coffee every morning until the day I die."

"Which might be today, if you freeze to death."

The cabbie snickered, steeling his face into a bland nothing when Jenks hummed his wings. "You got something to say, Mr. Peabody?"

The man—a Were, actually, as most of Cincy's cabbies were—found my eyes through the mirror. "You're Rachel Morgan, aren't you. The runner? No one else works with a pixy."

It hadn't really been a question, and I dropped the amulet to feel for the outlines of my splat gun through my bag. "What if I am?"

"Nothing." His gaze flicked to Jenks, giving him a respectful nod. "But if you were, I'd tell you that you're doing the right thing." He turned the wheel and pulled to the curb. "I can't get any closer. Sorry."

I frowned out the side window, suddenly reluctant. We were at the commons, the strip of town houses looking onto the open green space that dropped gently to the Twin Lakes Footbridge and the overlook beyond. It was usually a pleasant place to play Frisbee or have a sunny picnic, but now? It was a mess, the open space filled with angry people. Buses and cars lined the one-way drive all the way to the lookout. Hastily made, hand-lettered signs had been raised as if it was a primary, each one with a different pack tattoo on it to collect everyone in their factions.

Feeling the crush already, I hung the finding amulet around my neck.

"You going to keep wearing it?" Jenks asked, but he was looking at the chakra ring on my finger, not the amulet, and I nodded, thinking it worth the risk. Yes, it had been made with dark magic and could, in theory, be used that way again, but it also blocked Parker from simply cursing me, and I wasn't going to give it up.

"Only you and I know what it is," I said as I made a fist. "Thanks for the ride," I added as I reached for my wallet.

"Hey, is that Mrs. Sarong?" Jenks said, and I winced, recognizing the short woman with her small, pale features and wisps of gray in her otherwise jet-black hair. The owner of the Hollows baseball team was an island of class amid the chaos, her bevy of pretty boys keeping everyone back. Mrs. Sarong had never liked me after I magicked her field to force her to make good on an agreement, and I wasn't sure which side of the Parker fence she might be on. She hadn't had any beef with David, but the slim older woman *had* sided with Constance to kill me not four months ago in the name of keeping the peace. It hadn't even been a real game, either.

"And the news vans," I said with a sigh. They'd pulled up right onto the grass. Grimacing, I opened my wallet. There were two nervous people with a tiny dog waiting, their intent obvious.

"No charge." The cabbie cleared his meter, grinning. "I like the way things are. Hue is a good alpha. You're going to help him, right?"

I reached for the door. "If he lets me. Thank you."

The noise hit me as I got out, a low thrum that went to the pit of my soul—like fear given sound. I took a breath, jerking out of the way when the people with the dog rushed the car, diving in to claim it before slamming the door shut. "Thanks!" I said again, and the cabbie waved out the window as he drove off. Humans. What were they thinking, trying to walk their dog in this?

"Hey, Jenks," I said as a wizard-painted van took the cab's place and eight heavily tattooed people piled out. "Can you find David or Cassie for me in this?"

"On it," he said, darting straight up into the late, cloud-ridden afternoon.

It was windy, and I pulled my jacket closer as I took a moment to shoot David—or Cassie, maybe—a text that I was here. I felt alone as I stood on the sidewalk, out of place amid the tattooed, pierced, leather-wearing people. You could still move down here, but the closer you got to the bridge, the heavier the mob, and the more crowded it was.

I.S. cruisers were already aligning themselves at the outskirts, towing the cars at the curb and replacing them with fire trucks and ambulances. Three FIB cruisers were across the street in a parking lot, their occupants wisely staying where they were, standing on top of their cars with binoculars to watch what they dare not step into. I doubted very much that anyone here had put in for a gather permit, but clearly the city's police forces were going to wait and see.

Jenks could find me in a dust storm on Mars, so I took a deep breath and plunged in. The green glow of the finding amulet had become more pronounced, but I didn't need magic to tell me Parker was at the center of this. Trudging forward, I worked my way through the generally shorter Werefolk. I got maybe thirty feet before it became obvious that I was being noticed. Heads were turning and conversations became silent as I passed. Some of the looks were welcoming, some not, and I moved my splat gun to a front pocket.

The rasping of pixy wings gave me scant warning before Jenks dropped down. "Found him," he said, landing on my hastily raised hand. "He's at Al's ley line. Cassie, too."

"Of course they are," I muttered, tucking the amulet behind my shirt. It was only making it more obvious that I didn't belong. "Parker?"

"On the bridge," Jenks said, and my pace quickened. "So far, they're ignoring each other. I think they're waiting."

*For me?* I wondered, gaze rising at the garbled, dueling bullhorns. People had begun to push back as I passed, and I touched my braid, nervous.

"It's not your hair," Jenks said, and I followed his attention over my shoulder and winced. Several sign-toting packs had fallen in line behind me. They were silent as they kept up, but their very presence forced the people ahead to take notice and move out of the way.

"Ahh . . ." I murmured, not sure I was entirely comfortable with this, but it did make it easier to walk, and the crowd behind me grew and the one ahead thinned until, almost like magic, the way parted to leave a clear path to the bridge.

Weres couldn't see ley lines, but I suspected they could sense them, seeing as Al's ley line ran clear and true before me, not a single scruffy face or expensive leather boot even hinting at touching it. David's familiar silhouette paced before Romulus and Remus, the statue of the lactating wolf and the two infants a gift from Rome itself. Cassie was there as well, her arms swinging and her mood clearly bad as she argued with him.

"Why are you bein' so stubborn about this!" she shouted, her accent clear over the noise of the bullhorn blaring at the parking lot.

"Because it is *my* problem!" David yelled back, visibly starting when he caught sight of me and the nearly fifty Weres behind me.

"It's our problem, David," I said, then stopped, turning to the advancing horde with a frown. "It's *all* our problem, but go sit somewhere, will you? You're crowding my space."

Grins showed, and they began to break up, the packs quickly organizing to make a wall between us and the rest of the world. Parker was on the other side of the footbridge, and I warred with the desire to simply go over there and beat the answer of who the mage was out of her.

David limped forward with Cassie, worry hard on him. "Rachel," he said, tone bland.

Cassie stood behind him, hip cocked, arms over her chest, clearly upset. Her bruises were healing, but she still looked sore. "Hi, Rachel," she mocked, voice high.

But she wasn't mad at me, and I tugged David into a careful hug to reassure myself that he was okay. I breathed him in, thinking the scent of Were was a close second to the delicious danger of a pissed-off elf. "You shouldn't have tried to leave her behind," I said, meaning Cassie, and he winced, deepening his few wrinkles about his eyes.

"Yeah." Jenks hovered close, wings clattering. "It just pisses us off."

"How are you doing? Better?" I asked as I looked him up and down.

"Better," he said, and I let go of him, my attention drawn to Mrs. Sarong as she pushed through our living wall, her intent to talk obvious. Her expensive jewelry and stark white business suit with matching high heels made her look vulnerable out here on the grass amid her rougher, heavily tattooed kin, but I was willing to bet her thousand-dollar purse held a pistol.

"This is exactly why I came out here alone," David said, a shaky hand rubbing his attractive stubble in worry. "This was to be a quick, quiet meeting to beat the tar out of Parker and convince her to leave. No one else was supposed to even be here. No one was supposed to get hurt but me."

I knew how that felt, and I nodded. "It sucks to have people care about you," I said, and Cassie made a rude snort. "David, you can't fight her," I added, and his jaw set.

"The hell I can't."

The footbridge was beginning to clear, and my pulse quickened as I caught a glimpse of Parker standing on it as if it was a pulpit, brazen with a misplaced confidence, her bruises and bandages only making her seem stronger. "You fight her, and this turns into a full-scale riot," I said, and

David's eyes narrowed. "But I can end it today by calling for an alpha challenge. Her and me."

"This is not your fight," he said, and Cassie took a hasty breath, pushing forward.

But I was faster, and I shoved his shoulder, jerking his attention to me as he winced in pain. "The reason Parker is even *here* is because I gave you the focus," I said. "That makes it my fight. Cassie can abdicate her position for an hour. Parker can't refuse an alpha challenge."

"Rachel . . ." David whispered, seeming to be torn as he bowed his head.

"Excuse me," Cassie said, her color high. "I'm the female alpha of this pack. And I'm not abdicatin' anything. If anyone is challengin' that whacked-out bitch, it's going to be me."

"You're a werefox. A third her size," I said.

"And *you* aren't even a Were!" she said loudly.

"Well, at least I can turn into a wolf!" I shouted, and Jenks rose up on a column of red sparkles, the pixy clearly uncomfortable.

Cassie stepped forward, and my chin lifted as we stood toe-to-toe. "Back off," she whispered, our breath mingling. "This is my ground, my pack, and my responsibility."

"You see?" David gestured helplessly. "You see why I came alone? They told me to come alone."

"So they could take the focus and kill you," I said, and Cassie spun to the bridge, clearly done talking.

"I'm calling you out, Parker!" she shouted, and the bullhorn and mob noise abruptly dulled. "You tried to lure my alpha away, and I'm calling you out!"

"You?" Parker gripped the bridge railing. She probably thought the bridge gave her the high ground, but it only made her look vulnerable. "You're not even a werewolf."

But Parker was staring at David, and I felt a chill. She wanted him dead and the focus, deep in his bones, in her hands. She knew the chakra ring did not give her power. It was witch magic. It counted for nothing in the eyes of the pack.

"I am the female alpha of the Black Dandelions," Cassie said, and the crowd tightened behind us. "And I'm calling you out, Parker. Join me in challenge or be diminished."

"Cassie?" I touched her elbow, and the startled woman almost back-handed me. "This is not going to be a fair fight. Let me do it. Grant me temporary alpha status. I can Were into a wolf. A fox can't take down a wolf."

Cassie was fixed on Parker with an eerie intensity. "With all due respect, Rachel, you can go to hell." Lips pressed, she wedged her shoes off and handed them to me. "I'd appreciate it if you would be my second, though."

Frustrated, I weighed the chance of ruining a potential friendship and having her alive against downing her with a spell and saving her life. Parker was a savage—this was my task to do.

*Or is it?* I thought suddenly as I caught sight of Jenks hovering behind Cassie, a sorrowful, angry expression on his small features. I'd learned the hard way that small did not mean helpless, and I felt my anger twist to fear as I held Cassie's size five shoes in my hand, still warm from her body. "This is not what I had planned," I whispered, and then, louder, "but I would be honored." If Parker cheated, I could legally step in.

Shock flashed across Cassie's face, followed by gratitude, and then a renewed anger as she turned to the bridge. Though she had always been confident, it now flowed from her. My belief had given her strength. *God, please let this not be a mistake. . . .*

David groaned, and I handed him Cassie's shoes. Behind Parker stood a veritable bear of a woman—Parker's second. David raised his hands to the crowd. "All of you go home!" he shouted, but no one moved, and a laugh tittered through them.

Mrs. Sarong shook her head. "And let Parker claim the Weres of Cincinnati?" she said, her faint Japanese accent making her even more exotic. "That's not happening, Mr. Hue. Let your alpha settle this, or we will."

"I call you out, Parker," Cassie said again, looking strong with Jenks hovering beside her on the circular patio where the covens of Cincinnati had their solstice bonfires. "Before all the packs of Cincinnati, I call you. Meet me now or forfeit your place. Such as it is."

309

Parker stepped off the bridge. "I'm not the one hiding behind two bitches," she said, and Jenks's wings rasped in threat.

Cassie bristled as the watching packs murmured. "This doesn't concern David," she said. "It's you and me. If I win, I get the chakra ring and the identity of the mage. You can keep your foul pack. I don't want it."

Parker glanced at the ring on her finger, then me. Smirking, I waggled my fingers at her to make the light glint on its older sister. "And if I win?" Parker sauntered forward until her toes edged the paved circle. "I get the focus. I want Morgan to rip it from him herself and put it in me."

That wasn't going to happen, and an angry red dust slipped from Jenks as the watching crowd seemed to take a collective breath. "If you win, you can discuss the focus with him yourself, seeing as you'll be his alpha female," I said, and Cassie blanched.

David took Cassie's arm, the glint of his big-ass rifle showing as his duster furled. "This is hardly fair," he said. "Cassie, you're only twenty-five pounds to her hundred and fifty."

Parker laughed. "She called me. The challenge stands. No witchcraft assist. If there's even a hint of it, I win by default." Eyebrows high, she crossed her arms over her chest to show the breakaway cast. "That includes your spell pistol," she added, and I frowned, hand touching my pocket where it lay.

"I came out here alone because I didn't want to put anyone in danger," David said, his expression hardening. "This is not your fight. I'm the one she wants."

"And we're the ones she has to go through to get you," I said, handing him my splat gun so there would be no question about it. "You keep the peace. We keep your back."

Parker was snickering at something her second had said. She knew who the mage was. I could see it in her amused smile. "Are we doing this, or just talking about it?" she said, confident that the hour would end with her shoving David into a van and driving off.

But the truth was, even if Cassie should lose and I somehow failed to keep David safe, the watching mob would not let David go. It was the power of the focus, and the focus didn't care who died for it.

Jaw set, Cassie began to disrobe, taking her clothes off with a passionless disregard, as if she was cleaning her sink. Piece by piece, she handed everything to me until she stood alone, her brown skin gleaming in a shaft of late-afternoon sun and her peacock tattoo spreading its feathers in a stupendous display of body art.

Parker gave her a disparaging look, then began to do the same. I blanched at the scars that Parker's clothes had been hiding. Old and puckered, they said the woman knew how to fight.

"The I.S. is staying clear," Jenks said, his wings tickling my neck. "Tink loves a duck, she's got a lot of scars," he added. "Cassie's got this. Parker clearly doesn't know how to fight."

But that's not how I had read the story her body told, and I became more nervous yet.

"Challenger's choice," Parker magnanimously said, and Cassie nodded, her eyes taking in every imperfection, every scar before her, reading the damage, analyzing it, deciding where the woman's defense lacked.

"I choose to start from human form," Cassie said, and a soft hush rose from the surrounding mob. Making shifting part of the challenge was uncommon. Most Weres preferred to go to fur before the contest started, eliminating the pain of a forced, fast shift. But being able to shift quickly was an alpha trait and so including it within the challenge was acceptable. It would also give Cassie the advantage, as werefoxes were naturally fast shifters.

"Fine." Motions rough, Parker twisted the chakra ring off her finger and gave it to her second. Someone had died to make it, and if my pearl ring had gone black, I would be terrified.

Reluctant and slow, David moved to stand between them. "As it is I who hold what these two alphas contest, it is I who will begin it," he said. "Do both parties agree that the results be binding?" He hesitated. "I need a verbal acknowledgment."

"I agree," Cassie said, voice low.

"They had better damn well be!" Parker shouted, and a small cheer rose from the footbridge. Alphas. They were all alphas, and I didn't like the answering rumble of threat from the Cincy Weres behind me. If Cassie didn't bring her down, they would fight. People would die.

"Any who interfere will be removed," David said when the noise abated. "May I have six alphas to serve as adjudicators?"

Mrs. Sarong pushed her way to the front, smiling and flashing her jewelry. Her business rival, Simon Ray, was tight behind her, and then another, head-to-toe-leather-clad alpha with at least six pack tattoos, rough and garnering cheers as he made a fist and stepped forth. There was a quick scuffle at the bridge before two women and a man came forward, completing the thirty-foot circle around Cassie and Parker. They would officiate, and I felt a chill as I studied them. *That should be me*, I thought, but even as I took a breath to protest, David bowed his head and walked to the edge.

"Begin!" he exclaimed, voice broken, and a cheer rose from the watchers, some eager, but most had an edge of fear. Nearly all alpha challenges were symbolic shifts of power as lives and needs changed, such as when I had stepped down from the Black Dandelions because I didn't have the time or personality to attend to the growing pack. But everyone had seen alpha challenges gone wrong, when flesh was torn and neither would yield.

Breath held, I watched Cassie's expression become vacant as her mind fell deep within itself and she began to shift. Slumping to the pavement, she curled into a fetal position, trembling as she endured a bone-cracking pain to finish her transformation before Parker. Werefoxes were said to have sprung from witches, and seeing as Cassie could dump her extra mass into the ley line until she shifted back, it seemed to make sense. Weres were not able to do that, and though most Weres were small in their human shift, a two-hundred-pound wolf was enormous.

My head snapped up at a wild cheer. Adrenaline slammed into me as Parker ran across the space between them, still in her human form. "Cassie! Look out!" I shouted, and Cassie's eyes flashed open.

"Not fair!" Jenks shouted, darting up. "Not fair!"

But it was fair, and I stood, my toes edging the circle as Parker drew her leg back and, with the accumulated momentum of her run, slammed her foot into Cassie's ribs. The crowd reacted, and beside me, David groaned, helpless as Cassie rolled, shocked out of her transformation.

"Get up!" I shouted. "Cassie, get up!"

But she couldn't breathe, and I watched, horrified as Parker hammered on her with her cast, blows hitting her head and ears until Cassie found a handful of dirt and threw it at her.

Pawing at her face, the woman stumbled, teeth clenched in outrage.

Cassie rolled to her feet, panting and hunched, one arm protectively about her middle.

"Yield!" Parker shouted, and Cassie laughed at her.

"Slaughter her!" Jenks shouted as he hovered beside David, his belief in Cassie stemming from his confidence that need made one strong, not size. David clearly wasn't so sure, his hands clenched and his face pale.

Still grinning, the smaller woman flung herself at Parker, knocking her off-balance even as Cassie hit the ground in a controlled fall. Parker went down, too, and Cassie straddled her, gripping Parker's hair and slamming her head into the pavers until Parker figured out what was going on and shoved her off.

Cassie rolled easy, that smile still on her as she got to her feet, hunched and ready. "Come here, little puppy," she goaded, and, howling, Parker went.

And soon, the strength of Jenks's confidence was laid bare. Even as a human, Cassie was markedly smaller, but she was practiced in the martial arts, and as Parker swung at her, Cassie jabbed the palm of her hand out, scoring on Parker's chin, snapping her head back, and spinning out of the way.

Parker jerked in shock, her focus wavering for a half second before finding Cassie behind her. Snarling, Parker backhanded Cassie, and the small woman went flying.

"Cassie!" David shouted, reaching out as Cassie hit the ground and rolled. She kept rolling, but Parker had followed, coming down on her, elbow in her gut.

The watching crowd *oooh*ed in sympathy, and Jenks's wings rasped harshly as Parker continued to hammer on Cassie, the woman having curled into a fetal position to try to escape.

But then I realized that wasn't what she was doing. "She's shifting," I whispered, grabbing onto David's arm. "David, she's shifting!"

Parker suddenly realized it, too, as Cassie's curly reddish-black hair became a smooth red and black. Snarling, Parker picked Cassie up and threw her across the cleared area. I gasped as Cassie's misshapen, narrowing body rolled and stopped. Her limbs were too thin, and her head had become long. A muzzle was forming, and teeth. The crowd's savage calls had dulled at her weird mix of fur and human, and, panting in obvious pain, Cassie tried to escape as Parker reached for her.

"She's going to be too small," I whispered, and Jenks landed on my shoulder, safe from the fist-throwing, screaming watchers.

"Nah," the pixy said, his wings cool on my neck. "She'll be just the right size. If she can finish her shift, there's no way Parker is going to win."

But I didn't see how. "Get up!" I shouted, my gaze darting across the circle to Mrs. Sarong, wishing she'd call a foul so I could step in. But she didn't. No one said you had to be in fur to fight an alpha challenge.

"Why is she shifting?" David agonized. I could see why. Cassie was a breath away from being a fox, twenty pounds soaking wet to Parker's hundred and fifty. Parker towered over her as she paced forward, and, grinning, the scarred woman picked her up by the neck, shaking her by the throat as Cassie's muzzle elongated and wicked teeth showed.

"Yield, you fool of a bitch!" Parker shouted, her hands around Cassie's throat as she hung, helpless in her grip, a feathered tail and hind feet curled up. "This is your one chance. Yield, and live to watch your alpha die."

David groaned, his grip on her shoes becoming white-knuckled.

But then Cassie's eyes opened, and with a wild twist, she flung her clawed back feet at Parker's face.

Screaming, Parker flung the small fox away.

# CHAPTER

# 23

THE CROWD HOWLED AS CASSIE ROLLED, FOUND HER FEET, AND stood, tail switching. A tuft of her fur was clenched in Parker's hand, and the woman lurched across the pavement, bare feet slapping and hands reaching, an eerie howl rising from her throat.

Cassie, though, had finished her shift, and with a cackling chuckle, the fox jumped at her, latching onto Parker's hand and biting down.

Screaming, Parker tried to push her off.

Cassie let go, her black feet barely touching the earth before she jumped again, snapping at Parker's neck and ears as her back feet raked Parker's chest.

"Get her!" Jenks shouted, but the crowd was going silent, an eerie quiet beginning to spread. Cassie chittered as she sprang at Parker once more, and the woman swung, scoring on the fox to send her spinning to the ground.

"I'm going to fucking squish your neck!" Parker shouted as she went for her, and then I started as David swore, lurching away as Al was suddenly behind me.

"It's just Al," I said, and the imposing demon glowered.

"*Just* Al," he muttered, giving his exquisitely patterned gray and black scarf a twitch. "Rachel, we need to work on that. There is no *just* when it comes to demons."

"*Just* say no," Jenks said. "*Just* a pain in the ass. *Just* what the hell do you want?"

"Al, what are you doing here?" I said as a ripple of unease passed over the nearest watchers, carried by the light scent of burnt amber.

Al huffed, adjusting his blue-smoked glasses on his nose as he glanced at my book-heavy bag. "You are five steps from my ley line. Did you not think I'd notice?" he said dryly, his attention returning to Parker and Cassie. "Isn't subduing psychotic city rulers your job?"

I tensed, but Cassie stayed clear of Parker's reaching hands, snapping at her fingers and ankles. Death by a thousand nips. "Cassie took it from me." Parker thundered after Cassie, her ham-handed swipe missing again. *Cheat, Parker,* I thought. *Give me an excuse.*

"Throw me a gun!" Parker kicked at Cassie, missing. "I'll shoot the little bitch."

But even Parker's second shook her head, and for the first time, David's terrified expression began to ease. "You have teeth and claws," the large woman said, and a nervous murmur thickened from the watchers pressing in.

"And hands," Parker said, frustrated and hunched as she reached for Cassie. "Come here, you little rag."

Ears pinned, Cassie chittered, daring her.

Bent double and breasts hanging, Parker lurched forward in a last bid. It was a mistake.

Cassie jumped at Parker's face, feet clawing. Howling, Parker caught her, then screamed as Cassie's teeth found her ear, shredding what was left of it as Parker flung her off.

The crowd was silent as Al applauded, his gloved hands unheard as Parker bellowed in anger, blood dripping. I felt ill as Cassie found her feet and spit out a chunk of Parker. "Tink's titties, she's fox chow," Jenks swore in admiration.

"That's not going to grow back," Al said, and the pixy laughed, a cheerful gold dust spilling as he flew to sit on Al's shoulder, shocking the demon and me both.

"Stop moving!" Parker shouted, then shrieked in alarm as Cassie launched herself at her again, the werefox's sharp teeth taking a chunk of her breast before Parker got her off.

Tail switching, Cassie hit the ground, and Al applauded as he nodded to the six officials.

"Call this off," I said to David, and he shook his head, his focus never leaving Cassie.

"I can't," he said. "And I don't want to."

"Mother pus bucket!" Jenks shrilled, and my attention jerked to Cassie as the crowd gasped. "She got her eye that time!"

"My eye!" Parker shrieked, the high-pitched sound cutting the air. "You took my eye!"

Horrified, I watched Parker fall to her knees, one hand to her face to hide the ruin, the other casting about for Cassie, the woman half-blind and enraged. But the werefox had retreated, sinking down as if tired, her battered tail curling over her nose. Parker's tendon-draped eye sat next to her, ugly and stomach turning.

"She's shifting!" Jenks said, and my breath caught. Parker's alphas had begun to shout directions to Parker to find Cassie. But the rest of the crowd were doing the same, directing Parker away.

"Bad form!" Al called out, hitting his affected lordly British accent unusually hard.

"Where is she?" Parker shouted as she waved about, blinded by the blood running from her ruined eye and a nasty scalp wound. "Where is she!"

*Why is she shifting?* I thought. Cassie was helpless, and I took David's arm so he wouldn't interfere when Parker wiped the blood from her good eye, spotted Cassie, and staggered forward.

"Get up!" I yelled, throat raw as Cassie's limbs lengthened and lost their fur. Nearly human, she lay on the cold ground, curled in pain from shifting too fast. "Cassie, get up!"

"You took my eye. I'm going to squish the breath from your body," Parker said as she staggered forward. "And then I'm going to kill every member of your sorry-ass pack."

"Cassie!" I shouted as Parker reached for her, her blood-spattered arm shaking.

And then Cassie moved, a slim hand sporting a faint red fuzz lashing out to grip Parker's wrist. Her eyes still fox-like, she sat up and smoothly punched Parker in the throat.

Choking, Parker fell to the ground, a hand to her neck, unable to breathe.

The watchers screamed their approval, but I felt nauseous.

"I say," Al murmured as Jenks cheered from his shoulder. "That was beautiful. She shifts amazingly fast."

"Werefoxes are like that," I whispered. Cassie staggered to Parker. Both women were bruised and in pain, but it was obvious who the alpha was.

"Yield!" Cassie exclaimed, jerking to stay clear of Parker's lashing foot. "Yield!" she demanded again, pulling Parker's head up by her hair to expose her throat.

"I yield," Parker choked, and the crowd erupted into a wild noise.

David made a half sob, half cry of relief, lurching over the unseen boundary as Parker's words freed him. Arms moving in a graceful arc, he took his duster off, flinging it over Cassie's bruised body and drawing her from Parker.

"Tink's little pink rosebuds, she did it!" Jenks crowed, but I still felt ill.

People surged forward, buffeting me as I stood unmoving. The alpha pack was breaking up fast, and I lurched into motion, shoving through the press to get to Parker's second before she slipped away.

I shouldn't have worried, though, as the Black Dandelions had already surrounded her and Parker. Jenks, too, hovered to keep a sharp watch on the vehicles trying to leave.

Al harrumphed, glaring at the surrounding Weres until they gave him space. "Never underestimate small. She is amazing."

"She's in love," I said, a lump in my throat as David helped Cassie to the nearby statue of Romulus and Remus, where she could sit with her back against it. "Al, can you hold my books for a moment?" I added, handing him my bag, and he shook his head in bemusement.

"Why are these out of your belfry?"

"Because Vivian wanted to look at them, and I don't want her to see the rest of my library," I said, then pushed into the mass of exuberant, backslapping congratulations, secure in the knowledge that he'd keep them safe. This would mean nothing if I didn't get a name and that second chakra ring.

It had only taken a moment for my pack to come forth to claim the ground, and trying to get through them was a chore. They were celebrating, but I only felt sick. "Ms. Rachel! Ms. Rachel!" an exuberant, high voice called, and I jerked to a halt when the Were who had taken a beating for me in the I.S. lobby a few months ago stumbled forward.

"Garrett?" I said, and he widened his grin, breathless in enthusiasm. He pushed a ring into my hand, and I felt a moment of disconnection as the curse and the cure touched.

"I'm part of the Black Dandelion pack," he said proudly, shifting his collar to show the pack's tattoo. "Is it the right ring? It's the only one she had."

The small circlet in my palm was shiny and uneven, the bump where the Möbius strip had been folded into a circle sharp against my touch. It was sloppy. Still, it worked, obviously, and I stifled a shudder at the wrong feeling emanating from it. Someone had died to make it, and I doubted it was the mage. *This is so foul.* "It's the right ring," I said, and the enthusiastic Were whooped, hand fisted in the air as he shouted to the rest of the pack.

Lips twisted in distaste, I put the curse on the same finger as the cure. They sort of hummed and fizzed against my aura, and, uncomfortable, I straightened to see over the quickly dissipating crowd. Mrs. Sarong was long gone, but it wasn't hard to find Parker abandoned right down to her second and surrounded by my pack.

An ambulance crew was pushing closer, and I tensed as two went toward Parker with a stretcher. "Don't take her out of here yet!" I shouted, and Jenks spun in the air, his hand falling to the hilt of his sword.

The paramedics grudgingly halted, familiar with the ugliness of an alpha challenge gone wrong. Concerned, I began to push to Parker . . . and the way opened like magic. For a moment, I thought it was me—until Al chuckled from my shoulder. He wanted to see this, apparently. Either that, or he wanted the rings. *Not until Vivian looks at them. Sorry, Al.*

"David, I'm fine," Cassie complained as she got to her feet, and he finally relented, draping his arm over her shoulders as they limped forward to confront Parker.

Yes, Parker was the architect of my current nightmare, but my first ugly words evaporated as I took in the misery that Cassie had wrought. Parker's pack had scattered and she was alone. She was bloodstained and sore, her pride costing her an eye and an ear.

"Who is the mage?" I said, and the beaten woman peered at me from the ground. Someone had draped a gray blanket over her, and she stared at the two rings on my finger.

"Answer her!" Jenks demanded when Cassie came to a halt before her. "Let me poke it out of her," he added, a hand on his hilt.

"You yielded," I reminded her, and Parker spit at the ground. "She's your alpha. Talk."

"Yielding to that stunted whelp changes nothing. She isn't a Were," Parker whispered, and my pulse quickened when her ruined gaze landed on Cassie. "She's not my alpha," the woman breathed, close to collapse. "She is not." And then a low growl rose from her, eerie and spine-tingling. "You are not!" she screamed, flinging her blanket aside and lunging at Cassie, her bloodied hands reaching.

Shocked, Cassie stumbled back, falling to hit her head on the cement with a dull thud even as David pulled Parker off her. "Get off!" David shouted as he spun Parker away. But the woman had fastened on the rifle in his grip, and it pulled from him as he threw Parker aside.

The woman hit the earth, the weapon's aim focused on Cassie.

"Fire in the hole!" I shouted to get Jenks clear as the energy from the ley line crackled within me. The rings on my hand burned, echoing the force.

"You are not my alpha!" Parker cried out again, her desperation ugly as she aimed the rifle at Cassie slumped in David's arms. "I give you nothing!"

"End her," Al whispered behind me, and I flung out a hand.

"*Rhombus!*" I exclaimed, jumping at the thunderous boom of the rifle going off. The slug hit the inside of the circle I'd put around Parker and me. Cassie's eyes were wide as the bullet ricocheted three times before falling to the ground at my feet, spent.

Pissed, I grabbed the rifle from Parker's slack, surprised grip, then dropped the circle. Somehow I resisted the urge to smack the butt of it across her chin—but it was close.

"You should have snuffed her," Jenks said, a harsh expression pinching his brow as he hovered over my shoulder. "Crazy never tells you anything."

"She has to," I said, but Al was watching me over his blue-tinted glasses, his head moving in a slow denial. *Crap on toast,* I thought. She was under the same no-divulge curse? Why couldn't I ever catch a break!

"What is wrong with you!" David shouted as he pulled Cassie deeper into the pack.

Parker began to laugh hysterically, until the pain became too much and she gasped for breath.

"David, I'm okay," Cassie said, trying to soothe him, but the man was incensed. *And he loves her,* I thought, seeing it in his desperate hold on her.

"Go ahead," Parker taunted, her voice raspy. "Try to force me to tell you who the mage is," she chortled, and Jenks's wing hum eased in pitch. "I'll be dead before his name passes my lips." Her lip curled into an almost smile, ugly. "Once by accident, the coven might believe, but twice? You will rot in Alcatraz, Morgan."

It *was* that damn no-divulge curse. I couldn't break it even given time I didn't have. The last of the mob was beating a hasty retreat at the I.S.'s cautious advance, leaving only the Black Dandelions. The alpha challenge the I.S. could ignore, but the rifle shot? Not so much.

"I'm going to hound you all until the day I die," Parker burbled, her eye beginning to bleed again as she dragged that blanket over herself. "You'll never sleep safe. You'll always be looking. Or you will be dead."

*Well, screw that,* I thought, handing the rifle to Al and taking my bag back in turn.

Al's heavy brow lifted as he held the rifle as if it was a dirty rag before passing it to Garrett lurking behind us. "If she refuses Cassie's sovereignty, her life is forfeit," the demon said. "As Cassie's second, it's your responsibility to kill her."

"Whoa. What?" I said as David's expression lit up.

"He's right." David turned to Parker. "We won't know who the mage is, but she won't be his tool anymore."

"I am no one's tool," Parker whispered, and the watching paramedics shifted nervously.

"I'm not going to kill her," I said, horrified, and Al sighed. "What do you think I am?"

"A fool," Al grumbled. "Kill her and leave your people safe. There's no extradition from the ever-after, and the line is five steps away."

My thoughts flicked to Constance's belief that I'd continue to fail until I learned the art of killing those who opposed me, her claim that I was putting my own people, the ones who loved and supported me, at risk. *This is not who I want to be,* I thought as I looked at David and Cassie, beaten and hurt—because of me. Maybe the half-crazy undead vampire mouse was right, but there were worse things than death, and I knew what Parker valued to the bottom of her soul. The question was, Could I be that cold and take it from her?

Jaw clenched, I moved closer to the downed Were, my grip on the ley line becoming more sure. "I'm not going to flee to the ever-after," I said, and Al sighed dramatically. "And I'm not going to kill you," I added, and Parker grinned through the agony, thinking she had won.

"I'm going to take your ability to Were," I said, and David's protest choked to nothing. "I'm going to turn you into a human." Al's frown eased into a wicked smirk as Parker went ashen, and I eased closer still. "You are going to be stuck as a warped, half-blind, scarred woman who remembers what it is like to run under the moon when the snow is fresh and unspoiled." Exhaling, I drew the line into me until the stray strands of my hair began to float. I didn't know the curse, but Al did. It had to be in the collective. All I had to do was access it. That proud grin he was now wearing told me he'd do it.

"W-wait," Parker stammered, real fear in her voice. It went to my core and lit an ugly side of me, one I wish I didn't have. Bitter satisfaction rose up from a lifetime of being bullied, swamping the softer parts of my soul, silencing them. I would not live looking over my shoulder. Not for her. She was not worth it.

"You know him!" she choked out, panicking. "The mage. He was at the festival. You were there when I took the ring from him." Her focus sharpened on me. "You helped him," she gasped, then began to laugh hysterically. "You protected him from me. If not for you, I would have ripped his throat out and taken Cincinnati as mine. You know who he is!"

"Seriously?" I said as I fought with the urge to give her a smack. "The only people I protected at the festival were Trent and . . . Lee," I trailed off in shock.

Gasping in laughter, Parker held a hand to her ruined eye and nodded.

"That piss-poor excuse of my ex-familiar is the mage?" Al said, and I turned to him, my denial hot on my lips. Beside me, Jenks's dust went thin. *No. Lee tried to protect us at the festival. Didn't he?*

"He wants you in Alcatraz and Kalamack destitute," Parker said, a bitter anger swamping her laughter. "Vincent trusted that was all the mage wanted and that we would have Cincinnati and the focus both. The fool would have let the mage use and discard us like curs. So I got rid of him. The mage, too, after I got the new ring and I had no more use for him."

Cold, I made a fist, holding the foul rings to my chest as Parker began a rasping laugh. "And then Rachel Morgan blunders in to save the day," she gasped, trying to breathe around her cackling. "You not only helped him get what he needed to do the curse to bring you down, you stopped me from killing him once he twisted it!" Blood poured from her ruined eye as she shook. "*You helped* him find everything he needed to twist the curse."

"No," I said, but I knew it was true when Al dropped his gaze and pinched the bridge of his nose. *Lee?* He had pictures of the curse book, of the pentagram, everything. We caught him trying to steal the lens. Breath catching, I felt my shoulder bag for the book. I had it. But the lens . . . I had left the lens in the church. *Oh no* . . .

"Why?" David asked, expression drawn.

"He blames Trent for the death of his baby girl," Parker said, laughing. "He hates Kalamack and Morgan." Her gaze came to me. "I gave you what you wanted. Let me go."

I couldn't move. The sharp edges of the new chakra ring pinched my hand, tingling. Lee had tricked someone into casting the curse, killing them. Trent knew not to twist the curse, but what if Lee had pitted our lives against each other? Trent might willingly do the curse if it would keep me from doing it to save him. Hands shaking, I looked at my pinky ring, glowing as Jenks's dust hit it. The pearl was white, but I had to see Trent for myself. I had to see him.

"I have to go," I said. I took a step to the parking lot only to have Al jerk me to a halt.

"Trent's okay, Rache!" Jenks was so close I couldn't see him. "The timing is wrong."

"The pixy is right." Al's grip was tight as he pulled me back to his side with a rough yank. "Lee won't kill Trent outright. He wants to see you in Alcatraz and Trent a pauper first." Al hesitated, his hold on me easing as I stood frozen, panicking. "That's how revenge works, itchy witch. Your ring says he is alive."

Breathless, I looked at my pearl ring. It was still white. But I had left Trent with Lee at the hospital, and the fear wouldn't let go.

"Rachel, it couldn't be Trent who did the curse," Cassie said as she drew David's coat closer about herself, but I wasn't listening, fumbling for my phone. "The second ring showed up at the coffee festival. Whoever Lee tricked died before then."

"He's okay." Jenks hovered over my phone, his dust blanking the screen. "Finish this so we can go find him. Rachel. Listen to me. We have to finish this first."

My pulse hammered as I stared at Jenks. I was afraid to believe his logic, and I turned to Parker. "Who did Lee trick into making the ring?" I said. Trent might not be dead, but Lee had been with him when I left him, and all I had was a text to indicate he was alive. A text that Lee could have sent on Trent's phone.

The battered woman hung her head, lank hair hiding her face. "I don't know. Let me go."

But I couldn't, and I stood there, phone in hand as I shook. She was right. I was twice the fool. Lee had opened Hodin's room, taking pictures of the book and even trying to take the lens needed to perform the curse. All for the love of a child he had let die so as not to be indebted to Trent for saving her life?

*Parker went to the festival to get the ring and kill Lee with it,* I thought. And whereas she had clearly gotten the ring, Trent and I had saved him before she could use it. The ring had probably been held by one of her people when she shifted—seeing as she hadn't used it until her people recovered her in the undead emergency drop-off.

My breath came and went, and I stared at my pinky ring, the pearl holding a steady white glow. Slowly I put my phone away. Jenks was right. I had to finish this first.

David edged closer, his lips holding a hard derision as he stared at Parker, daring her to move. "Lee got one thing right. He has to take you both out at the same time. You're too strong when you're together."

"It's been that way since you were twelve," Al said, his gaze fixed on his white gloves.

*At camp,* I thought, my focus blurring as I remembered how Trent and Lee's relationship had changed when I had taken a liking to the bullied but powerful boy Trent had been, balanced even more finely than the rest of us between adolescence and death as his father struggled to repair his shattered genome and draw one more generation from the failing elven population. Lee's bullying had been subtle from long practice, and Trent, desperate for a friend, overlooked it until I had rubbed it in his face and given him an alternative. *What wonders would Trent and I have done already if Trent's father hadn't quashed our friendship in his war with the demons?*

"He hates you both," Parker said, and my wandering thoughts snapped to her. "The mage can't beat Trent with you in the way, because as strong as our alpha males are, they are nothing without us," she added bitterly. "You know everything now. Let me go."

"You are not going anywhere but the I.S.," David said, and my worry shifted. Handing Parker over to the I.S. would only give the woman free hospitalization and a chance to recruit people for her next attempt—best case. Worst would have her out in twenty-four hours. *We* knew what she had done, but all the I.S. had was our word and a really ugly alpha challenge. The I.S. didn't like me, and they had ignored my findings before.

Cassie's grip on David's arm was white-knuckled. "The I.S. won't hold her forever, even if they do believe what we tell them. I'm not living my life looking over my shoulder."

"Agreed," I said, and Parker's jaw clenched. I couldn't let her walk away. She had only told me the truth to avoid a fate she considered worse than death. As soon as she was able, she'd come in the night and kill what threatened her: me, David, Cassie, Jenks maybe. It was more than that, though. I was the city's subrosa, and Parker had proven to be a clear and present threat. "I will give you a choice," I added, refusing to believe that Constance was right in that only by killing could I remain in control. I didn't have to kill Parker, just take her power. "Forever on four feet, or forever on two."

Jenks bobbed up and down in confusion as Parker's breath rasped in, her remaining eye widening as she saw a way out. "I choose four," she blurted, and the pixy went ashen.

"Four," I agreed, only half-aware of Cassie's confusion as she whispered to David. My gaze was on Al, my eyebrows high in question, and when he nodded, a chill tightened my gut. I'd have to use a curse from the collective, one that couldn't be broken by salt water. Lee might be the problem, but Parker was his sword—and I was going to break her.

"I choose four," Parker whispered again. Red streaked her face, but there was hope there, and gratitude, maybe. She lived in a world that fought her at every side, and this, though harsh, might be a gift.

"Al?" I said, reaching out for him, and he put a hand on my shoulder. Eyes closing, I gathered his charred and burnt presence to myself and then dropped both of our thoughts into the demon collective. He'd know where the curse was.

I jerked, almost flinging myself free as an unexpected pain raked over my mind. Al's grip on my shoulder spasmed, and I scrambled to claim the pain as my own before he could pull away. It was because of his burnt synapses, the line's energy trying to flow through blocked and twisted channels. I was feeling his pain, but with both of us taking it, it was halved and tolerable for each of us.

*Al?* I thought, hearing his breath shake in his lungs. *Some of this is mine. Don't take it all.*

*None of this pain is yours,* he thought. *A moment,* he added, and then, to open the vault, *Reserare, Algaliarept.*

My breath sucked in as I felt my mind drop into what had to be the demon's weapons vault. With the sudden shock akin to finding a missed step, my thoughts expanded, and not in a pleasant way. I cowered beside Al's pain-racked presence. Whispers of long-dead demons rose to tug at me, luring me to taste their power . . . curses twisted in anger and fear. They demanded my attention when I tried to ignore them, pulling at me when I said no.

Alarmed, I cleaved to Al's thoughts to hide. I groaned as his pain redoubled, and in reality, I felt someone catch me as my knees gave way. Al's thoughts were burning. It was too soon for him to be here, and, teeth clenched, I reached for handfuls of his pain, pulling them to me so he could better search as he rifled through the whispers and hints, disregarding the memory of agony and the hint of rising screams.

*Do you see?* Al's thoughts lifted through me as if they were my own. *Lupis seculo seculorum. Res ispa loquitur. It is not a curse to Were. It's to transform another into a wolf. She will have no memories. She will be a true animal. It cannot be untwisted.*

I balked. An animal? But she would be alive and free. To forget might be her only relief of the pain her life was. What waited for her at the I.S. would be hell.

*You have it?* he asked, and before I could answer, he shoved me out of his mind and the collective both.

I gasped, my eyes flashing open as the pain vanished. "Al?" I called, blinking at Jenks hovering inches from me. It had been David who caught me, and I was coated in pixy dust. I had dropped my bag, and I pulled it to me before my books could spill out onto the cold cement.

Jenks exhaled as he flew backward. "She's all right."

I lurched upright and out of David's arms, books tight to me. The park had all but emptied, leaving only the I.S. at the curb and the paramedics waiting at the parking lot. "Al!" I exclaimed when I saw him passed out on the ground. Cassie knelt worriedly beside him, her small frame lost in David's coat. *Crap on toast. I think I killed Al!*

I fell to my knees on his other side and patted his cheek. I'd never seen him so slack and empty of emotion, and it scared me. If Al was anything, it was exuberantly alive. "It was too soon," I said, more to myself than anyone else. "He took me into the vault, and it was too soon."

"Should I get some water?" Cassie said, and then she yelped, jerking back when Al's eyes opened.

Unmoving, he looked at us staring down at him, his red, goat-slitted eyes flicking from face to face. "Did you see the curse?" he said, and I nodded. "Good. If any of you ever speak of this, I will turn you inside out."

Cassie's smile was tight with relief as I extended a hand to help him rise. Decidedly sheepish, he let me take his weight and pull him up. "He's not kidding," I said.

The werefox's expression faltered, and, nervous, I turned to study Parker's misery. The bloodied woman was beginning to feel the pain through the amulets, head down and shaking as she sat naked under her gray blanket.

Al tugged his frock coat straight. "Do not tarry," he said, his attention on the I.S. cars at the curb. "The fear of demon justice won't keep them there much longer."

My worry for Trent loomed. Pushing it down, I pulled my bag up higher on my shoulder and focused on Parker. "You will be a true wolf if I do this. Your alternative is to be human. Tell me again what you want."

She lifted her head. "I want you dead," she rasped, clenching in on herself to keep from moaning in pain. "But being a wolf will do."

David shifted from foot to foot, his grip on Cassie tightening. That was enough for me, and I took a stronger hold of the ley line. We were practically standing in it, and I felt a twinge of guilt as it poured through me without pain. My hands began to glow with its strength, and the tips of my hair began to float.

*Reserare, Jariathjackjunisjumoke,* I thought to open the vault, my eyes closing as I felt myself fall into it again, my awareness brushing past the whispers of anger and hate, finding what I needed. It would make Parker a wolf. A real wolf. Only that would grant both of us peace.

*"Lupis seculo seculorum."* I whispered the words, drawing the curse through me and settling it into the haze in my hands. *"Res ispa loquitur."*

"A wolf, forever and ever," Al said, and I blew the magic to her. "You are judged."

Parker stiffened as the glowing haze settled over her. "Wait. No!" she cried out, lurching as if to stand, only to fall prostrate, a white leg showing from under the blanket now covering her. "Oh, God . . ." she gasped, shaking.

"Don't touch her," David said, catching Cassie's arm and drawing her back.

I slumped as the magic left me, cold and empty. Parker's pale leg showing from under the blanket was changing, becoming unnaturally thin and bony. Her foot lengthened, toes turned to claws and finally became furred. Her cries became whimpers, and stopped.

Jenks hovered close, his green eyes wide. "Is it done? Is she a wolf?"

Slowly, Parker pulled her leg under her and lurched to four feet. The blanket fell away.

She was a wolf, silver with black feet. One ear was savaged nearly to her skull, and she was missing an eye. Both were raw with new damage, marring her beauty.

"I'm sorry it came to this," Cassie whispered, and the wolf's remaining ear swiveled. There was intelligence in her gaze, but it was that of a wolf. Parker was no more.

David pulled Cassie closer in protection, and with that slight movement, Parker bolted. There was the sound of rustling leaves and grass, and she was gone, lost in the rain-wet urban wilds surrounding Cincinnati. *Maybe I should give Doyle and Glenn a heads-up.*

"Damn, Rache!" Jenks said, clearly approving. "Hey, the amulet still works."

I looked to see that the amulet had swung free of my shirt, the green glow slowly fading as the wolf vanished.

"She is an animal," David whispered. "Did you see?"

I felt sick, but it was done and could not be changed. I had killed everything that was Parker except perhaps her will to survive, and I was unable to meet Al's eyes when his hand touched my shoulder and dropped away.

"It was a gift," Cassie said, her expression pinched in heartache. "Rachel, don't you ever think you could have let her go. She would have come after all of us. Her mind was broken."

"I have to go." The thought of Trent struck through me like fire. "I have to find Trent," I said as I tugged my shoulder bag high. "Can I borrow someone's car?"

# CHAPTER

# 24

IT WAS RAINING AGAIN, AND IF IT WASN'T SATURDAY, TRAFFIC WOULD have been nearly at a standstill. But as it was, I zipped through a yellow light at an empty intersection, taking the corner too tight as I tried to simultaneously call Trent and drive. He hadn't answered the first two times, but hey . . . third time's the charm.

"Tink's titties, Rache!" Jenks shrilled as he hung on to the stem of the rearview mirror. "Put the phone down and drive. Let me call Quen. He might know where Trent is."

"Thanks." I set the phone into David's nifty cell caddy, and Jenks dropped, his sparkles an annoyed green and gold. "David's car corners as if it's on ice," I added.

"I'm telling you, Trent is fine." Jenks used the palm of his hand to scroll through my recently called list. "You left him in a hospital, for Tink's sake."

I left him with Lee. Exhaling, I looked at my pearl ring, and my hands clenched the wheel harder. My phone was ringing, and I almost grabbed the phone when Quen finally picked up.

"Rachel. Can I call you back?" the older elf said, his low voice holding a distracted, irate tension: one hundred percent annoyance, zero percent interest.

"Where's Trent?" I blurted, and he seemed to hesitate.

"Ah . . ." There was the click of a door closing, and then, louder, "About that . . ."

My hands were white-knuckled on the wheel, and I came to a too-short halt at a stop sign, tires squeaking on the wet pavement. "Quen, Lee is the mage. I got it from Parker herself. I left Trent with him at the hospital, and he isn't answering his phone. I believe her. Where is he?"

Jenks's wings were slack and unmoving as he stood by my phone, and when Quen said nothing, fear struck me, quick and sharp. "Quen?" I prompted, and he took a breath.

"I would question if Parker was lying myself, except this makes my morning make sense," Quen said. "The I.S. is here with a warrant to search for unspecified contraband, both drug and magic. They are being unusually thorough."

"Lee blames Trent for the death of his little girl," I said, not liking Quen's almost blasé reaction. "Trent isn't answering his phone. He doesn't know that Lee has gone off his rails. Someone died to make that second chakra ring, and, ah . . . Parker . . ." I pushed the guilt for her down deep. The woman would rather have died than been incarcerated. Now she was free.

Jenks's wings hummed. "Quen, Trent's fine. The second ring showed up at the festival."

*Stef,* I thought. But I'd seen her at the hospital. It wasn't her. "Trent is not fine. If he was, he'd answer his phone."

"He's not answering his phone because I told him not to," Quen said, and I turned onto Oak Staff, forcing myself to slow, wipers striking a too-fast beat. "When the I.S. showed up at the estate, I told him to lie low and not answer it. As long as that pearl ring is still white, he's okay." He hesitated. "It is, right?"

"Yes." I stared at the ring, my hand trembling as I drove. *No flashing lights at the curb. That's good.* "Don't you have a GPS amulet for him? I mean, you didn't even let him drive a car until he was twenty-three."

"I do not," Quen said softly. "He's wanted for questioning on some very disturbing charges. I'd be surprised if you weren't implicated as well. Get off the phone and disappear. Stay clear of the church and everyone you know."

Annoyed, I looked up at the steeple. "Hide. Sure. Right after I make a finding amulet for Trent."

"Rachel, this is not a joke," Quen began, and I hung up on him.

Jenks's wings were a soft hum as he rose to the dash. "Disturbing charges?"

"Pick one," I muttered as I made the sharp right into the church's carport. "If Lee is behind the warrant, it could be anything." We both worked above the law when we had to. Hell, I had just irrevocably transformed a woman into a wolf. I'd done it because it was my job, but it was still illegal. The city would let me get away with it only as long as I served their interests. It was a new place to be, and I wasn't sure I liked it.

"Rache, give me a minute to check the grounds," Jenks said, and I nodded, frustrated as I cracked the window for him.

"Watch your temps!" I shouted as he darted out into the rain, and he flashed an impatient red before vanishing over the wall and into the back garden. I lingered in the car, bent at an awkward angle to peer at the steeple. It was empty. Bis had fallen asleep on the top of Carew Tower this morning, and he wouldn't wake up until the sun was down.

I slumped deeper in the car's seat, my fingers tracing the expensive leather as the rain pattered down. The yards were quiet and empty. Soggy leaves were piled at the curb, and the first of the carved pumpkins sat on front steps, ready for Halloween. I hadn't even thought about what I wanted to dress up as this year to hand out candy. Perhaps a DMV officer. Those guys were scary.

Anxious, I grabbed my bag as I got out, shutting the door carefully to minimize the noise. Phone in hand, I called Doyle's direct line. It went immediately to voice mail. *He's still at the hospital?* I mused as I headed for the front stoop, boots slick on the leaf-wet walk. Jenks was still on his recon, and I searched the sky over the garden for his telltale dust.

"Hey, Doyle," I said when his outgoing message quit. "I'm sorry that you're last on my list, but seeing as you were cut pretty bad, I figured you'd be out for a while. Ah, Lee Saladan is the mage. Parker told me, and she probably wasn't lying, seeing as it makes perfect sense."

I hesitated as I hiked my shoulder bag higher. "Let me know when I can come down with Vivian Smith and uncurse your people," I continued.

"I'd do it now, but she wants to see it in action. I'm going to hold on to the ring for a few days until we're sure there aren't any more chakra curses lurking in the hospitals, and then I'm giving it to Al. Oh, and if I can talk to the family of whoever Lee tricked into making it, I'd appreciate it. They need to know what happened and that we are going to prosecute the person who murdered him or her."

I winced as I remembered Parker roaming Cincy's streets. "One last thing. Parker is a real wolf," I said, my boots clumping as I went up the stairs. "Torn ear, missing one eye. Could you let everyone know not to shoot her? She needs to be humanely caught and relocated to the wild, not a zoo. I have a finding amulet if it helps. And, um, whatever it is that Lee says Trent and I have done . . . er, call me if you need me to make a statement. I might be hard to find for a while, but Jenks will know where I am. Bye."

A sigh brought my shoulders down as I eased the door to the church open and slipped inside. It hadn't been a very good day. Tonight wasn't going to be any easier between finding Trent, then locating Lee. Not to mention some serious groveling for having stood Vivian up. Having her there when I uncursed the I.S. agents Parker had downed was an excellent idea. I figured I had a little time before the I.S. showed up, but the sooner I found Trent, the better. *Told him not to answer his phone, huh?*

I closed the door by leaning against it, unmoving for a moment as I stared at a slice of dimly lit sanctuary. *Grab my bug-out bag, a few more books, detangler charms, leave a note for Bis.* If Trent was in hiding, we might end up in the ever-after. Perhaps we could grab something to eat and the news at Dalliance.

I pushed away from the door, already tired as I headed for the belfry stairway. Everything I needed apart from the detangler charms was up there. But then I hesitated, my nose wrinkling at the scent of burnt amber and redwood.

"Al?" I questioned as I toe-heeled back to look into the sanctuary. My ley line was nearby in the graveyard. He might have popped over to tell me to stay out of the vault—now that I had access to it.

But I stopped short at the open archway, my knees becoming watery. There was a new yellow-wax pentagram traced on the old oak timbers. It was huge, using the circular outline of the decorative replaced floor as its center. Burnt-out candles were little more than empty shells at the six corners. Half-charred satchels rested at each point, each a different chakra color. An ominous mound of greasy black ash spilled atop the floor beside it, and my largest copper spell pot lay in the corner, discolored as if from flame.

"Jenks?" I called, a sick feeling trickling through me. Someone had done some major spelling in my sanctuary. It could have been Stef, but she would have cleaned up. Not to mention it smelled like burnt amber. That meant illicit magic. *Someone twisted a dark curse in my church.*

But Jenks never showed, and I stared at the glyphs, sure they were the ones we had seen in Hodin's room.

Son of a bastard, Lee had twisted the chakra curse in *my* church. Hand over my mouth, I stared at the pile of sticky ash beside the circle, knowing it had once been a person. Bile rose, and I forced it down. The scent of ozone was long faded, but it was obvious that someone had died there.

"When . . ." I whispered, books held tight to me as I inched forward. But the answer was obvious. He'd made it last night when I'd been at Trent's apartment. Lee had killed someone in my church to make a spell, then coolly gone to the festival the next morning. He must have been surprised to find me there.

"Stef?" I whispered. I reached for my phone to call her, fingers trembling. She was okay, seeing as she'd been at the hospital all night, but I didn't want her to walk in on this.

The stairs behind me squeaked, and I spun. "Stef, is that you?" I called, and then froze, expression empty. It wasn't Stef. It was Lee. And he had a stack of books in his arms. My books.

"Rachel," he said, his smile as pleasant as if there wasn't a dark pentagram adhered to the floor behind me. "I thought I heard someone come in. That wasn't your car I heard drive up. I was hoping it was Stephanie."

"Where is she?" I said, my fear for Trent redoubling.

Lee sniffed, his gaze going to the rafters before dropping to me. "Work?" he guessed. "They were incredibly busy when I left. I imagine they're asking everyone to stay late, and she is so conscientious."

The grip on my bag tightened as I looked at the books in his arms. *How the hell did he get past Al's wards?* But then I remembered he had been Al's familiar once. He probably knew the password.

"I know you're the mage," I said. "So does the I.S."

He frowned, a hand going to a shirt pocket. "Thank the Turn I don't need to wear that stupid costume anymore. I bought it for Trent's little party in the hopes of doing some snooping in his lower labs. But the costumer could never get the eyes right. Or the voice."

My gut tightened when his smile became predatory. "Rachel, what *have* you been doing?" he mocked as he pushed me deeper into the sanctuary one step at a time. "Illicit, dark magic?" he added as he dropped my books on Kisten's cracked pool table and tugged his sleeves down as if ready to do a trick. "Do me a favor." He settled his feet, balance firm. "Run, so I have a reason to use excessive force to bring you in."

I shook my head, retreating until that greasy ash circle was between us. "You know I didn't do this. It's not going to stick. Parker . . ." My voice faded. Anything Parker had said was now hearsay. It was my word against his. "Vivian knows I'd never do anything like this," I said instead. "Where is Trent?"

"Illicit magic books," Lee said, glancing at the pile he'd taken. "Check. Possession of illegal artifacts to perform dark magic, check. Evidence of using them to perform dark magic . . . big red check there. You are so screwed. Right to an Alcatraz wall."

*Alcatraz?* An icy drop of remembered fear slid through me, and I retreated again until my heels found the small rise to the stage and I stepped up onto it.

"Refusal to meet with coven representative to explain possession of illicit materials," Lee said, ticking off his fingers. "Absolutely. You stood Vivian up."

"I had to go," I said, not knowing how he knew, or why I was explaining this to him. The ugly yellow-wax pentagram was between us, like a guilty secret laid bare. Even if I could scrape it off, the oil from the candles and the residual fat from the ash circle would stain it forever.

Lee halted three feet from the pentagram, an ugly smile quirking his thin lips. "You are a hot mess on steroids." His chin dropped, and he eyed me from under a lowered, sarcastic brow. "You murdered someone in your own living room. I'm going to have the pleasure of bringing you in. Straight to Alcatraz. No hearing. No trial. You're a bad witch with a reputation."

I shook my head, the threat of Alcatraz stiffening my spine. "You threw Trent under the bus, didn't you," I said in disgust. "Seriously, Lee? Do you really think—"

I stiffened as Lee yanked on the ley line. Instinct pushed me into motion, and I sprang to the side as he threw a spell at me. Gasping, I hit the stage and rolled off, books sliding out of my bag. The wall behind where I'd been flared a brilliant purple as Lee's magic dripped to the floor and dissipated.

"Hey!" I shouted as I stood, safe under my protection circle. *Please don't come in, Jenks. Stay in the garden.* "Watch the walls! And what's your game, Saladan? You and Trent are two sides to the same coin. Getting greedy?" I mocked, and Lee's lip twitched. "Half the world not enough? You need it all?"

"This has nothing to do with Brimstone," he said, his clenched hands dripping an oily magic. "It's necessary. Made illegal by frightened humans who don't want an Inderland drug to be the only thing between them and a set of sharp teeth and a short life of servitude. I make it. I sell it. I don't care who buys it. Trent is the one playing *God*! Choosing who will live and who will die. Tinkering with people's lives. Selling life from death for a dollar."

*His daughter,* I thought. Revenge moved him, not money. I was in deep shit. Money I might be able to reason with him, but not revenge. Not the broken heart. "Lee, I'm sorry about your daughter," I said as I dropped my protection circle and looped my bag over my shoulder again and out of the way. Maybe if I looked as if I wanted to find a peaceful solution, he might calm down. "You should have talked to Trent. He would have—"

"You know nothing!" Lee shouted, and I flung out a hand, energy arching through my palm as I sent a ball of unfocused magic to slam into his. The two struck, hissing and sparking between us until Lee's magic overloaded and popped.

"Trent would have cured her," I said, coming closer as he did the same, both of us shifting around that perverted pentagram.

"I will not be owned by a Kalamack elf!" he shouted, and my clenched jaw eased.

"Maybe once he might have wanted to own your fealty, but he's changed."

"Such naivety," he mocked. "Nothing is free. No one changes."

Lee stopped, standing almost on the stage. He had given me the door. I could sense my books behind me, and my pulse quickened. *Plan B. Grab the books and run like hell.* But if he wanted me to run, that was the last thing I should do.

"I suppose you're right," I mocked as I shifted to get between him and my books. "How terrible would it be if he saved your daughter? Don't make me defend myself, Lee," I said as I backed up to my books. "We both know I haven't done this. Vivian knows I wouldn't *ever* twist that curse. Who do you think she's going to believe? A wax pentagram carries the aura of the one who makes it. Your signature is all over it. This is not going to stick."

Lee rubbed his chin as if amused. I could feel him slowly bringing in line energy, his aura almost visible as he gathered all he could hold. "It will," he said. "Vivian wanted me to tell you, but I convinced her that it would be easier to catch you in a lie if you didn't know."

My books were right behind me. I didn't like that he had touched them. "Know what?" I said as unfocused power dripped from his fingers.

Not answering, he flipped his lapel up, showing me its underside and the emblem there.

*Shit.* It was a Möbius strip—it was a dull copper instead of the bright, sparkling silver that Vivian wore, but it was still a Möbius strip, the emblem of the coven of moral and ethical standards.

"I'm the coven's new plumber," he said, and my gut twisted. "Seems after finding out witches were stunted demons, they wanted one in their club."

"N-no . . ." I stammered, cold as I remembered seeing him and Vivian at the spell shop and the directive tone she had with him. It was true. He was coven.

"Now you understand," Lee said, his low voice almost gleeful. "And as coven, what I say counts more than what you can twist to your advantage. Better yet, I can do whatever I need to bring you in. The coven has wanted you dead for a long time. I bring you in, and I'm set for life."

Suddenly plan B had a new appeal. Lee was allowed to do illicit magic to uphold the law. He would frame me with the ease of erasing one answer and scratching in a new one. There'd never be an analysis done on the magic etched into my floorboards. No one questioned the coven. Lee would be listened to, believed. And with me in Alcatraz and Trent fighting whatever claims were made against him, Lee would champion Trent's legal woes, leaving Trent a pauper and everyone who trusted me in the lurch. I'd had one shot with Vivian, and I blew it because I was afraid to trust her.

*Well, no more,* I thought, my resolve strengthening. "Yeah, okay," I said, and his expression hesitated, surprised at my reaction. "But I let you beat me the last time we fought."

Face twisting, Lee shouted a word of Latin and threw a spell. I deflected it with a word, and it went spinning into a corner. "You did not let me win!" he said, his cheeks reddening. "I beat you to a sniveling pulp. Left you crying over your dead father!"

"Sure, I cried," I admitted, chin high. "But I let you beat me. I didn't want to be Al's familiar, and why would he take me, a sorry-ass milksop crying over her dad, when he could have you? Big, strong, powerful witch with demon blood. How did that go, anyway?"

Furious, Lee lobbed three spells at me. Moving like a dancer, I evaded the first, blocked the second, and then caught the third, holding it hissing in my grip as my aura slowly absorbed his, making the curse mine. The books in my bag seemed to glow, and I took strength in it.

Suddenly unsure, Lee retreated a step.

"You might have fooled everyone, Stinklee," I mocked, using the insulting moniker Jasmine had saddled him with. "You might have the law in your pocket and Trent scrambling. But you forget one thing."

Lee traced a circle with his toe, rightfully concerned I was going to throw his own magic at him. "What's that?"

I tossed his spell from hand to hand, hearing it sizzle, watching it shift as it left my aura and then returned. "I'm not just a witch with demon blood. I fought them. I bargained with them. I flew on the hunt with them, watched them destroy their deranged son, Ku'Sox. I caught the demon Hodin, who sold them out to the elves. You think a witch can do that? I *am* a demon, Lee, the only one welcome on both sides of the ley lines, and I'm going to prove you twisted that curse. It will be you in Alcatraz, not me." Smirking, I absorbed the spell in my hand, stifling a shudder as the foul thing untwisted in me and raced back to the ley lines as pure energy. "Now, if you will excuse me." I picked up the books he had left on Kisten's pool table and put them in with the rest. I could replace everything that had been in my bug-out bag with a quick stop. "I have to find Trent. He owes me a coffee."

"Good luck with that."

Lee's words brought me up short. He was smiling bitterly.

Ice dropped through me. Lee knew where he was. And he wasn't going to tell me. I glanced at my ring, pulse hammering. The pearl was white. *And yet . . .*

Anger flooded me. Ticked, I dropped my book-heavy bag on the table with a thump. Lee's confident expression faltered, then vanished when I pulled on the ley line, inhaling power as if it was a drug. "Where is he?"

"He wanted to be somewhere safe, so I put him where no one will find him. It's cold up there this time of year, though. Rains a lot. He's going to—"

I'd had enough. *"Voulden!"* I shouted, throwing the curse at him. It hit

Lee's fast-implemented protection circle, popping and hissing before it spent itself.

"He's going to die," Lee said, safe in his circle as I paced forward.

"You first," I said, then threw a pool ball at him, following it with a new spell.

Lee incinerated the eight ball with a puff of magic, and then my spell hit him. Gasping, he staggered away as his magic rose to beat the spell out. He was out of his circle.

Hands reaching, I lunged, plowing into him and sending us both to the floor. "You can't win, Lee," I said as I clawed my way up his body as he fought me. "You aren't nearly pissed enough."

I reached for his head, and he hit my arm, shoving me off him. Wiggling, he stretched for a wand stuck in his sleeve. "*Teneo!*" he shouted, and I dodged the arc of power, feeling it as it hit my quickly invoked circle— and burn, and burn, and burn, until it broke through.

It was coven magic, and I tried to douse it, failing as fire and ice tingled over me.

Black coils of smoke wrapped up and around me, imprisoning me in a grip that tightened with my every movement. I was bound by legal, dark magic, and I lurched to fall against Ivy's piano. *Caught.*

"Where is Trent!" I shouted, furious, and Lee grinned, his confidence restored.

"Cold, wet, and out of your reach," he said. "Probably treading water by now, if he's still alive. I hope he is. I really want to see him living in a hovel and visiting his girls for an hour on the weekends."

*He is alive.* Fear for Trent twisted my gut. Panicked, I wiggled and twisted, gasping when I felt my balance shift, and I toppled from the piano to hit the floor with a thump. His shoes inched closer, and I hated him as I heard the familiar sound of his phone taking a picture.

I needed a knife. I needed a magical knife.

And then I had it. "Hey, Lee," I said, and he looked up from his cell phone. *Reserare, Jariathjackjunisjumoke,* I thought, jerking as my mind fell into the vault. The presence of long-dead demons seemed to start, rising up at my hatred of Lee, clamoring for me to take what they made, use it to kill those who threatened what I loved. Ugly, unspeakable curses, but that's not what I wanted, and as they pushed and shoved to force a way into my mind, I reached for the memory of Al and the dagger he had made from a curse. It was here. It had to be.

*Quaere!* I thought, and in my mind, a dagger made of light exploded into existence. *Serve me as you serve Algaliarept. I offer you the blood of a total ass.*

But I truly didn't need to ask for its help. I had summoned it and it was mine. My eyes flashed open, and satisfaction was a warm balm as I saw Al's dagger in my hand, called from the demons' vault. All I had to do was angle the blade to touch the black coils withering around me like smoke, and with the sound of nails on stone, the coven-sanctioned dark spell was overwhelmed and it parted.

I was free.

I spun, rising from a crouch and into a stand in one smooth move as Lee gaped at me.

*He's not afraid. Not yet. Dumbass.* "You might have shared that picture a little too soon," I said, and my grip tightened on the hazy dagger made of energy.

"Al gave you access to the vault?" he whispered, and I sprang forward, pinning him to Ivy's piano.

Lee snarled as my arm went under his chin, pressing on his neck. "Where is Trent?"

Lightning sprang from his fingers and palms as he tried to force my grip from him. Fiery tiger teeth pierced my arm, and I welcomed them, grinning wildly as I took his energy and turned it against him. Yelping, he dropped the line. "Where is Trent!"

He shoved himself away from the piano, and we fell. I never let go, hooking my foot behind his and spinning us around to land on him. His head hit the floor with a thunk, and I pressed my arm against his throat again, the dagger hovering over his neck as he tried to focus.

"Where. Is. Trent," I intoned, Quaere's blue flame gleaming on his neck.

"Three days," he snarled up at me. "You left me there for three days."

I pulled the knife from him in shock. "You put him in the camp's well?" I said, and then he shoved me. I rolled to my feet, Al's dagger in my grip. "The well was dry!" I shouted, my heels edging that dark pentagram. "It wasn't as if you had to tread water!"

"You left me to sit in my own shit and piss for three days!" he exclaimed, spittle spraying from him.

"Then maybe you shouldn't have killed Jasmine's baby duck!" I exclaimed, only now remembering it. She had been in tears. And though he insisted it had been an accident, we had played jury and executioner, dropping him in the well as punishment. One day became two, then three before the reality of what we'd done hit us and Jasmine and I "found" him, almost comatose from cold and starving at the bottom of a dry well. Lee had never told on us, but it had been the end of all our innocence, and the very next week, they kicked me out of the camp for good.

*That's why I threw Trent into the tree,* I realized, only now remembering it. He had wanted me to leave Lee to die there, and I had said no. *Son of a bastard . . .*

In a mental fog, I turned to the front door. "I gotta go," I said, not sure what to do with the dagger. I couldn't just shove it between my sock and calf. My books were still on Kisten's pool table, and I paced forward, fear for Trent filling me. It had been raining for three solid days. The camp was closed. It wasn't as if I could call someone to go out there. I was going to have to buy a line jump, and the only demon I halfway trusted other than Al was Dali. *No, I have to buy three. One to get there, and two to get back.*

"You'll never make it. Trent is going to die," Lee said, his voice ringing in the rafters with the surety of a minister preaching hell and brimstone. "And you are going to live with the knowledge that you couldn't reach him in time."

I jumped, shocked when Lee's spell slammed into the pool table, engulfing it in a weird purple and blue flame.

He hadn't been after me. He'd been after my books.

"*Dilatare!*" I cried, throwing the explosive ball of air at the flames, and the fire vanished, blown out to leave only smoke rising from the burnt felt. My bag was singed, but the books were fine. Not even warm when I gathered them to me like kittens. *Dumbass. He tried to burn my books!*

"What is your problem!" I shouted as I spun to him, my books held to my chest. "I'm sorry about leaving you in the well for three days. But I was twelve. Everyone is stupid when they are twelve. It was a mistake."

Lee shook his head, unfocused magic wreathing his hands. "The only mistake you made was telling them where I was before I died."

"Yeah. That's what Trent said." And then my eyes widened at his sudden pull on the ley line. Words dripped from him, unclear and muffled. His hands gestured, pulling energy up and over him in branching rills, sparking in the charged air. This was pure anger I was seeing in him, rage possessing his every thought.

And it didn't have to be this way.

"I am so sorry, Lee," I whispered, books tight to me as I came forward. I needed a secure circle to ride out whatever he was going to throw at me. I didn't have time to scribe one, but that ugly wax and fat circle might save my life. "I wish your daughter had been a normal witch," I said, grief for his loss filling me.

And then I stepped onto his dark pentagram.

I jerked to a halt in surprise as a residual energy seemed to rise through me, fastening on my grief and loss, pulling it away, taking it in . . . harnessing it? Pain cramped my hand, and I cried out as the chakra rings burst into a quickly quenched heat.

*What the hell?* I thought as I shook the imaginary fire from me. But then my breath caught. Lee's dark magic pentagram was glowing. I had triggered something, something latent and left over.

"Lee!" a familiar, feminine, and very pissed voice shouted.

My head snapped up, and Lee spun, staggering in shock as he half turned.

It was Vivian, her expression tight in anger as she stood before us on the stage. Mystics wreathed her, making her short hair into a halo and her white clothes spark as she moved. "You and me," she said, pointing, and Lee retreated to the windows. "Right here. Right now."

"How," Lee gasped, the magic in his hand faltering as he gaped at her. "You're . . ."

"Not happy," she finished for him. "I can see everything now. And what I can't, others can. They whisper to me, saying you lied. You lied to me. You lied to the coven. Consider your conditional plumber position revoked. Better yet, let me revoke you."

"You're—" he exclaimed, and then he yelped, cowering as he flung up a protection against Vivian's white-hot stream of unfocused energy.

I staggered back, my feet slipping on the ugly ash lines. My grip on Al's dagger tightened as Vivian's energy flowed over his circle, eating away at it layer by layer. I could barely see Lee within it, cowering as he frantically etched symbols into my floor, trying to stave her off.

"He's the mage!" I said, so grateful that she believed me, I could have cried when Vivian's magic faded to a flicker as she nodded sagely. "I have to save Trent. Do you have this?" She must have come to the church to find me, ream me out about standing her up. Thank God she had hidden in the shadows, listening to Lee's confession as we fought.

"Go," she said, and I swear I heard Lee whimper, whispering his words that might or might not save his ass. Vivian had been born to the coven. She had skills Lee had never dreamed of. I almost pitied the man. She was practically floating over the wooden-plank floor. "And thank you."

I shifted my books higher up on my hip, and Al's dagger hissed in the highly charged air. "For what?"

She shrugged, confusion pinching her brow. "You gave me this chance to make things right. Go save Trent," she said, her smile now a benevolent knowing. "I have this piece of slime. Oh, and, Rachel? Don't you *ever* feel guilty for putting him in the well. Jasmine says he deserved it for killing her duckling. It wasn't an accident. He did it on purpose."

*How did she know?* I thought, then looked at my pinky ring. The pearl was still white.

"Go!" she shouted as she faced Lee again. "He's treading water."

I had no idea how she knew, other than it had been raining for three solid days, and I stood for one horrible moment, fixated as Vivian threw ribbons of blue and gold energy at Lee. The bands crackled and popped, tightening around his protection circle, squeezing them until his bubble began to warp and twist. The energy distorted, and Lee screamed.

"Thank you," I whispered, then I ran out the door, hardly slowing as the rain pelted down, cold and stinging. Vivian was here. Everything was going to be okay. She knew the truth. The coven would disbar Lee. Put *him* in Alcatraz. The charges against Trent would be dropped. Everything would return to normal.

Books still tight against me, I ran for the ley line out back. I needed a line jump. No, I needed three.

# CHAPTER

# 25

MY ENTIRE LIBRARY TINGLED A WARNING AS I RAN FOR THE LEY LINE, shoving through the gate and racing into the garden. I didn't need my second sight to find the glowing haze; I was the one who had pushed the shimmering band of energy from the middle of the sanctuary out into the garden where it belonged. Behind me, Lee howled in anger, or maybe fear. No doubt. I'd learned the hard way that you didn't piss off Vivian.

A soft rattle of windows sounded—and then a brilliant light flashed through the stained-glass windows to set the garden in high relief. With a silent boom, darkness returned. I jerked to a halt, pulse fast as I stared at my church. *At least the windows are still intact.*

"Rache!" Jenks shrilled, and I spun. His dust was an unreal dark red— the color of old blood. "I thought you were still in the car! Did you go in there for your books? I finally found Getty. She's six feet under the ground. All those times I couldn't find her she's been hiding with Constance. You won't believe what she said Lee did."

"I heard. He put Trent in the well at camp," I said, and Jenks's wing pitch shifted, his eyes widening as he saw the dagger still in my grip.

"He did what?" the pixy said, and I pushed past him, looking for the ley line.

"Jenks, you got the con. I'm going to buy a couple of line jumps from Dali to get him. Stay out of the church until Vivian brings Lee down."

"Vivian?" he questioned, flying backward before me as I trudged through the gravestones. "Ah . . ." Still flying backward, he lifted his gaze from the dagger in my hand to look to the church to the garden and back again. "Getty said that Lee—"

"Is a coven member. I know. Jenks, I have to find Trent," I said shortly as I stepped into the ley line and a wash of tingles rose up through me, warm, like a puddle long under the sun. I squinted at the church, curious. Seeing it from within the line, it almost had an aura, as if it was a living thing. I'd never seen that before, and I'd stood in the line hundreds of times. *That's weird.*

"Yeah, but, Rache," Jenks tried again. "Getty says—"

"Is she okay?" I said, interrupting him. The pearl on my ring was still white, but it had been raining for three days, and the need to move was growing. The caves had been out-of-bounds because they filled with water every time it rained. Trent was in trouble.

"She's scared is all." Jenks hovered, his tiny features pinched. "But, Rache, Vivian—"

I sank my awareness into the line, feeing it hum through me. Stepping to the ever-after would be a small thing, and then I could reach Dali easier. "When Bis wakes up, tell him I might need his help," I said, then closed my eyes, willing my aura to match the line.

"Listen to me, witch! Vivian is—" Jenks shouted, his voice cutting off as I let my soul return into its normal resonance. That fast, I was in the ever-after.

My breath hissed in as a sudden, cold wind gusted to knock me down. Hunched, I squinted at the brilliantly colored sunset. Autumn-dried grass whipped my legs, and it was bitterly cold. I held my heavy bag closer. The scent of burnt felt clung to my books, but Lee's fire had done no damage. Demon tomes could not be burned, and that's all that Lee had taken from my library.

Dalliance was a five-minute walk from here, but I was hoping that if I called Dali from this side of the lines, he'd answer. Closing my eyes again, I willed myself into the collective.

Breath catching, I wavered, dizzy as both the wind and a mental uproar buffeted me. They were arguing, everyone thinking as loudly as they could to be heard. *Dali?* I called, throwing my will into the void only to have it dissolve like an unheard echo in an ocean wave. *Dali!* I shouted, putting my fear and worry behind it.

With a frightening suddenness, an eerie silence fell. For a heartbeat, there was nothing, and then a nervous titter and whispered questions. I heard my name, and Al's. *It's her. She's alive,* I sensed Dali think, and then, *I'll find out. No one does anything until I return. Got it? Or the only thing you'll find in the jukebox will be that slutty strip bar.*

*Ah, Dali?* I questioned again, and then his presence was wholly in my mind, oppressive and domineering. *Hey, back off,* I thought as I fell deeper into myself, not liking his lack of social graces. For all his failings, Al gave me some space. *I need to talk to you.*

And then I started as he left my mind. I took a breath to yell at him, my eyes flashing open as he was suddenly before me. The slightly overweight demon squinted up at the brilliantly colored sky and gathered his robes around him in the unexpected wind. There were no bells on his sash, and the hem was tattered, a sordid black rising to blood red at his collar. It was old, and he only wore his old robes when he wanted to remind everyone he had been one of the first to escape the elves, second behind Newt and Al.

"So it's true," he said, his goat-slitted gaze touching upon my books before dropping to the dagger still in my grip. "Al took you into the vault. Gave you access to our toys. Is he alive?"

"Of course he's alive," I said, appalled. "Are you serious?"

Dali shrugged, the portly demon giving the impression of both indifference and worry. "Gally has been making questionable decisions lately. Most concerning you. His agony rippled through the collective oh, say, not two hours ago, and here you are, with one of his prize possessions in hand."

Dali eyed me in expectation, and I shoved a feeling of guilt down. "He was helping me take care of Parker. I need three line jumps."

The demon snuffed, but still that wariness hung over him like a shroud, coloring his every move. "And you think I'm going to give them to you? Because you need them?" he practically sneered, robes fluttering, hissing against the grass.

I glanced at my ring. The pearl was white, but my gut said every second counted, and I pushed forward into his space until my newest elven book sparked at his presence and he jerked away in shock. Worry crossed him, and then it was gone. "Look, you," I said, trying to get my wildly whipping hair out of my mouth without stabbing myself with Al's dagger. *Maybe I should have asked Al how to turn this thing off.* "Lee dumped Trent into a well. The camp is closed, and it has been raining since Thursday. I need three jumps. Now!"

Dali grinned, his flat white teeth catching the fading light as a secret tried to escape him. "Yes. I know. Who do you think he bought a line jump from?"

"You?" I said, ticked. "You sold Lee a jump to put Trent into a well?"

But the demon shook his head, hands going to his ample waist as he squinted into the rising wind scouring the utterly cloudless sky. "Actually, it was Trent who bought the jump," he said, shocking me. "I'm sure he didn't know that's where he was going to end up. I'm astonished, actually, in the utterly foolish way your elf applies his trust. Blindly believing Lee when he told him he knew of a safe place, and then not even questioning where he was going. I suppose it was Lee's promise that he'd send you along in due time that did it. I guess he was right, because here you are." He hesitated. "Asking to buy a jump as well."

"Why . . ." I whispered, then realized that Trent hadn't known. He had no clue that Lee was the mage and had plotted wheels within wheels to bring him down. The need to reach him doubled, and my gut cramped with fear. "Are we making a deal or not?"

"Are we?" Dali mocked as he took in the beauty of the sun sinking in an angry sky.

"I have books," I said, words tumbling over themselves as I opened my shoulder bag. They were all I had of any worth, but I'd give them up for Trent's life.

Dali's gaze flicked down. "Most of which are Newt's and of questionable value, and one that I can't touch, apparently. How is it you can? It is ancient elven."

I pulled the books closer, anxious and frustrated. "Trent handed it to me. Dali . . ."

Dali's lip curled. "As if you were his servant to fetch and carry."

"Hey!" I shouted, the word ripped from me by the wind. "I don't care what the book thinks I am. I can touch it. Do you want them or not!"

"That is a fine dagger," he said, eyeing Quaere, and I froze.

*Ahhh . . . shit. He wants Al's dagger?* "It's Al's," I said, but Trent might be drowning, and the need to move was almost a pain. "How about a favor?" To owe Dali might cost me my own life. I didn't care.

"What, and have you bankrupt me as you do everyone you have close ties with? No." Dali's head tilted as he scowled at the wind as if its presence was my fault. "I suppose I will never hear the end of it if you don't get what you want. A jump, you say?"

Hope lit through me. He was still looking at that dagger. "Four," I said, reconsidering my first request. Al would get over it. "When I want them, immediately and with no delay. One to get me to Trent, and two to get Trent and me to Al's clearing. I need to talk to him. Yes or no."

Al was going to be pissed, but I held Quaere out to Dali, my hand shaking. *Yes or no, you uncaring spawn of hell.*

"That is three jumps," Dali said, his fingers twitching. "What is the fourth? You want one on credit? No. I'll not be at your beck and call."

Frustration clenched my jaw, and the dagger hissed and popped in the damp air. "The last is to pay for Trent's original jump. Whatever it was he gave or promised you, it's null and void."

"Mmmm." Dali's gaze went distant as he thought about it, the icy wind buffeting us both, almost knocking me down. And then he grinned, thick hand reaching for the dagger. "Done and done."

My breath exploded from me in relief as the dagger left me.

"Al is going to wring the life out of you. This dagger is worth a lifetime of line jumps, and you sold it to me for four." Holding it up to the fading light, Dali studied it in greed. "I rename you Revenge," he said, and it vanished.

Anxious, I held my books closer. "I didn't sell it to you for four line jumps. I sold it to you for Trent's life." Dali's glee faltered, and I shifted my weight from foot to foot, eager to be gone. "Could you hold these for me for a moment?" I shoved my bag with all my books at him, and he scrambled to find the straps as if fearful the elven book might sting him. "I want them back," I added as he held my bag like a husband at the mall. "Don't open them. They aren't yours."

"If you survive." Thick lips quirking, Dali tried to shift the cover of the elven tome, and it jolted him with a blue fire. "Putrid, filthy elves and their biolocks!" he shouted, and I pulled my jacket closer, anxious to leave.

"Thank you," I said, desperate to be gone. "Send me to him. Please."

Dali's expression shifted as his thoughts left the book he couldn't open, treasure he couldn't see. "Before I do, I need—" he began, then hesitated. "*We* need, or rather, we'd like to know what you took from the vault besides the dagger. What unholy hell did you release upon the world, Rachel Mariana Morgan?"

He was using all three of my names. This was more than a polite request, and I tried not to scream at him in impatience. "Al showed me the curse to turn Parker into a wolf. A real wolf. No return. That's it. I didn't touch anything else. It was that, or I was going to turn her into a human and she would have killed herself. I saved her life." But really, I had taken it.

Dali's gaze dropped to my bag, full of my books. "And yet you managed to summon Al's dagger, ungifted. You clearly saw more than he intended. Than *we* intended."

"Hey, I really need—" I began, and then I gasped as my body evaporated into nothing but a thought. Flustered, I snapped a protection circle about myself before the chiming roar of creation energy could singe my thoughts. I was in the lines. All of them. Simultaneously.

And then I felt an aura blossom about me, pulling me to its match. *I will never be able to do this,* I thought, suddenly having the need to breathe as I regained my lungs.

"Hey!" I yelped as a dropping sensation filled me.

*Damn it, Dali,* I thought, cursing the perverse demon as I hit the water. Bubbles and froth beat at my ears as I flailed to find the surface and pushed into the air, gasping. I couldn't see, and I trod water, the sound of my fall still echoing in the flooded cave that had once been the camp's well. "Trent?" I coughed, kicking off my boots as I pulled in air stinking of frogs and slugs. *No wonder they don't use this anymore.* "Trent!"

"Rachel?"

*He's alive!* Elated, I spun to his voice and a sudden splashing. It grew close, and I reached for him at an icy, fumbling touch on my face. "Thank God," I whispered, legs kicking as I found him cold and wet. "Are you okay?" I asked, pulling him into a hug that nearly sent us both down, and he shivered as the scent of spoiled wine rose from him. "I got here as soon as I could," I added, my chest tight with worry. "Are you all right?"

"I'm fine. Where's Lee?" he asked, sounding more peeved than angry. "I've been clinging to the wall for hours. He tricked me here. He tricked both of us," he said, the first hint of real anger in his voice.

"Thank the Turn you're okay," I breathed, wanting to hold him. "He's trying to kill you." Tears threatened, and I blinked them back, glad it was too dark to see.

"Lee? No," Trent said with a scoff. "But he's gone too far. I can't reach a ley line to get out of here, otherwise . . ." He hesitated. "Lee?" he shouted, neck craned up to the unseen well house far overhead. "This isn't funny! Get us out of here!"

His voice echoed against the hard walls, not a hint of worry that Lee might not be up there. My eyes had begun to adjust to the ever-so-faint light from the well house, and Trent looked awful. His hair was flat to his head, and though he was clearly cold to the point of pain, his green eyes seemed to hold more annoyance than anger. Arms and legs moving, I started an awkward paddle to the wall. I couldn't reach a line surrounded by water, either, but if I could ground myself, I could probably reach Dali's thoughts. "Trent, it's not a joke. He's trying to kill you," I said between sodden splashes.

"No more than usual." Trent began to follow. "Have you talked to Quen? He said not to call you. That's the last time I do that," he muttered, moving far more efficiently through the water. "Quen said to find a place to lie low, to not tell you, or him. *Lee*," he added sourly, "offered to help. I thought he was going to put me up in a hotel, not drop me in the camp's well. Someone is coming after me with both barrels this time."

"It's Lee," I said flatly, lip curling when I found the wall, slippery with slime. I still couldn't tap a line, but I could feel the collective, and I shivered in relief.

"Because he dropped me in a well? No." Trent looked up in expectation, but the door to the shed covering the hole was not opening. Lee was not standing up there, laughing at us, and doubt pinched Trent's eyes.

"I bought a jump out of here. Ready?" I said, my hand fumbling to find his and hold it with a scared determination. *Dali?* I thought, closing my eyes as I found the collective.

*That took too long.* Dali's annoyance slid into me as if it was my own. *I am not your personal lackey.*

*Thank you,* I managed, and Trent shuddered as if getting a glimpse of the demon's mind.

And then I stumbled, practically thrown out of the ley line to land before Al's smoldering fire pit. Gasping, I slid to a soggy halt: wet, cold, and dripping. "Hey!" I exclaimed as I shook the clinging dirt from my hands, then ducked to avoid my entire library of books falling from nothing. "Trent?" I spun to a muffled groan. He was on the ground, soaking wet and cold.

The sun had set, and with it the wind had eased. Twilight reflected down from the clear skies. It made Trent's smile hard to see as he shivered, his hair flat to his head as he got to his feet, staggered to the fire pit, and muttered a word of Elvish.

Flames leapt up, and Trent sat on one of the flat stones arranged before the fire and held his hands out, inches from the new flames. "The Goddess take me. I don't recall ever being that cold before."

"I do," I said, remembering dragging him out of the icy Ohio River, and he nodded ruefully. "Are you okay?" I asked, shivering as I stacked my books, trying not to get them wet. They were all present, but Dali had kept my shoulder bag and everything in it. I hadn't stipulated its return, and he was always eager to be petty. *Son of a moss wipe demon . . .*

"Getting there," Trent said, and I tossed a few more logs onto the flames before I sat my soggy rear beside him on the rock and pressed against his cold body, giving him a sideways hug. There was probably a blanket in Al's wagon, but I wasn't going to rummage around to find it, especially if he wasn't here. It wasn't as if we were being especially quiet. His gargoyle, Treble, was not on the roof, and I guessed that Al was at Dalliance. Either that, or he didn't want to come out and admit that he couldn't spell us dry.

"Lee went too far this time," Trent said, hunched and blowing on his damp, shaking hands. "He knows it's the rainy season. At least it was dry when we put him in there."

Trent was okay, and the overwhelming relief of that was shifting to anger. "Trent. I'm sorry. It wasn't a joke," I said, my hands shaking as I held them to the flames. "Lee is the mage. He's behind the warrants. He wants you dead or broke. I can't tell anymore and I don't think he cares at this point."

Trent jerked stiff, clearly horrified. "No," he said, clearly not wanting to believe.

"The only reason I was able to beat your location out of him was because I had a knife at his throat." *That, and Vivian.*

"The Goddess take him," Trent swore. "No wonder he wasn't surprised when Quen told me to go into hiding." A muffled groan slipped from him as he peeled one sock off to show his foot, pale and wrinkled. "All this because I want him to up his purity?"

"Taking you out of the market will bankrupt you. He's looking to pay you back for his daughter."

Trent was silent as he took off his second sock. "I told him the cure was free."

"Clearly that's not how he saw it." The fire wasn't making any inroads into warming me, and I pulled my socks off, inside out. "It gets better," I said as I dropped them into a sodden pile. "He tricked someone into making a new chakra ring in my church." My eyes filled, and my throat tightened. "I thought he forced you to make it," I added, my voice going high.

"Oh, Rachel." He gave my hand a squeeze as he tugged me into a sideways, frog-smelling hug. But someone had died there, leaving nothing but a fatty ash stain, and my gut hurt at their probable pain and anger. *Please let it be no one I know.*

"He was going to blame me for it," I said as Trent's grip eased. "It might have stuck if Vivian hadn't intervened. Did you know he was the coven's new plumber? That's why he is in Cincinnati." *Not some dumb Halloween party.*

Trent leaned away, but his hand never let go of mine. "No," he muttered flatly.

I watched our twined fingers, our pearl rings glowing orange in the flames. "No wonder he jumped at the chance to get into Hodin's room. He wasn't only looking for evidence to frame me as a dark practitioner"— *which I am*—"and you as a drug lord"—*which you are*—"but the recipe for the chakra ring."

"That's why he tried to steal the lens." Trent slowly shook his head, little drips from his hair spotting the dry earth. "He's been playing us since he got here." Disgusted, he tossed another split log onto the fire to send sparks up into the clearing sky. "I have to call Quen," he added as he took his cell from his pocket, shoulders slumping as he set the ruined phone down.

"Quen knows about Lee," I said, quickly adding, "The girls are fine. We're going to be okay. Vivian heard him admit that he twisted that curse."

Jaw tight, Trent frowned. "I hate to see him in Alcatraz. They won't let him run his Brimstone from there, and I'm not eager to deal with his replacement. I spent a lifetime getting to know him, and now it doesn't mean squat."

"Good God, Trent. He tried to kill you!" I exclaimed, and he shrugged, gaze distant on the fire. "Um, I really wanted to talk to Al, but I suppose we should get back," I said, not relishing the coming walk loaded down with my books and in soggy underwear. I wasn't looking forward to putting my socks back on, either. "You've got a change of clothes at the church." I stood, glancing at Al's dark wagon.

"Sure." Pride softened his features as he rose as well and tugged me closer. "You learned how to line jump. I knew you could do it."

"Ah, actually, no," I said, head down in a pinch of guilt. "I bought the jumps from Dali. And I repaid the one you bought from him, too, so don't let him try to double-dip on you."

"Oh, Rachel." He took both my hands, turning them over to see if I had a demon mark. "You shouldn't have done that."

"What, and let you die?" I said, jerking my hands from him. "You might think it's a joke, but Lee wants you dead or penniless! To him, they are the same thing."

"Okay." He steeled his expression. "What did you give Dali if not a future favor?"

"Al's dagger. The one from the vault."

The door to Al's wagon crashed open, thumping into the wall of his van to make us both spin. "You gave *Quaere* to Dali?" Al bellowed, half-dressed in a billowing red nightshirt as he stumbled down the narrow, ladderlike steps. "Do you have any idea how long it took me to make?!"

"Al! Uh, hi," I said, shocked. "Just who I wanted to see," I added, cursing myself for the guilt in my voice. "I was going to—"

"Six months!" Al tugged his nightshirt straight as he paced forward. "It can only be twisted during an absolute full moon on the summer equinox. Do you know how rare those are? It was worth more than four line jumps!" He jerked to a halt, red eyes narrowing as he saw Trent. "But it might have been worth your elf's life." Slumping, he sat on the stone closest to the fire, his nightshirt up about his knees. "He renamed it, didn't he."

I still felt guilty. "Yes. I'm sorry. He called it Revenge. I'll make you another one."

"Pffft, all gone," Al said, gesturing to the darkening sky. "Like you will ever have six uninterrupted months in a row." He turned to me, his lip curled. "You brought books instead of shoes and sequined dresses. Perhaps you will survive after all."

I motioned for Trent to stay back, then cautiously sat on the flat rock beside Al. "Ah, I was hoping I could stay here for a few days?"

Al frowned at Trent as the elf sat down as well and tried to get his phone to work. "Yeah?" the demon said flatly, the word holding an entire conversation of "no."

"Until Vivian clears my name," I said. "She's totally ticked that Lee used the coven to further himself. Everything will be fine by Monday." I hesitated. "Probably."

"Monday?" Al mocked, and then he stiffened, his gaze going to the woods. "Ahhh, excuse me," he said, springing to his feet. Fumbling in a pocket, he threw a charm on the fire. Immediately it whooshed up higher, throwing back the shadows until I could see all the way to the encroaching woods.

"What is it?" I asked, jumping when the door to his wagon slammed shut. He was gone.

"That's Lucy." Trent set his phone down and stood to face the woods. "Lucy?" he called, and a little-girl shriek split the night.

"Hi, Daddy!" Lucy's clear voice was like sunshine. "Down, Abba. Down!" she demanded, and I inched closer to Trent as the fallen leaves in the woods rattled, sounding like an entire scurry of squirrels was descending on us. But it was only Lucy tearing out of the dark woods in her pj's with the surety of running through her own house.

"Hi, Daddy!" Lucy flung herself at Trent when he crouched to meet her. Beaming, the little girl gave him an enthusiastic hug only to push away with a frown when he stood with her on his hip. "You're wet!"

Trent gave her a loving kiss. "I spent the day in a well, my lovely."

And then I was scrambling to take her when he shifted her to me. "Hi, Lucy. Why are you out of bed?" I asked as I got a squishy hug and she pushed from me as well.

"You're wet, too!" she said, sounding betrayed, and I tweaked her nose.

"Someone needed to rescue your daddy."

Trent smiled, glancing at his bare feet before turning to the woods and the sound of slow hooves. "It's Quen," he said in worry as the branches snapped and Tulpa stepped into the chancy light, a small wagon behind him. Ray was beside Quen on the bench, and the little girl stood, reaching.

"Sa'han," Quen called, then clucked and crooned to Trent's horse, pulling him to a halt before the fire. Ray was wobbling precariously at the edge, and Quen scooped her up, jumping effortlessly to the soft, leaf-strewed meadow. "I was hoping Rachel would bring you here," Quen said as he set the wiggling girl down and she ran to Trent.

"Hi, my lovely," he said, cuddling her close and listening to a whispered little-girl request as she touched his wet collar.

I was very glad to see them, even if their presence meant something had gone wrong. The girls were supposed to be with Ellasbeth. If Quen had spirited them away, she was going to be ticked.

"You're wet," Quen said, his forehead furrowed as he noticed both Trent's and my bare feet.

"Daddy was in a well," Lucy said importantly, and Quen's expression went cross.

"A well?" Quen echoed, then seemed to reset himself. "Sa'han, I have news."

"I imagine so." Trent's focus brightened as he went to his horse, softly greeting him before continuing on to the wagon. "Rachel has told me Lee is the mage," he said as he rummaged. "Fortunately the coven won't continue to entertain him or his ridiculous claims." Clearly pleased, he opened a plastic tub and took out a new set of clothes, right down to his tighty-whities. "Can I assume that the correct, ah, deposits are being made?"

"Vivian heard him admit to everything," I said, pleased until Quen's shoulders drooped in a heavy sigh. "What," I said flatly.

He took a breath, but his words remained unsaid as Al shoved his wagon's door open and strode down the steps as if entering a ballroom. He was in his usual crushed green velvet frock coat, but I couldn't help but notice that his boots were scuffed.

"My girls!" the demon called, falling to a knee to take both Lucy and Ray when they ran to him. "I have something to show you," he said, rising with them in his arms. "In the creek."

"Mermaids?" Lucy asked, and Al's brow furrowed for a moment in distress. Mermaids? Maybe once, but now it was probably frogs.

"You never know," he said. "But you must be quiet. Can you be quiet, my Lucy?"

The little girl shook her head, and Al laughed. But it faded fast as he walked away. His eyes almost glowed in the fire as he looked over his shoulder at me. Stifling a shudder, I turned to Trent and Quen at the wagon. Al had taken the girls to the creek so we could talk, but he would stay near enough to hear.

"You brought a wagon?" I said as Trent continued to rummage through it.

"It's my bug-out bag," he said shortly. "Quen, where are the bath wipes?"

"I'll find them, Sa'han."

"You can keep rolling that wagon along," Al said from the stream. "You aren't moving in with me." He beamed at the girls, now throwing leaves into the stream to watch them drift. "Unlike you, my elven sunshines, who can stay as long as you like."

That worried feeling in my gut began to grow stronger. "Come on, Al," I coaxed. "You can put up with us for a few days. It's the weekend."

Trent was stripping off his shirt, eagerly taking the packaged shower-in-a-bag that Quen handed him. "Tal Sa'han?" Quen said, somewhat snarky as he extended one to me as well, and I shook my head.

"I'll wait to get back to the church."

"That would be ill-advised," Quen said, and Trent's motions hesitated, his damp, bare chest gleaming in the firelight.

"Oh no," I whispered. "Did they burn it down? Did Lee burn down my church?"

"The church is fine." Quen's expression was a severe nothing, and yet my worry tightened. "Your assets have been frozen, Sa'han, pending the results of an I.S. investigation into your genetic endeavors and, ah, Brimstone trade. The investigation into accusations of practicing illicit magic are a deeper concern."

Trent set the cloth aside, shuffled into a new shirt, and unzipped his pants as he moved to the shadow of the wagon. "Lee will drop the accusations. It will pass."

"Not this time, Sa'han." Quen frowned at me as if it was my fault. "Rachel, you have been implicated as well. I hope you brought more than your books, because the church has been impounded."

From the creek, Al chuckled. "If they are the right books, that's all she needs."

"Finnis is en route to Cincinnati," Quen said, and I jerked.

"Wait. What?" I interrupted. The undead vampire had already tried to take Cincinnati once. "Why?"

Quen opened a second shower bag and handed the thick cloth to Trent. "Possibly as early as tonight. His people have taken possession of Piscary's. With Finnis in charge of the I.S., I will not be able to quash the investigations no matter how much money we throw at it." Quen became tight-lipped, still staring at me as if it was all my fault. *It isn't, is it?*

"Please tell me Constance is still a mouse," I said, and from behind the wagon, I heard a zipper go up.

"I have not heard either way," Quen said. "Word on the street says Ivy, Nina, and Pike have made it to a safe harbor thanks to Piscary's children. It's unraveling, Tal Sa'han."

He had said the last with a bitter accusation, and I felt myself cringe. Tal Sa'han, as in most trusted advisor to Trent. And look where that got Trent. "David? Cassie?" I asked as Trent came from the shadow, his hair spiky and sticking up from a probable towel rub.

Quen began unhitching Tulpa. "Hiding. The streets are surprisingly quiet. Everyone is waiting to see what you will do."

"As are we all, itchy witch," Al said, then congratulated Ray for having set her floating leaf on fire.

"But Vivian," I said, at a loss. "She had Lee pinned down. She will fix this. Make it right. There is no way that Lee can best her, even if he used demon magic."

Quen stood before me, Tulpa's harness in hand. "Vivian is dead. Lee tricked her into making a second chakra ring last night. You're wanted for her murder."

*Wait. What?* Stunned, I turned to Trent, but he seemed as shocked as I was. "No, you're wrong," I said. "I don't know who Lee tricked into making that ring, but it wasn't Vivian. I texted her this afternoon. She texted me back. I *saw* her not more than a few hours ago."

But Quen shook his head, his gaze on Tulpa as the horse eagerly ambled into the dark to graze. "If she texted you, it was probably Lee. I'm sorry. I know she was a friend. Jenks says Getty witnessed the entire thing. Tried to stop it. Lee told Vivian that you wanted to meet her at the church last night to show her everything. When you weren't there, he set the curse up and convinced her the only way to know if it was illicit or not was to do it. All he had to do was get Vivian to stand in the right spot and say the invocation phrase. It's unfortunate that Getty's statements are inadmissible in court."

"But I *saw* her," I said, not believing this. "So did Lee."

And he had been terrified. As if seeing a ghost.

I felt sick, and I sat down hard on the low stone before the fire. Jenks had tried to tell me, but I had been in too much of a hurry to listen. "I saw her," I whispered. "She said . . ." My words faltered, and I looked at the chakra rings on my finger, my hand shaking as I recalled the fiery sensation cramping my gut when I had touched the pentagram. Had Vivian died there, leaving enough of an imprint in the fabric of time and space that she had lingered? My God. Had she become a ghost to warn me? She had been covered in mystics, almost floating over the floor. And how would she know what Jasmine had said if she hadn't talked to her? *Jasmine is a ghost?*

I could do nothing, and I stared at the fire even when Trent pulled me to a stand and gingerly took me in his arms, damp clothes and all. "I'm sure you saw her," he whispered. "She was the coven's most proficient practitioner, adept at high-level manipulations. She might have found a way to linger, to avenge herself and you."

*Vivian . . . no,* I thought, grief swamping me. "I . . . I have to go," I said, taking a step out of his arms. Al stood at the stream with the girls, eyes bright and watching. There was no one left to say that I didn't kill Vivian. There was no one to vouch for me in the coven. No one but Vivian knew Lee was the mage. If Lee had survived, Lee would be believed. Everything was falling apart. But mostly it was my grief that Vivian was . . . dead.

"I have to get to the church." I had to see if it was true. I had to know for myself, talk to Getty. *Damn it, Jenks had been trying to tell me, and I hadn't listened.*

"Tal Sa'han, perhaps now is not—" Quen said, and I rounded on him.

"I am going to the church!" I shouted. *Not Vivian,* I thought, my eyes spilling over, hot tears dripping down my face. *Please, not Vivian . . .*

And then my grief found an outlet. *Lee . . .* Like a switch, my tears vanished. Trent saw it and let go of me. He knew what it meant.

Quen did not. "Rachel, you can't best five coven members. That you are free is the only thing keeping the lid on Cincinnati. From what I've pieced together, Lee cut a deal with the I.S., the DC vamps, and the coven, promising them all a share of, or a return to, power if they forced Trent out. David is the only one still in control of his people. Ivy and Pike are in hiding, and Trent is now a persona non grata. Zack is trying, but if he says too much, they will silence him. Don't ruin what little power he has."

I sank back down onto the stone, focus distant as I reached for my soggy socks and struggled to put them on for the trip home. David was okay because I had gotten rid of Parker, but everyone else?

"I can't get these damn socks on!" I shouted. Frustrated, I slumped where I sat, not sure what to do. In one ill-defined moment, I had lost it all. Lee had not only ruined me but taken down almost everyone who had stood with me. Lee's sword had been my fear for what Vivian might think of me. I'd waited too long to show her what I'd done. It was my doing.

"I have to go." Giving up on my socks, I rose, an arm wrapped around my middle so nothing spilled out.

"We will fight this, Rachel." Trent tried to pull me close, but I'd have none of it, and I stepped away, my bare feet finding sticks and tiny rocks. "It will only take time," he said. "The girls are safe. David is strong. Ivy and Pike are in hiding. We reassess and move forward. I've got a tent in my bug-out bag. Everything will look better in the morning."

Silent, I turned to the woods. Loss crushed me. It felt too late. Everything was gone. Everything.

"Rachel?" Trent called as I started walking. I could get to my church easy from the ley line. Five minutes. Six if I kept stomping and cut my foot.

"I'm fine!" I shouted back, but I wasn't fine. Lee had killed Vivian. If I had shown her the stupid curse, she would have known it was lethal. She would have known Lee was lying to her. It could have ended right there. But I hadn't, and everything she'd been was gone.

"I'll talk to her," Al said around a breathy groan. "Before it begins to rain again."

*You think so, you old demon?* I thought as I passed his mushroom ring and my damp hair briefly lifted.

Behind me, branches began to snap, and a muffled swearing rose. "Rachel, stop," Al demanded. "Mother pus bucket, which one of you thought trees with thorns was a good idea?"

Relenting, I drew to a halt. The moon was high, mirroring the one in reality, and I clenched my jaw, chin lifting as he came even with me, his eyes dark in the dim light, pinched with a shared heartache.

"You are going to reality?" he asked, and I pushed past him to start walking again.

"I need a new pair of jeans," I said. "And boots." *And maybe a lamp.*

"Tomorrow," Al said, and I jerked to a halt when he touched my shoulder.

Shocked, I looked at him as he hid his hand as if he'd done something wrong. I could count the number of times that he had touched me, but it was the pain in him that struck me.

"You need to pause," he said, voice low. "I've survived through ugly turns such as this. Much as I am loath to admit it, your elf is right. Those who pause to think, survive. Those who react . . ." His eye twitched, and his focus went distant. "Tend not to," he finished.

I bit my lower lip to try to keep from crying in front of him. I knew he was right, but Vivian was dead because I hadn't trusted her, and I couldn't simply help Trent set up camp and go to sleep. "His name is Trent," I said instead, and Al frowned in confusion. "He's not *my elf.*"

Al grunted as if pained. "*Trent* is right," he grumbled. "Your power structure is still there. Sleep. Eat. Give Lee a chance to think he's safe. Find out his next move. Counter it. This is not unexpected. It is only unfortunate."

But my heart hurt, and all I wanted to do was pound Lee until he quit moving.

"Please, Rachel," Al whispered, his hand finding my shoulder again. "Don't try to do this alone. You are not alone. Don't force yourself to be."

His hand was warm on me, and my head bowed. "Just go back to the fire," I said bitterly. "Wait until morning. Like I'll even sleep. You make it sound so easy."

And yet, Al exhaled, clearly relieved as I let him turn me around. "I know this pain," he said softly. "The pause isn't easy. But it will keep you alive."

# CHAPTER

# 26

"HOT IT, DADDY! HOT IT!" LUCY WHINED, AND I PULLED THE COVERS over my head. The girl's high-pitched complaint cut right through the thick sleeping bag to let the sunshine in. I was awake.

Sitting up, I found myself inches from the double-insulated tent's ceiling. The air mattress under me squished until my butt hit the cold earth, and I didn't move, staring at the hazy sunrise through the trees and feeling tired as Lucy continued to wail. *At least it's not raining.*

Trent's "bug-out bag" was a little more complex than mine, but in all fairness, he did have a more complicated life. Or so it seemed on the surface.

I exhaled as Lucy continued to cry, waiting for the will to breathe in again. The spot beside me where Trent had been was long cold, and I tugged the sleeping bag straight. My pearl ring was glowing after I'd spooned against Trent all night. Vivian had once told me it was on the wrong finger, and my gut hurt as a pang of heartache found me. She was gone. Vivian had died because I hadn't been forthright about the curse. If I had, she would have known it was lethal and still be alive. That she wasn't was my doing.

It was the smell of coffee that finally pulled me crawling from the tent. Bits of sticks and grass stuck to my palms as I got to my feet, and I was in desperate need of my toothbrush currently sitting an entire reality away. Al had said I'd feel better in the morning, but all I felt was cold and slow.

Trent was at the smoldering fire with Lucy, trying to braid her hair through the distracting birdsong. Across from them were Ray and Al. They both had their eyes closed as if sleeping, but I'd be willing to bet he was teaching her how to still her thoughts. Bis had come in during the night, and his hunched silhouette beside Treble on Al's roof made him look tiny. The only one missing was Jenks, and I felt a pang of guilt as I silently sat down beside Trent and Lucy. Jenks had been trying to tell me about Vivian—and I hadn't listened, utterly blowing him off in my concern to get to Trent.

"Good morning," Trent said, his concentration fully on Lucy as I poked at the fire. She was singing about spiders and waterspouts, and I smiled. "Coffee?"

"Please," I whispered, and Al cracked an eye, chuckling as he resettled Ray and the two resumed their drowse. The demon was positively content, and I wondered at the restorative power of children, grounding us in what was real. Ellasbeth was probably angry that Quen had cut her weekend short, livid that he was on the run with them. The only child she had any legal right to was Lucy, and I wondered if Quen had done something drastic to take custody of her.

The bright chattering of the coffee into a mug was more than pleasant, and I lost myself for a moment, my bare feet on the cold ground, a warm mug in hand, me breathing in the nutty scent and enjoying my first sip. Trent nodded in satisfaction, then turned to reorganize the burning logs to a brighter flame. He seemed different in jeans and a thick wool shirt, his hair unstyled and woodsmoke on his clothes. As I huddled on the dew-damp cushion before the warm fire and hitched a blanket smelling of burnt amber around my shoulders, I wondered if perhaps it might be time to quit. Someone else could save the world from here on out.

Done with the fire, Trent jammed the poker into the ground. "Sorry about the early wake-up. They've camped before, but never without hot and cold running water."

I slumped deeper into myself and glanced at the low sun. "It's okay." I blearily scanned the shadowed clearing, realizing Tulpa was gone. "Where's Quen?"

"Getting the news." Shoulders hunched, Trent touched his empty pocket where his phone usually was, then squinted in worry at the woods. "He should have been back half an hour ago."

"Mmmm." I squirmed, sensing a sudden need. "Thanks for the coffee. You, ah, don't happen to know where the little girls' room is, do you?"

Trent smiled, his attention going to Al's wagon behind me. "The woods, I'm afraid. He won't let anyone inside."

I stood, blanket pulled tighter around my shoulders. "Al?" I questioned hopefully, and he opened one eye. "Can I . . ."

"No," he muttered, brightening when Lucy came to him with an acorn and asked him to turn it into a spider.

Fine. I could pee behind a bush, but someone was going to have to dig a latrine before too much longer. Steps slow and awkward from my bare feet, I started for the tree line, pulling up at the sound of horse hooves.

"Quen?" I called, all wistful thoughts of my beautiful bathroom gone. But it wasn't Quen, it was David sitting atop Tulpa, looking as if he was coming in off the prairie in his duster and hat. *David knows how to ride?*

"David." I shifted to intercept him. "Is everything okay? Where's Quen?"

"He stayed behind," David said, and the horse picked up the pace, tail high as he trotted to Trent despite David reining him in. Trent had risen at the sound of hoofbeats, and he cooed and murmured at the horse when it headbutted him, clearly glad to see him.

"You are a splendid animal," Trent whispered, fondling the horse's ears before turning to David. "Coffee?"

"Yes, please." David slipped down, hitting the ground with a faint grimace. "Quen was right. He knew exactly where you were."

Smiling, Trent began to unsaddle the horse. "He's my familiar."

David gave Tulpa a pat, beaming at the domestic scene. "Wow," he said, his breath visible with his words. "It's cold over here."

Al made a harrumph as he set both girls down and gave them a trinket to keep them occupied. "It is. Today," he said, glancing accusingly at me. "At least it isn't raining."

*And that is my fault?* I thought as I gave David a hug and pulled in deep the complex scent of Were. "So, what's the news?"

"About what you would expect." Shifting, he took a phone from a pocket and handed it to Trent. "Quen sent a replacement for you."

"Thank you," Trent muttered, immediately immersing himself in it, head down and almost walking into the fire as he went to sit before it.

"Jenks?" I pressed as I led David to the fire and filled an empty mug. "Did you talk to Stef?"

"No, but they're both okay." David sat, mug almost lost in his laced fingers. He glanced at Ray and Lucy as they ran past him to play under the wagon. "Doyle has a car at the church. Jenks and Getty are there, making life hell for anyone who tries to get into your room. Lee has been especially persistent."

"He's alive?" I blurted. "I thought Vivian . . ." My words faltered as Al and Trent exchanged a worried look. "I saw her," I said, feeling myself warm. "She helped me."

David raised a hand. "Rachel, I'm sorry, but if you saw her, it was a Saladan trick."

"One that tried to kill him?" I said.

"Maybe it was to get you to leave," Trent said, and I frowned, resettling myself on the cold stone. I knew what I'd seen. Vivian had helped me. Ghosts were like that. Sometimes.

"Regardless," David said, clearly uncomfortable. "Despite Jenks and Getty's valiant efforts, the coven has been through the rest of the church. Confiscated everything not in your room, down to your spelling salt."

"Really." Anger stained my grief for Vivian. "At least my books are safe."

Trent put his new phone in a breast pocket, his gaze on the girls. His phone wouldn't connect to anything in the ever-after, but Quen had probably downloaded his messages before David had crossed. "Ivy and Pike?" he asked.

"Hiding," David said. "Nina, too. You know the toxic hospital grounds that you tricked Constance into buying?"

I found I could still smile. "No kidding," I said, figuring they'd be safe there for a while. No one went into the abandoned hospital campus, afraid there might be a lingering T-4 Angel virus on a doorknob.

"Bad news is that Finnis is coming in tonight to take over for, ah, you."

*Great.* Leaning over my knees, I sighed at my bare feet. My hair was in ugly straggles, and I pushed it behind my ear, angry at the world.

"That is," David continued, "unless you want to do something about it?"

I had no words, and I simply stared at the fire, poking at it with a thin stick.

"What do you expect Rachel to do?" Trent said, surprising me. "Vivian was her voice in the coven. With her gone, no one will believe Rachel. She's accused of murdering a coven member with dark magic. She's got the books to do it and the motive, if they believe Lee." He hesitated, focus shifting to the fire. "Regaining my assets will be a trick, too," he muttered.

The tip of the stick smoldered as I sketched out Pike's logo in the dirt. It was no fun being poor. It wasn't anything to be ashamed of, though, and I'd been poor before. The shame was in being rich off someone else's work. Unfortunately, it was a cold, immutable fact that I had twisted illicit magic in the past and likely would again. Vivian had been the only one who had trusted me to not hurt anyone with it. "Maybe it's time to take a break," I whispered, tossing the stick on the flames.

David was silent for a moment. "You mind if I give you some advice?"

"What," I said flatly, and Trent got to his feet, his smooth, uncalloused hands brushing his jeans free of dirt.

"I should check on the girls," Trent said as he turned to Al. "Al?"

"I'm not missing this," the demon said.

Trent took a breath as if to protest, then changed his mind and walked away.

David was smiling, and it ticked me off. "What's so funny?"

Silent, he hunched over his knees and shifted the logs for a better airflow. "You are."

"Me?" I said, not liking that Al was listening. "Please. Tell me what's funny. I could use a laugh."

"Just how long," David said slowly, "do you think you will be content to sit here in self-imposed isolation and watch Cincy flounder before you step back in?"

My anger evaporated and I slumped. "It's gone," I said. "There is nothing left."

David shook his head. "It's not gone. It's underground. Where it should have been all the time, if you ask me. When power is obvious, it gets challenged. And you were. By Constance. By Hodin. And now, Lee. Unlike the rest, Lee learned from their mistakes. You can't be beaten by outright power, so he manipulated you. Frankly, you deserved it. You got cocky."

"Gee, thanks," I muttered, but a sliver of guilt was rising, and I hated it.

"You hid when Lee accused you of murdering Vivian, thereby giving up your freedom. Trent lost his money, and with it went your pull with the elves. With Finnis coming in, whatever influence you had on the I.S. and the vampires will shrink. Frankly, all you have left is me, and that's not enough."

My frown deepened as I tugged my blanket tighter about my shoulders and watched Trent sit cross-legged under the wagon with the girls. "If you're trying to cheer me up, you're doing a sucky job of it."

"I'm not done yet," he said, lips quirked. "Everything you think you lost is still there. But it won't last if you stay here," he cautioned. "The coven is gathering support to curse the demons into exile in the ever-after."

Al sat up with a grunt. "They are what?" he said, and Trent turned our way.

"Lee would be exempt," David continued. "He's not in the demon collective, but you are. If it works, you'll be stuck here, and everything you worked for will slowly and painfully decay, and I say painfully because no one in their right mind wants Finnis and Lee in charge. And that's assuming no one has found out your summoning name, in which case, you are in Alcatraz."

My chest hurt, and I stared at Al, scared when his expression stiffened.

"Okay," David said, knees spread as he took in the fire's heat. "I get that it's a challenge to avoid incarceration or death when the coven is out to get you. You have a definite home base. You're easy to track on social media. It doesn't help that you haven't been up-front with the coven. Unfortunately, with Finnis involved, the I.S. is more than willing to bring you in."

"I've already fought one I.S. death threat and won," I said. Trent was coming back to the fire, and I shifted on my stone to give him a place to sit down.

"That's what I'm saying." David smacked a hand on his knee. "You got this. But not if you're camped out in the ever-after eating s'mores and drinking coffee made over an open fire." His gaze went appreciatively into his cup. "As good as it is. That's why Quen pushed me through a ley line so I could ask you, one city power to another. What are you going to do?"

Guilt, anxiety, and a little thread of panic iced through me as I looked from David to Trent, and then finally Al. The question in David's eye remained, but he knew I wasn't going to sit here and feel sorry for myself for very long, because he was right. Everything was still there. It was in hiding. As it should have been from the beginning.

Slowly I nodded, and Al's furrowed brow smoothed.

"I need to talk to Dali," the demon said as he stood. "May I borrow your horse?"

"If he will accept you," Trent said dryly, and the horse nickered, ears going flat when Al boldly strode across the field toward him.

"Al?" I called as the demon stopped four feet from the horse, the aging gray's lip now lifted in threat.

"The coven can't be allowed to exile us from reality again," Al said as he took a step forward, shifting sharply to the left to avoid a thrown hoof. "Rachel's efforts to get that curse removed nearly bankrupted me the first time." Moving like fire, Al snagged Tulpa's bridle, dragging it off the horse as Tulpa lunged to bite him. Shocked, the horse waggled his head. "I'll be with Dali. If you need me, call him."

In an enviable smooth move, Al grabbed a handful of mane and swung himself atop Tulpa, bareback and no bridle. The horse made one stifled whinny, his alarmed prance quickly dissolving into an even, in-place trot. Even his ears lifted.

"I didn't know you could ride," I said, thinking he looked really good there. Almost as good as an elf.

"Ride?" Al patted the horse, now standing still and blowing. "I invented dressage. Well, the fighting horse, actually. Dressage is all that's left." He hesitated, something new passing through him as he sat atop a horse. "Kalamack, the ever-after is lacking. When you have time, I'd like to talk to you about introducing a semi-wild herd."

"Ah, sure," Trent said, clearly stunned that Al was atop his familiar. And then Al shifted his leg and the horse wheeled around to canter slowly into the woods.

"Huh," I said, surprised, but I really shouldn't have been.

"Rachel?" David asked. "I'm going to fix what I can. What is your decision?"

The I.S. truly wasn't the problem, or Finnis, or even the coven. It was Lee. If I took his power, it would all fall back to me. I couldn't best a city, but I could best a man. "Can you get a message to Ivy for me?" I asked, and David stood and extended a hand to help me up, his smile wide in anticipation.

"I can do one better. Find some boots. I know where she is."

# CHAPTER

# 27

"THEY USUALLY GO DOWN AROUND NOW AND SLEEP FOR SIX hours," Trent was saying to Al. The demon was holding both girls, a flicker of annoyance on him as we had drawn him out of Dalliance and his conference with Dali to babysit. The demon eatery was currently that vampire strip bar, and the modern, unkempt building with its cracked parking lot and paint-peeling fence was surreal at the bottom of an earthen bowl with Tulpa cropping the tall grass surrounding it.

"Please don't keep them up, or they will crash too early tonight and throw off their entire schedule," Trent added, squinting in the high sun. Between the girls' needs and finding a pair of Trent's slippers for me, it had taken us a frustrating four hours to make the twenty-minute walk to Dalliance, and I was antsy to see Ivy.

"I have cared for elven children before." Shifting them higher, Al beamed at the sleepy girls in turn. "We will have so much fun at Dalliance, my darlings!"

Trent's expression blanked. "Ah, I thought you'd take them back to your wagon to nap," he said, his hands twitching as if he was having second thoughts.

"They'll be fine." I linked my arm in Trent's to draw him away, but he resisted even as his gaze went to David, waiting on the crest of the hill. "If the demons can't find a way to slip the witches' curse, they'll be stuck in the ever-after, and if Al isn't here, he won't be able to give any input. But you don't have to come," I added, and Trent's focus sharpened on me. "The I.S. and coven still have a warrant out for you."

"I'm not staying here," he said, his attention flicking to the strip bar when the door banged open.

It was Dali, the portly demon striding across the cracked pavement toward us with his formal black spelling robe furling about his heels. "Rachel!" he bellowed, voice echoing in the cupped valley. "A word with you and Gally. Alone."

Trent sighed, and my hands went to my hips. "Trent—" I started, annoyed.

"Isn't a demon," Dali finished, and I scowled.

Trent took my hands. "It's not a big deal," he said as he tugged me forward and gave me a small kiss to make Al stifle a groan. "Actually, I think it's great. They are seeing you as one of their own," he added as he tweaked Lucy's neck to make her squirm and arranged Ray's hair. "Be good for your uncle Al," he told the girls, his voice light, and then to me, "Rachel, I'll wait for you with David." Pausing, he gave Al a respectful nod. "Al."

"Kalamack," Al said, just as blandly.

"You don't have to leave," I insisted, but Trent only gave Dali an amused smirk before heading for the rise, his long legs taking the hill with ease.

"You know I'm going to tell him. Whatever it is," I said as Dali settled in before us. His goat-slitted eyes held worry, but anticipation had tightened his stance, making him seem almost aggressive. Clearly something was up.

"This doesn't concern the elves," Dali said, his gaze lingering on Lucy and Ray falling asleep in the noon sun, their wispy hair shifting in the breeze. "Your recent failure with Kalamack Senior's lab experiment is embarrassing, but it *has* brought to light a dangerous situation we need to remedy."

"Kalamack Senior. You mean Trent's dad?" I said, and then, after a moment's thought, "Hey. I am taking care of Lee. I haven't failed anything."

Dali made a face in a silent rebuke. "In light of the situation, we have decided that we will endeavor to close the lines to simple translocation travel to prevent witches and elves from crossing into the ever-after by standing in a ley line. Their fear of us once kept our reality free of them, but you broke that, and such an action is long overdue. Your presence is both needed and requested."

"Lee isn't an experiment," I said, annoyed as I watched Trent trudge up the rise, Tulpa following close behind. "Is that what you think I am? An experiment?"

Al took a breath, but Dali was faster. "Time will tell what you are," Dali said. "Inside."

But I shook my head, arms over my middle to become as unmoving as a salt pillar. "I'm not going to help you close the lines to translocation travel," I said, and Al chuckled knowingly. Doing so would only stop witches and elves from coming to the ever-after. Demons were not about to give up their oat milk cinnamon lattes and could move from reality to reality without needing to stand in a ley line. That is, unless the witches cursed them into exile. Either way, I was going to be stuck in whatever reality I was in when it happened. "Look, I appreciate the gesture, but Lee is not that big of an issue. I've got this. Besides, closing the lines might negate the legislation that Trent has done on our behalf. I lose everything, you lose everything."

Dali's lips pressed together, but Al was clearly not going to side with him, and his eyes narrowed. "You have already lost everything," Dali said sourly. "Into Dalliance. Go."

"I said I can handle Lee," I muttered, and Al nodded, boosting my confidence. "Once I get him out of Cincy, things will course correct. I already took out his primary muscle, and he's scared to death of you all. He won't dare cross the ley lines." Because despite my cold-morning thoughts, I wasn't about to stay here for the rest of my life. It was a place to catch my breath, to regroup.

"I do not share your optimism concerning . . . Lee." Dali's lips curled as Al patted Lucy's shoulder and sniggered. "And despite your lofty opinion of yourself, not everything is about you. If Lee was indeed Hodin's student, there's a chance, however slim, that he could tamper with the tulpa that holds him. Closing the lines will prevent Lee from entering the ever-after. He can't line jump, and no demon will sell him one."

"And there's the sticking point," Al said softly as I bristled.

"Neither can I, yet," I said, feeling a hit. "Nor Al at the moment."

Dali's lips curved into an ugly smile. "Learn?" he said insincerely.

"No," I said as Al jiggled on his feet and patted Lucy drowsing in the sun. "I'm not going to help you close the lines. Not for any reason. Isolation is a bad idea no matter what you think you might gain from it."

"It doesn't matter," Dali said. "You are outvoted. We are doing this with or without you."

"Hey!" I started, and Al cleared his throat.

"You can try," Al said sourly. "But you will not manage it, even with her help. Our collective has become too small for such a curse. Without Newt, we are too few." He beamed at Dali and hitched Lucy higher up his hip. "Unless you suggest we ask for the Goddess's aid?"

Dali's expression became dark. "You jest."

"Of course," Al coaxed, but I wasn't convinced, and I doubted Dali was, either. "Regardless, I will not burn what's left of my synapses tilting at windmills. Rachel is correct. Lee will not cross the lines for any reason, and not to rescue Hodin, the very demon who had been grooming him to perform a lethal curse."

I took a breath, then let it slip from me. I had assumed the initial S in Hodin's notes regarding his potential sacrifice had meant Stef, but it could have been Saladan.

"Despite Rachel's convictions, the problem isn't Lee," Al insisted. "It is the coven, and Rachel is taking care of that." His gaze sharpened on mine. "Right?"

"Ah, yeah," I said, still trying to figure out who Hodin had been intending to off.

"Fine." Dali's expression soured. "We do this without you."

"Dali," I said, but he had spun away. Five seconds later, the door to the bar closed with a dull thud. In hindsight, I could see why the demons wanted to close the lines, because once you knew how to translocate from reality to reality, it wasn't that hard. Not like line jumping. Now that the fear of demons was abating, it wouldn't be long until people would be crossing to take a picnic or ride their four-wheelers over the pristine fields.

"Everything okay?" Trent shouted from the top of the hill, and I winced, not knowing.

Al hitched the girls higher, neither of them stirring. "Is it?" he asked.

"It will be." Not convinced, I arranged Lucy's and Ray's hair as they slept. "You're okay with them?"

He nodded. "I will keep them safe," he assured me. "Do what you need to do."

"Thank you," I whispered, and then I turned and trudged up the hill. The bar's door closing sounded odd amid the soughing of the dry grass, and I managed a smile when Trent came forward, his horse trailing along behind him like a half-ton dog.

"You don't have to tell me," he said, and I laced my fingers in his.

"Dali wants to shut down the lines to all translocation travel before the witches can exile them to the ever-after, but Al says they don't have enough pull to do it," I said, worried. "Dali thinks Lee might find a way to tamper with the tulpa that holds Hodin, but it's more than that. Lee is an excuse. Fear used to keep the ever-after free of witches and elves, and the demons have lost that. Maybe Dali is right. If people keep coming over here, demons won't be able to resist abducting them." And I'd be right back where I was three years ago.

"Mmmm." Trent's steps slowed as we made our way to David, Tulpa slowly trailing us. "What do you think?"

"I think Lee likes Hodin right where he is," I said. "I'm more concerned about the coven." Because for all my bravado, both the coven and the I.S. had warrants out for my arrest—all of which would make it hard to stop the witches from exiling the demons *and* to prove I didn't murder Vivian. But as difficult as it was today, it would be impossible if Finnis took the city.

"All set," I said as we joined David, but instead of going to the nearby ley line that came out at Eden Park, he faced north, striding through the waving grass, heading into nothing. "Ah, we're not going to Eden Park?" I said as I hotfooted it to catch up.

"The coven is watching all the lines," David said as he checked his watch. "But we have clear passage at the university's ley line. That's where Quen is. He can take us to Ivy."

*And from there?* I wondered, not liking my lack of a plan. But seeing as Ivy probably already had one, what was the sense in making my own?

Pulse fast, I met them, stride for stride, the grass hissing about my calves as the afternoon sun slowly became lost behind the clouds and the wind picked up. Trent looked good in his black, uniform-like slacks and top. David, too, fit the part in his faded jeans, tidy shirt, and ankle-length duster. As for me? Despite having tied my hair back with one of the girls' ribbons, I was still a mess, wearing stiff, fire-dried jeans and one of Trent's black sweaters. The man's bug-out bag was better equipped than my entire closet. *Not that I'm complaining,* I thought as I glanced at my feet, a pair of Trent's slippers between me and the earth.

My books were safe at Al's wagon, but Dali still had my bag with all its stuff, and it made me twitchy. Fortunately, the ever-after was a small reality, and the university ley line was a ten-minute walk instead of the hour-long hike that it would be in reality.

"Hey, ah, could you tell me when we're getting close?" David asked. "I can't see the line, but it's around here somewhere. This was where Quen brought me in." The Were slowed, eyes on the ground. "You can see where Tulpa trampled everything."

"There," Trent said, pointing, and I scuffed to a halt on the flattened grass, bringing up my second sight to find the ley line a mere fifteen feet away.

Unlike the narrow, tidy thirty-foot line in my garden, the university's ley line was huge, the shimmering red haze at chest height spanning almost the width of a road and running at least four blocks. Dali had remade it to match the original ley line that had vanished when the lines had gone down. If I remembered correctly, it had taken Dali a very long time to extradite himself from the nothingness of what lay between realities when they had created the original ever-after, scraping a ley line into existence in the process.

"I don't see Quen," Trent said, and I squinted to bring a chalk line image of reality into focus. Slowly the flat, grassy plain became superimposed with the image of Cincy's streets. Walls were transparent, and cars and people hazy shadows. Seeing the sun and sky simultaneously made them almost too intense to bear, but the longer I studied it, the easier it became.

"Ah, this is not a clear crossing," I said as I spotted an I.S. vehicle at the curb.

"We have a plan for that." David took his phone and turned on its flashlight. "All I can see is grass. Let me know when he flashes back."

Not sure what I was supposed to be looking for, I watched the passing people and cars, thinking it was a rather busy street to shift realities on.

"There," Trent said, and though David couldn't see the small haze of pixy dust, I could.

"Jenks," I whispered, my worry for him cascading through me. "What is he doing here? It will be too cold when the sun goes down."

"Not where we're going." David put his phone in a pocket. "In a few minutes, an entire pack of Weres will come walking down the street with protest signs. When they hit the line, we are going to cross realities right into the middle of them. With some luck, the I.S. won't notice you. Once we get to the end of the block, we should be clear. They're watching the line, not the adjacent streets."

"Nice." I reached for Trent's hand and gave it a squeeze. Energy tingled against my fingers, and his grip tightened. Still, that hint of worry pinched his brow, and I wondered if the threat of incarceration was bothering him. It never had before, but he had two girls waiting for him now and a jealous, wealthy woman eager to gain custody rights.

"I won't let them put you in jail," I whispered, then stiffened. "There they are."

So faint it could have been my imagination, I heard excited voices chanting in unison. The traffic ceased, and hazy, ghostlike images of angry people wavered before us, marching as if in a forgotten war. Weres couldn't see ley lines, but it was obvious they could sense them. Straight as an arrow, they paced down the street, an open area in the middle waiting for us.

"Okay, let's go." I took David's arm and stepped forward, shivering as I walked through the protesters to find the center open area. David shuddered, the man positively gray, and I wondered if it was the people we'd just passed through like ghosts, or me shifting his aura to match the lines so we could use it as a conduit.

"Ready?" I said, and, much as Trent and I had been training the horses to walk down a ley line as we translocated them to another realm, I sent David and me to reality.

That fast, we were home. Noise and color slammed into us. David shook on his exhale, his furrowed brow easing. The Weres around us started as well, more than a few swearing under their breath as the rest continued to shove their hand-lettered signs into the air, shouting, "Con-stance! Lo-cal rule! Con-stance. Lo-cal rule!" A few pedestrians watched and took videos, but mostly we were ignored. Car alarms were going off on the next street over, and I jumped, eyes going to the sky when a firework exploded into hard-to-see sparkles.

"That was as freaky as all hell," David muttered, but Trent's grin faded fast as we walked past the parked I.S. cruiser. Head bowed, I risked a glance. The two officers inside were gesturing at the protesters, but they were clearly too interested in their sub sandwiches and supersize Mountain Dews to interfere. Uneasy, I pulled Trent into a half-hunched slump. Weres tended to be small, and a redhead next to a paper-white blond would stand out.

"David, this worked amazingly well," Trent said, and the Were nodded. "It was Jenks's idea."

"It was a good one," I said, still scanning for Jenks. "Where are we going?"

"Down," David said, and my gaze went to the sound of metal on pavement. The protest had halted at an intersection, waiting for the light to change.

"Into the sewer?" I squeaked at the open manhole, and Trent's expression went empty.

"Yup," David said as I stared at the ugly black hole. Three Weres held the heavy manhole cover up, but I balked. "Now. The light is going to change," he added.

"I thought we'd take a car," Trent said, and Jenks darted close, his wings rasping.

"I tried to pix the light," he said, scowling at me. "But the traffic fail-safes are insulated. You got fifteen seconds to get your lily-white asses down that hole."

"Jenks!" I exclaimed, then staggered when David shoved me forward. "I'm so sorry," I babbled as I sat on the filthy pavement and dangled my legs. "You were trying to tell me about Vivian, and I didn't listen."

"Go!" David said, and I pushed forward, teeth clenched as I hit the bottom of the tunnel. It was warmer down here, and it stank. Breath shallow, I moved aside as Trent eclipsed the light.

"Don't try to butter me up, witch." Jenks's dust was an angry red as he hovered before me, lighting the narrow tube. "You left!"

Trent dropped in, his slight stumble graceful compared to my fall.

"I know. I'm sorry," I babbled, hating Jenks's angry expression. "I was so worried about Trent. Is Getty okay? That must have been horrible to watch. I'm so glad she didn't interfere. She did the right thing by hiding. Lee would have killed her."

The light dimmed again as David entered, and then Quen, the elf landing with hardly a whisper. The man was dressed in security black, scowling as if ready to slit someone's throat. I stifled a shudder as the manhole cover scraped back into place, and then it was just Jenks's sparkles lighting the curving walls.

"Getty is fine," Jenks muttered, wings rasping when Trent whispered a word of Latin and a globe of light blossomed. "Why by Tink's little pink dildo can't I stay mad at you?"

"Because you love me," I said, and the pixy's dust brightened.

"Damn straight," he said, and Quen pushed past me, silent as he took Trent's light in hand and stepped off the raised platform and onto the curved floor of the tunnel.

"This way." Quen paced forward. Trent was next, and then David, leaving Jenks and me last. "I really am sorry," I whispered, and the pixy's wings rasped as he landed on my shoulder and tugged at my hair to make room for himself. "I thought Trent was drowning."

"Was he?" Jenks asked.

"Just about," I said, and Jenks grunted.

"Then it was probably good you went to get him." His wings tickled my neck. "Great. They have no idea where we're going," he added, eyeing the three men bunched up at a fork, arguing.

"It's left," David said, his attention on a faint glimmer of reflective paint. It was Pike's logo, and I nodded as I scuffed to a halt.

"Left leads down," Trent said, clearly unhappy. "Any lower, and we get wet."

"You aren't the one in slippers," I grumped as I pushed past them, and Jenks snickered. The light behind me held steady for a moment, and then it began to move, bobbing against the walls as Trent and Quen reluctantly followed, whispering about city maps and pre-Turn records.

David came even with me, a faint smile playing about his lips. "I would have thought that elves would be comfortable in the dark."

"It's not the dark that bothers me," Trent said from behind. "I'm not familiar with a direct, belowground, pre-Turn hospital access."

"Vamps and humans weren't the only ones making tunnels before the Turn," Jenks said.

David tilted his hat back to study the low ceiling. "I don't think anyone has been down here since the hospital was abandoned."

"Is it far?" I asked, nose wrinkling at the scent of mold.

"No," David said, and then I jerked, startled as my foot found an ankle-deep puddle.

"Water ahead," Jenks said.

"Thanks," I said sourly, my slippered foot suddenly cold and heavy. "So, Jenks, if you're here, who's watching the church?"

"Stef," the pixy said. "She got most of your ley line stuff upstairs before the I.S. showed up. You would have lost everything if not for her," he added, his sparkles brightening at the memory. "She was parked on the top stair of the belfry when I left. Getty is with her."

"Really? Thanks."

"Lee's been the biggest problem. No one else really wants to go up there, and I think he just wants to make mischief." Clearly content, Jenks shifted to sit on Quen's shoulder, looking back at me as he ate a wad of pollen he'd brought. "Lee is hell-bent on convincing anyone who will listen that you killed Vivian, but no one believes him. Even the people who don't like you. The I.S. won't move from the curb until Finnis takes over, and the Weres are tooling around as if they own the city. It's the humans who have me worried. They bought up all the bread and toilet paper as if we got a hundred-year snowstorm coming."

David glanced over his shoulder, his amusement brightening his face.

"Good," I said. "They should be hiding. What about Pike and Ivy? She has a plan, right?"

"Did the sun come up this morning?" Jenks grumped, and my tension began to ease.

Up ahead, Quen's stiff silhouette slowed and stopped at a rust-laced door. Pike's logo glittered in the glow from Trent's light, and the elf's frown deepened. "What is the sense of having a safe house if you tell everyone it exists," Trent said as David smacked the heavy door with a tire iron—three distinctive taps.

"If you can handle Lee, Ivy has an idea for Finnis," David said as the noise echoed. "But I don't think you're going to like it."

"Yeah." Jenks took to the air, tiny features bunched. "Wait until you see who she's plotting with."

"You will not like that, either," Quen added, his expression sour as the lock slid from the inside and the door began to open.

"Mrs. Sarong?" I guessed, balking when the scent of stale water and old wood rolled out. *And Ivy* . . . I thought in relief as I followed David and Quen into the small room lit by a dim, industrial, battery-operated light.

"Hi, Rachel." Ivy rose from a makeshift cardboard-box table. Pike was there, too, giving me a preoccupied smile and wave before going back to his maps. Eyes black in stress, Ivy came forward, weaving through the three metal folding chairs and Pike's brother nestled in a beanbag chair, his knees almost to his ears. The memory-challenged vampire didn't even look up as the door squeaked shut; he was entirely focused on his handheld game.

"Hi, Ivy." But my reach to give her a hug faltered as I saw the mouse cradled in her long-fingered hand. It was wearing jewelry.

Suddenly the ceramic bowl on the cardboard-box table was making sense.

"What is she doing here?" I said, and the mouse glared, whiskers trembling.

# CHAPTER

# 28

"I TOLD YOU SHE WASN'T GOING TO LIKE IT," DAVID SAID, AND IVY frowned at him.

"Constance?" Trent said, and the mouse hissed, showing him her long canines. "Ah, shouldn't she be in a cage?" he added.

Cooing, Ivy raised the incensed mouse to her face, soothing her with little whispers.

Jenks snickered, hands on his hips as he hovered over Ivy's shoulder where his dust could "accidentally" spill onto Constance. With a shriek, the vampire mouse turned her anger on him. "Constance hasn't been in a cage for months," Jenks said. "You know how I could never find Getty? Well, she renovated a fairy bolt-hole in the garden, dug it six feet down below the frost line in case, ah, things didn't work out in the church. She showed it to Constance the first night."

"And they both lived happily ever after," I said, all of which explained how Getty knew where Constance was hiding.

Jenks rasped his wings, clearly proud of the independent-minded pixy woman. "If you ask me, half the reason Constance wants to shift back is because Getty won't be able to visit once the weather closes in."

Quen stood beside Pike, his arms at his sides, stance disapproving. "I do not agree with this plan, Sa'han," he said, and the mouse began squeaking, gesturing wildly.

"Why? Because it involves Constance?" Pike said, surprising me. I'd thought he hated her, but perhaps six weeks of getting his undead fix from Ivy's mom was leaving its mark. "There's nothing more trustworthy than a long undead who sees you as their way to survive."

*Until they don't need you anymore,* I thought.

Quen crossed his arms, his pox scars in bright relief. "You can trust they will do whatever is in their best interests, and nothing else."

Constance hissed, and Ivy flashed him an irate look before turning to coax the rodent into a better mood. Pike left the makeshift table, giving his brother's shoulder a reassuring but ignored pat in passing. "Which in this case is seeing that Finnis stays out of Cincinnati. Finnis wants Constance twice dead. That's why the DC vamps sent her here in the first place for Rachel to off."

Worried, I frowned at the mouse staring at me. Allow Constance to resume her city-master status? Even if it was only a shell position, I'd have to uncurse her. True, Constance could have turned herself back any number of times when I'd been spelling and had a salt vat set up. That she was considering it now meant she wanted something more than being herself again. *Protection?* I mused, seeing as that's what she'd been getting the last six months, living in a hole in the ground in my garden.

Ivy set Constance on the table, and the mouse immediately went to the empty bowl and rocked it. "Rachel, I've been over it a hundred ways," Ivy said as she sat beside her. "Even with the substantial force at David's disposal, Pike and I can't overpower Finnis, Nina's and my mother's help aside."

Leaning against a damp wall, David pointedly cleared his throat. "I disagree."

"Without a lot of bloodshed and major news coverage," Ivy amended. "And someone going to jail for illegal death."

Grinning, David touched the rifle under his duster. "They have to catch you first."

I sighed as Quen and Trent began arguing in quiet, terse voices. I wondered if this was to be my life now: making decisions underground with a few people—a few powerful, good people. *I'm not sure Constance fits that description.*

"Ah, no," I said, and Trent spun, blinking in surprise.

"See?" Jenks took to the air as Constance began squeaking. "I told you she'd say no. She's smarter than she looks. Constance stays a mouse. Curse her like you did Parker. Keep her that way."

"Hey!" I said as Constance turned her wrath at him, and Jenks merrily flipped her off.

Thinking it was settled, Trent turned to David. "What do you have in terms of firepower? I might be able to help."

"Wait. Slow down." Pike held up a hand as Ivy's expression darkened. "Rachel, I truly believe Constance will help. She hates you, but she hates Finnis more."

"That's not convincing me," I said, and Quen sniggered.

"Maybe I'm not explaining it correctly." Brow furrowed, Pike put a hand on his waist and thought for a moment. "I agree that Constance hates you. But most undead vampires hate the person seeing to their needs. That's not a reason to say no. She's not suited to hold a city," he said, voice softening. "She knows it. The DC vamps know it. That's why they sent her here for you to kill."

"Still not convincing me," I said, and Trent bobbed his head, agreeing.

"She knows you are stronger than her," Pike coaxed. "Not just physically, but politically. She knows that if she returns to DC, they will find a way to kill her twice. She needs the protection that you have been giving her."

"I haven't—" I started, glancing at the mouse—then I sighed. I had.

"You have," David affirmed, a faint smile on his face. "A city's master vampire firmly believes he or she is the alpha and omega, *A* to *Z*. Constance knows she is not—and she's terrified. That's why she is so brutal. Take away her fear, and she will be easier to live with. Guaranteed."

Unsure, I turned to Ivy. Her expression was empty, but I trusted her, and when I lifted my shoulders in question, she gave Constance a look to stay put and came forward.

"Why is she really doing this?" I whispered, but I figured Constance heard me, as she began squeaking, gesturing wildly at the ceiling, floor, me. I thought about giving her a phone, but I wasn't sure I wanted to know her exact thoughts.

Eyes dark, Ivy took a slow breath. "She's been watching you since you cursed her," she said. "What you can do. How you operate. Obviously she thinks she can manipulate you, but mostly, she wants Finnis out of Cincy and she can't do it. She needs you."

I leaned to see past Ivy to where Constance had gone silent, her little white feet planted at the edge of the cardboard box, staring at me. Behind her, Brad snickered and laughed at whatever game currently occupied his entire world. His new wrist cast had so many signatures, it was almost black. "And when Constance gets what she wants, she will try to get rid of me."

"I don't think it will come to that." Ivy took a slow breath. "Finnis molded her. She's not mentally capable of ruling a city, but she's not stupid. She knows she can't return to DC. I say uncurse her. Once she feels safe, she will relax."

"Besides," Jenks said, his dust shifting an eager gold, "if she doesn't behave, you can always curse her again."

"True." But even as I nodded, I felt a massive foreboding grip me. I was going to uncurse Constance. I was going to uncurse the crazy vampire, give her a voice, a way to hurt me.

"Okay," I whispered, and Trent stiffened. "Keeping Finnis out of Cincy is more than half the battle."

"Ah, Rachel?" Trent started, and both Ivy and Constance glared at him. The tension thickened, and I shrugged. As Jenks had said, I could always curse her again.

"Great!" Clearly excited, Pike turned to the table. Constance was squeaking, her thin, furry arms waving dramatically. "I've got it. I've got it," Pike added. "Hold your little furry tail." Beaming, he took the folded paper that Ivy stoically handed him. "Ah, Rachel? Constance has a few conditions before agreeing to help."

Trent's eyes narrowed. "There it is," he muttered, but I took the paper, not surprised.

"Of course she does," I said, glancing from the mouse eagerly waiting at the edge of the table to the literal mouse-scratching on the paper. The words were tiny and sloppy, and I squinted at them. "Ah, I can't read this . . ."

"I can." Jenks dropped to hover over the page. "She says she will keep Finnis out of Cincinnati, but in return, she wants your protection."

"From Finnis," I said to be sure, and Constance made a "go on" motion. "And the DC vampires who sent you here," I added, and she bobbed her head dramatically. "Okay. I can do that within reason, but I'm going to want acceptable behavior from you, or my protection vanishes. What else?" There was a lot of tiny print there. I was sure there was more.

Jenks eased closer to the page, squinting. "She wants the I.S."

"Seriously?" I said, wishing I could say I was surprised.

"Absolutely not," Quen said, and Trent grimaced, clearly agreeing.

"That's not happening," I said, and the mouse began to scream, her tail whipping the air as she threw her diamond necklace at me. It fell far short, and Jenks darted down, snagging it before it hit the filthy cement. "What I will give you is a voice in city matters equal to that of everyone else I work with. You can have a lower suite in the I.S. with a small staff. Two . . . no, three living vamps. Your choice. Good?"

"I'd take it," Pike said, and the mouse sullenly nodded, glaring at Jenks as he modeled her necklace.

"Ah . . ." Jenks chuckled. "She also wants all the credit and half the proceeds from the soul curse when it goes public."

My eyebrows rose. "Really?"

"Whoa. Wait up." Trent pushed forward. Behind him, Quen pinched his forehead as if in pain. "That's not anywhere near going to happen. Rachel developed that curse. She gets the credit for it. You get credit for championing it through the FCSA."

The mouse rubbed her thumb and finger together, and Pike smirked.

"Ah." Trent glanced at me, and I gestured for him to have at it. "How about five percent of the profits, post-tax, once it's approved and regulated. Twenty percent until it *is* approved, but you pay for distribution until it is."

"Twenty percent?" I questioned. "Why does she get more before it's approved?"

"It works out to be nearly the same when you include the bribes and kickbacks needed to get it on the street before approval," he said, and Constance's beady little eyes fixed on him. Her perfect little tail whipped around . . . and then she nodded.

"Anything else?" I asked, and Jenks shook his head, wings rasping as he sat on my shoulder. "Okay. In return for my protection and a slice of the profits from the soul curse, you agree to play the part of city master vampire to keep out Finnis and anyone else the DC vampires send. In actuality, Ivy, Pike, and I are handling city issues, though I will solicit your advice as the occasion warrants it. Good?"

There was a lot we hadn't agreed upon, but as Jenks had said, I could always turn her back. Constance nodded, clearly eager. Ivy and Pike were obviously on board. Jenks was confident in my ability to bring her down should she renege on it. Trent wasn't so keen, but he trusted me. Quen was not happy, but David had gone to watch Brad play his game, either knowing how this was going to end or simply not caring.

Apart from the soul curse, it was very close to the deal I'd offered her six months ago, the same that she'd spit on. In hindsight, it was fortuitous that I hadn't killed her then. Still, there was one more thing I wanted, and I came forward, looming over her, to make Ivy and Pike nervous.

"I like this," I said, and Constance flicked her tail, hearing the *however*. "I have a condition of my own."

The mouse stared up at me, whiskers trembling.

"Me, my family, my team, and my team's families are entirely off-limits." I put a hand to either side of her, remembering what it was like to be so small. "Including but not limited to Ivy," I said, to make things perfectly clear. "Jenks, Pike, Trent, David, and Zack. If I come to you and say no—on any person—you back off."

Hunching, Constance hissed.

"Also, I want you to take lessons on how to act the part," I added. "Ivy can teach you." Ivy's eyes were wide, and I wondered if I'd gone too far.

"She's been training for this her entire life. She knows how to keep the peace in Cincinnati through enormous respect and a little fear, not the other way around. Listen to her."

The mouse went silent, clearly thinking.

"Well?" I prompted. "I need some kind of acknowledgment. We doing this, or not?"

Whiskers trembling, the mouse spun to Pike and Ivy. Ivy had her arms over her middle in a rare show of unease, but Pike was bright and eager. Finally the mouse nodded.

"Great!" Jenks said, startling me. "Who has the salt water?"

Pike turned to his brother. "Brad, do you still have that jug you brought down?"

Brad looked up from his game. "No," he said, but then David found it, giving the forgetful vampire a reassuring pat on his shoulder before handing it to Pike.

Constance stood at the bowl's edge, holding it as he poured it in.

"Wait," I cautioned her as the last glugged in, and she hesitated, clearly afraid. "I want to make sure it's the right concentration," I said, dipping a finger in and finding that, yes, it tasted right. "It's all yours." I glanced between the surrounding faces. "You brought something for her to wear, right?"

But it was too late. Constance had scrambled up and over, landing in the water with an ungraceful flop.

"There she goes!" Jenks shrilled, and with a startling pop and whiff of burnt amber, a haze enveloped the bowl, expanding in a muffled woof.

Constance shrieked, the high-pitched sound raking over my nerves, and then, with a sodden thump, she hit the floor, her sudden weight crushing the box and busting the bowl into three shards underneath her. A small, brown, naked, heavily scarred woman sat and shook, trying to figure out what had happened.

"Maybe you should have put the bowl on the floor," Quen said sourly, and Constance glared at him, her red lips pulling away to show her teeth.

"Mother pus bucket, that never gets old!" Jenks exclaimed, and Constance turned to him, her eyes pupil black as she flipped the wet coils of her hair back.

"Give me my necklace," she rasped at the pixy.

Brad stood, hooting and tugging on his brother's arm, pointing as if it was a grand trick.

"Jenks, give her the necklace," I said, nervous as the scent of the long undead thickened in the stale air. My neck began to tingle and my pulse quickened.

"Why? She can't wear it."

"Give it to her," I said again, not sure I liked the submissive way Ivy was helping the woman stand up and shrug into a robe. Clearly they had come prepared. I would have been upset, thinking that my decision was a foregone conclusion, but Ivy would have brought the water and robe even if there'd been no chance that I'd uncurse her. And if you had asked me yesterday, those were the odds I would have given you.

"Jenks, give her the necklace!" I exclaimed when he balked, and, sullen, he took it from around his neck and dropped it into her damp, shaking hand.

Immediately she put it on her finger as a ring. "We're good, right?" I said, and she wiggled her hand to make the jewels catch the light.

"We are . . . adequate." Constance's gaze went sidelong to Pike. "I'm hungry."

I couldn't tell if her eyes were dark from the dim light . . . or something else. Quen had gone ashen, his back to the wall as he drew Trent away. I'd forgotten that Piscary had given him a scar. It must be hell at the moment. "That's from the transformation spell," I started, my words faltering when she held her hand out for Pike.

"Um . . ." I began. "We agreed hands off my people."

"It's not my hands that I'm going to touch him with," she said, but Pike only grinned, taking her tiny fingers in his own and kissing the top of them. For such a small woman, she had a lot of ugly charisma.

"Ron is waiting for you," Pike said, his voice throaty. "And Jessica. And if you're still hungry after that, Abbie and Chuck."

"Four?" Constance made a rude scoff. "You misjudge me, Welroe. Acquire a fifth."

"Can you find your way out?" Ivy said, her own eyes edging toward a dangerous black. "Sundown isn't for a few hours, but Finnis won't be able to fly until then. If we're lucky, we can ground his plane before it leaves DC."

David pushed from the wall, his stance tight with tension. "I have a car. Ivy, my people will be looking out for you. They'll get you where you need to go, but I'd stick to the surface streets. The expressway has too few outs."

She nodded, but her hands were shaking. "Go. None of you can stay here."

David immediately went to the door. Trent and Quen were quick behind him, Jenks's wings a tight hum in the tense air. "Are you going to be okay?" I asked Ivy, and she glanced at Constance sitting in one of the rickety chairs as if it was a throne. "Did we make a mistake?"

"No, but you need to leave. We'll take care of Finnis. You finish off Lee."

"Morgan, we are moving!" Quen exclaimed from the tunnel, and I gave her hand an encouraging squeeze. I wouldn't give her a hug with her eyes that black.

"Gotta go," I said, walking backward. "So, where is Lee?" I asked, and Quen exhaled loudly, clearly glad when I shut the door and it cycled to locked from the inside.

"Hiding in some back office," Quen said. "But come sundown, he'll be at Fountain Square to help close the circle and curse all demons to remain in the ever-after. You want to grab something to eat in the meantime?"

Trent took my hand, and my worry eased as his strength tingled against mine.

"Food sounds good," I said, my stomach rumbling.

# CHAPTER

# 29

JENKS DUSTED A CONTENTED GOLD AS HE SAT ON THE REARVIEW mirror and cleaned a spot of ketchup from one of his wings as we made our way to Fountain Square. Dinner had been fries and paper-wrapped burgers out of brown bags, the five of us sprawled on a sagging queen-size bed as we watched the local news on bad cable. Trent had sulked at the delay, but I was firmly of the opinion that full bellies and informed decisions would serve us better than driving all over Cincy to find Lee. Especially when we only had to wait for sundown for him to show. Trent's mood could have been because there hadn't been enough ketchup for his fries, though.

Even better, I had taken a long, hot shower, rinsing the scent of damp cement and woodsmoke from me before slipping into the same worn jeans and sweater. The hotel shampoo hadn't come close to taming my hair, but Jenks and David had gone out for some hair charms and shoes so I wouldn't have to kick coven ass in a second-rate braid and soggy slippers. David, I wasn't surprised, had very good taste in footwear, and I tapped my new ankle-high, stylish boot against the car's door to release some tension.

My focus blurred on the passing city as I slumped deeper into the cab's stiff cushions and curled a strand of clean hair around a finger, wishing I had my bag and my splat gun. The front windows were cracked open, but not enough, and I gave Trent's knee a squeeze. The sun still had yet to slip below the horizon, and the reflected light made the clouds pink and blue. Bis would join us after sundown to bring our number to six.

*Five too many,* I thought, worried. Everyone but Jenks was stressed, and there was more than a hint of excited Were and the familiar tang of snickerdoodles and good wine. Quen was up front with David, giving us three magic users, a Were, a pixy, and an adolescent gargoyle against the entire coven—now supported by who knew how many of Cincy's resident witches after Lee's afternoon of propaganda. Witches *were* the largest minority demographic, and whereas they tended to keep a low profile, getting them riled enough to curse the demons into exile wouldn't be difficult if the coven was behind it. Spelling with the coven of moral and ethical standards was on everyone's bucket list.

The streets had been suspiciously clear at the city outskirts where we had spent the afternoon, but here, downtown, it was curb-to-corner cars and excited people. With only a few blocks left to go, getting out and walking *was* an option, but it felt dangerous even with the fading light. Overly casual I.S. agents and bright-eyed vigilantes were on every corner. Trent and I were both wanted, and though we could handle ourselves, there was a time issue. Magical fights were often fast but seldom discreet.

"We are not getting any closer to Fountain Square in this traffic," Trent grumbled. "It's worse than game day. I've never seen so many people trying to get into one square mile."

David, who was driving, glanced at him through the rearview mirror. "Which is exactly how we want it," he said as his gaze returned to the crowd, his pride obvious.

"The I.S. is everywhere," Quen muttered, clearly not happy.

"Ya want me to distract 'em so you can get out?" said Jenks, and David took a breath.

"It's too cold," I interrupted, and when Jenks turned to me to protest, I cut him off. "The sun is almost down, and it's *cold!*" I exclaimed. "You either promise me that you will find somewhere warm to serve as lookout and watch my back, or you will be in my bag."

"You don't have your bag," Jenks practically barked, and I leaned over the seat.

"Then you had *better* find a light to *park your ass on* and be a *lookout!*

I'm not going home to Getty and telling her I let you fall into an ill-prepared hibernation coma."

"Fine!" he yelled, sullen as he went to sit on Trent's shoulder.

Trent cleared his throat, clearly uncomfortable as Jenks belligerently checked his garden sword before slamming it back into his scabbard.

"Okay, then," David said as he sent his window all the way down. I thought he was proving a point until he made a sharp whistle, following it up with a rolling motion.

Immediately several heavily tattooed Weres jogged from the crowd, our headlights brightening against their jeans as they went not to us, but the I.S. cruiser parked at the curb.

"A distraction," I mused as I leaned farther over the seat. "Nice!"

"On steroids," David said in pride as two of the Weres engaged the officers, leaving a third to hop in behind the wheel and slam the door shut.

The officers spun, but it was too late and the cruiser took off, lights and sirens blaring.

"Tink's a Disney whore. That was slicker than snot on a doorknob, Mr. Peabody," Jenks said as the I.S. cruiser slowly outdistanced the furious agents.

Lips quirked wryly, David slipped in behind the stolen vehicle and accelerated.

"I like," I said, settling deeper into the seat as we ran a red light. "Do you do weddings?"

Jenks snickered, but Quen, clearly not amused or impressed, cracked his knuckles, the play of line energy dancing about them obvious.

The last few blocks took less than a minute, but my tension returned tenfold when the ambient light suddenly brightened and our stolen escort slowed to a crawl.

Fountain Square was packed. People made a living, moving, noisy wall, and when our escort whooped his siren and continued on, David double-parked so we could get out.

"I'm not sitting in no bag," Jenks muttered from Trent's shoulder, and I reached for the door handle, suddenly unsure. My memories of being cuffed and dragged onto the stage were not that old, and whereas one person is hard to convince, a mob is ready to believe the worst.

Trent gave my hand a squeeze and I got out. The wind from the river lifted through my blessedly clean hair, and I squinted up at Carew Tower. The noise was tremendous, sound rocking between the shaded buildings to build upon itself. Over it all, a woman onstage yelled through a bullhorn. I couldn't understand her, but the crowd cheered at every other sentence.

Trent took my elbow and led me to the curb as I gawked. Behind me, a tattooed Were dove into the cab and drove away, leaving us to melt into the crowd and avoid the I.S. officers still trying to recover their stolen cruiser.

"Is that Lee with the woman with the bullhorn?" I said, and Jenks darted from Trent's shoulder to check. "This is worse than the solstice," I added, shouting to be heard.

"We've got all three major demographics down here, not just one." David frowned, his good mood tempered. So far it had been a mischief-and-annoyance campaign. Neither one of us wanted those looking to him to do more—but they would if pressed. It was up to me to see that it didn't come to that.

"It's Lee," Jenks said as he returned, his dust dull from the cold. The wind coming up from the river ripped away any heat that the streets might have held. This was not a good situation, but as I took a breath to say something, the pixy practically exploded. "God, woman!" he yelled, hands on his hips and dusting red. "I'll find a light!"

"Wait, Jenks?" I said as he darted off, and he came back, clearly frustrated. "Will you do something for me?" I asked, knowing he would risk his life if I didn't get him to leave. "Will you find Doyle? He's got to be out here. You own the church. You can request that he take a scraping of that wax pentagram. I want it tested against Lee's aura on file."

Jenks's angular face tightened. "You're getting rid of me," he muttered.

"Bet your lily-white ass I am. Will you do it?"

Hand on his sword hilt, Jenks scowled at Trent. "Keep her alive."

Trent lifted our laced fingers, and I stifled a shiver when our internal energy balances equalized. "With my last breath," he said, and Jenks darted up, his dust an angry red.

"Last breath?" I leaned to put my lips to his ear. "Let's hope it doesn't come to that."

"He's not happy," Trent said as he tugged me protectively closer.

"True, but he'll be alive tomorrow." Trent's grip tightened as I went up on my toes, using him for balance as I tried to get a better view of the stage. Lee stood quietly beside the woman with the bullhorn. His coven regalia was impressive, the black robes fluttering about his ankles and a ribbon embroidered with a Möbius strip whipping about his neck. Four more people had taken to the stage, all dressed as he was. Brow furrowed, I dropped to my heels. The entire coven was here—well, apart from Vivian— and they were children.

"Trent . . ." I said, worried, and then I stumbled, jostled by the crowd. Most coven members were born to the position, trained by their predecessors from an early age. I'd thought it odd that Vivian had asked Lee to be a coven member, but clearly the last few years of dealing with me, the demons, and Ku'Sox had taken their toll, and the members in waiting had been forced to step into vacant shoes—far too soon.

Quen immediately stiff-armed the guy who'd knocked into me, staring at him until the man retreated, cowed by Quen's toothy aggression. "They have yet to organize a circle," Quen said, gesturing for us to put our backs against a large planter.

"They will soon. The sun is almost down," Trent said, but I wondered if that made any difference. It felt as if it might already be too late. The I.S. was at the outskirts, simply waiting. As soon as Finnis took control, they'd move. We had hours, maybe, and an entire city to convince I was not responsible for Vivian's death.

David's focus was on the crowd as he lifted a hand to acknowledge someone. "You got this?" he asked. "I'm no good in a magic fight, but I can prep for a sudden mass exodus."

"Thank you. Go," I said, and he gave me a quirky smile before striding off, two heavily tattooed men in torn jeans and Howler caps quickly converging on him. That fast, David was gone. *Three still feels like too many.* "You want to help him?" I offered to Quen, and the older elf grunted, amused I'd even asked. Trent's eyes, too, had a decidedly mischievous slant.

With one lurching step, Trent gracefully stepped up onto the planter, turning to extend a hand so I could join him. Torn, I took it, ignoring Quen's pained expression as we were suddenly taller than anyone else.

"Sa'han," Quen coaxed. Yes, we were now obvious targets, but at least we could see the entirety of the large plaza. The tables and chairs had been stacked to the side, and the food wagons were gone apart from Good Grounds. Three news vans had set up beside the stage, and the fountain was off. Every now and then, some smart-ass would climb onto it to get a better view, falling into the crowd with a yelp and singed synapses from the fountain's built-in security.

There were too many people to see the huge inlaid circle, but as soon as Lee got everyone organized, it would be defined by the people themselves. It was large enough to need several well-versed practitioners to close, but any witch or elf who cared to participate in cursing the demons could partake as long as they were nearby. As much as I wished it was otherwise, there were too many people still afraid of demons.

*Perhaps they're right,* I mused, overwhelmed by the noise. My adopted kin hadn't exactly been toeing the line since regaining the ability to come and go within reality at will.

The woman with the bullhorn continued to stomp across the stage, riling them up as Lee went to confer with two city officials at the rear. Slowly my jaw tightened; he stood upon the very same stage where I had knelt not a year ago, judged by a mob and waiting to be killed. *Not this time,* I thought.

Taking a deep breath, I pulled on the ley line. Hard.

Trent sensed it, his expression becoming decidedly vicious. His chin lifted, and I felt him do the same, drawing in line energy until his unseen aura tingled against mine.

People began to turn, suddenly nervous as they noticed us gathering enough energy to make the tips of my hair float.

"That's Rachel Morgan," I saw a woman say, her eyes widening as she tugged on her friend's arm. "Morgan is here. We need to leave!"

"Where?" Shouting, her friend pulled from her grip, searching. "I've never seen . . . that's Morgan? What's with her hair?"

"She's tapping a ley line," the woman said, her outright panic beginning to draw attention. "She's got enough line energy in her to fry a cow. Let's go!"

*Well, on a good day, maybe,* I thought, a hand going to my hair.

Trent leaned close, a faint smile about his lips. "You're fun, you know that?"

I was not amused. The two women had fled, alarm rising in their wake. A slow wave of fear pushed out from us to make a growing pocket of silence. The people here had gathered to curse me, and, seeing me ready to stop them, they were clearly having second thoughts.

"Quen. Let's move. Stage," Trent said, and I made the jump to the pavers. Someone shrieked, and that fast, a way opened as people pushed back. More heads began to turn, and an obvious movement to the curbs began. David was there, standing ready to keep the flood from becoming a dangerous stampede. And whereas I appreciated the path that was opening before me, something felt broken. I didn't want to be feared. I just wanted some respect.

Our matched steps slow and measured, Trent and I went to the stage. Quen lurked behind us as a rear guard. Lee still hadn't noticed us, and as he talked to the media, I studied the four young people with him. None of them could be more than twenty. One looked twelve.

"Trent," I said, suddenly unsure, and the tallest girl turned, stiffening as she realized who we were. Her brown skin and straight black hair melded into her black robes, and her Möbius strip pin glinted. I balked when our eyes met and her anger slammed into me. *Vivian's student?* I wondered. Her rage appeared personal.

"I don't want to fight children," I whispered as a slim, blond, gawky boy stared at us in fear. He couldn't be more than twelve. No wonder they had made Lee their plumber. He was the only one with enough experience to handle the big, bad uglies.

"Don't let their age fool you," Trent said grimly. "They've been studying magic since they could walk, and I guarantee you they won't pull their punches."

"Well, I will," I said, slowing as the media focused their cameras on us. "Look at them. They might know their magic, but they don't know shit about the way people use each other. Lee's tricked them. That's not a reason to get hurt."

"Rachel . . ." Trent began, and I drew him to a halt before the stage. The plaza was going empty apart from a tightening knot of angry people, and I sent a silent thank-you to David.

Lee stood on the stage before the coven, a smile on his thin lips, a hint of line energy dancing at his fingertips. I could sense him drawing on the same ley line I was, and I yanked on it, satisfied when his face blanked.

*Feel that, did you? Come closer and I'll smack you with enough energy to land you in next week.* "Hey, Stinklee!" I shouted, and he frowned at the hated childhood nickname. "You got a permit to convene a coven on public property?"

Trent winced, rubbing the bridge of his nose before he lifted his head. "Lee?" Trent's voice rang out as the crowd continued to retreat to the surrounding buildings. "Please tell me you aren't trying to illegally curse the demons into exile?"

But Lee smirked as if amused. "How did you get him out so fast?"

"I bought a couple of line jumps from a demon," I said, anger warming me as my gaze lifted to the young people behind him. "Same as you," I added, but I doubted they would believe me.

Lee's jaw clenched as the taller of the two young women pushed up even with him. Brow furrowed, he waved her softly spoken question away. "She lies," he said. "But it doesn't matter. As soon as Finnis resumes control of the city, there won't be a place on earth that the I.S. can't find Trent."

"Ahhh," Trent said, desisting when Quen pointedly cleared his throat. The older elf's presence made me feel better. Quen's priority was Trent, and with that assurance, I could concentrate on grinding Lee under my boot.

"Probably," I said. "Good thing he has two realities to hide in. I'm surprised you survived Vivian's ghost."

"Ghost?" the tall woman blurted as she turned to Lee. "She made Vivian a ghost?"

Lee flushed. "Vivian is dead," he said flatly. "I told you everything that comes out of her mouth is a lie." But I could tell he was nervous, and a hand went to his middle as if covering a remembered hurt. "She murdered Vivian."

"Yeah?" I took a step forward. Trent grabbed my arm to keep me within Quen's magical reach, and from the outskirts, an alarmed gasp rose. "I'm not the one her ghost attacked. Run the test," I demanded. "See whose aura links to the pentagram that killed her."

"You're the one with the chakra rings!" he shouted, red-faced.

"Because I took them from your lackey!" I exclaimed, stumbling when Trent drew me to him. "This is pathetic, Lee. I nullified your pack of power-crazed Weres, and now you are tricking children into doing your dirty work?"

"So you admit you attacked an incoming pack who threatened your power structure? Killing one alpha, and transforming another into an animal?" Lee said, his cheeks spotting red.

"Perhaps a different tactic," Trent whispered.

"Murder by magic," Lee taunted, finding strength in Trent's reaction. "You can't fight the coven."

But I had before. And I would again. Even if they were down to children pushed into their positions decades before their time.

"Lee, I'm sorry about your daughter," Trent said, coming right to it. "You need to stop this. Can we get a coffee? Talk this out?"

Energy crackled over Lee's fisted hands as the coven clustered behind him. "This isn't about my daughter!" he shouted, his broken voice echoing on the buildings. "This is about Rachel using illicit magic to kill a coven member and you creating and distributing illegal genetic cures!"

Lee knew I hadn't killed Vivian, and his very anger said it was everything to do with his daughter.

"Lee. Please. Stop this," Trent implored, and my gaze went to the young people behind Lee. The tall woman in black was slowly pulling in line energy. I never would have noticed if I hadn't been doing the same thing. That, and her outright hatred burring into me.

"I've heard enough," she said, my very passivity pissing her off. "I'm not here to talk," she added, and then, without any fanfare, she threw a spell at me.

It hissed through the air, glittering a bright red and purple. The media panicked, scrambling for cover as Lee spun to her. "What are you doing!" he shouted, clearly angry.

"Got it!" I shouted, then yelped, ducking when Quen's counterspell smashed into her charm. The twin powers coiled and hissed against each other, spinning violently across the emptying plaza to slam into a cab. The car lifted with an echoing boom, flipping end over end down the street until it hit a cement road divider and rocked to a halt.

Cries of fear rose up, and even the vengeful crowd that had lingered ran for the buildings. Trent turned to Quen in annoyance, and the dark elf lifted a shoulder. "I make no apology, Sa'han," he muttered.

My focus returned to the young woman, her jaw tight and her stare fixed on me even as Lee reamed her out. "Hey! Bright eyes!" I shouted, and Lee's harangue cut off. "Give everyone a chance to clear out before you exert your godly cosmic powers, okay?"

Her expression twisted, and I felt another large draw on the ley line. "You murdered Vivian!" she shouted, her hands wreathed with unfocused power.

"Elyse, don't!" the youngest boy in black robes begged, and Lee grabbed her arm.

"Stop!" Lee demanded, and the woman, Elyse, apparently, jerked her arm free. "We are not here to break the law," he said, but his attitude said different. "We are here to curse the demons into the ever-after. Your task is to gather the witches of Cincinnati into a functioning coven. If you engage her, we will never garner enough people to spell the demons into exile."

"It's a curse, Lee, not a spell. Get it right," I said, and Elyse's brow furrowed. Angry, she pulled from him again, sullen as the youngest coven member tried to talk to her. The plaza only seemed empty. Enough people were huddled in doorways and under the overhangs to make an effective coven. Even the news vans had found a dubious shelter in the lee of the stage.

*I know how you feel, babe,* I thought when Elyse shook her head in frustration as the boy at her elbow begged her to stop. The demons were in trouble. Their idea to close the lines to translocation travel would give them the isolation they wanted—needed, perhaps—but it would fail. They were too few to manage it. It wasn't as if they could convince an entire city's demographic of witches to help them.

I blinked, going still at a sudden thought. True, the demons couldn't gather enough communal energy to close the lines. *But they might have enough to bounce the coven's own curse back on them,* I thought, pulse quickening. Making witches the focus of the curse would leave the demons free to travel as well as exile the witches to reality. The demons would be happy with that, and it might drum up enough anti-coven sentiment that someone might consider that Lee had killed Vivian, not me.

My breath came in fast. Trent's eyebrows rose. He knew I had an idea. "What?" he asked, but I had already sent a sliver of my awareness into the demon collective. *Dali?*

"I will not ignore that she murdered Vivian!" Elyse said, pointing at me. But I knew how to fix this, and excitement tingled to my fingertips. Breath held, I glanced at the I.S. agents standing with David's people, both sides waiting, both smart enough to not want to actually engage. In the foggy patches of my thoughts, I could hear the demons arguing, their quarrels going in circles. *Dali!*

"I'm with Elyse," the youngest coven member said, the last two coven members at his shoulders. "We can't fight Morgan and twist the spell at the same time. Subdue Morgan first, then curse the demons. If not today, to-morrow."

"Why aren't they arresting her?" Elyse exclaimed as she pointed at the I.S. "She's wanted for murder. They have a warrant!"

"Because they know I wouldn't kill Vivian," I said, and Elyse spun to me. "She was my friend. Elyse, please. Lee is using you. He knows the coven can't best me. That's why he's trying to curse me to the ever-after. Don't do this. Ask yourself, Who is going to gain the most?"

*Dali!* I shouted into my thoughts, starting to get ticked. This wouldn't work if the demons weren't ready.

Elyse wasn't listening to me, either, and Trent pulled me closer as the woman's long black hair begin to lift, sparkling with the energy she was gathering. "I did not take the coven's oath to talk. *Per fas et nefas!*" she shouted, looking magnificent as she threw the spell, red and purple twining into a binding force to twist and rend.

"Got it!" I shouted to keep Quen clear, simultaneously sending an arc of unfocused energy out to meet it. They hit with a roar, shaking the ground. I staggered, finding my balance as I pulled the energy to me instead of letting it dissipate. Absorbing it, I made it mine.

"Rachel!" Trent called, and then another thunderous boom rocked between the buildings as he deflected a second blast.

But I stood firm, breath shallow as I took in Elyse's anger-driven energy. Her frustration made a bitter tang on her aura. It lingered in her magic as I funneled most into the ground, keeping enough to make my hair float and my fingers tingle. "Elyse." Hands fisted, I stepped free of Quen and Trent. "I didn't kill Vivian. Lee—"

"Down!" Trent shouted.

I dropped and rolled. Trent was there when I rose, and I started, surprised to see his circle around us. That is, until I saw the stone melted where I'd been. *Damn, girl!*

"How do you want to play it?" Trent said, his attention fixed on Elyse. Lee had spun her around, arguing with her. Quen stood ready, the dark elf looking like Death himself as green and black dripped from his hands to hiss against the stone. The I.S. was beginning to move, no longer able to ignore us, and pushing forward with a smattering of witches in front.

Elyse was shouting at Lee, neither one of them giving an inch. Behind them, David was beginning to struggle as living vamps began to emerge into the dusk, feeling stronger as the sun crept to the horizon. "I'll take Elyse," I said, feeling the pinch of time. "You and Quen keep Lee and the rest off us. Elyse isn't going to let this go. I'll draw her into the street so Lee can organize the circle."

"You want to what?"

I ducked, startled at the sharp crack of a breaking spell. Apparently Elyse didn't like Lee trying to tell her what to do. "Keep the I.S. busy, but let them take the plaza," I said as Lee and Elyse argued. "I need Lee to twist the curse."

"You want the demons cursed?" Trent's face held a tinge of heartache, desperate as he looked from me to the advancing I.S. force. "We can beat this. I'm not going to let you be cursed to live in the ever-after."

I touched his jaw, loving him. "Make sure they do the curse," I insisted. "The demons can take control of it mid-cast. Shift its focus. Bounce it back on them. Elyse wants me. I need you do to this."

He blinked, realizing what I was saying. "Bounce it back, and the witches will be exiled in reality. They won't be able to cross to the ever-after by standing in a line anymore." He tensed, a wicked delight making his mien devious. "Elyse is yours."

I pulled him to me, breathing him in one last time. My eyes closed, and I sent my thoughts back into the collective, even as Trent's lips met mine. *Dali! Talk to me, you short-horned, whiptail midnight flier of a dead earth!*

And then Trent started, our lips parting when a purple and red spell slammed into the Good Grounds truck. "Go," I said as coffee beans rained down, and his arms slipped away.

Nodding, he strode forward, breaking his protection circle as he passed through it. His lips moved in silent Latin as he joined Quen, little trills of power dripping from his fingers.

*Okay, Elyse. Lesson one. Don't piss off the demon.*

# CHAPTER

# 30

"MORGAN!" DAVID CALLED FROM ACROSS THE PLAZA, AND I SPUN, lips parting to see a ball of who knew what coming at me.

Again I rolled, this time to the street to draw Elyse from Lee. *Rhombus,* I thought as I settled on the pavement, cowering under my hastily crafted circle. Her spell hit with a thump, popping and crackling as it bubbled against the asphalt to try to find a way in, expending itself as Elyse strode forward.

Crouched, I blew the hair from my face as I waited for her spell to dissipate. There was a growing chance that I had underestimated her. She'd clearly had a heady will, and her long hair was a black halo of unfocused energy. Behind her, the I.S. was pushing into the square to keep Lee and the rest of the coven safe. David continued to funnel people out and maintain an eye on me, and Trent lobbed spell after spell, a light distraction as Lee organized whoever was left.

Elyse wouldn't be able to help them craft the curse, but all Lee needed was the will of enough of Cincy's witches. They were the ones who would power the spell, and a thrill tinged with worry sparked through me. *Dali!* I shouted into the ether. *I have an idea!*

But he ignored me, and I rose when Elyse's spell finally spent itself. My circle's energy cascaded over me like rain as I broke through it, and I toe-heeled to the street, never letting go of her gaze.

"Elyse, keep Morgan off me!" Lee shouted. "Don't listen to her. Everything she says is a lie."

"Way ahead of you, old man." Elyse's steps left glowing footprints as she followed me to the street, her young features twisted into anger. "Morgan, you murdered my teacher, and I will hold you accountable!"

Behind her, the circle at Fountain Square rose up, thin at first, then stronger as the witches of Cincinnati returned. Encouraged by the promise of I.S. protection and the chance to expel the demons from their nightmares, they came from the shadows of alleys and storefronts.

But it was easy to forgive them. I'd been afraid of demons, too, once. Still was.

"Fight me!" Elyse exclaimed, and I gestured helplessly, my grip tight on the ley line.

"I didn't kill Vivian," I said, stumbling as I found the curb. "She was my friend."

"Fight and die," she whispered, voice like ice. "Or you will simply die."

"Elyse . . ." Gasping, I dove for the shelter of a car. Energy cracked the air, and I yelped as her spell hit the vehicle. Lips parted, I fell on my butt, staring as wisps of red and purple raced over the car and it began to shake. It rattled and groaned, and then it sank inward. I watched, shocked as it imploded to the size of a basketball. Air smelling of gas and oil shifted my hair as I found myself sitting on the damp pavement, nothing between us as little rills of energy raced over the crushed car and vanished. *Holy crap on toast, what are they teaching these kids?*

"Lee killed Vivian," I said, then lurched to my feet and simultaneously threw a ball of unfocused energy to meet hers. "He did it in my own church to hide his blame!"

"You lie!" she shouted as our energies hissed and popped against each other. "You're a liar!"

"Then why won't he let anyone take a sample of the pentagram?" I inched away from the smoldering car. Little pings of sound still came from it, audible over Lee's directive shouts at the circle. "Why is he hiding evidence, Elyse?"

"Because you tampered with it," she said as the first chants rose from the circle. They were beginning to gather their power. And when the sun fell? After that, they would do the curse.

"You are a dark practitioner," she said. "You are a demon!"

"I am a demon." I'd reached the center of the street, and I stopped. This was where I wanted her, and I would retreat no more. "But I didn't trick Vivian into making a second chakra ring. Think, Elyse. I already had one. Why would I need another? She was my friend, and my only crime is that I failed to trust she could protect me from the rest of you. Maybe if I had, she wouldn't have trusted Lee."

"You are a demon. I will never believe *anything* you say." Smooth expression twisting in heartache, Elyse threw another spell.

I deflected it with a burst of power, but my confidence faltered when it hit a light pole and spun toward a bus. There were people in it.

*My God*, I thought, remembering the crushed car. *"Detrudo!"* I shouted, imagining a huge bubble of force under the bus. I couldn't reach the spell in time, but I could move the bus, and with a sodden thump and groan, the bus majestically tipped up onto its right wheels . . . and slowly fell over. The chanting at the circle faltered as the bus hit the pavement with a terrifying crunch, but Elyse's spell spun through empty space to hit a stunted street tree instead.

White-faced, the young woman stared as the thin trunk exploded, and I ducked to avoid splinters and branches flying like shrapnel.

"You need to stop throwing that shit," I said, shaky as yellow burning leaves sifted down to eddy about my feet. Cries for help were coming from the bus, but the riders were alive, bruised at the worst. Elyse was out for blood. She didn't care about the truth, only her hurt. She moved from grief, not true hatred—and I understood that.

"Vivian was my friend, and I am going to miss her," I said, choking as the heartache of her loss hit me hard. "You are doing exactly what Lee wants you to do," I added as the glowing embers of red and yellow leaves spun up in a whirlwind about me. "If you down me, no one will stand up to him. He will take this city to the detriment of everyone in it. That's why he killed Vivian. That's why Vivian's ghost attacked him. She's there. Still in my church. Ask her."

Elyse hadn't moved, her sudden uncertainty obvious. Either my words had finally reached her, or the wonder that I had saved a busload of people from her lethal spell had broken through. She licked her lips and glanced toward Lee, clearly unsure. "You saw her? You saw her ghost?" she asked, and I nodded, my grip on the ley line never easing.

"She was angry when she died, betrayed and angry enough to linger. I should have shown her the curse when I found it," I said. "But I was afraid of what she'd think of me, and I don't have enough friends to lose any. And I lost her anyway." I swallowed hard, my throat closing. "Please don't let your grief give Lee what he wants. I've known him since I was ten, and he's a selfish, manipulative, cruel bastard, all the way to his core."

Again Elyse half turned to the plaza, the red and purple haze about her fingers faltering. "I can't let myself believe you," she said, but there was doubt, and my pulse hammered.

"Then maybe you can believe everyone else," I said as I gestured to David orchestrating the Weres to keep everyone at a safe distance.

For an instant, I thought she might understand as she scanned the plaza—until her eyes narrowed on me. "Why is Kalamack just standing there? You *want* us to curse the demons? You'd be trapped in the ever-after as much as them."

"Ah . . ." I took a step forward, and her face blanked, her returning mistrust making her expression hard and unforgiving.

"You want us to do the curse," she said again, thinking. "Why?"

*Damn, she is smart.* "Um . . ." I hedged. Then I shouted, "No! Elyse, wait!" when she spun, her black cloak furling.

*Mother pus bucket, can't I catch a break?* I thought, frantic as I imagined a circle around both of us. *"Rhombus!"* I exclaimed, trapping Elyse before she could reach the curb. The woman saw it go up, skidded to a halt, and spun. I was stuck in here with her, and the only escape would be to knock me out or throw me into the circle itself.

"Elyse, we need to talk."

Her young features twisting in hate, she howled, hands dripping energy.

Gasping, I darted around a car. *Al!* I threw the thought into the demon collective. Dali clearly wasn't going to answer me, but Al would be there if the rest had agreed to share the pain of his burnt synapses. Yelping, I dodged another fireball. Grabbing an abandoned bike, I flung it at her.

*Do you have any idea . . .* came drifting into my thoughts.

It was Al, and I fastened on him in relief. *"Stabils!"* I shouted to curse Elyse, simultaneously throwing a distracting ball of unfocused energy at her. As expected, she focused on the glowing ball and my initial joke curse hit her square in the chest. With a yelp, she dropped, falling to the pavement in an ungraceful heap.

*The coven is bound and ready to curse us,* I thought, even as Al's surprise that I was in a battle shocked through me.

*Move,* he advised, and I lurched to get out of Elyse line of sight. She was still spewing Latin, and anything she could see, she could spell. *It's too late, Rachel,* he thought as a ribbon of white-hot magic arched from the enraged woman to hit the ground where I'd just been, bubbling and frothing to a black ash. *Even if you lent your strength, we don't have enough force to stand against them.*

*Will you just listen!* I yelled into the demon collective, frustrated as the huge circle before the fountain began pulsating a gold-tinted purple. Crap on toast, the sun was down, and Al's bitter thoughts stained my excitement.

*Look,* I thought as I scanned the sky for Bis, and the nearest demon within the collective began taking notice of our semiprivate conversation. *We can't stop the coven. It's a thousand to our three hundred. But you don't have to. They're doing all the heavy lifting. Twist their curse back against them. Take it, and change its aim. Exile them to reality. All of them, not just the ones twisting the curse.* My gut tightened as Elyse twitched. She was figuring out the *stabils* curse. It was, after all, just a joke curse. *Bounce it back to every last one of them,* I thought as Elyse shook herself and got up, hair in disarray and her black cloak filthy with street dirt.

*Curse the entire body of . . . Dali!* Al thought, and then he was gone. I was alone in my mind.

"Hey!" I shouted as Elyse crashed into me and we went rolling. "Ow!" I shrieked, jerking my arm close when my funny bone hit the curb and twanged. Eyes wide, I did nothing when she gripped my neck, her lips pulled back from her teeth as she dumped a massive wash of line energy into me. I took it all, funneling it into the circle imprisoning us to make it stronger.

"You don't deserve Alcatraz," she snarled from atop me, utterly oblivious that I had taken everything she could dish out—and not replied in kind. *Holy crap, is this how Al feels?*

"No one deserves Alcatraz," I rasped, then brought up my arms to break her hold. Twisting out from under her, I found my feet. "Have you been there?" I said as she stood uneasily before me, watching my circle around us pulsating with our combined energies. "Perhaps you should do a walk-through before you start sending people to the island."

From behind her, a silver bell chimed. It was the start of the curse. Elyse turned in dismay. My circle still held us both, and I felt a twinge of satisfaction.

"Lee! Stop!" she shouted, running to the barrier's edge and punching at it. A bright pop flung her away, and she cried out as her butt landed on the pavement again.

"*Si Peccabus poenam mers!*" Lee exuberantly shouted, the force of Cincinnati's witches behind him as he invoked the magic to bind the demons to the ever-after.

And as the circle at Fountain Square began to glow with their combined will, from the depths of my mind rose a thunderous roar of denial. *Pacta sunt servanda!* Dali exclaimed in my thoughts, and I staggered as, with one voice, the demons grabbed the will of an entire city of witches . . . and slowly turned it to the demons' desires.

"Trent!" I shouted when the witches' circle flashed a sudden black. It was the demons' spell, now twisted to their will and hanging before the witches, as yet uninvoked. As one, the gathered witches gasped—and when the first person broke and ran, the spell engaged.

"Fire in the hole!" I shouted, relieved when Trent's protection circle flashed into play an instant before Quen's.

The circle at Fountain Square exploded outward with a building-rocking boom. Gasping, I lurched for Elyse, dragging her down and circling us both within a second protective bubble. The woman shrieked, fighting me as I held her tight, almost smothering her as the demon-turned curse burst upon the world, ringing through the planet and setting the atmosphere glowing with a black aurora borealis. My teeth clenched as the curse found me with the sensations of maggoty pinpricks. *Not me,* I thought, gripping Elyse tighter—and it dissolved and broke up, repelled by my circle.

It had passed me over.

With a wondering jolt, it hit me anew that I really *was* a demon. Whatever had been a witch in me was gone. I blinked fast as the reality soaked in, but when I looked up, the spell exiling the witches to remain within reality still hung in the atmosphere, a shimmering black and gold with the first of the stars peeking through like diamonds. "My God . . . it's beautiful," I whispered as it began to fade.

"Get off!" Elyse shouted, and my hands sprang away at the first hint of tingling ley line energy. Her elbow rammed into my gut, and she spun to a stand. "Drop your circle," she intoned, and I did. I didn't need it anymore.

Elyse turned from me, her face aghast as she stared at the plaza. Cries of dismay and fear echoed as people got to their feet, ashen as they felt the curse settle deep into their souls. Some sobbed, some were angry, but most of them ran, weaving through the holes in the I.S.'s net like fish.

Lee stood as if in shock, what was left of the coven of moral and ethical standards surrounding him. Pushing past their shouted questions, he stomped over to the thickest gathering of I.S. agents. I felt no victory, only a tired acceptance.

"You bounced it back," Elyse said. She wasn't retching or in shock as were all the other witches, and I wondered if the spell had passed over her, seeing as she'd been under my circle at the time. "You turned it against us and bounced it back," she said again, staring at her hands. "How? You couldn't . . . Lee said there were only three hundred of you left."

"Thereabouts," I agreed. I stayed where I sat on the pavement, my knees to my chest and my arms about my shins. It felt good to be doing nothing. But she was still staring at me, and I probably should drop some demon wisdom on her. "Maybe you need to rethink who you're following if you're going to be responsible for an entire demographic's morality." *Yeah, that was good.*

Groaning, I rolled myself over and up. Smacking the dirt off my jeans, I started for Trent, slow until I knew how bad my hip was going to hurt. It seemed to be over, but that's usually when the rug got pulled out from under me.

The media had predictably recovered first, loud and disorganized as they struggled to get their equipment linked to the studio again. The sun was down, and I squinted up at Carew Tower, wondering where Bis was. "Thank you, Ivy," I whispered as the vampiric I.S. agents ignored Lee's increasingly agitated demands to arrest me. Most had turned their backs to the square, clearly waiting to see who owned the streets before they acted.

"But you are so few," Elyse whispered, and I jumped, startled to see her at my elbow. The curse might not have seen her hiding under my circle, but she was still confused. They taught these kids from the time they could walk that they were invincible. And they weren't. No one was.

"True." I paused, one foot on a wide step. "But apart from me, Lee, and the surviving Rosewood babies, every demon in existence is over five thousand years old." Silent, her gaze went to Lee, and I snickered. "Yep. He's biologically a demon. But seeing as he's not in their database, I'd be willing to bet that when the demons twisted the curse and sent it back to you that it fastened on his witch heritage." Sighing happily, I slumped. "He doesn't look too happy. Elyse, I think I could like you. Here's a word of advice I found out the hard way. You need to exhaust all options before trying to curse someone, much less an entire people. Even if it hurts."

"Then I will take her myself!" Lee howled, and I frowned as he started my way, arms swinging. "You *canicula*!" he shouted, and I renewed my hold on the ley lines as his hands began to glow. "You twisted it against us! You stupid whore of a demon. Elyse! Take her!"

Elyse took a symbolic step back, retreating as two I.S. agents jogged forward to intercept Lee. Doyle hastened to join them . . . a sparkle of pixy dust at his shoulder. *Jenks!* I thought, my hand rising as I saw Bis's angular shadow cut through the early dusk.

"Bis!" I called, and he flipped end over end, his red eyes reflecting the lights from the I.S. cruisers as he oriented on me.

"Hi, Rachel!" the kid almost crowed, and the wind from his wings pushed the hair from me as he landed on my shoulder. Shocked, Elyse took a step back. "I would've been here sooner, but I wanted to find Jenks. It's too cold for him, and I figured he wouldn't leave you."

"You figured right," I said as his tail wrapped securely behind my shoulders. The tingle of the line I was holding seemed to grow, and Bis rumbled low in his chest, feeling it as well.

"Elyse!" Lee demanded as the woman looked at her hands, then the overturned bus, her complexion a sickly gray. Brow furrowed, she shook her head. Snarling, Lee pulled on the line.

I was ready for him, and I flung a hand out, meeting his energy with my own. Snapping and popping, the two forces collided until I took hold of the wildly gyrating energy and drew it into me with the sharpness of a cracked whip.

Lee skidded to a halt, suddenly unsure as I pulled every last erg from him. On my shoulder, Bis seemed to thrum, wings extended as the ley line filled us both.

"How . . ." Lee stammered, and then he jerked, starting when Doyle caught up. The living vampire spun Lee around and adroitly snapped a ring of charmed silver around his wrist.

"What . . . I am a coven member!" Lee protested, his cheeks reddening in his entitled anger. "Get that off me. Get it off!"

"Read him his rights," Doyle said, and Lee's face went ashen.

"You," Lee said as his eyes found me.

"Me," I said, tired as two I.S. agents began to muscle Lee to a car. "Me," I said again, softer this time as I saw Elyse cross the plaza to join the rest of the coven. Seeing her slow, beaten pace, the first inklings of relief began to unknot my gut. Smiling, I put a hand on Bis's craggy feet as both of us oriented on the sound of pixy wings.

"Hey, Jenks," I said, flipping my hair out of his way as the cold pixy dropped down. Dusting a dismal blue, he landed to press against my neck, his wings a frigid shock. "Tell me it's good news," I added, and he sighed as my body heat warmed him via his wings.

"The best," he said. "Someone had scraped off the wax pentagram by the time I got Doyle to the church, but I told him he could dig out a chunk of floor. There was enough embedded in the floorboards to do a positive ID." He took a breath. "Thanks for the lift, Bis."

"No prob," the gargoyle rumbled, his dark, pebbly skin lightening as he blushed.

At the curb, Lee began to fight the two I.S. agents. "This wasn't my fault," he said, refusing to get into the car. "It was Morgan. She galvanized the demons. It's not my fault you can't go to the ever-after anymore. It's hers! Arrest her!"

Doyle sidled up beside me, his grin wide to show his pointed teeth. "Maybe tomorrow, Sir Coven Leader Stanley Saladan," he said loudly, and Lee went stiff at his mocking tone. "Right now, you're wanted for questioning in the matter of the murder of Madam Coven Leader Vivian Smith, fabricating evidence, tampering with an I.S. investigation, falsifying information on a government form, and obstruction of justice."

"No!" Lee went limp to try to wiggle from of their grip. "Elyse, she lies! She murdered Vivian. It was her!"

Doyle shrugged, clearly satisfied as he turned to me. "You do understand this all goes away if Finnis—"

"Yeah, I got it," I said, and, giving me a cheerful nod, Doyle walked off, almost strutting to the media vans.

"Thanks, Jenks," I whispered, none too eager to join Trent, cornered

by the press. No way was I going over there. Elyse, too, was occupied, surrounded by the remainder of the coven. All three of them were sneaking
glances at me as she gestured and spoke.

"Thanks, Jenks?" Jenks mocked me, but I could tell he was pleased. "I
pull your lily-white ass out of Alcatraz, and all I get is a 'Thanks, Jenks'?"

"Yep." Tired, I pushed into motion. I should talk to the coven before
they decided to do something stupid. "Elyse?" I called as I got closer, and
they froze, their sudden silence and fear striking me cold. "Um." I slowed,
wondering if Bis and Jenks on my shoulders helped or hindered my case.
"Guys?" I whispered. "Could you check on Trent for me?"

"Tink's a Disney whore, Rache," Jenks grumbled as he lifted from my
shoulder, his dust again a warm gold. "If you want to be alone with the
coven, you only have to ask."

Bis's feet gave me a comforting pinch, and then he was gone, the wind
from his wings sending my hair flying until he found the air. As Bis did
barrel rolls around Jenks, they flew over the plaza, gathering stares in their
wake.

Elyse and the coven hadn't moved, and I bowed my head, trying to
look innocuous and wondering if this was a mistake. "Elyse, I am so sorry
about Vivian," I said as I scuffed to a halt, an awkward eight feet between
us. "I have a white spell that might bring her back for a night. It would give
you a chance to—"

"Rache!" Jenks shrilled as someone pulled on the ley line. Hard.

"Trent?" I spun, my expression emptying.

It was Lee. He'd gotten free of his charmed silver. I.S. agents at his feet,
he stood by the car, his dark robes snapping as he swung his arm and the
ley line roared into him. Snarling in anger, he threw dark magic at us.

"Fire in the hole!" I shouted, aghast as Lee's spell sped through the air.
*It's not aimed at me,* I suddenly realized. "Elyse! Get down!" I called, but
she had frozen, shocked into immobility.

"Down, down, down!" Doyle shouted, and three agents fell on Lee,
smothering him.

His magic, though, had been loosed, and Lee watched from the pavement as it sped toward us, his anticipation and delight disgustingly obvious.

*"Corrumpo!"* I exclaimed, directing the energy at Lee's blast even as I flung myself at Elyse. Eyes clamped shut, I collided with her, slamming her to the pavement. She shrieked as we hit the ground, pain a sudden shock racing up my hands and arms as we slid.

Elyse's sudden struggle under me pulled my eyes open. Flustered, I rolled to sit beside her with my hands to my middle. *Damn it all to hell, that hurt.*

And then Lee's deflected magic hit Carew Tower. A collective gasp rose as everyone looked at the old building. Purple and green sparkles rained down, pitting the sidewalk and sending everyone running for safety.

"That was Lee. I only deflected it," I said as Doyle frowned at me from across the square. Trent was already jogging across the plaza, but Jenks and Bis were quickly outdistancing him. Feeling sheepish, I rolled to my knees to stand up, only to jerk my hands away when they hit the pavement. I sat back on my heels as I hissed in pain. My hands were scraped and bleeding. *Worth it,* I thought as I saw Elyse being helped to her feet.

"Rache, he's gone!" Jenks said, and I winced, breath held when the pixy dusted my hands to stop the bleeding. "He knocked the I.S. on their cans and ran off!"

"Swell." I had been hoping we could finish this all with a nice ribbon and go home, but nooooo, Lee was going to make me sweat a little.

"Leave her alone," I heard Elyse say, and then louder, clearly annoyed, "I said leave Morgan alone! Are you deaf or just blind? She saved my life, you idiots!"

But my snicker petered out into wonder as she extended her hand to me to help me rise. "Ah," I said, reluctant, and she grabbed my arm instead, hauling me to my feet in an ungraceful lurch.

"Thank you," she said, glancing to the car where the I.S. agents Lee had downed were still sitting, shaking their heads and trying to focus. "That would have killed me."

"Yep." I sighed, realizing it wasn't as over as I would have hoped. "If he can't use you anymore, he'd rather see you dead."

Suddenly tears threatened as Trent closed the distance between us, his love and worry pouring from him. "Could you excuse me?" And then my throat turned into a lump as Trent yanked me to him. I couldn't breathe as his arms wrapped me tight, pulling me into a painful squeeze until I gasped.

"Are you okay?" he said, smiling at I carefully wiped a spot of dirt from his shoulder. "That looks bad," he added as he took my hands in his.

"Relax, Cookie Maker," Jenks said as he hovered, his dust shading to blue. "She's okay."

"Thanks for the warning, Jenks," I said, then hid my hands as Doyle strutted up.

Bis glided in from the fountain to my shoulder, his frown one of suspicion. Jenks immediately dropped to Bis's head, and my entire body seemed to relax when a warming heat emanated from the gargoyle. Elyse and the coven had moved off a short distance, but they weren't leaving, and I wondered if they wanted to talk, as they were again shooting glances at me. I could hear sirens, and I hoped it was fire trucks, not ambulances. I had a better chance of snagging a pain amulet if it was fire trucks. Dali still had my shoulder bag.

"You let him get away?" I said to Doyle, and the living vampire gave Trent a respectful nod. "There are like a hundred witches out here. Didn't anyone think to circle him?"

"I'm not in charge of this circus," Doyle said, his smirk widening at Bis's glare. "I'm only responsible for evidence gathering and testing."

"So . . . we can go?" I was not going to hide in the ever-after. This was my home, and I couldn't do my job from another reality by virtual meetings and remote ass-kicking.

"You?" Doyle's chest shifted as he sighed as if unhappy. "You can. There's an eighty-eight percent likelihood that the curse that killed Vivian came from Lee. You pinged at twelve percent. That is a statistical zero when the sample comes from an area you occupy. Residual aura settlement."

"Told you," Jenks said, the dust spilling from him a bright silver. Trent's arm slipped around my waist, and I leaned into him, tired.

"Good." My attention went to the lingering I.S. agents, all of them ignoring me. For now.

"Mr. Kalamack, though . . ." Doyle added, and Jenks's wings hummed a warning. "Things are not so clear."

Trent's hold on me tightened. Doyle, though, was looking up at Carew Tower, not us, and I gave his hand a squeeze to relax.

"Word is that Finnis's plane never got off the ground," Doyle said, his voice carefully casual. "Seems that Constance made a few calls this afternoon, right before sunset." He hesitated, wincing. "You freed her? I fail to see how this is any better than Finnis."

"Give her some time," I said, beginning to think we might have done it. Or at least, put it off for a while. "I took a lot of stress from her, and she is not dumb, just frustrated. Can you arrange a suite in the I.S. for her? Small staff of three. She's going to take classes on properly directing anger and city management." I hesitated. "She's not in charge. I am."

Doyle sucked on his teeth, clearly not happy as he glanced at the remaining coven members being checked over by the arriving paramedics. "Yeah, I can do that."

"We good, then?" I asked, needing to hear it from him.

Doyle smiled, lips closed. "I imagine so. Everyone will be busy trying to figure out who has the longest teeth for a while." He hesitated, and Trent stiffened when the living vampire reluctantly pulled an envelope from an inner pocket.

"That doesn't look like a check, Rache," Jenks said, and I frowned.

"It's a warrant for Trent." Doyle tapped it against his palm. "I'll hold on to this for twenty-four hours," he said, gaze going across the plaza to where Quen was talking with David. "Seeing as you are busy cleaning up our mess."

"Seriously?" I almost whined as I prodded my ribs, and the vampire laughed, his low voice pulling the attentions of everyone within earshot.

"Sorry," he said, and Bis's grip on my shoulder tightened. "The only act you were wanted for was killing Vivian with illicit magic. Kalamack's business efforts, though appreciated, are still illegal. We could turn a blind eye to that as usual, but the claims of illegal genetic treatments can't be overlooked." He hesitated, head inclined to Trent. "At least, not without the proper kickbacks."

It was as good as I was going to get. Twenty-four hours would be more than enough time for Trent to find the money. *I think.*

Grinning, I wound up and punched Doyle in the arm, slowly so he knew it was coming. "Thanks, Doyle. You're not bad for a living vamp."

Doyle flicked his arm as if brushing off an insect, showing his teeth to make a drop of remembered vampiric heat fall through me. "Excuse me," he said, smirking as he sensed it, and then he strode to the I.S. van, yelling at his people to get the cars moved so the ambulances could get in here.

"I need to sit down," I whispered, one arm around Trent, the other holding my ribs.

"Room service is half a block down the street," Trent offered, and I slumped deeper against him. Half a block, yes, but between reporters and the crush of emergency vehicles, it was going to take at least five minutes. Elyse was looking at me, and I gave her a respectful nod before shuffling into motion. One of the younger members protested, and she told him to back off, making me smile. Looked like the coven had their new leader.

Eventually we would talk, and until we did, I probably didn't have to worry about the coven. Lee had vanished but the world was onto him now, and the warrant for Vivian's death had his name on it, not mine. David and Cassie clearly had the Weres under control, and though Constance was again a potential threat, we had an agreement.

All that was left was getting my bag from Dali.

"Jenks, thank you," I whispered as we turned to Carew Tower. "You are seriously the difference between me walking away from this and having to hide in the ever-after." I hesitated. "And Trent," I said, my head thumping onto his shoulder. "And Quen. David. Ivy, Pike . . ." I added. "But mostly you," I finished.

"Yeah, I know," the pixy said smugly. "Hey! Your plan worked!"

I chuckled, leaning deeper into Trent as we angled to find Quen and hopefully a quiet ride up to Trent's penthouse. "First time for everything," I whispered as I closed my eyes, trusting that between Jenks, Bis, and Trent, I'd get there okay.

# CHAPTER
# 31

"THANK YOU!" THE KIDS ON THE STOOP CHORUSED, THE PREOCCU-pied lilt to their high voices telling me they were already thinking of the next door.

"Be safe out there," I said as they ran for the sidewalk, costumes fluttering. "Don't take any black tomatoes!"

That got a wave from their waiting parents, and in a flurry of commotion, the pack of superheroes and anime characters trundled to the next house. The small gesture went right to my gut, making me feel as if I belonged. I'd thought I'd lost that.

The sounds of the night were wonderful, and I lingered on the cold stoop with my bowl of candy, soaking in the excited calls of "Trick or treat" and the thumping of running feet. Cars prowled, their headlights cutting the darkness into angles of black and white. And above it all was the moon, just shy of full, as the night moved and lived.

I turned to go in, my gaze lingering on Doyle parked across the street. He'd been there since sundown. He'd been there every night for the past week, waiting for Trent, I think.

"Hey!" I shouted, and he looked up from his phone. "You want to come in? I have hot cider."

Brow furrowed, the I.S. detective actually considered it before shaking his head.

"If you change your mind, come on up," I said, smiling as I felt behind me for the open door and went inside.

The TV was a soft murmur, and I took a foil-wrapped pumpkin from the bowl as I went into the sanctuary. There was a distinct possibility that Jenks and I had overestimated our candy needs. It was hard to know from any given year to the next if I would have people driving from across town to knock on the demon's door, or if even my neighbors would be avoiding my porch light. But it was early yet. The real action never started until after midnight.

Sighing, I fell onto the couch before the TV and dropped the wad of orange foil on the little pyramid already there. The TV was tuned to the news, and I reached for the remote to toggle up the sound when they went to a live shot outside of Trent's estate.

"As you can see," the no-nonsense blonde in her Halloween-inspired snake dress was saying, "Trent Kalamack's annual Halloween fundraiser is in full swing. The highly anticipated yearly event is one of Kalamack's major community outreaches, bringing in high society to fill Cincinnati's pantries as well as fund the city's many programs designed to help the underprivileged rise to self-sufficiency. Mr. Kalamack has not yet made an appearance, and questions to Cincinnati's I.S. branch have gone unanswered. It is still unknown if Mr. Kalamack is in custody on charges of manufacturing genetic medicines, or if the former councilman is in hiding evading justice. Either way, he knows how to throw one hell of a party."

I looked up at the sound of pixy wings, recognizing Jenks's heavier thrum.

"She said *hell*," Jenks said. "I didn't know you could say *hell* on national TV."

"It's a local channel," I said as they went to commercial and I turned it down. "Sometimes you have to use the right word, fines or not."

"Mmmm." Jenks landed on the lampshade, fidgeting as he adjusted the new shirt that Getty had made him. It was purple and gold, like pansies in the sun, and I didn't know if I should say something or not. "Is Doyle still out there?"

"Yep." Stretching, I reached for another chocolate pumpkin. *Chocolate for dinner. Adulting at its finest.*

Jenks swung his feet, wings softly moving. "If you want to go to the party and spend some time with your mom, I've got this. Leave the candy on the front steps. I'll make sure no one trolls the bowl."

"Thanks, but we had lunch together. Besides, seeing my mom dressed up as Madonna might scar me for life."

He snickered, the dust spilling from him shifting a brilliant gold. "So . . . Trent still camped out in the ever-after?"

"Mmmm." I nodded, the chocolate mirroring my thoughts of the night perfectly: sweet, bitter, fleeting. The usual bribes weren't working, hence the warrants on Trent still being active. It could have been Lee, but I was betting it was Finnis. Or Constance maybe, just to irritate me.

It had only been a week, and Constance had already begun to test her influence, making forays to deplete a few high-end jewelry stores, and of course to Piscary's to cull a few blood donors from its namesake's orphaned and willing children. I'd sent her a bouquet of roses three days ago to remind her of her end of the deal, but it seemed that she was being as good as her word. I'd gotten news this morning that the soul curse was again in active FCAS consideration, and apart from Doyle camped out on my curb, the I.S. seemed to be off my case.

Ivy, though, was struggling to keep Constance within reasonable bounds. I think she enjoyed the challenge, if the truth be told. I'd never be able to trust the undead vampire, obviously, but at least the ex-mouse was not actively trying to take me out. At the moment.

All in all, it had been a quiet week. The demons were smug in having turned the exile curse back on the witches, and their restored pride meant they were less likely to do anything disruptive anytime soon. Most witches didn't care that the ever-after was now denied them, wrongfully thinking it made them less likely to be abducted by a demon, and those who did mind kept their mouth shut lest someone claim they were dark practitioners. Parker had been captured outside the zoo and was currently in quarantine, scheduled to be relocated to that island off Mackinaw City, which I thought criminally ironic. David and Cassie had eloped and were on their honeymoon. Stef had gotten a promotion at the hospital and was currently looking at new apartments. And Trent?

I sighed, reaching for another chocolate. Trent was hiding in the ever-after, evading that stupid warrant.

"Relax, Rache," Jenks said, wing in hand as he smoothed out a small rip. "If the coven wanted to see that curse you used on Pike's brother, they would have asked already."

My head snapped up at a sudden knock. There was no following "Trick or treat."

"But I could be mistaken," the pixy added, rising up on a column of silver dust.

"That was the back door," I mused aloud, wondering if it might be Trent. Yes, he was in the ever-after, but the ley line in my backyard was hard to watch and easy to use. And unlike the witches, elves could still stand in a ley line and move from reality to reality.

I got to my feet even as Bis swooped in from the foyer, the gargoyle clearly having slipped in through a belfry window. "It's the girls!" he said, his skin a pebbly black in excitement. "Can I hold the bowl?"

I nodded, worried as my gaze went to the front door. Doyle was at my curb, but unless he had a winged backup—which was highly unlikely—he wouldn't know Trent was here. Eager to see what the girls were for Halloween, I started for the porch. Bis grabbed the bowl and flew out before me, Jenks in hot pursuit.

"Trick or treat!" Lucy yelled from the porch as I came into the kitchen, and my smile widened.

Bis and Jenks were already there, and the girls were silently staring into the bowl as if it was the most important decision in the world. Behind them, Trent stood with two little pumpkin baskets in hand, pleasure softening his face. The blond beard and mustache he now had were new, making him look like a rangy Viking.

"It's a pixy and fairy come to my garden!" I said, seeing as both girls were in gossamer and lace. Ray sported a set of orange butterfly wings, and

Lucy was in pink pixy wings. "Jenks," I added as I sat on the top step. "Do you think they want to work for acorns?"

"No!" Lucy shouted. "Trick or treat!" Her little face scrunched up as she tried to get her fingers into a glitter pouch. "Pixy dust!" she yelled, throwing the sparkling silver in the air.

"Then treats it is, you little goblins," I said, and Trent fumbled for his phone to snap a picture. "Take your candy. No tricks here, please."

Lucy flung herself at my knees, her eyes sparkling. "It's me, Aunt Rachel."

"Lucy?" I put a hand to my chest. "That's Lucy? And Ray?"

Ray beamed, a foil-wrapped pumpkin tight in her grip.

Clearly content, Trent sat down on the step beside me. "You are our only house tonight," he said, then leaned over the bowl to give me a kiss.

"Then you should take two treats," I said, a hand lifting to touch his beard. I had yet to decide if I liked it or not. "Ray, Lucy, you are so . . ."

"Pink," Jenks said flatly, and Bis flipped his tail to shove Jenks into the air.

"Formidable and dangerous," I finished, and Ray gripped her plastic bow tighter. Lucy, though, began dancing about, throwing her glitter and smacking her wings into everything. Stumbling, she bumped into Ray, who promptly shoved her down. Lucy hit the porch boards, her eyes widening as she looked at Ray and began to cry. No, I wasn't ready for this.

"Ray," Trent coaxed, staying where he was instead of running to stand Lucy up as I would have done. "Think about Lucy's intention before you shove her down. It was an accident."

"Ray pushed me!" Lucy wailed, but Ray had already gone to give her sister a hug. Snuffling, Lucy gave her a hug back, and peace was restored.

"I am so not ready for being a parent," I whispered, and Trent tugged me closer.

"No one is," he said, but I seriously had my doubts.

"I thought Ellasbeth would have them tonight," I said, and Trent's eye twitched.

"I get Halloween. She gets the solstice."

"Maybe you should come in," I said as I noticed Jenks's dust shifting to a cold blue. "Doyle is at my curb."

"Still?" Trent let go and stood.

"Yep. And another in the street behind the church." I hesitated. "You hungry? All I've had tonight is chocolate."

"Well, shoot." Hands gentle and firm, Trent began to corral the girls to the kitchen door. "I had been hoping to check on the progress at the apartment. At least I can update my phone."

In a quick patter of feet, the girls ran into the sanctuary, Bis and Jenks hot behind.

I followed them as far as the kitchen, smirking as I drew him to a halt and ran a hand over his week-old beard. "Sneak into Carew Tower?" I said. "With nothing but a beard and mustache? Trent, they are serious about bringing you in." My hand dropped. "I thought Quen would have settled this by now. You said two days, and that was a week ago."

Trent's phone hummed, and he turned it facedown on the counter after a brief glance. "I don't get it," he said. "It's as if my money is from a Monopoly game. Even the offshore funds are frozen. My laborers have gone on strike because I can't pay them, food is rotting in the fields. Trains aren't running for the same reason. Zero movement on the reno. The only thing that *is* still working is the Brimstone."

"Finnis?" I guessed as I leaned against the counter, then sighed. "Lee."

Trent nodded, brow furrowed. "Probably. I'm beginning to think I'm stuck in the ever-after until we find him."

Depressed, I peeled off the foil, thinking, *Fun size? Who are they kidding?* It wasn't an ideal situation, and I pulled the candy bowl closer. "I don't know if putting him away is going to help anymore. The entire situation has taken on a life of its own."

Trent's breath seemed to catch. "Why? What have you heard?"

But my words stayed unsaid as Jenks darted in, a bright red dust spilling from him. "Rache!" the pixy sputtered, clearly angry. "I told him he can't stay, but he won't leave."

Alarm tightened my gut. "Who?"

"Al," Jenks practically snarled, and my worry turned to confusion. "That Tink-blasted troll gigolo of a moss wipe parked his van between the Davaros plot and Pierce's pylon."

"This is a joke, right?" I said as Trent and I peered out the window. Sure enough, Al's huge, brightly colored wooden van was there amid the dead grass and tombstones, a dark figure moving about in the moonlight as if settling in. "What the devil?" I whispered.

Trent made a soft, regretful sound. "Maybe I shouldn't have asked to use his kitchen again."

"This is not happening." Grabbing a handful of chocolate, I headed for the porch, skidding to halt when I realized Trent wasn't with me. "Aren't you coming?"

Trent shrugged, appearing unusually helpless. "I . . . I tried," he said. "He . . ."

"You need to fix this," I demanded, and he cringed, wincing when Jenks made a rude snort. "Chicken," I added as I pushed onto the porch and stomped down the stairs.

It was cold, and I focused on Jenks as he flew along beside me. "I told him he couldn't stay," the pixy said. "He laughed at me. Rache, I can't make him leave. He's a demon!"

"I can." But I wasn't sure how, and my pace slowed as I stepped over the low wall and into the graveyard. Al must have known I was there, but he didn't even glance up from arranging his rock ring as I closed the distance. He had dropped his van next to Pierce's tombstone, right where the ley line ran. The van was potentially here or in the ever-after at will. And if I had my way, it wouldn't be here.

"What are you doing?" I said as I halted before him.

Al pushed back onto his heels from where he was kneeling on the cold, matted-grass earth, his red eyes glinting in the faint moonlight. "What does it look like I'm doing?" he said, then rose to his feet to dust his dark slacks and vest clean. "I'm renting the graveyard from your pixy. Your fairies are in Mexico, and Jenks can't string lines in the snow."

Jenks rasped his wings in frustration. "I never said that," he blurted.

"Rache, I never said he could move in. The graveyard isn't zoned for an RV. I gots standards!"

I raised a hand for patience, then took a slow breath. "Trent doesn't want to be in the ever-after any more than you want him there," I said, and Al made a rude sound. "Give him a few more days. You can't stay here."

"I have *given* him a week." Lip curled, Al leaned against Pierce's stone. With a sudden snap, the tall, cracked stone broke to send two shards to the blasphemed earth. "This is a paranormal shelter, is it not?" he said as he shoved one toward the fire with his foot. "I am sheltering."

Not believing this, I gestured to the sky. "From who?"

Al gave Pierce's gravestone a second nudge into place. He was going to use it as a fireside seat. "From your elf," he said. "He is driving me crazy. Him and those sweet, charming, noisy girls of his. Up at the crack of dawn. As long as he is there, I am here."

"See?" Jenks said, then he spun to the church, his dust going thin. "Someone is at the front door."

"It's trick-or-treaters," I said, but Jenks had risen straight up to check. "Al." I turned to see him hunched before the fire pit. I had no idea what he thought he was going to burn. They had firewood at Home Depot, didn't they?

"It's the coven," Al said, and a pang of angst raced through me.

"On Halloween?" Nervous, I handed him all but one of the candies.

Jenks dropped down, his dust a pale hint. "Rache, it's Elyse."

"Told you." Beaming, Al unwrapped a chocolate and bit it in two. "Mmmm, cheap chocolate. Nothing better. Would you like me to come in? Smile at her, perhaps?"

"No." Trent in the kitchen, Al in the garden, Doyle at my curb, the coven on my front steps. Damn, couldn't I catch a break? "Ah, Jenks, give Trent the heads-up and let her in. I'll be right there."

"'Kay," the pixy said, then darted off.

Al was beaming as if it was all a great joke. "Don't get comfortable," I said. "You are not staying."

"I'm surprised they waited this long," he said as he sat on Pierce's stone and threw a charm into the fire pit. A blue and gold fire whooshed up, burning who knew what. "But they are young," he mused aloud. His brow furrowed, his amusement gone. "You may have been cleared of that murder charge, but you're still wanted for questioning concerning practicing illicit magic. That's not going to change."

I hesitated as I took in the church, worried. It was beautiful with all the light spilling out into the night, and I stifled a shudder at the memory of Alcatraz. "No, it isn't," I said softly, wondering if this was why he had dropped into my garden. *Trent, eh?* "Thank you," I said, and he closed his eyes as if he hadn't heard me, settling back against the stone as if to go to sleep.

Head down, I began walking to the church, my arms wrapped around myself from more than the cold.

"Rache . . ."

It was Jenks, and I flicked my hair from my shoulder. "Trent and the girls know she's here?" I said, and he landed to press his cold wings to my neck.

"Yeah. Can't you make him leave?"

"How?" I said, not sure I wanted to. "Besides, he's right. Until Lee is in custody, we could use the extra security."

"Tink loves a duck," he muttered, and I took the porch steps two at a time. "I gots a demon in my summerhouse."

A faint smile quirked my lips. I knew it was still there when I went in to find Trent, desperately trying to keep the girls quiet with a box of cereal. Bis was atop the fridge, and his ears pricked as I came in, his red eyes hopeful.

"Everything okay?" Trent asked, a hint of worry in his voice.

"Ask me tomorrow," I said. "Jenks, you want to watch the girls with Bis?"

"Sure," the pixy said, dropping down to stand on the cereal box, hands on his hips. "You going to be quiet for me, right?"

Mouth full, Lucy nodded, and Trent stood to follow me into the sanctuary, tugging his lightweight shirt down as if it was a dress coat.

"Hold up, there," I said, blocking his path. "I got this. You are going out into the garden and work things out with Al."

Trent's brow furrowed. "Ah . . ."

"Neither one of you is staying here," I whispered as I leaned in and gave him a kiss. "My insurance won't cover either of you."

"Damn! I mean, darn," Jenks said, glancing at the girls and their cereal. "She got you there, Cookie Man."

"I mean it," I added lightly, my hand trailing from his jawbone as I left him and went down the hall. *Elyse. Not what I need tonight.*

My pleasant expression froze as I saw Elyse standing at the broken pool table. Her fingers resting on the burnt felt made me wonder if she sensed the magic I had once twisted on the slate underneath.

"Hi, Madam Coven Leader," I said, and she spun.

Cheeks flushed, she touched her smooth black hair in what was probably a nervous tic. Black jeans and a gold top showed past her long cashmere coat, and a small clutch purse sat on the table's bumper. "Elyse is fine," she said, her eyes going from me to the floor where the shadow of that dark curse still lingered. "So this is what a paranormal shelter looks like."

I came in and gestured for her to sit down. "On a good day," I said, my thoughts winging to Al and Trent in the garden, then Doyle at my curb. "You're not here to arrest me, are you?"

Elyse's gaze dropped from the open rafters. "I'm honored to entertain whatever agreement you had with my predecessor. Besides, I'd need a warrant to arrest you, and we can't issue one until we have a full forum. You're safe until June, when I will likely deem the curse you used on Welroe illegal unless you can prove to me it isn't or that you truly were ignorant of its origin." She smiled as she took her purse and came over. "But that's not why I'm here."

*June,* I thought in relief. That was like forever. I had some time. "You sound just like her," I said, wanting to sit, but until she did, I wouldn't.

And then my expression blanked as Elyse froze, blinking fast to ward off the tears.

"Elyse, I am so sorry," I said as I came forward, feeling like a jerk. "I can't tell you how sorry I am. I should have—"

Elyse lifted a hand, clearly not wanting me to touch her. "I came here tonight because I wanted to thank you." Her head lifted, showing me her unshed tears. "For saving my life. For your patience when I tried to hurt you." Her breath shook on her exhale. "For stopping Saladan. For opening our eyes. My eyes."

I slumped where I stood, feeling awkward. "You're welcome. Is everyone okay?"

Elyse nodded as she opened her purse. "Vivian had been my teacher since I was ten. She didn't have any family except for me, which means I'm the one going through her things. I'm guessing this might mean more to you than me," she said, holding out a shot glass with MARGARITAVILLE emblazoned on it in a garish gold paint.

I took it, a smile so wide on me it must have looked as if I didn't care. But really, it was the opposite. "Thank you. It's from our trip."

"I figured." Elyse snapped her purse closed. "Vivian thought that having a witch-born demon in the coven would open up possibilities that have been closed to us for thousands of years. Clearly Saladan was a mistake. He was using us for his advantage, not furthering our standing or creating a safer environment."

I heard the back door shut, and it grew quiet in the kitchen. "That has nothing to do with his biology," I said. "Lee is a bastard. You don't have to be a demon to be a bastard." Though it did seem that when push came to shove, most demons were.

Jaw tight, Elyse stared at the circle stained into the floor. "Lee was supposed to forge a link to the demons, become a conduit for dialogue and the beginnings of understanding our heritage," she said, but her tone was rising as if she was having trouble keeping it together. "And I find myself in a situation where I am tempted to make the same mistake twice," she added, voice light and sort of weepy.

"Uh . . ." I said, an entirely new worry trickling through me.

Elyse's smile was clearly forced. "As the acting lead member of the coven, I have the authority to invite candidates to be considered for the honor of wearing the Möbius strip. It's usually a formality as active members tutor and mentor their replacements. Exceptions can be made. Were made."

She took a breath and I froze, feeling everything tighten.

"Rachel, I intend to submit your name into the pool of potential candidates this June, provided the curse you used on Welroe checks out."

"Sweet mother of Tink," came a tiny voice from the rafters, and I stared, not believing the words that had come out of her mouth. The honor was heady, but immediately my suspicious nature asked, *Why?*

"Vivian was right," she said, glancing at the faded pentagram. "We need a closer tie to the demons. They have a lot to teach us."

"Not really," I said, wondering what they really wanted. "Lee about covered it."

"It would be beneficial to you as well," she said, clearly sensing my lack of excitement. "Coven members have a license to curse. If you are chosen, your past indiscretions would be expunged and future issues would be covered—provided there was no loss of life."

I was glad now that we weren't sitting companionably about my coffee table eating chocolate, and I shifted my weight to one foot. "Provided I give you free access to my demon books."

Jenks's wings hummed, but not a glimmer of dust showed.

"Lenny says they are unique," Elyse said, and it was all I could do to not throw her out. They didn't want me. They wanted what I knew. That wasn't the same. *No wonder Al is camped out in my backyard.*

"They are," I said. "No."

"Atta girl" drifted down from the rafters, but Elyse stared, clearly shocked.

"No?" she repeated.

"Yeah, you're right. That was kind of short," I admitted. "Let me try again. Thank you for the invitation to be a member of the coven of moral and ethical standards, but I will have to respectfully decline. I will show you a copy of the curse that I was going to show Vivian because I owe it to her and myself, but I will not become a coven member and betray the trust of the demons."

Elyse had lost her smile. Actually, she looked a little pissed. "I'm not asking you to betray the demons. I'm giving you a chance to . . ."

"Redeem myself with my peers?" I suggested, glad that Trent wasn't hearing this. He would probably say it was a mistake, and maybe it was. Even so, I should probably try not to piss her off, and I ducked my head, trying to ease the tension. "Elyse, I can't express my humble thanks enough, but I know where my loyalty needs to be. Please accept my apologies, but it's not with the coven." *Firm yet polite. That should do it.*

Elyse seemed stunned. She had come to me with what she probably thought was a chance of a lifetime, and here I was, dumping all over it. "This would absolve you of all your indiscretions," she said. "You wouldn't have to fear Alcatraz ever again."

From the rafters, Jenks said, "She doesn't fear Alcatraz now." Dropping down, he landed on my hastily raised hand. "Do you, Rache?"

My attention flicked to Bis as the kid crawled into the room on the ceiling. He had shifted his color to match the paint, and I stifled a shudder. "No," I said, and his ears waggled at me as he smiled to show his black teeth. "I don't." I hesitated to give my next words more weight. "Should I?"

"You are seriously turning me down." Elyse was clearly confounded. "I thought . . . this would be a mutually beneficial situation. You'd be free to pursue your demon studies, and we'd gain the help of a powerful practitioner when such strength was needed."

I shook my head, my arms going over my chest. Coven member? Not likely. I would be fighting them on everything, pushed into being their enforcer when things got tough. Not happening.

"Rache has her own thing going," Jenks said. "We don't need your favors."

"It's okay," I said softly, then louder to Elyse, "Again, Madam Coven Leader, I am honored that you would ask, but I respectfully decline. I simply can't abandon my responsibilities here."

Jenks snickered. "Which is a shame, really, because you all obviously need the help."

I flicked my hand, and Jenks took off, laughing merrily.

"I see." Elyse tightened her grip on her purse. "I am done here, then. Happy Halloween."

My breath caught as the proud woman turned to the door. This was not how I wanted our relationship to start or end. "Elyse? Wait," I said as I followed her. "This is not what I wanted . . ."

I jerked to a halt, my words cutting off when she suddenly spun.

"What did you want?" she said, her color high and eyes pinched in anger.

I stood before her, not sure what to say. I wasn't even sure what I wanted. Elyse didn't need a friend. *Even if I do.*

I put a hand up as I asked her to give me a moment to figure this out. "What are you doing this winter solstice?" I said, and her gaze flicked past me to the sanctuary.

"I don't know," she said stiffly. "I haven't assessed my new responsibilities yet."

"See if you can be in Cincinnati," I said, hoping Jenks stayed right where he was and out of this. "You can go over that curse I was going to show Vivian, and maybe you can help me with a spell I want to try out." I managed a weak smile, feeling vulnerable. "It takes the ambient power of a citywide coven to stir, but perhaps with the two of us we can manage it."

Elyse slumped, her anger gone as she looked at the stained pentagram with longing. "I know that spell," she whispered. "That's the one you used to bring back Pierce when you were eighteen, yes? Gives a ghost existence for a night? It's a nice spell but limiting, seeing as you can only do it a couple times out of the year and only if they are in purgatory."

"Maybe you need to try it here," I said. "Where she died."

The young woman took a slow, steadying breath. "Maybe," she finally admitted even as she turned to the door. "It's a shame you didn't say yes," she added as the door opened and the sounds of the night filtered in. "The spell you have is good, but it's a bastard spell. The original is so powerful it can return even the undead for more than a single night. If I couldn't bring back Vivian with that, then nothing will."

My reach for the door faltered, and I stared at her, the confident woman now standing on my front steps. "You have a spell to recover the undead?" *My God . . . Kisten.*

Eyes on the night, she pulled her coat closed. "Yes, but you will never see it." Her expression became mocking. "Coven business."

"Elyse." I reached after her, but she was already flouncing down the stairs to a little white car parked behind Doyle. It had been Vivian's. I recognized it.

"Good-bye, Rachel Morgan," she said with such smugness that I began to wonder if all her melancholy and shock had been an act. "I'm sure we will be in touch." Her brow lifted. "Don't leave Cincinnati without telling me."

"What a moss wipe," Jenks said as she gave Doyle a little wave and got in her car, but I couldn't speak, my thoughts tumbling as my knees suddenly felt like water.

Unseeing, I stumbled backward into the church and shut the door. From outside, I heard Vivian's car start and Elyse drive away.

"How dumb do they think you are?" Jenks said as I took out my phone. "Trying to lure you into becoming their muscle when you got everything you need here."

He was almost right, and my fingers shook as I hit an icon and waited.

"Ivy?" I said when the line clicked open. "There's a way to bring him back."